ALSO BY TODD RITTER

Death Notice

BAD MOON

BAD MOON

TODD RITTER

Minotaur Books ⚞ New York

BAD MOON. Copyright © 2011 by Todd Ritter. All rights reserved. Printed in the United States of America. For information, address St. Martin's Press, 175 Fifth Avenue, New York, N.Y. 10010.

www.minotaurbooks.com

Library of Congress Cataloging-in-Publication Data

Ritter Todd.
    Bad moon / Todd Ritter.
        p. cm.
    ISBN 978-0-312-62281-7
    1. Children—Crimes against—Fiction.   2. Murder—Investigation—
Fiction.   3. Missing persons—Fiction.   4. Small cities—Fiction.
I. Title.
    PS3618.I79B33 2011
    813'.6—dc22

                                                    2011018799

First Edition: October 2011

10   9   8   7   6   5   4   3   2   1

To my family

BAD MOON

JULY 20, 1969

It was the baby, of all things, that woke her up. Not her husband. Not the police. Just the baby and his crying.

Maggie had grown accustomed to the sound. Having two kids did that to you. Sometimes she'd accidentally sleep right through whatever racket one of them was making. But that night was different. The crying was different. It wasn't the irritated wail of an infant who was tired or the pained whimper of one who was teething. It was, Maggie realized, a cry of terror, and the noise tugged her out of sleep, out of bed, and out of the room.

Along the way, her bleary eyes caught the clock on her dresser. It was almost eleven. She had been asleep for more than three hours. Not as bad as some days, but not good, either. Not good at all. And despite the rest, she still felt weary as she crossed the hall to the nursery. Still utterly exhausted.

In the nursery, Maggie flicked on the overhead light. The sharp, sudden glow made her eyes sting in addition to being bleary. It didn't matter. She could navigate the room with her eyes closed, which is exactly what she did. The memories of hundreds of similar trips guided her—rocking chair to the right, dresser to the left, don't stub your toe on the toy chest. Once she reached the crib, Maggie opened her eyes.

The crib was empty.

The crying, however, continued.

Maggie heard it, loud and fearful. She rotated in the center of the room, looking for a possible explanation. Had the baby somehow escaped the crib and crawled into the closet? The dresser? Another room?

It was only after two more twirls that Maggie's sleep-addled mind caught up with her spinning body. When it did, she realized the source of the crying wasn't in the nursery at all. It was coming from downstairs and had been the entire time. Only now it sounded more urgent, more frightened.

Maggie left the nursery and clomped down the stairs. At the bottom, she expected to see Ken reclining in the living-room La-Z-Boy, the baby wriggling in his arms. Instead, the chair was occupied by Ruth Clark, whose spindly arms struggled to stay wrapped around the writhing child.

Ruth, who was only sixty but looked at least a decade older, lived down the street. She and Maggie were friends, but not friendly enough for Ruth to be in her house, holding her child, at almost eleven o'clock at night. Yet there she was, trying to hush the baby in the gray glow of the television.

"Ruth? What's going on?" Blinking in confusion, Maggie noted what her neighbor was wearing—a nightgown stuffed into threadbare trousers, flip-flops on her feet. She had dressed in a hurry. "Where's Ken?"

"You were asleep," Ruth said with forced cheer. "So he asked me to come over and keep an eye on the baby. He had to step out for a minute."

"Why?"

Ruth stayed silent as she pressed the baby into Maggie's arms. He had been wrapped tightly in a blanket, which covered everything but his face. Whether it was Ken's doing or Ruth's, Maggie didn't know. Either way, it was a bad move on such a muggy night. Both the baby and the blanket were drenched with cold sweat, which explained the bawling.

The crying softened once Maggie settled onto the couch and loosened the blanket. Ruth sat next to her, uncomfortably close. She was hovering, Maggie realized. And watchful.

"Did Ken say where he was going?"

Ruth's reply—"He didn't"—was rushed and unconvincing.

"What about when he'd be back?"

"Soon."

"I'll wait up for him. You don't need to stick around."

"I think I should stay."

Maggie didn't have the energy to protest, not that Ruth would have allowed it. The finality of her tone made it clear she intended to stay. With nothing left to say or do, Maggie stared at the television.

What she saw astounded her.

The screen was mostly a grainy blur—fizzy patches of black and gray. Then an image took shape through the haze. It was a figure in a bulky uniform, looking like a ghost against a background of endless darkness. The figure was on a ladder, hopping downward rung by rung.

It paused at the bottom. It placed a foot onto the ground. It spoke.

"That's one small step for a man, one giant leap for mankind."

"Sweet Lord," Ruth said. "He's really standing on it."

He was Neil Armstrong. *It* was the moon. And Ruth was correct—the astronaut was standing on its surface just as easily as Maggie now sat in her living room.

Eyes fixed on the TV, she immediately thought of Charlie. Nine years older than the baby, he had been moon crazy the past year. Earlier that afternoon, when *Apollo 11* actually touched down on the moon's surface, Charlie had cheered, jumped, and cried until he made himself sick.

He would want to see this, Maggie knew. History was taking place.

"I'm going to wake Charlie."

Ruth trailed her to the stairs. "Maggie, wait!"

Maggie didn't stop, continuing up the stairs with rushed purpose. At the top, her bare feet made slapping sounds on the hardwood floor as she moved down the hall to Charlie's bedroom. Ruth remained downstairs, calling up to her.

"Please come back! Charlie's not there!"

Maggie stopped, hand against the closed bedroom door. "What do you mean?"

"Come back downstairs," Ruth said. "I'll explain."

Maggie did the opposite, pushing into the room instead. The streetlight outside the window cast a rectangle of light that stretched across the floor. Just like in the nursery, she didn't need it. She knew every inch of the bedroom, from the telescope in the corner to the model rockets lined up on the bookshelf.

The window was open, letting in a rainy breeze that dampened the curtains. Beneath it was Charlie's bed, draped in a comforter dotted with moons, stars, and planets. Holding the baby with one arm, Maggie used her free hand to lift the comforter and whip it away.

The bed, much like the baby's crib earlier, was empty.

"Please come downstairs." Ruth now stood in the doorway, breath heavy, face pinched.

"Where is he? Did Ken take him somewhere?"

Ruth moved into the room and tried to clasp her hand. Maggie yanked it away. "Answer me, Ruth. Where is my son?"

"He's missing."

"I don't understand."

But Maggie did. She understood quite well as she shuffled backward and plopped onto the empty bed. The bed that should have contained Charlie. Her boy. Whose whereabouts were now unknown.

"Is that where Ken went? To look for him?"

"He called the police," Ruth said. "Then he woke me and Mort."

Mort was Ruth's husband. Maggie presumed he was also looking for Charlie, along with the police and God knows who else. Apparently everyone but her knew her son was gone.

"Why didn't you tell me?"

"Ken didn't think you'd wake up. And if you did, he knew you'd be worried."

Damn right she was worried. Her body might have been motionless on her son's bed, but her mind was a whirling dervish of fears and bad thoughts. Where was Charlie? How long had he been gone? Was it too late to find him? When Maggie's brain settled down, her body started up again. She rose from the bed and stomped past Ruth into the hallway.

"I have to look for him," she said. "I have to find him."

Again, Ruth tried to stop her. "I'll take the baby."

"No."

Maggie tightened her arms around the infant. One of her children was missing. She wasn't going to let the other out of her sight until he was found.

She descended the stairs into the living room. The TV was still on, still broadcasting surreal pictures from another world.

A second astronaut had joined Armstrong, both of them leaping like jackrabbits across the moon's surface. Maggie moved right past it, not caring. Her only concern was her children, not the moon, or the astronauts, or the fact that she was running outside in the rain in bare feet, denim cutoffs, and a T-shirt stained with baby puke.

She made it to the end of the driveway before seeing two men approach the house. One of them was Ken. The other was Mort Clark. Maggie looked past them, hoping to see Charlie lagging behind. He wasn't.

"Did you find him?" Maggie asked as she met them in the middle of the street. "Where is he?"

"I don't know," Ken said. "I have no idea."

He looked pale and haunted—more ghostlike than those astronauts on TV. The rain had flattened his hair. Large drops of it clung to his beard.

"We were watching TV," he said. "They were showing stuff about the moon landing and Charlie said he wanted to go for a bike ride and look at it. He said he thought he'd be able to see the astronauts from here."

It was a ridiculous notion, but very much in line with Charlie's thinking. Maggie easily pictured him hopping on his bike—midnight blue with badly painted stars—and pedaling off in excitement.

"How long ago was that?"

"About an hour."

"Where did he go?"

"The falls."

One of Charlie's favorite places was the creek that rushed through the woods behind their cul-de-sac. There was a dirt path there, perfect for biking, that led to a footbridge. From that perch, you could see the water hurtle over Sunset Falls, which plunged thirty feet into a rock-strewn pool. They had allowed Charlie to ride there alone for the first time this summer. Maggie now regretted that decision.

"Did you check the bridge?" she asked.

When Ken sighed, Maggie suddenly felt the urge to hit her husband. She would have done it, too, had she not been holding the baby. She would have let loose with a few good punches while asking Ken why he didn't go with their son, why he couldn't find him, why he was talking to her instead of still looking for Charlie.

"Of course I checked the bridge. It was the first place we went. The police are still there."

Then they needed to look somewhere else. *She* needed to look somewhere else, since Ken had made it clear his searching was over for the night. Maggie felt herself moving away from him, compelled to do something. Charlie wouldn't be found with her just standing there.

"Where are you going?" Ken asked.

Maggie didn't answer. Wasn't her destination perfectly clear? She was going to find her son. End of story.

Ken called after her, his voice muted in the rain. "I think you should leave the baby with me. I don't—"

He stopped himself, but it didn't matter. He might as well have just finished the sentence and let the truth escape. He didn't trust her with the baby. Not after what happened in May. It's why he hadn't bothered to wake her when Charlie went missing. It's why he had sent Ruth to watch the baby earlier. It's why he was trying to stop her from leaving now.

But Maggie couldn't stop. Her body wouldn't let her. She had no choice but to cross the street, even as the rain increased in force. Even as Ken begged her to come back. And even as the distance between her and her husband grew wider with each passing step.

There were four houses on the cul-de-sac, set apart by wide lawns and rows of sycamore trees. Ken and Maggie's was by far the smallest—practically a cottage—and the most full. Two parents and two kids, crammed together in a house that Maggie struggled to keep clean. Across the street, in a cruel reflection of her own abode, sat the home of Lee and Becky Santangelo. It was everything Maggie's house was not—large, rambling, spotless.

With Ken watching her from the driveway, Maggie crossed the Santangelos' yard. It was so much larger than her own, an expanse of crisp green kept trim by a local teenage boy. At the moment, though, it was soggy with rainwater. It squished between her toes as she made her way to the front porch. Once there, she grabbed the giant brass knocker that dominated the door and rapped twice. When no one answered, she knocked again, this time slamming continuously until Lee Santangelo eventually opened it.

Like their disparate houses, Lee was the complete opposite of Ken. He was taller, for one thing, and far more handsome. Strong build, matinee-idol looks, always clean shaven. Normally, he was pleased when Maggie dropped by with Charlie and threw the door wide open for them. But this night was different. The door opened only a crack as Lee peered at her with a mixture of surprise and annoyance.

"Maggie," he said, pretending to be happy to see her. "What's going on?"

They were the same three words Maggie had used to greet

Ruth Clark. Hearing them directed at her, she realized just how rude and suspicious they sounded.

"It's Charlie. We can't find him."

Music was playing loudly inside. Something psychedelic that Maggie couldn't place. Beyond that, barely audible, was a constant whirring sound. When Maggie tried to peek inside, Lee blocked her view with a quick side step. Seeing the length of his body, she realized he was wearing next to nothing—a pair of boxer shorts and an unbuttoned shirt, tossed on no doubt for her benefit. It didn't matter. He could have been stark naked and she wouldn't have cared.

"And you think he could have come here?" Lee asked.

"With all this moon business going on, I thought he might have stopped by. You know, because—"

Because Lee Santangelo was an astronaut. Or had trained to be one. Or had almost been one. Maggie didn't know the details. She only knew that Charlie had driven him crazy with questions all summer.

"He hasn't been by tonight. I'm sorry. But I'll definitely keep an eye out."

"If you see him, please tell him we're looking for him. And that we're worried."

She added that last part in the hope that Lee would fling open the door and let her look around the place. Instead, he tried to close it. Maggie, thinking fast, blocked the door with her foot. The squeeze of it against her big toe made her wince.

She persisted, despite the pain. "What about Becky?"

"What about her?"

"Maybe she saw him tonight."

Maggie knew Charlie had a crush on Lee's wife, even if the boy didn't know it himself. It was well within reason that

Charlie could have bypassed Lee and instead sought out Becky, who offered him cookies, tousled his hair, and tut-tutted over his scraped knees.

"She's not here," Lee said slowly. "She's gone until tomorrow. I'm the only one here."

And that, Maggie realized, was all the information she would get at the moment. Time was ticking, and every second spent with Lee Santangelo was another second wasted in the search for her son. So she thanked him for his time, apologized for bothering him, and moved on.

She was halfway across the lawn when a sudden movement from the Santangelos' house caught her eye. It was a curtain being rustled in a second-story window. Maggie saw a shadowy face peek out from behind it and stare down at her. She kept walking, pretending she hadn't noticed. But when she reached the edge of the yard, she allowed herself one last, quick glance. What she saw was a silhouette standing in front of the window. Maggie could make out a thin frame and shaggy, shoulder-length hair.

A woman.

Maggie didn't have a clear enough view to see if it was Becky Santangelo. But who it was didn't really concern her. What mattered was that Lee had lied. He was definitely not alone.

Pebbles jutted into the soles of Maggie's bare feet as she crossed the street. Each stone she stepped on caused a small flare of pain. For that, she was grateful. It took her mind off the knot of worry lodged in her chest. The distraction was only momentary, but considering the circumstances, she'd take what she could get.

In front of her house again, Maggie noticed that Ken had finally gone inside. Through the front picture window, she saw him pacing in the living room. His mood earlier had been maddeningly unreadable—equal parts annoyance, worry, and prickliness. But the unfiltered view through the picture window showed a man who was clearly distressed. He stared at the floor. He tugged at his beard. He closed his eyes and pressed a thumb and forefinger against the bridge of his nose, which Maggie knew meant he was trying to stave off a headache.

Part of her wanted to return to the house and comfort him. Despite all the mistrust of the past few months, she still loved him deeply. But Maggie needed comfort, too. She knew that would only come once Charlie was found safe and sound. So she pressed on, even though her arms were tired from carrying the baby and her legs were weak with worry.

She was also running out of neighbors. Besides the Clarks and the Santangelos, there was only one other house on the street, and it was the last place she expected to find Charlie. Still, she at least had to ask, even though she dreaded doing it.

Her destination was the house next door to her own. The oldest on the street, it was an exhaustingly ornate Victorian that looked ancient compared with her own home. Charlie liked to pretend it was haunted. He claimed children were buried in the backyard and that their ghosts roamed the house at night. Maggie had no clue what gave him such ideas, but she understood how the house's appearance played a part in fueling his imagination. Black shutters flanked the tall windows. A widow's walk on the roof seemed to lean in whatever direction the wind was blowing. The wraparound porch had an unused swing and brittle steps that threatened to break when Maggie climbed them.

Although the house was dark, she knew its owner was home. He was always home.

"Mr. Stewart?" Maggie shifted the baby's weight to her left shoulder and knocked on the door with her right hand.

No one answered, which didn't surprise her in the least. Glenn Stewart never answered his door. Nor, as far as Maggie could tell, did he go outside.

"Mr. Stewart? Are you there?"

Maggie knocked again, remembering the last time she had seen him, during that awkward homecoming party. The whole debacle had been her idea. Glenn had no family that she knew of, and she felt sorry he was returning from Vietnam to an empty house inherited from his grandparents. So she baked a cake, rounded up the neighbors, and marched next door, intent on creating a happy homecoming through sheer force of will.

Glenn had wanted nothing to do with it. He wasn't rude when he opened the door and saw seven people (seven and a half, if you counted Maggie's very pregnant stomach) applauding on his porch. He looked more scared than anything else, twitching like a rabbit facing a pack of wolves. But he refused to let them inside and declined the cake, which Maggie thrust at him desperately. Not knowing what else to do, she had left the cake on the porch, hoping Glenn would retrieve it later. Then they left, taking the hint. Glenn Stewart wanted to be left alone.

But now Maggie couldn't leave him alone. Not until she knew if he had seen Charlie. So her knocking turned to pounding.

"Mr. Stewart? It's Maggie Olmstead from next door."

Dropping her head in frustration, Maggie noticed something sitting on the porch floor, about a yard away from her feet.

It was the cake—ravaged by birds, bugs, and four long seasons—sitting exactly where she had left it a year earlier.

Retreating from Glenn Stewart's house, Maggie saw two police cars at the end of the cul-de-sac, where the asphalt ended and the footpath into the woods began. Twin beams of light swooped through the trees. Flashlights, scanning the darkness for her son.

One of the lights suddenly stopped. A voice rose from the woods.

"I think I see something!"

The second light bobbed swiftly toward the still one. Maggie moved, too, running toward the forest. She no longer felt the pebbles under her feet or the rain stinging her face. The only things she felt were the baby wriggling in her arms and the knot of worry expanding to all points of her body.

Her other senses, however, were heightened to an alarming degree. When she reached the path and pushed into the woods, her eyesight never dimmed. The smell of wet earth, moss, and maple sap clogged her nostrils. Her ears practically buzzed at the sound of boots tromping through the underbrush and voices murmuring to each other.

Then there was the creek. She saw the water's glint, smelled its banks, heard the discordant rush as it approached Sunset Falls and plummeted over.

Two men were standing at the footbridge when Maggie reached it. One of them was Deputy Owen Peale, his face obscured by a hooded poncho. The other was the police chief, Jim Campbell. He eschewed the poncho in favor of a wide-brimmed hat. Maggie's presence startled both of them.

"You shouldn't be here, Maggie," Jim said.

"Did you find Charlie?"

He tried to turn her around, away from the water. "What are you doing out here with the baby? You're sopping wet."

Maggie refused to budge. She craned her neck until she could see over the chief's shoulder. Behind him, Deputy Peale had his flashlight pointed toward the stream.

"Is Charlie there?" she asked. "Is he okay?"

"Let's get you home," Chief Campbell said, his voice telling Maggie everything she needed to know. It was falsely optimistic, bordering on condescension. Something was wrong.

The baby began to stir in Maggie's arms, more forcefully than before. A cry erupted from the infant, as loud and fraught with terror as the one that had awakened Maggie in the first place.

"How about you give me the baby," Jim said. "I'm drier."

When he held out his arms, Maggie made her move. She swerved past him and sprinted up the path. Deputy Peale lunged for her at the bridge, but she scooted right, just out of his reach. Then she was on the bridge, bounding across it until she was directly over the water. In the distance, about twenty yards away, the creek ended and the falls began.

Looking down at the water, she saw a branch emerge from under the bridge, riding the rain-swollen creek. It floated along the surface before hitting a rock and briefly stopping there. But the persistent current didn't allow it to stay in place for long. Water swirled around the branch like tentacles until it was dislodged. The branch was whisked onward to the edge of the falls, where it slid from view.

Over, down, gone.

Maggie heard Jim Campbell yelling her name. She saw

Owen Peale now on the bridge, approaching slowly and saying "It's okay, Mrs. Olmstead. It'll be okay."

Her eyes turned back to the falls, where the branch had just tumbled into darkness. She traced its path, gaze swimming against the current. Soon she was looking off the other side of the bridge, her back to the falls. The creek there looked just as wild. Leaves, sticks, and globs of trash floated toward her and slipped beneath the bridge. There were rocks there, too, large boulders that poked out of the water like icebergs.

Owen Peale had reached her by that point. He clutched her shoulders and shook his head. "Don't look. Please don't look."

That was when Maggie saw what she wasn't supposed to see. It was an object caught on the rock closest to the bridge, pinned there by the current. It was blue. A blue so dark she could barely make it out. There were spots of white, too, ragged blotches that vaguely resembled stars.

Maggie screamed.

It was Charlie's bike. Right there in the water. The current caught the spokes of the front tire and rocked it back and forth.

Jim Campbell joined them on the bridge. One of the men, Maggie didn't know which, took the baby. The other tried to pull her away from the bridge railing. Maggie allowed herself to be moved. She didn't have the strength to fight it. She simply went limp as she was dragged off the bridge. Along the way, she took one last glance toward the creek, even though she knew she shouldn't. She had to see it again. Just to make sure it was real.

She saw the water dislodge the bike, just as it had moved the branch earlier. Caught on the current, the bike was submerged for a moment. It poked out of the water again on the other side of the bridge, riding inexorably toward the falls. When it reached the edge, the bike overturned, rear tire spinning. Then it slipped away, riding the falls.

Over.

Down.

Gone.

WEDNESDAY

ONE

Five minutes.

That's how much time Kat Campbell had until she needed to be out the door. Five lousy minutes to brew coffee, feed the dog, pack her son's lunch, and toast two bagels for them to eat in the car. On a good morning, all of that could be accomplished in ten minutes. But this wasn't a good morning. Not by a long shot.

The coffee was brewing so slowly it made Kat wish someone would just hurry up and invent a caffeine IV drip. One bagel was trapped in the toaster, quickly turning from golden brown to charcoal black. The other sat on the kitchen counter, waiting to meet the same fate. James's lunch so far consisted of two slices of bread and a cup of chocolate pudding. His beagle, Scooby, had already given up on the prospect of breakfast and was now chewing an empty toilet paper roll dug out of the bathroom trash.

"James? Are you almost ready?"

Kat didn't move from the kitchen counter. She was well aware how far lung power traveled in her house, and her voice would have no trouble rushing up the stairs and into her son's bedroom.

"In a minute," James called back. It was punctuated by the sound of a dresser drawer slamming shut. Never a good sign.

"It's the first day of school. We don't have a minute."

In reality, they had three, but Kat was too busy making his lunch to correct herself. She slapped some cold cuts on the bread, coated it with mustard, and dropped it into a Ziploc bag. This was tossed into James's lunchbox with the pudding, a granola bar, and milk money. Then it was on to the bagels. The one stuck in the toaster was freed with some shaking, tapping, and the strategic use of a butter knife. The untoasted one remained that way.

Next came Scooby, who had dropped the toilet paper roll into his dinner bowl, presumably to make Kat feel just a bit more neglectful. She replaced it with kibble, refilled his water dish, and let him go to town.

By that time, the coffeemaker was squeezing out a few last drops. Kat grabbed the pot and poured half of it into a thermos. She was done, with a minute to spare.

Pausing to catch her breath, she turned to the small television sitting on the kitchen counter. James sometimes watched cartoons on it while eating breakfast on Saturday mornings. That day, it was turned to CNN, where a blandly handsome anchor was sharing breaking news.

"The space race has officially restarted," he said. "Early today, the China National Space Administration successfully launched its first manned voyage to the moon."

The screen switched from the anchor to a clip of China's president hailing the launch. That was followed by footage of the launch itself—a distant shot of an ivory tower streaking across the sky. After that was a view of Tiananmen Square, where thousands of spectators cheered.

"As the entire nation watched, three Chinese astronauts took off for the moon. They are expected to reach it Friday afternoon. A successful mission would make China only the second country, after the United States, to send a man to the moon. It would also be the first time since 1972 that man has set foot on the moon's surface."

Kat checked her watch. Time was up. Switching off the TV, she called upstairs once more. "James, we've got to go. Even if you're still naked, we're leaving this house."

Two seconds later, her son stomped into the kitchen wearing jeans, a Phillies T-shirt, and sneakers. The clothes and shoes were new. And expensive. At first, Kat had balked at spending so much on back-to-school clothes, but James swore up and down that he needed them to fit in. Kat realized, sadly, it was most likely true. James was entering fifth grade, a tough year for any kid, let alone one with Down syndrome. But he was a smart boy, able to keep up with the others in his class, and so far he had made it through elementary school with a minimum of teasing. In order to keep it that way, Kat was willing to shell out for new clothes. And sneakers. And a backpack, even though the one James had used last year was in perfectly good condition.

The only holdover was his lunch box, which featured characters from the movie *Cars*. Kat had assumed James would want a newer, cooler one, just like everything else. But when he didn't mention it, she didn't bring it up. She was all too happy to save a few bucks and pack his lunch inside good old Lightning McQueen.

Yet when Kat handed him the lunch box, James looked at her like she had just grown a second head.

"What's this?"

"Your lunch. Or at least something that resembles lunch."

James wasn't amused. "Fifth graders don't use lunch boxes."

"I didn't get that memo. And we don't have time to deal with it now."

"But I'll look stupid," James protested as he slung his backpack over his shoulder.

"You didn't look stupid last year."

"But that was fourth grade. It was cool in fourth grade."

"And you'll be cool tomorrow." Kat handed him his bagel and nudged him toward the back door. "But today it's either the lunch box or no lunch at all."

James sighed dramatically. It had become his usual way of demonstrating that he was right and she was wrong. Whenever she heard it, Kat felt a twinge of nostalgia for the boy who used to think everything she did was wonderful.

Once James was out the door, she reached for a small rack on the wall behind it. One hook contained the keys to her patrol car. The other held her holster. Kat removed both, putting the keys in her pocket and the holster around her waist. Below the rack was a small safe that contained her Glock. She opened it, removed the gun, and checked the safety before quickly sliding it into her holster. Then she grabbed her own bagel and thermos and left the house.

Although James didn't bring up the lunch box again during the drive to school, he was certainly thinking about it. He spent the entire trip staring at it with resignation and, Kat sensed, no small amount of trepidation. He was nervous, which was understandable. Kat was nervous, too. She remembered entering the fifth grade and discovering how different it was from the previous year. It was the same way with sixth grade. And then junior high, which was a whole other world of cliques, peer pressure, and petty cruelties.

"You'll be fine, Little Bear," she said as they approached the school. "And we'll brown-bag your lunch tomorrow."

James's nervous gaze moved from the lunch box to Kat. "Promise?"

"I promise."

After sending James off with a peck on the cheek that he quickly wiped away, Kat headed to work. Perry Hollow's police station sat a few blocks southeast of the school, but instead of taking a shortcut to get there, she turned onto Main Street and drove its entire length. Taking her time, she scanned the quaint shops and restaurants that lined both sides of the thoroughfare.

They were the heart of Perry Hollow now that the lumber mill that had given the town its name was gone. Part of her job as police chief was to make sure that heart was beating strongly. If Big Joe's, the town's de facto Starbucks, was closed, it meant something was wrong with its aged proprietor, Ellen Faye, and that Kat needed to check up on her. When passing Awesome Blossoms, the flower shop, she made a point to note the presence of its delivery van, which had been stolen in the past.

It was still too early for most of the businesses to be open, but the lights were on at Big Joe's, which meant Ellen was still chugging along. The same was true at the Perry Hollow Diner, where pickup trucks outnumbered cars in the parking lot by a three-to-one margin. And sitting in front of Awesome Blossoms was a white Ford delivery van.

The sight made Kat sigh with relief, considering the hell the town went through when it was stolen. Almost a year had passed since the end of those dark days, and Perry Hollow seemed to have gotten over the worst of it.

For the most part, Kat and James had, too.

Once she finished the inspection of Main Street, Kat maneuvered the Crown Vic down a side street and into the police station's parking lot. Two other cars were already there. One was a patrol car similar to her own. That was driven by her deputy, Carl Bauersox, who was finishing up his usual night shift. The other was a Volkswagen Beetle that belonged to Louella van Sickle, the station's dispatcher, secretary, cleaning lady, and all-around indispensable presence.

When Kat entered the station, Lou was already at her desk. She eyed the thermos and blackened bagel in Kat's hands.

"Stuck in the toaster again?"

"Yup," Kat said. "It was one of those mornings. I predict the coffee sucks, too."

She took a sip, proving herself right. The coffee was far too strong, with a bitter aftertaste that stuck in the back of her throat.

Lou shook her gray-haired head. "Bad coffee. Burned bagels. You need a man in that house."

"And you," Kat said, "need to get your mind out of the fifties."

Lou, who had been married for forty-three years, took it as a compliment.

"Call me old-fashioned, but I like not having to worry about making the coffee in the morning. Al does that. And he fixes the toilet. And mows the lawn. Plus, he's still pretty good in the bed department."

Kat didn't need to know that. Nor did she need a man,

despite Lou's insistence otherwise. She had enough on her plate already—job, son, dog. There wasn't any room on her schedule for finding and keeping a mate.

"All I'm saying is keep an open mind," Lou told her. "One of these days, the perfect man could walk through that door and you'd dismiss him immediately."

At that moment, a man did walk through the door. But Carl Bauersox, who was nice enough, wasn't Kat's type. Plus, he was married, with two kids and another on the way.

"Do you make coffee?" Lou asked him.

Carl answered with a nod. "And I fix the toilet and mow the lawn."

"So you heard our conversation."

"Yes," Carl said, his baby face growing red. "But I don't want to talk about the bed stuff."

"That's fine," Lou said. "I'll call your wife and ask her."

The deputy looked mortified, as if she'd actually do it. Lou didn't help matters by reaching for the phone. Kat beat her to it, pressing palm to receiver and assuring Carl that no calls would be made to his wife about their sex life. Ever.

"How was your shift?" she asked him. "Anything to report?"

"Not really. Speeding ticket on Old Mill Road. The Wellington kid again."

Kat arched an eyebrow. "That's his third ticket in four months, right?"

"Yup," Carl said. "I can't wait until they suspend his license so I can take a break from writing the darn things."

"And nothing else suspicious?" Kat asked. "Nothing at all?"

She knew she was being paranoid. If something had been amiss during the night, Carl would have told her about it. But she needed to be thorough, especially after the events of the previous year. Once a town goes through the experience of having a serial killer on the loose, it's hard to return to the way things were.

Carl laid a hand on her shoulder. "Relax, Chief, everything is fine. Now I'm going to go home and give my wife something to brag to Lou about."

His uncharacteristic stab at bawdy humor made Kat laugh out loud. Lou did her one better: she catcalled at him. Blushing even more than before, Carl waved weakly and left the station.

"That's what I'm talking about," Lou said. "You need a Carl."

"What I need is a toaster oven and a gift certificate to Big Joe's."

Kat grabbed her bitter coffee and burned bagel and headed to her office. She took two steps before being stopped by another man entering the station.

"Chief Campbell. Just who I wanted to see."

Once again, it wasn't Prince Charming. In fact, Burt Hammond, the town's mayor, was the complete opposite of charming. He was tall, slightly over six feet, and as fit as someone in his early sixties could be. Yet an aura of sleaze always seemed to surround him. Maybe it was his too-white smile. Or the spray-on tan that made him the same shade as a glazed ham. Or the fact that he was a lawn mower salesman who just happened to be holding a half-price sale on election day. He won by a landslide.

Kat didn't have to deal with him very much, which was good, because she didn't like him very much, either. She had learned through the grapevine—in which Lou van Sickle was the head grape—that Mayor Hammond felt the same about her. On the occasions when they were forced to meet, their conversations were terse but cordial.

Widening his lips into that fake grin that seemed to afflict all politicians, Burt said, "Sorry for the intrusion, but I was wondering if I could have a word in private."

"Sure thing." Kat led him to her office and settled behind her desk. "What can I do for you, Burt?"

The mayor remained standing, hands behind his back, head bowed ever-so-slightly. From her seat, Kat had a dead-on view of the prominent mole on his chin. Burt had been known for the mole long before he was known as the mayor. Roughly the size of a dime, it wasn't unsightly, nor was it particularly dark. It was just so large that, once you spotted it, you couldn't stop looking at it. Plus, it made Burt instantly recognizable, a fact he capitalized on in ad campaigns for his lawn mower dealership. There was even talk that the real mole had been removed years ago and that Burt now sported a fake one just so he'd still be recognized.

"We've been doing some number crunching," he said. "Just trying to see where we stand before digging in and starting the budget for next year. You know the drill."

Kat was well acquainted with submitting requests for more staff, better equipment, new patrol cars. Every year, all but the smallest requests were turned down on the excuse that money was tight across the board and that every department had to share the burden. So while she and Carl got to drink from a new watercooler, their eight-year-old Crown Vics would have to spend another twelve months on the road.

"This year," Burt continued, "you're asking for new patrol cars."

"New Dodge Chargers," Kat added.

Top-of-the-line ones at that. The department in Mercerville, the next town over, got some two years ago. They were sleek and safe and fast as hell, an asset Kat never really thought was necessary until the events of last year.

"Unfortunately," Burt said, "you're not getting them. There's just not enough money in the budget. Nor is there any money for a new hire, even though you've made it abundantly clear that you want another officer in the ranks."

"I *need* another officer."

Burt never stopped smiling. Kat had seen more sincere grins on corpses, and she wanted to wipe it off Burt's face with the back of her hand.

"I'm just doing my job," he said.

"And I'm doing mine. Which is looking out for my department."

"This isn't just about your department. We're all making sacrifices here."

The word made Kat roll her eyes. "Sacrifices? Talk to the families of the people who died last year. They'll tell you all about sacrifice, Burt."

"I know things were bad—"

"It was a serial killer." Kat spoke slowly, elongating every word. "Living in this town. And every day I think about the lives I could have saved if there had been one more cop on the streets."

"Considering that death toll, you should feel lucky to still have a job at all."

Jumping out of her chair, Kat stood chest to chest with Burt. It didn't matter that he was a foot taller than her. Nor did it matter that the mayor, along with the rest of the town council, was technically her boss. He was implying that she hadn't done everything in her power to protect her town at the height of the Grim Reaper killings, and Kat couldn't let that slide.

"I don't like you, Burt," she said, anger heating her cheeks. "You don't like me. That's fine. Neither of us gives a damn. But if you ever doubt my commitment to this town again, I swear to God, I'll—"

Kat didn't know what she was going to say next. A thousand different responses popped into her head, each more risky than the last. The one on the tip of her tongue, just waiting to be set free, was "yank that mole right off your face."

Fortunately, she never got the chance. Just as she was about to say it, her cell phone rang, cutting off her torrent of anger. Saved by the bell. Literally.

She paused, breathing hard, as the cell phone continued to ring. She backed away from Burt Hammond, finally noticing just how much he towered over her five-foot-tall frame.

"I think you should go now," she said.

Burt nodded and said tersely, "That's a good idea. We'll discuss this later. Hopefully after you learn to control your emotions."

He left Kat alone with her pounding heartbeat and her ringing cell phone. She answered it with a rattled "Hello?"

"I'm just outside of town."

The caller was Nick Donnelly, who had never met a greeting he didn't like to forsake. The lead state police investigator during the Grim Reaper killings, he was fired after assaulting an employee at the county hospital. Normally, Kat frowned upon such behavior, but since his actions saved her life, she cut him some slack.

"Outside of what town?" Kat asked.

"Yours. I'm meeting a client there."

When he was booted from the Pennsylvania State Police, Nick started a nonprofit foundation devoted to cracking unsolved cases. His clients were mostly families of victims seeking answers to long-forgotten mysteries. If one of his clients was in Perry Hollow, that meant the crime most likely occurred there, too.

Only there weren't any unsolved crimes in Perry Hollow. It was a tiny town, a speck of commerce amid the mountains and forests of southeast Pennsylvania. Before the Grim Reaper murders, the crime rate had been almost nonexistent. If there was a cold case buried among the old files that filled the station's basement, Kat didn't know about it.

"Who's the client?"

Nick played coy. "I'll tell you when I get there. Let's meet at Big Joe's in fifteen minutes."

"Not until you tell me who hired you."

"I'll do you one better and tell you who the case is about."

"Fine. Who?"

"Charles Olmstead."

The name made Kat gasp. She couldn't tell if Nick heard it or not. Knowing him, he did. But at that moment, she didn't care. She was too busy wondering why someone was interested in the Olmstead case—and how Nick's involvement would quickly and inevitably drag her into it.

TWO

A storm was coming. Nick felt it in his right knee as he shuffled up the sidewalk to Big Joe's. It was a steady throbbing at the joint, which was held together by titanium pins and polyurethane supports. After the surgery, Nick joked that he was a few bolts shy of being the Six Million Dollar Man. In reality, though, he had become a walking weather vane, able to pick up a low-pressure system from miles away.

The one he detected that morning was a whopper. He had no idea what direction it was traveling or when it would reach Perry Hollow, but the buzzing pain he felt told him it was most definitely on its way. The knee didn't lie.

The downside to feeling the weather was that it also made walking difficult. Nick's right leg felt like jelly whenever he put weight on it, which made his limp more pronounced. By the time he entered Big Joe's, he was leaning on his cane so much he felt like Tiny Tim.

Kat was already inside, as Nick knew she would be, and waved when she saw him. Nick tried to wave back, which wasn't easy with one hand still holding the door and the other firmly gripping his cane. The end result was an awkward shifting of limbs and jabbing of elbows that ended with him simply nodding a greeting.

The coffee shop was laid out in such a way that walking a straight line from the door to the counter was impossible. Instead, patrons had to wind their way around tiny tables scattered across the floor. It was annoying for someone with two good legs. Since Nick was technically working with one and a half, he found it to be a royal pain in the ass.

"Sit," Kat said. "I'll get your coffee."

Nick declined the offer. "I can do it. My physical therapist says I need to learn how to do things for myself. The bitch."

His physical therapist, a brick house of a woman named Shirley, also told him he needed to rely less on the cane and more on his leg. He was using the cane as a crutch, she said, which made Nick logically ask, "Isn't that what it's for?"

Shirley hadn't found that very funny. Nick did, because he had no intention of laying off the cane. For one thing, it helped him get around. It also, he had to admit, was a pretty cool accessory. The staff was solid teak. The handle was bronze, sculpted into the shape of a pit bull. A gift from his former colleagues in the state police, its meaning was clear—never stop being tenacious.

He took that message to heart, even if it meant limping to the counter of an overpriced coffee joint and ordering an extra-large house blend. Once the coffee was in hand, he returned to the table, sat down, and let out a relieved sigh. The knee felt better with some weight off it. And now that he was indoors, the Weather Channel embedded inside it had been muted.

"How's the leg?" Kat asked.

"Still hurts, but I'll live."

"And because of it, so will I."

Nick had shattered his knee while saving Kat's life, although she didn't make a big deal out of it and neither did he. Both of them liked it that way.

"Have you heard from Henry?" Nick asked.

He was referring to Henry Goll, the other person he had

destroyed his leg to save. Like Kat, Henry had come face-to-face with the killer known as the Grim Reaper and lived to tell about it. Barely. Now he was in Italy. Maybe. Nick wasn't sure anymore. All he knew was that Henry was no longer in Perry Hollow, and the town was poorer for it.

"Nothing since New Year's Day," Kat said, frowning. "And I honestly doubt I'll hear from him again."

Nick took that as a sign that he should drop the subject. He did, turning his attention to a sheet of paper that he removed from a jacket pocket and placed on the table. The page was a reproduction of an old newspaper article, accompanied by a photograph of a boy who had a tiny nose and jug-ears. He wore a shirt and tie and had spit-slicked blond hair, leading Nick to assume it was a school picture. And although the boy was giving a lopsided smile, there was sadness in his eyes.

Above the article and photo was a simple, devastating headline: PERRY HOLLOW BOY, 10, MISSING.

"Charlie Olmstead," Kat said.

"So you know the story?"

"Everyone in town has heard about Charlie."

"What happened to him?"

"No one knows. Which is probably why everyone has heard about him."

Nick stabbed the article with an index finger. "The story is pretty vague. Although it quotes the police chief at the time. Jim Campbell. Does that name ring a bell?"

The man in question was Kat's father, who had been Perry Hollow's police chief until he died when she was eighteen. Nick knew this bit of information, and Kat knew that he knew. He had hoped it would make her smile. Instead, she frowned at the page.

"This was a long time ago, Nick."

"I know."

"And it's really the foundation's next case?"

"As a matter of fact, it is."

The Sarah Donnelly Foundation was named after Nick's sister, who was murdered when he was ten. The killer was never caught, but Nick had a pretty good idea who did it. Since that man had died in jail years ago, there would be no closure for him. That's where the foundation came in. The Philadelphia newspapers referred to Nick as a cold case philanthropist. Nick couldn't have said it better himself. His mission was straightforward—find unsolved cases and solve them. It didn't matter if his clients were rich or poor, young or old, city slickers or backwoods hillbillies. They needed closure and Nick tried to help them get it.

Other than himself, everyone who worked on a case did so on a voluntary basis. Kat had helped him out in the past, flipping through files, riding with him to distant crime scenes, even calling a few police colleagues in other towns and asking for information. Only this time, the situation was different. Her town was involved. So was her father's police work. It understandably put her on edge.

"You know I'm happy to share whatever information I have," she said. "If you want, we can go to the station's basement right now and take a look at the report. But if you're expecting me to help, I can't. The case has been officially closed for decades."

"Would it change your mind if I told you who hired me?"

Kat sighed. "Not likely."

"His brother."

"You talked to Eric?"

She had done a good job of trying to temper her surprise. Her voice remained steady. Her body stayed loose. The only thing she couldn't control was a slight widening of the eyes, which Nick naturally noticed. He was good at spotting the little things that betrayed people's emotions. It's what had made him a great cop.

"I guess you two knew each other," he said.

"We did."

Nick watched her closely, searching for the slightest sign that told him the whole story. But Kat was on to him. She remained as still as a stone, her face and voice a complete blank. This was uncharacteristic for Kat, whose emotions were usually so transparent they could have been pinned right next to her badge. She knew Eric Olmstead better than she let on.

"What can you tell me about him?"

"It was a long time ago," Kat said. "You'd get more accurate information from the Internet. He probably has a page on Wikipedia."

"He does."

Nick had looked at it five minutes after getting off the phone with him. He'd done a Google search, too, finding out lots of useless tidbits about Perry Hollow's most famous native son. Eric Olmstead, forty-three, author of seven bestselling mysteries. Two-time winner of the Edgar Award. Sometimes played baseball with John Grisham and guitar with Stephen King. The search yielded links to his official Web site, to fan fiction based on his most famous creation, private eye Mitch Gracey, to online retailers that sold all of his books.

What Nick couldn't find was any reference to his brother or why, after more than forty years, Eric Olmstead was so interested in finding out what happened to him. Their conversation had been brief, covering only the basics of his brother's disappearance—who, what, and when. The why part had been omitted, although finding that out was the point of Nick's midweek jaunt to Perry Hollow.

"Do you know why he'd ask me to look into Charlie's disappearance?"

Kat nodded while simultaneously taking a sip of her coffee—the skills of a hard-core java junkie. "I suspect it has something to do with his mother. She died two weeks ago."

"Interesting. I guess I'll find out soon enough. Want to tag along?"

"Where?"

"To pay Eric a visit. I told you I was coming here to meet a client."

This almost made Kat drop her mug. "Eric's still in Perry Hollow?"

"So he says," Nick replied. "Might be nice to see him. Catch up on old times."

"I never said we had old times."

"You didn't need to."

Kat abruptly stood, pushing in her chair so hard that it slammed against Nick's good knee. While she acted apologetic, Nick remained suspicious. The topic of Mr. Olmstead seemed to bring out the worst in her.

"So are you going with me or not?" he asked.

Kat paused at the door, holding it open for Nick and his cane. "Of course."

"Good. In the car, you can tell me all about how Eric Olmstead broke your heart."

And with that, Kat let go of the door. It slammed shut inches from Nick's face, forcing him to struggle once again to open it while wrangling with his cane. Through the glass, he saw Kat watching him with what could only be described as bemusement.

"That," Nick yelled through the door, "was not an accident!"

Kat smiled sweetly. "Neither was the chair."

THREE

Sitting in front of his laptop, staring at the blank screen he had faced so many times before, Eric typed two words: FIND HIM.

He sighed, reading the slim columns of black against the wide expanse of white. This was not what he was supposed to be writing. He had told his editor—promised, in fact—that he would be hard at work on the latest adventure of sports-reporter-turned-detective Mitch Gracey. Yet the two words on his screen were the most he had typed in two weeks, and they had nothing to do with hard-drinking, Mets-loving Mitch.

Still, Eric couldn't delete them and start over. In fact, he typed more. FIND YOUR BROTHER.

Eric deleted it immediately. He needed to focus. He needed to write. And fast. He was nearing a head-on collision with his deadline and had nothing to show for it. Sitting up in his chair, he cracked his knuckles and let his fingers hover over the keyboard.

They remained motionless.

As much as he tried, Eric found himself incapable of forming a sentence. It was that way in the days before his mother died and had only grown worse in the two weeks that followed. At first, he had chalked it up to a variety of factors. Location was a big one. The rickety desk and the bedroom he grew up in were a far cry from the Brooklyn apartment that served as his usual writing base. Timing was another. He normally wrote at night, when darkness made it easier to come up with the brutal scenarios required for crime fiction. But in Perry Hollow, he woke early. His mother's condition had required it. Now that she was gone, he still couldn't shake the habit.

Yet deep down, he knew these weren't the reasons. They were simply excuses he used to justify spending the day napping. Or surfing the Internet. Or eating peanut butter sandwiches while watching *Animal House* for the sixteenth time. The real reason Eric Olmstead couldn't write was because the well had run dry. He wasn't sure what had sapped his creativity. Grief, probably. Guilt, definitely. But it was gone, not to return anytime soon, no matter how much time he spent at his laptop.

That morning he vowed to stay there until he wrote five pages or until noon rolled around, whichever came first. But with no inspiration in sight, Eric had a feeling noon was going to be the winner, so he was happy when the doorbell rang at quarter after nine. It meant he had a distraction on his hands, and writers loved distractions almost as much as they loved royalty checks.

Reaching the front door, he found a man in a black suit standing on the porch. Had he been a character in a Mitch Gracey book, Eric would have described him as worn but handsome. The cane gripped in his right hand hinted at a troubled past. Also he had been a cop at some point. Eric knew that from the searching green eyes that tried to take in everything all at once.

"Eric Olmstead?" the man asked.

"Yes, sir."

The man extended a hand. "I'm Nick Donnelly."

Eric must have looked confused because the man added, "We spoke on the phone on Friday. You told me I could stop by this morning."

Eric slapped a palm against his forehead, stunned he hadn't realized it was Wednesday. The days tended to blur when you were trying to avoid writing.

"I'm so sorry. It completely slipped my mind."

He moved out of the doorway and Nick Donnelly entered, taking another one of those sweeping gazes. Behind him, someone else crept tentatively up the porch steps. Her uniform indicated that she, too, was a cop. But Eric didn't need to see a badge to confirm that. He already knew Kat Campbell had followed in her father's footsteps.

Twenty-five years had passed since Eric last saw her. Time had been generous. Although older, she still had that sharp chin that would lift when she was angry and lower when she was sad. Her eyes still sparkled with kindness, and the formation of her lips suggested everything from tension to boredom to the barest hint of a smile.

"Please tell me we're not so old that you've forgotten me."

"We're older," Eric said. "But I didn't forget you, Kat."

The hint of a smile remained on her face as she leaned forward and gave him a brief, nervous hug. It was the reaction Eric had been hoping for but not entirely expecting. He had done nothing to deserve a hug, not now and certainly not then.

"Let me get a good look at you," Kat said.

As she stepped backward to take him in, Eric foolishly wondered how he looked now compared with his eighteen-year-old self. He had changed a lot since those high school days. His contacts were new. So was his thatch of curly brown hair. His body, too, had undergone changes, getting leaner and more muscular as he got older. Each passing year made him hit the gym harder in an attempt to stave off old age.

His face, however, had stayed the same. At forty-three, his skin remained free of wrinkles and age spots. He didn't know how long it would last, but he thanked good genes for making it this far. Sometimes he'd look at photos of himself from high school and be amazed at how little his features had changed. Same jawline. Same strong nose. Same crooked smile.

"You look great," Kat said. "And I'm so happy for your success. Truly and deeply."

That last part had been added for a reason, Eric knew. It was her way of saying that, yes, she remembered everything but that she was prepared to let it go.

"So you work for the Sarah Donnelly Foundation, too?" Eric asked.

Kat looked at Nick Donnelly, who had been watching their reunion with an impatient lean on his cane. "No, although Nick would like that."

Eric glanced between the two of them. "Then why are you here?"

"Just trying to be a good police chief," Kat said, at last stepping inside. "And in that role, I'm curious about what you think happened to your brother."

"I don't know what happened to him," Eric replied. "But my mother had an idea."

"Which was?"

"That Charlie was kidnapped."

* * *

They sat at the scuffed table in the shabby dining room, Eric on one side, Nick and Kat on the other. The arrangement forced him to focus on either the private investigator who might take his case or his old flame. Not knowing who to pick, Eric settled on the space between their shoulders, which offered a view of the faded wallpaper. There had been roses on it once. Tiny pink ones with thornless stems that twisted around each other. Now the roses were barely visible, their stems vague gnarls of color.

"Before I take on a case," Nick began, "I like to get a grasp on the situation to see—"

Eric finished the sentence for him. "If it's worth your time. I completely understand."

In his books, Mitch Gracey did the same thing. He didn't waste energy on cases that couldn't be solved. It made things easier. But Eric already knew that Gracey wouldn't for a second take on Charlie's disappearance. He hoped Nick Donnelly thought otherwise.

"Good," Nick said. "So let's start by your telling me how much you know about your brother's disappearance."

"Not much," Eric said. "I was a baby when it happened."

"Did you parents ever discuss it?"

"Never. My father's been mostly out of the picture since I was two. My mother didn't like to talk about it."

Not that she needed to. Her actions spoke volumes. There were no photos of Charlie on display in the house. Eric hadn't even known any existed until he accidentally found a box of them in the basement one December when he was snooping around for Christmas presents. He spent the rest of that afternoon staring at image after image of his brother. Ten years of photographs, hidden away in shame.

The same was true of his brother's bedroom. Instead of clearing it out and putting it to different use, Eric's mother had sealed the room off like a tomb. The door was locked. The key was God knows where. Usually, Eric didn't think about it. But sometimes he'd walk by the door and pause, wondering what was on the other side. He always imagined something empty and pristine, like the room of a Benedictine monk.

Eric never brought up the photos, not even as his mother was dying. He never asked about the bedroom, either. He knew Maggie didn't mention them because it was too painful, and that talking would only bring the pain back.

Fortunately for Eric, the rest of Perry Hollow had no such reservations. They talked plenty about his brother. Everything he knew about the incident came from people in town—classmates, store clerks, parishioners at the church his mother had dragged him to during a brief religious phase. He didn't know how much of it was the truth, but growing up, he didn't care. Any morsel of information was a feast to him.

What he learned—and what he told Nick—was that on the night of July 20, 1969, Charlie left the house and never returned. The only trace of him was his bicycle, which his mother, Kat's father, and a deputy saw drift over Sunset Falls. The bike was found the next morning, smashed against the rocks at the base of the falls. His brother was never seen again. After several days of news coverage, search parties, and tense living-room vigils, Chief James Campbell made his official ruling. His brother, Charles Olmstead, accidentally rode his bike into the water, tumbled over the falls, and was swept away by the current.

"But your mother didn't believe that?" Nick said.

"Apparently not."

Kat, who had been quiet up to that point, leaned forward. "What do you believe?"

"I honestly have no opinion. Charlie's gone. In my mind, he's always been gone. I'm just hoping you'll be able to find out what exactly happened to him."

"But why now?" Nick asked. "It's been more than forty years since your brother disappeared."

"It was my mother's dying wish."

Eric had inherited it, along with Maggie's house, her car, and whatever money she had managed to tuck away over the years. He planned to sell the house. The car would be donated. The cash, too, would go to charity. When it was all gone, Eric would only be left with the words. Although nearly two weeks had passed, he still heard his mother's urgent whispers, riding on her final breaths.

They didn't believe me. They'll believe you. Find him. Find your brother.

At the time, Eric had been too overwhelmed by emotion to fully comprehend those last words. He thought Maggie had been delusional as death approached and wanted him to summon his brother, gone so many decades before. It was only a few days later, after a funeral service mostly attended by people he didn't know, that he realized the importance of her words. His mother had truly meant what she said. She wanted him to find Charlie. It was the last order from mother to son in a lifetime that had been full of them.

This was confirmed the day after the funeral, when his mother's lawyer contacted him about the house, the car, the cash. The lawyer then dropped this bombshell: for the past four decades, Maggie had been convinced that Charlie was kidnapped.

In her will, she had set aside a small amount of money devoted to finding out if that actually was the case. Eric's responsibility was to oversee it.

He waited a few days before making a few calls to private investigators he had interviewed as research for his books. All of them told him the same thing Nick Donnelly did—that details of the case were so sparse it would be hard to uncover anything. Yet Eric proceeded to ask each of them for help. All politely declined.

A few more days went by as he considered his next course of action. Then he stumbled upon an article in the *Philadelphia Inquirer* about the Sarah Donnelly Foundation. Eric appreciated its mission of offering hope to the hopeless. He finally got around to calling Nick Donnelly on Friday. Now it was Wednesday, and Nick was sitting in front of him asking, "Do you have any idea why your mother thought kidnapping was involved?"

Kat added, "All this time, she could have talked to me or to my father."

"I wish I could tell you," Eric said. "She never shared her abduction theory with me."

Nick piped up. "I would love to help you try to uncover the truth about your brother's disappearance. But in order to do this, we're going to need a lot more information."

Eric looked to Kat. The uniform she wore managed to seem both fitting and surprising. Knowing her sense of duty and honor, Eric realized it was appropriate that she wore a badge, yet when he looked at her, he still saw the sweet-faced teenager he had known so many years ago.

"I assumed Kat would help with that," he said. "Or is this not an official police matter?"

"It's not," Kat quickly answered. "I already told Nick he

could have full access to our records. But I doubt abduction is mentioned in them, so they likely won't tell us anything."

"That leaves family," Nick said. "Is your father still alive?"

Eric nodded, although he knew Ken Olmstead would be of little help. When Eric was growing up, his father was never there when he needed him. Eric saw no reason why he would start now.

"Or neighbors," Kat suggested. "Lee and Becky Santangelo are still around. So is Glenn Stewart."

Of course she would know that. But Eric assumed that, like his father, none of them would be useful. Although the Santangelos had lived across the street his entire life, he barely knew them. His mother had a falling-out with them before Eric could even walk. Their only exchanges were icy stares when their paths crossed while pulling out of the driveway or fetching the mail.

And when Lee was stumping for votes, of course. During election time he was happy to come over and chat. That was politics for you.

Then there was Glenn Stewart next door. Amazingly, Eric knew less about him than he did the Santangelos. His presence on the street was so minimal that Eric usually forgot about him entirely. His house—so tall and rickety—might as well have been empty, just like the one Mort and Ruth Clark used to live in.

"That's a start," Nick said. "I'll talk to them and see what they remember about that night. If we're lucky, maybe one of them saw something suspicious around Sunset Falls."

Eric shrugged, something Mitch Gracey never did. Even though Eric was his creator, Gracey was the complete opposite of himself—decisive, hard-charging, certain of everything. For instance, Gracey would already have been pounding on the Santangelos' door, demanding they spill their secrets. He wouldn't have remained in the dining room like Eric did, listening to Nick Donnelly move on to the next order of business.

"About this waterfall," he said. "Where is it?"

Although the question was directed at Eric, Kat Campbell was the one who answered. "Just beyond the woods at the end of the cul-de-sac."

"You can walk to it," Eric added, trying to be helpful.

"That's a good idea." Nick grabbed his cane and used it to help pull himself to his feet. "Let's have a look."

When Kat also stood, Eric reluctantly followed suit. He had no desire to visit Sunset Falls. Even as a boy, he never wanted anything to do with the spot that had shattered his family. But that morning it was unavoidable. Nick Donnelly wanted to see the falls and Eric was obliged to show him. It was where his brother's existence ended. Hopefully, it would also be the place where the answers to what happened to him began.

FOUR

The cul-de-sac was quiet. Forbiddingly quiet, like a graveyard at night. Part of that could be attributed to its status as a glorified dead end, an afterthought by town planners, which jutted into the woods toward the water. But there were other streets in Perry Hollow just like it, and none of them were this silent, this still, this—

Haunted.

That was probably too dramatic a word to describe the cul-de-sac, but it perfectly summed up the vibe Kat got from it.

There was no sidewalk, only high sycamores that towered next to the road, blocking out the bulk of the sun. In their leafy shadows, the street's four houses looked dark and empty. Their lawns were vacant. Their front porches bare. It seemed to Kat like a ghost town.

She was sure Nick and even Eric Olmstead, who grew up there, felt the same way. The three of them walked down the middle of the street slowly and quietly, as if they were afraid of disturbing whatever spirits might lurk there.

Nick was the first to speak, pointing to a large brick home set far back on the opposite side of the street. It reeked of ostentation, from the curving driveway to the giant brass knockers on the front door.

"Who lives there?"

"That's the Santangelo residence," Kat said. "Lee and Becky."

"Lee Santangelo. Where have I heard that name before?"

"He was a politician. State representative for, like, twenty years."

Until Eric Olmstead hit the bestseller list, Lee Santangelo had been Perry Hollow's most famous resident. The highlight of his tenure in Harrisburg was never taking a stand on anything and voting in whatever direction the popular wind was blowing. But people loved him. He was a former fighter pilot handpicked by NASA to train for the space program. His wife was a stylish beauty queen turned homemaker. They were Perry Hollow's own JFK and Jackie.

Kat remembered how Lee would visit the elementary school each year, giving rambling speeches that encompassed everything from the importance of space exploration to state government. Even as a girl, she had thought him a bit too full of himself, a little heavy on the preening. Other girls disagreed. Even as Lee entered his forties, Kat still heard classmates talk about his sheer dreaminess.

"When was the last time you talked to Lee Santangelo?" she asked Eric.

"We've barely said ten words to each other our entire lives. The most we talked was when he'd put campaign signs in our yard every election, despite the fact that my mother always pulled them up and threw them in the street. They didn't get along."

"Why not?"

"My mother never talked about it. Which makes me think it had something to do with Charlie."

Kat shot Nick a glance. Whether he meant to or not, Eric just gave them their first suspect.

They came to a stop again at the next house on that side of the street. About half the size of the Santangelo residence, it was a two-story clapboard. And although the lawn was mowed and curtains were hung in the windows, Kat didn't need the FOR SALE sign at the end of the driveway to tell her it was vacant. It had that air of emptiness homes on the market often possessed.

According to the sign, the Realtor was Ginger Schultz, a former high school classmate. She and Kat had taken algebra together, and they'd spend the class sitting in the back row giggling and slipping notes. Now that Kat thought about it, a lot of those notes had to do with Eric Olmstead. That he and Kat were once again in the same place at the same time would amuse Ginger to no end.

"Who used to live here?" Nick asked.

"Ruth and Mort Clark," Eric said with noticeable affection. "My mom actually liked them. They were good people."

"When did they move?"

Kat, whose job required her to know as much as she could about everyone in town, took the liberty of answering. "They didn't. They died. Mort sometime in the late eighties. Ruth was in the early nineties. The house has been on and off the market a lot since then."

"Any particular reason?" Nick asked.

"No idea."

Eric started walking again. "I'd say it was the street. People know what happened here. Word gets around. It makes the place feel . . . "

His voice trailed off, but Kat knew what word he had intended to use. It was the same word that had popped into her head earlier. *Haunted.*

As if they needed further proof of that feeling, Kat turned to the house across the street. Absurdly tall and run-down. The only way it could have looked more haunted is if there had been a cemetery in the front yard. Kat's gaze started at the widow's walk on the roof and slid down the house's façade. The windows were wide and rounded at the top, giving the impression of many eyes staring outward. Some were cracked. Others were missing shutters. The siding—Kat assumed it had once been white—desperately needed stripping and a fresh coat of paint. The front porch was in equally bad shape. Holes gaped willy-nilly in the floorboards and a whole section of railing had broken off. It now lay on the ground, partially hidden by knee-high crabgrass.

"Let me guess," Nick said, "this one is also vacant."

"You'd think that, from the looks of the place," Kat replied.

Nick jabbed his cane in the house's direction. "Someone actually lives there?"

Kat nodded. "Glenn Stewart. He's the town's recluse."

Other than the fate of Charlie Olmstead, Mr. Stewart was Perry Hollow's biggest mystery. Kat, who could recognize almost every one of the town's residents, had never knowingly laid eyes on the man. She also didn't know too many people who had. In order to see Glenn, you'd have to go inside his house or he'd have to come out. As far as she knew, neither of those things happened very often.

"He was here in 1969?" Nick asked.

"Yes," Eric said. "But according to my mother, he didn't leave the house back then, either. He just stays inside, in his own little world. If it wasn't for the occasional light in the window, you wouldn't know he was there at all."

Craning his neck, Nick scanned each window that faced the street. "He can hear us," he whispered.

Kat whispered back. "How can you tell?"

"Because he's watching us."

She tilted her head upward until she, too, saw what Nick was looking at. It was a lace curtain hanging in the window, yellowed by the sun. Holding it away from the glass was a pale hand. After a few seconds, the hand retreated and the curtain dropped into place.

"Weird," Nick said.

"Very."

"How much do you know about this guy?"

Kat struggled to come up with something—a random tidbit, a minor piece of gossip—and failed. She knew absolutely nothing about Glenn Stewart, a fact that bothered her immensely.

They moved forward, not speaking, until they reached the end of the cul-de-sac. A thick swath of trees created a green wall in front of them. Emerging from deep inside it, barely audible, was the muffled rush of water.

"It's this way," Eric said, pointing to the remnants of a path that had once cut through the woods but was now camouflaged by weeds and brush.

He led the way, tamping down the weeds in front of him. Kat went next, kicking away anything that had the potential to trip up Nick. When she checked to see how he was faring, she saw his eyes narrowed in concentration as he carefully made his way.

In the distance, the roar of Sunset Falls grew louder as they continued to trudge through the woods. Soon they cleared the trees and emerged along the water's bank, where the sound enveloped them. It was a steady thrum that echoed off the trees and forced them to raise their voices.

"This is it," Eric announced. "Sunset Falls."

In front of them, the creek rushed along with abnormal speed. It had been an unusually rainy summer, with the clouds opening up more often than not. The result of all that precipitation was a swollen creek that sparked into white water near the lip of the falls.

A wooden footbridge spanned the width of the creek, about fifty feet. It was narrow—barely wide enough to let two people pass—and of dubious strength. The trail continued on the other side, although it looked more neglected than the one on which they stood.

"Where does that path go?" Nick asked.

"Nowhere," Kat said. "It just slopes down to the bottom

of the falls, where it dead-ends. It used to be a popular place for picnics and pictures. Then Charlie Olmstead vanished, and no one wanted to go down there anymore."

"Is there any other way to get there?"

Kat knew where he was going with the question. If an abduction did occur at the falls, he wanted to know all the ways to get in and out of the area.

"Nothing. This street is the only way to reach it."

She should have said it *was* the only way to reach it. The bridge leading to the trail was now closed, a decision made sometime between her father's reign as police chief and her own. Signaling its closure was a rusted sign nailed to a decrepit sawhorse that sat in the way.

"Do you think it's safe?" Eric asked.

Kat, who hadn't been on the bridge in probably twenty years, said, "There's only one way to find out."

Moving the sawhorse aside, she contemplated the span. Age and exposure to the elements had turned the wood slate gray, and cracks and termite holes were visible everywhere. But the bridge seemed sturdy enough, so she took a single step onto it.

Nothing happened. So far, so good. Only about fifty more steps to go.

"You guys coming?"

Nick shook his head and backed away. "No thanks."

Kat bobbed up and down on the bridge's first plank, testing its sturdiness. "It seems fine to me. Where's your sense of adventure?"

"The last time I felt adventurous," Nick said, tapping his right knee, "this happened. So I'll just lean against a tree and watch."

This was unlike him, cane or no cane. Kat knew only one

thing could keep Nick from going out on that bridge: an ulterior motive. He was giving her time alone with Eric, presumably so the two of them could get reacquainted.

As Nick gingerly backed himself against a nearby oak, Kat faced forward again. She took another tentative step, practically on her tiptoes. Although the bridge seemed fairly solid, she did the same with her next two steps as she gripped the waist-high railing. After another two steps, she eased up on the caution and was walking normally.

The bridge creaked slightly under her weight, but that wasn't cause for concern. All bridges creaked. It wobbled, too, which worried Kat more than the creaking. But by that time it was too late. She was at the halfway point. Through the cracks between the bridge's planks, she saw the creek flowing swiftly beneath her. If the bridge collapsed, there was nothing she could do about it.

To her left, the creek was a ribbon of water that curved slightly through the trees. A couple of large rocks jutted through the surface, sending the water swirling around them in ripples that caught the sun. On the right side of the bridge, the water picked up speed. It gathered in long white streaks that slipped over the falls and vanished from view. If she fell in, there was very little to prevent her from tumbling down the falls.

Her only hope, Kat noticed, was a low-hanging branch from an oak tree next to the creek. Strong and sturdy, it stretched over the water at the point where the stream ended and Sunset Falls began. If she managed to grab the branch and hold on tight, she could survive. If she missed, then she'd be dead.

Thankfully, Eric caught up to her and she no longer had to think about survival plans, which made her nervous. To put her mind at ease, she engaged in small talk instead.

"How long are you going to be in town?"

"A few more weeks," Eric said. "I still have to pack everything up and put the house on the market."

"Your mother was a good woman. I was sorry to hear about the cancer."

Kat had considered going to Maggie Olmstead's funeral but eventually decided it wasn't a good idea. Seeing Eric again under those circumstances would have been awkward for both of them. Being alone on the bridge with him was awkward enough.

Yet it was also oddly exhilarating. For a moment it felt as if she was once again that shy freshman finally freed of braces and Eric had become that cute senior in Buddy Holly glasses. Memories she hadn't thought of for decades suddenly flashed through her mind. Most of them were good. Only one was bad.

"Should we push on?" she asked.

They crossed the bridge to the other side, where the path was practically invisible. Now a strip of dirt, it slanted downward, pointing the way to the bottom of the falls. Kat took a deep breath and began the descent, with Eric following close behind. It was rough going. A few rogue branches swiped at their heads while weeds scraped their legs. The waterfall, plunging directly to their right, sent off clouds of mist that stuck to their skin and made the ground muddy and slick beneath their feet.

"So," Eric said, "are you and Nick Donnelly . . ."

His voice trailed off, letting Kat pick whatever euphemism she wanted. Dating? An item? Lovers?

"We're just friends," she said. "Good ones."

"How do you two know each other?"

"Nick used to be with the state police," Kat said. "He helped me with a murder investigation last year."

"I heard about that. It's hard to believe something like that could happen in Perry Hollow."

It was also difficult to imagine Eric's brother being snatched by a stranger in the woods. Certainly, it was possible. About 80 percent of child abductions by strangers were committed a quarter mile from the victim's home. But this was a remote area, with only one way in or out. Someone on the street would have noticed a stranger coming or going.

They had reached the base of Sunset Falls. The path leveled off and the trees receded a bit, giving way to a pebble-strewn shore. The waterfall emptied into a deep pool that swirled and churned from the impact. According to official town records, the drop was thirty feet. But from Kat's vantage point, it looked much higher.

"If someone went over, do you think they could survive?"

"I doubt it," Eric said. "But someone could get lucky."

They'd have to be very lucky. A handful of ragged rocks jutted from the water at the base of the falls. They looked sharp and menacing, making Kat think of dinosaur teeth waiting to catch and destroy whatever fell their way.

Beyond them, the creek continued its journey, cutting a path through the land toward the horizon. Was Charlie Olmstead's body somewhere along its banks? Maybe dragged underwater by branches or lying somewhere in the trees, hidden from view. That was assuming, of course, that he had gone over the falls at all.

"Do you really think my mother was right?" Eric asked.

"I don't know. But Nick will find out as much as he can."

Despite tagging along with him, Kat still didn't want to get involved in the investigation. Her intention had been to stop by, see how Eric had changed—for better or for worse—and let the two of them try to solve the unsolvable mystery that was Charlie Olmstead. She had no desire to waste time before coming to the same conclusion her father had reached.

So Kat took one last look at the falls before retracing her steps along the path. This time, the climb made it even more arduous. By the time they reached the top, both she and Eric were out of breath. Back on the bridge, Kat saw Nick climb to his feet with the help of his cane. Apparently alone time with Eric was over.

"I think the native is getting restless," she said.

Eric took the lead and crossed the bridge quickly. "Nick seems like a pretty determined guy. Am I right?"

"You have no idea. Once he sets his mind on something, he doesn't quit until he gets it."

Kat, following Eric off the bridge, heard a loud creak that stopped her cold. The noise came from beneath her feet, soon changing from creaking to outright cracking. Then, before Kat had a chance to move, the plank beneath her splintered and fell away.

She managed a strangled yelp before falling with it, slipping helplessly into the gap the missing board had created. She came to a stop halfway through it as her rib cage and chest lodged between the boards on either side of her. Kicking her legs, Kat felt one foot splash into the creek. The broken board knocked against her ankle as it floated on the water's surface. It soon slipped past her and headed toward the falls.

In a flash, Eric was standing over her, gripping her arms. Kat, who had a prime view of his sneakers, saw the board beneath him start to bend from the weight and movement.

"Stop," she said. "Get on your stomach. Distribute the weight."

Cautiously, Eric moved into a crouch. Then he was on his stomach, sliding toward her. Just over his shoulder, Kat saw Nick step onto the bridge.

"Kat? Are you hurt?"

He took several quick steps, his cane smacking against the boards. Beneath them, the support beams groaned under the sudden addition of a third person. Kat felt herself drift backward an inch or so as the entire bridge shifted. She and Eric proved that it could support two people. There was no way of knowing if it could handle a third.

"Get off the bridge!" she yelled. "It's too much weight."

Nick shuffled backward until he was once again on land. Eric moved backward, too, gripping Kat's forearms and shimmying until she had enough space to pull herself up and out of the hole. When she heaved herself forward onto its surface, the bridge shifted again, this time in the opposite direction.

Kat got to her feet with Eric's help. The bridge still felt wobbly as they crossed to solid ground, but she suspected the sensation was just her body, which was shaking uncontrollably. She took a few deep breaths to calm herself. For the most part, she was unscathed. Other than her trembling body, the only sign of her close call was a streak of dirt across the front of her uniform. Kat tried to wipe some of it away as she turned back toward the bridge.

"Someone," she said, "needs to take a chain saw to that thing."

A half hour later, Kat was on the phone in her office. She was talking to a skeptical Burt Hammond about the danger posed by the bridge over Sunset Falls. The mayor, probably because he was still miffed about earlier that morning, wasn't buying it.

"I understand your concern, Chief," he said, "but that bridge has been closed for going on fifteen years now."

"Putting a sawhorse in front of it isn't the same as closing it. It needs to be demolished. I practically fell through the thing this morning."

"Why were you on the bridge in the first place?"

It was a question Kat should have seen coming. But still rattled from the bridge incident, she hadn't considered what the mayor would say once she called him. She only knew she couldn't give him the real reason. Burt Hammond would consider that a waste of manpower.

"It doesn't really concern you," she said weakly. "But the condition of that bridge should concern everyone."

"The town council and I will consider that."

Which meant they wouldn't consider it at all. In order to get any results, Kat needed to put it into terms the mayor could understand.

"If someone steps on the bridge and falls through it, he'll most likely go over the falls," she said. "If that happens, he'll probably die and his family will sue the town. Now, I don't know about you, but I don't want an expensive settlement on our hands."

When Burt responded, it was with a subdued, "I hadn't considered that."

Kat couldn't resist a smug smile of satisfaction. Her mission had been accomplished.

"I'm glad we agree on this matter," she said. "Maybe it means we can agree on a police budget, too."

Her smile faded when Burt said, "Considering all you're asking for, I highly doubt that." He then bid her a terse good-bye and hung up.

"Asshole," Kat muttered.

Nick, who was sitting in front of her desk, looked up in surprise. "Was that for me or the mayor?"

"The mayor, of course."

"I was just checking. You did slam a door in my face earlier today, although I think I deserved it."

"You did deserve it," Kat said. "But I'll forgive you if you forgive me."

"Deal."

Between them was a club sandwich and French fries picked up from the Perry Hollow Diner. Kat grabbed a quarter of the sandwich and nibbled off a corner. Nick practically inhaled a fry and grabbed the file on Charlie Olmstead, which they had retrieved from the basement. When he opened it, a tuft of dust rose from the pages.

He read the report with care, not skipping a single word. In all her years as a cop, Kat had never known such concentration existed until she met Nick Donnelly. When he investigated something, it was like a spell had been cast over him.

"This is interesting," he said. "After Charlie vanished, your father questioned everyone on the street."

"Including Glenn Stewart?"

"Yep. He said he went to bed at nine and missed all the commotion."

"Convenient alibi," Kat said.

"Speaking of alibis, Lee Santangelo also said he was home alone that night. His wife was out of town. But according to Maggie Olmstead, Mrs. Santangelo was also there. She saw her in an upstairs window."

"What did Becky Santangelo have to say about it?"

Nick grabbed his own piece of club sandwich and chewed

slowly, lost in thought. With his mouth full, he said, "That she was visiting her sister that night. The sister backed up her story. So did half a dozen other guests."

"At least my father was thorough," Kat said, grabbing a French fry, "although I doubt he ever imagined I'd be looking through one of his old police reports."

"Your father didn't write the report."

Kat froze, the French fry drooping an inch from her mouth. "Who did?"

"Deputy Owen Peale. Know him?"

"No. But I know someone who most likely does."

They left her desk and edged out of her office. Lou van Sickle sat at her workstation, chowing down on her own club sandwich. When Lou saw them approach, she instinctively covered her fries.

"What do you know about the Charlie Olmstead case?" Kat asked.

"That was forty-two years ago," Lou said. "How old do you think I am?"

Kat called her bluff. "Old enough."

Lou gave her the stink eye, which was reserved for occasions when she was especially pissed off. Still, she answered the question. "I know what everyone else does. It's no great mystery what happened to him. Or is it?"

Kat loved Lou like family, even though she was the town's gossip champion. There was no way she was going to tell Lou how they were investigating the Olmstead disappearance.

Nick, however, showed no such discretion.

"His mother thought he was kidnapped," he blurted out. "And we want to talk to the deputy who wrote the report."

Since she had already used the stink eye, Lou gave Kat a

you-know-better-than-to-get-yourself-messed-up-in-this look. Kat had seen it many times before, most notably when she had started sleeping with the colleague who would later become her ex-husband. That time, Kat should have followed Lou's silent advice. This time, she plowed ahead.

"His name was Owen Peale," she said. "I didn't know him, so he had to have stopped working here when I was very young."

Lou swiveled her chair until she was once again facing her lunch. "He quit before you were born. Went into private security because it paid more and he had three mouths to feed. Left without incident or animosity. I baked his good-bye cake. Vanilla with chocolate icing. Not my best work, if I recall. Anything else?"

"Is he still alive?" Nick asked.

"Last I heard he was. You can find him at Arbor Shade nursing home in Mercerville, because I know that's what you're going to ask me next."

Kat gave her a hug and a peck on the cheek. "You rock, Lou. Seriously, you do."

Nick also approached Lou, but instead of a kiss, he stole one of her French fries. Lou slapped his hand until he dropped it.

"Try that again," she said, "and I'll break your other leg."

FIVE

Sitting on the back porch, Eric held his cell phone in one hand and a lit cigarette in the other. He lifted them simultaneously, placing the phone against his ear and the cigarette against his lips. Both made him inhale.

He blew out a stream of smoke as the phone rang. And rang. And rang. He had never been much of a smoker, limiting it to a few bummed cigarettes in college dive bars and during breaks at stultifying writing conferences. He didn't start in earnest until after he returned to Perry Hollow to care for his mother. The excuse he told himself was that it was spurred on by stress. That might have been true, but the real reason was more complex. It was his own little rebellion—a reckless laugh in the face of the sickness all around him.

Eric inhaled again as the phone ceased buzzing. In its place was a small blip, the telltale sign his call was going to voice mail. It was followed by a voice more tired and hoarse than the last time he had heard it.

"This is Ken. I'm not around. Leave a message."

Eric closed his eyes. He wanted to hang up but resisted the urge.

"Dad," he said. "It's Eric. I guess you're on the road making a delivery. Or—"

Drunk. That's what he almost said. Drunk in the living room of whatever crumbling trailer he now called home or in some shithole roadside bar outside some shithole town along his trucking route. Instead, he settled on the more generic "somewhere."

"Listen. I hired someone to find out what happened to Charlie. Mom wanted me to. I guess she always wondered what happened. Anyway, this guy asked me to ask you if you knew anything about it. I told him you probably didn't, but he—"

Eric heard a sharp beep, followed by a click as the line went dead. He had rambled so much he was cut off.

"Crap."

He dialed his father's number again and waited through the requisite ringing before being connected to voice mail again. This time he was brief.

"Just call me back."

Eric dropped the cigarette, ground it out with his sneaker, and went inside. In the kitchen, he placed the phone on the table and stared at it, more to kill time than anything else. He didn't expect his father to return the call. He and Ken rarely talked. Just the usual birthdays and holidays, and sometimes not even then. So his hopes weren't high.

Even if he did call back, Eric was certain Ken would have no idea why his mother suspected something more sinister about Charlie's disappearance. As far as Eric knew, they rarely communicated after the divorce. His mother never talked about him. Ken Olmstead was another part of her painful past. Just like Charlie and his sealed-off bedroom.

The bedroom.

Eric knew he needed to look there eventually. The house was his now. In order to sell the place, he'd have to clear the whole thing out, including Charlie's room. If there was something inside that could help the investigation, that was even more reason to search it.

"No time like the present," he told the phone. It responded with silence.

He trudged upstairs and stopped in front of Charlie's room. Unlike the rest of the doors in the house, which had been replaced over the years, this one was an original. Brass doorknob. Old-style keyhole. Although he knew the door was locked, Eric tried the handle anyway. It barely turned. In order to open it, he'd need one of two things—a key or a crowbar. Mitch Gracey would have gone straight for the crowbar. Eric opted for the key.

Wherever that was.

Before his mother's death, little had been done in terms of planning. Other than the instructions in her will, Maggie did nothing to ensure Eric knew what to do when she was gone. Some of it, like learning when bills had to be paid, he had picked up easily. Other bits, such as knowing where the key to Charlie's room was hidden, had eluded him.

He started the search in his mother's room, rooting through her dresser and closet shelves. Then it was on to the kitchen, where every open drawer yielded only utensils, household minutiae, and Betty Crocker recipes.

Eric decided the next place to look would be the only spot in the house where he knew there was a visible trace of his brother—the basement.

Creaking down the stairs, he saw that little had changed there since he was a snooping kid. It was still strewn with dust-encrusted junk. Crates sitting upon boxes sitting upon chests. An array of appliances that spanned decades. And books. Stacks of them, some almost as tall as Eric herself.

Cutting a swath through all the debris was a foot-wide path that led to the furnace. Eric followed it to the end before he turned left. With his back pressed against the wall, he had just enough room to skirt past the bulk of the more recent junk and reach a section of old junk.

He cleared a space on the floor and sat down next to an eight-millimeter film projector he never knew his mother owned and sifted through box after box. Each one unearthed a long-neglected memory—Halloween decorations, mothballed clothes, Christmas ornaments that tapered into silvery points and had once seemed as delicate as stained glass. After an hour of searching, he opened a box and saw his brother staring back at him.

Eric recognized it instantly as a school picture. His own class portraits had been taken in front of the same blue background at Perry Hollow Elementary School. In the photo, Charlie looked uncertain. He was smiling, yes, but it was slightly crooked, with a hint of sadness at the edges. Eric saw the same sadness in Charlie's eyes. He looked like a boy who knew he didn't have many class pictures left.

There were more school photos beneath it, each one taken a year earlier than the one before and showing Charlie getting younger in a distinctly Benjamin Button–like fashion. There were pictures of him at Christmas. Blowing out candles on a birthday cake. Posing one Easter in a powder blue suit that Eric would have torn off had he been stuffed into it.

Below that was a photograph of Charlie holding a baby in his lap. The baby, Eric realized, was him when he was only a few months old. He and his brother were on the brown couch his mother had kept until 1982. Charlie looked at the camera, beaming, as Eric wriggled in his arms. Charlie looked so happy then. Eric saw that he did, too. It reminded him that although he had grown up an only child, he once had a brother, and it might have been nice to grow up that way, too.

There was one more photograph in the box. So many years there had left it flattened facedown against the bottom. When Eric pried it up, he saw it was a picture of his parents standing on a beach. His father wore a crisp white T-shirt and dark shorts. His mother had on a two-piece bathing suit. Both of them grinned madly for the camera.

Also in the photo were a man and woman Eric had never seen before. The man had a deep tan, slicked-back hair, and a devil-may-care smile. The woman wore a flowing white dress that fluttered in the breeze. Eric had no idea who they were. Friends of his parents, he assumed. He also had no clue when the picture was taken—certainly years before he, or even Charlie, were born—and he was struck by the sight of his parents in their youth. His mother had been so beautiful then, with a smile brighter and wider than any he had ever seen. His father, too, was good-looking—strong and handsome, with the confidence of someone who had yet to be defeated by life's disappointments.

After studying the picture a few moments longer, Eric placed it back in the box with the others. Then he slid the box back into its original position, noticing something unusual just behind it. A large piece of plywood had been propped in front of an alcove beneath the basement steps. It wasn't meant to hide the space. Bits of darkness could be seen above it and on each side. Rather, it looked to Eric like it was put there to hide something *inside* the alcove.

Like more of Charlie's possessions, Eric thought. Perhaps even a key.

Sliding the plywood aside, he didn't see a key or anything that might contain one. But he did find another one of Charlie's possessions—his bicycle.

It stood alone in the center of the alcove, unsteadily resting on its kickstand. The front tire was flat. The rear one was badly mangled. Four decades' worth of cobwebs dangled from their spokes. Rust had taken over the base years ago, and there were too many dents and nicks to count. Yet Eric could still make out bits of blue paint and tiny white marks that he guessed were stars.

When he slid a hand across its surface, his palm came up black with dust. He wished his mother had shown him the bike when she was still alive. He wished she had opened the door to Charlie's room and let Eric roam around it. Most of all, he wished his mother had trusted him enough to at least express her suspicions about what happened. And her hope. And her frustration and sadness and regret.

Tears welled up in Eric's eyes. He wiped them away with his clean hand. Since Gracey sure as hell didn't cry, Eric wasn't going to, either. Not when he still had work to do. He still had to find a key, and other than making him emotional, the trip to the basement had been fruitless.

Backing out of the alcove, he bumped against the plywood board. It tipped over, landing against the boxes behind it. Eric spun around, startled. What he saw unnerved him even more.

A map of Pennsylvania has been tacked to the other side of the board. It showed the entire state from border to border. Perry Hollow was marked with a large red circle. Five other spots on the map had similar circles. In the center of each was a thumbtack that held a length of red string in place. Each string stretched to an area outside the map, their ends also secured by tacks. Pinned next to every strand was a newspaper article.

Eric scanned the entire board, stopping at the string that

led to Perry Hollow. The article that accompanied it was illustrated with a picture of Charlie—the same class photo Eric had seen in the box. The headline was a punch to the gut: PERRY HOLLOW BOY, 10, MISSING.

His gaze jumped to another article. And another. And another. Each one sent his heart racing a little faster and tightened the knot that had suddenly formed in his stomach.

"Mom," he said in astonishment, "what the hell were you up to?"

SIX

There were no arbors at Arbor Shade. As far as Nick could tell, there wasn't much shade, either. While the name conjured up English gardens and rolling meadows, what he and Kat encountered was a clay-colored building just off the highway. Despite some shrubs by the front door and a smattering of trees on the lawn, the place looked anything but bucolic.

"Promise me something," Nick said as they neared the entrance.

"What?"

"That you'll shoot me before I ever end up in a place like this."

Kat agreed, adding, "Only if you do the same."

Arbor Shade wasn't much nicer on the inside—more dentist office waiting area than living room. Gray walls. Mauve carpet. A meager array of magazines on a crooked coffee table.

Next to a fake potted palm was a small receptionist's window, where a matronly woman peeked out at them.

"Are you here for a tour?"

Nick hobbled up to the window. "We need to talk to one of your residents. Mr. Owen Peale."

"I'm afraid it's too early for visiting hours. Most family members come on evenings or weekends."

Kat joined Nick at the window and flashed her badge. "I'm Chief Campbell of the Perry Hollow Police. We really need to speak with Mr. Peale."

The receptionist's eyes widened and she put a hand to her chest. "Is he in trouble?"

"No," Kat said. "Should he be?"

"Of course not." The receptionist checked the area for prying coworkers before leaning forward and whispering, "But we've had some complaints."

"What did he do?" Nick asked.

The woman at the window wouldn't say, which made her the worst kind of gossip—a tease. Nick much preferred Lou van Sickle's all-or-nothing approach.

"I've already told you too much," the receptionist said. "You can usually find Mr. Peale in the common room at this hour. And a word of warning: it would be wise to watch your wallets."

She gave them directions to the common room before pressing a black button on the wall. There was a low buzz, followed by a click as a door to Nick's right unlocked.

"Security," the receptionist explained.

Nick assumed the system was intended not to keep visitors out but to keep residents in. It was understandable. Thrown into a place like this, his first order of business would be to hatch an escape plan. But on the way to the common room, he saw that most of the residents seemed, if not content, then at least resigned to their fates. They roamed the halls aimlessly, using a wide array of mobility devices. Orthopedic canes. Walkers. Wheelchairs. Gripping the pit bull handle of his own cane, Nick realized it was all downhill from there. Soon he'd be making the same sad progression. At the entrance to the common room, he and Kat were cut off by a woman riding a motorized scooter. At least that was something to look forward to.

The common room was nicer than Nick expected, and a far cry from the waiting area. There were real plants there, catching the sun from a row of windows along one wall. Plush armchairs ran the perimeter of the room, broken up by shelves loaded with books and board games.

In the center of the room, a silver-haired cluster sat in front of a television, watching the news. Giving the TV a cursory glance, Nick saw yet another report about China's trip to the moon. The mission had been in the news all summer, with so-called experts squawking nonstop about what it meant for the United States and the rest of the world.

The attention had reached fever pitch now that the mission was finally under way. Nick couldn't turn on the TV or open a newspaper without seeing something about it. He understood why it was big news, yet he just couldn't bring himself to care. The moon had been there since the beginning of time and would exist until the end of time. It didn't really matter who walked on it and what country they were from.

Turning away from the TV, Nick asked an elderly woman sitting nearby to point out Owen Peale. She did, gesturing to a man in sweatpants and a plaid robe sitting alone with a deck of cards. Next to his elbow was a tattered shoe box.

Nick approached the table. "Mr. Peale?"

The man studied first Nick, then Kat. "That's me."

"Do you have a minute to speak with us?"

"Am I in trouble?"

That question again. Hearing it a second time made Nick wonder just how much of a handful Owen Peale really was.

"Of course not."

"I was just wondering," Owen said, cocking his head in Kat's direction. "Because most people who visit me don't bring a cop along."

Kat extended a hand. "Mr. Peale, I'm Kat Campbell—"

"Jim Campbell's girl. I know. You look like your dad."

"So you remember working for him?"

Owen started shuffling the cards while muttering, "Of course I remember. I'm old, not senile."

"Then if you remember that," Nick said, "you most likely recall an incident involving a boy named Charlie Olmstead."

"I remember. I wrote the report."

"I know. That's why we're here. To ask you a few questions about the incident."

"That's an old case, son. Let sleeping dogs lie. That's my motto."

"Even if the boy's mother thought he was kidnapped?"

That seemed to get Owen's attention. The former cop eyed Nick's cane. "Looks like you need to sit down, son. You're in worse shape than me."

Nick took a seat. Kat remained standing. It was a wise decision, because Owen Peale started dealing cards as soon as Nick got situated.

"What's this?" he asked, staring dumbly at the cards being tossed in front of him.

"Poker," Owen replied. "Five-card draw. No wilds."

"I don't play poker."

"If you're staying, you're playing. That's the only way I'm going to answer your questions. Now ante up."

"Ante?" Nick said. "You're joking, right?"

"Poker isn't played for fun, son. This is a money game. Now, I need to see some cash on that table or you and your cop friend can take your questions elsewhere."

Nick sighed his response. "How much are we betting?"

"Five dollars to start." Owen opened the shoe box, which was filled with loose bills and rattling change. He placed a five-dollar bill in the middle of the table. "We can go higher if you think you can keep up with me."

"Five? That's extortion."

"But I might have some juicy information about the Olmstead boy. You'll never know if you don't play."

Nick opened his wallet. Save for three ones, it was empty. He thought of the four dollars he had spent for a coffee at Big Joe's. Without the java, he could have played at least one hand. Unless the old coot decided to raise.

He turned to Kat. "Could you spot me?"

"This is ridiculous," she announced, digging through her own wallet. Still, ridiculous or not, she found a five and slapped it on the table.

When Owen saw the cash, a wide smile spread across his face. "Let's look at our cards."

Nick peeked at his hand. It was weak—a pair of twos, a four, a seven, and a king.

"You going to start asking your questions?" Owen said from behind his own cards.

"The report states you were with Chief Campbell and Maggie Olmstead the night Charlie vanished," Nick began.

"That's not a question," Owen said. "But I'm gonna answer it anyway. Yes, I was there."

"Who was the first person on the scene?"

"The chief. Normally, it was just me on duty at night, but the chief thought it'd be a good idea to have more manpower on the streets in case something happened with the moon folks. The whole town was buzzing about it. Parties and singing in the streets and worrying about something bad happening up there."

"What does the moon have to do with any of this?"

Owen lowered his cards and flashed him a look seen only from grandmothers, teachers, and other exasperated authority figures. "Don't you know your history, son? *Apollo 11*. Man walked on the moon."

"I know what *Apollo 11* is," Nick said, bristling. "Was that the night Charlie Olmstead vanished?"

"It sure was. July twentieth, 1969." Owen jerked his head toward the TV across the room. "And what's going on in China right now was going on in America back then. I raise you five."

A raise. Of course. Nick should have seen it coming. Kat, apparently, had. Clenched in her hand was a five spot, which she threw onto the table with an audible growl.

"So my dad was there first," she said. "Do you know for how long?"

"A few minutes, I guess. It was about quarter to eleven. I met up with him at the end of the street. He told me that Ken Olmstead just reported his son missing and that we should have a look around the creek and bridge."

"Why there?" Nick asked.

"Because that's where Mr. Olmstead said Charlie was heading. How many cards do you want?"

Nick got rid of the four and the seven. They were replaced by a six and a ten. Still a crappy hand, especially compared with the one card Owen took.

"I raise you another five," he said.

Nick dropped his cards. "I fold."

Grinning again, Owen Peale lunged for the money and slid it toward his side of the table. "Feel free to ask me another question."

"Was Ken Olmstead also there when you arrived?"

"He was. So was a neighbor. Mort Clark. They looked around with us for a little bit before going back home to tell Mrs. Olmstead the bad news. The chief and I continued looking."

It was Kat's turn for another question. "Did you see anything unusual?"

"Other than Mrs. Olmstead clutching her baby in the rain and getting hysterical?"

"When did this happen?"

"About fifteen minutes later. Right after I spotted the boy's bike in the water. She came out of nowhere and ran onto the bridge."

"Did she see the bike?"

Owen had collected the cards and was shuffling them again. For a man pushing seventy-five, his hands were quick. The cards seemed to dance in his capable fingers, a blur of reds and blacks.

"I told her not to look. Just in case the boy was dead nearby. But she saw it anyway. Then, while we were standing there, the bike broke free and went over the falls. That was the moment all of us realized the same thing probably happened to the boy."

Nick took note of his word choice. "Probably?"

"At that point, it wasn't a certainty," Owen said. "Still isn't."

"What do you think really happened?"

"Ante up."

Kat dug into her wallet and huffed. "I'm out of fives and I only have three ones. After that, it's all twenties."

"Don't worry, Officer," Owen said, grinning. "I can make change."

Kat reached across the table and traded a twenty for four fives. She placed one of them on the table.

"The bike went over the falls," Owen continued as he dealt Nick his new cards. "I saw it with my own eyes. So did the others. And I think everyone jumped to the same conclusion without asking one basic question: How did the bike get there?"

"Charlie Olmstead rode it into the creek," Nick said. "That was the official ruling, right?"

"It was. But when was the last time you heard of someone riding their bike into a creek?"

"Never," Nick said. "But it was dark."

"It certainly was." Owen stared at him expectantly. "You raising or checking?"

Nick examined his hand. It was much better than the previous one—a nine, a ten, a jack, and a queen. The odd card out was a five of clubs that he intended to get rid of immediately. "I'll raise you five."

This time, Kat shook her head before placing the money on the table. "I'm keeping track of how much you owe me."

"Think of it as a donation," Nick told her.

"Donation, my ass."

Owen called, tossing in his own money. "It was also raining that night. Made the ground soft."

"That only boosts the argument that Charlie lost control and accidentally went into the water."

Nick placed the five of clubs facedown on the table and Owen drew him a new card. It was a king. He had a straight on his hands.

"Sounds to me," Owen said, "like you think the Olmstead boy went over the falls."

"I don't know what to think," Nick replied. "I only know what I've been told."

"Then what if I told you that in that soft ground I mentioned, well, there weren't any tire tracks, bike or otherwise, leading into the water. So if Charlie Olmstead was on that bike when it went in, then he must have been levitating."

"How do you think the bike got there?"

"Someone tossed it in," Owen said. "After grabbing the boy."

Nick's mind spun so rapidly that he actually started to get dizzy. During the course of the day, he had slowly come to accept the official story about Charlie Olmstead's disappearance, mostly because there was no evidence to refute it. Until now.

"Did you tell anyone about this?" Kat asked. Taking a seat next to Nick, she leaned forward with anticipation.

"I told your father," Owen said. "Not that he needed telling. He noticed the lack of tracks, too."

"But why wasn't any of this in the report? Certainly the two of you should have investigated it further."

"We did. We interviewed everyone who lived on that

street. Even that crazy neighbor of theirs, although he wouldn't let us inside. We had to talk to him through the screen door."

"The report said Mr. Stewart claimed to be asleep at the time," Nick said. "Did you really believe that?"

"We had to," Owen said. "We knew there was no one to confirm or deny it. Besides, taking the Olmstead boy would require him leaving his house. And you're more likely to see Howard Hughes rise from the dead and give you a lap dance than be invited into Glenn Stewart's place."

Nick had a habit of creating mental files about cases, crimes, and suspects. It helped him organize his thoughts and keep ideas on track. Owen Peale's Howard Hughes line was immediately secured there, but not because it had anything to do with the Olmstead case. He simply wanted to be able to use it someday.

"What about the Santangelos?" he asked. "The report mentioned a disparity in testimony about whether Becky Santangelo was home or not."

Owen waved the words away like he was swatting at a fly. "That was just a simple misunderstanding. Maggie said she spotted Becky in an upstairs window. I think she saw someone, but not Mrs. Santangelo, if you get my meaning."

Nick most certainly did. "Lee was having an affair?"

"That was the assumption, which is why I left it out of the report. What Lee Santangelo did in his spare time was none of our business. Although why he'd want to step out on someone as fine as Becky is beyond me. I'd turn into a foxhound for a piece of that tail."

"You should change the subject," Kat told him, "before I decide to shoot you."

Owen shrugged off the threat. Nick decided that, scam artist or not, he liked the man.

"What did the Clarks have to say?"

"Not much," Owen said. "They were asleep. Ken Olmstead woke them with the news that Charlie was missing. Mort Clark joined the search. Ruth went to watch the baby. Even though their house was closest to the creek, they heard nothing. Not even a splash."

"That leaves the Olmsteads," Nick said. "Did you interview them alone or together?"

"Together. Although there seemed to be tension between them. Angry glances. Crossed arms. Stiff posture. There was some bad body language going on."

"Do you think some of that was grief?" Kat asked.

"Yes. And blame. It seems Maggie was sleeping when Charlie left the house. That put Ken Olmstead in charge."

"What was he doing?"

"He said he was resting, too. On the couch. Awake but with his eyes closed. He said it was about nine thirty when Charlie asked if he could ride his bike outside. Mr. Olmstead told him he could, but to make it quick. Again, with his eyes closed."

"So he never actually saw Charlie leave?" Nick said.

"No."

Owen continued recounting his conversation at the Olmstead residence, painting a picture of a very unhappy household. He told them how Maggie faulted her husband for not going outside with Charlie. Ken said he couldn't go because, since Maggie was asleep upstairs, that meant an infant, Eric, would have been left unattended. When Maggie said he should have just roused her from sleep to watch the baby, Ken countered by saying they both knew that wasn't an option.

"I don't know what he was referring to," Owen said. "When his wife disagreed with him, Ken responded with only one word—bathtub."

Nick had no idea why that innocuous word would have been significant, but it must have meant something to Maggie and Ken Olmstead. He tossed it into his mental file, just in case it popped up later.

"Did you mention the lack of bike tracks to the Olmsteads?"

"We told Mr. Olmstead about it the next day," Owen said. "He decided it was best not to tell Maggie, knowing she'd get worked up over it."

"Did he have any ideas as to why there weren't any leading to the water?"

"He wondered if the reason there were no tracks was because the rain washed them away. Chief Campbell agreed that it made sense. And since the bike had already been found at the bottom of the falls, all of us started to suspect the obvious had happened. So when Ken asked us to focus more on trying to find his son's body, that pretty much ended the investigation. I wrote up my report. The search party went on for a few more days. And Charlie Olmstead's body might still be out there somewhere."

However misguided they were, Nick understood the actions of Kat's father and Deputy Peale. Other than the lack of tracks, there was no real reason to suspect foul play was involved. Nor did he think the request by the Olmsteads was out of the ordinary. They were sad. They were grieving. They were trying to make sense of a senseless situation.

He and his parents had gone through the same thing after his sister vanished. Waiting for months. Riding a stomach-churning tide of hope and despair. Having an official police declaration that Sarah Donnelly had died in a tragic accident would have allowed them to stop questioning and start recovering. Nick suspected the Olmsteads just wanted to do the same.

Only one of them never stopped questioning.

"Maggie Olmstead," Nick said to Owen. "You told her about the lack of tracks, didn't you?"

Owen hedged slightly. "I did. Years later. Long after her son's case had been closed."

"How much later?" Kat asked.

"Early seventies. Maybe 1973. I was through with police work by that time. She came to my house late one night. She had her son with her. Eric. He was asleep and Mrs. Olmstead was carrying him. Other than the boy's size, it was just like the night Charlie vanished. She asked me if I thought Charlie really went over the falls or if he might have been kidnapped."

"But how would she even know to ask you that?"

"Beats me," Owen said with a shrug. "But something gave her that idea."

"And you told her what you just told us?" Nick asked.

"For the most part."

"How did she react?"

"Stoic," Owen said. "I got the feeling she had been expecting that answer. And disappointed, like I had let her down. Which I did, I guess. Every time I see a missing child on the news, I can't help thinking about that Olmstead boy and if I had failed him."

Nick didn't need to ask him any more questions. Even though Owen Peale hadn't told him exactly what he wanted to hear, it was enough. Nick knew the Charlie Olmstead case was anything but closed. Standing and stretching his bum leg, he thanked Owen for his time.

"Now, wait a minute," the former deputy said. "You can't just walk away in the middle of a hand."

"The game is over, Mr. Peale. Keep the money."

"I don't want to keep it if I haven't earned it."

"Fine." Nick huffed as he returned to the table and revealed the straight that had been hiding in his hand.

Owen turned over his cards—a three of hearts, followed by four aces. Raking the winnings toward him, he gave Nick a shit-eating grin that let Nick know he had just been played.

"Guess I earned it after all," he said.

The drive back to Perry Hollow was unusually quiet as both of them processed the information they had gleaned from Owen Peale. For Nick, that meant flipping through his mental notes, focusing on words that didn't make much sense on the surface. *Falls. Bike. Bathtub.* But he knew they were related somehow, just as he knew that Charlie Olmstead's disappearance wasn't what it seemed.

Kat knew it, too. Nick could tell by the way she gripped the steering wheel and worked her jaw, lost in thought.

"I don't understand," she eventually said, "why my father . . ."

Although her voice drifted off into silence, Nick knew what she was trying to say. She wanted to know why her father would just drop the issue of the missing tire tracks.

If Nick had been working the case, there's no way he would have stopped investigating. Family request or not, there was no reason to ignore even the slightest bit of evidence in a missing child case. But he also understood the actions of Kat's father. More important, he understood his mind-set.

"You shouldn't think less of him," Nick said. "Your father

probably truly believed Charlie went over the falls, most likely because the alternative was unthinkable to him."

He remembered how dazed Kat had seemed following the first Grim Reaper murder. She was still tough, of course, and impressively smart for a local chief, but Nick had also registered the shock in her eyes and disbelief in her voice. She couldn't fathom something so terrible happening in her tiny town.

"Cops don't ignore the facts just because they don't like them," Kat said. "And the fact was, there should have been tire tracks leading into the water."

"But there weren't," Nick countered. "There was no boy, either. Just a bike at the base of a waterfall. So, given two choices and knowing your town's crime statistics, which one would you believe? That the boy was abducted or that he somehow rode his bike into the water and went over the falls?"

Kat's face was expressionless as she stared out the windshield. "I hate when you're right."

"Then you must hate me a lot."

"Don't push it, Donnelly."

They were in Perry Hollow by that point, gliding down the Main Street of the place Kat had called home her entire life. Nick hadn't been back to his hometown in Ohio in ages. He suspected that if he ever did venture there again, he'd be haunted by his past. He wondered, not for the first time, how Kat dealt with the daily onslaught of memories.

"So," he said, "would you like to tell me about you and Eric Olmstead?"

He thought the question would make her angry. It didn't. She seemed to have become more mellow about the subject since seeing Eric again. Nick hoped that was a good sign.

"I thought you already had it figured it out," she said.

"I do. Boyfriend. Girlfriend. Puppy love. Like something out of *Gidget*."

"Yes, we dated," Kat said. "He was a senior. I was a freshman."

"For how long?"

Kat sighed. He was annoying her now. So much for being mellow. "Four months."

"How did it end?"

"Badly."

She turned left onto the cul-de-sac where Eric lived and Charlie had vanished. Just like that morning, it had an abandoned feeling about it. There were no signs of life in any of the houses except for the Olmstead residence, and there it was only Eric, sitting on the front porch. There was a cigarette in his hand and a beer bottle at his feet. He stood up and rushed toward them when he saw Kat's car.

"I know why my mother thought Charlie was kidnapped," he said.

Nick scrambled out of the car as fast as he could, which wasn't very fast at all. Sometimes he hated his leg, hated his cane. This was one of those times.

"Why?"

Eric pushed them toward the house. In the process, he knocked over the beer bottle. Foam bubbled up from the neck and spread across his sneakers. He didn't seem to notice.

"Because he wasn't the only victim," he said. "There were others."

SEVEN

The board, four feet wide and three feet long, covered most of the dining-room table. Kat circled it warily, overwhelmed not only by the sheer size of the display but by all the things crammed onto it. A map. String. Newspaper clippings. Photographs. Kat didn't know where to look first. She settled on the map, simply because it occupied the most space.

It had been marred by dozens of red circles. Some were made with pencil. Others with Magic Marker. Most of them were crossed out with a large X made of thick, black ink. That left only six red circles untouched. The first was in a southeastern corner of the map, exactly where Perry Hollow was located. Next to the circle, someone had scrawled a number, also in red—one.

"You think your mother did all this?" Kat asked Eric, who stood against the wall, arms crossed. He looked dazed and unsteady, like someone trying to shake off a massive shock. In his hand was a fresh beer, replacing the one he had spilled outside.

"I assume she did. That's her handwriting."

Kat took a closer look at the number next to her town. It had been cleanly written, the lines straight and letters methodical. A lot of precision had gone into its creation.

Poking right into Perry Hollow was a thumbtack with a string attached to it. The string led off the map, where Kat saw the same newspaper article Nick had shown her earlier in the day. She didn't need to read it. She knew exactly what it was about.

Surrounding the map were other newspaper clippings. Just like the red circles, only six of them remained.

"Look for a number two," she said.

Nick, standing on the other side of the board, leaned over it, index finger circling above the map. It landed in the northern part of the state, probably twenty miles from the New York border.

"Number two," he said. "Fairmount, Pennsylvania. Ever hear of it?"

Kat shook her head as Nick slid his finger over the string attached to Fairmount. It led to a newspaper clipping at the top of the board. The headline was an echo of the first. BOY MISSING FROM FAIRMOUNT.

"Is there a date on it?"

"He vanished the nineteenth of November, 1969. Four months after Charlie."

Nick read the article out loud. "Police are searching for a ten-year-old boy who vanished yesterday in Fairmount. The parents of Dennis Kepner reported him missing after he failed to come home last night. The boy was last seen playing in the park across the street from his house. A thorough search of the area by authorities yielded no clues as to the boy's whereabouts."

Just like the article about Charlie Olmstead, the one for Dennis Kepner ran with a picture. Instead of a school photo, it was one provided by the family. It showed a chubby, towheaded boy standing next to someone taller, probably a parent. The other person had been cropped out, leaving just a stray hand in the frame next to Dennis's elbow.

"Number three is nearby," Nick said, pointing to a circle less than an inch from Fairmount. "There's no town here. Just a blank space."

Kat hurried to his side. Surrounding the thumbtack was nothing but paper turned yellow with age. She let the red string attached to the tack guide her to the corresponding headline. BOY, 9, VANISHES IN STATE PARK.

The photo under the headline identified the boy as Noah Pierce. He smiled for the camera, grinning like a fool. His hair was neatly combed, except for one cowlick on the top of his head that couldn't be tamed. The image made Kat's heart break just a little.

She scanned the article and began to read it for Nick and Eric. "A boy from Winter Haven, Florida, was reported missing yesterday in Lasher Mill State Park. Noah Pierce, age nine, was visiting his grandparents in Fairmount. His grandmother said they went to the park because Noah wanted to play in the snow."

"Snow?" Nick said. "When did it happen?"

Kat looked for a date somewhere on the clipping and found none. Lifting the paper gently, she looked at the other side. There was a date there, slightly cut off by Maggie Olmstead's scissors decades earlier. Still, Kat could make out a month, a day, a year.

"February sixth, 1971," she said. "Considering this was the next day's newspaper, Noah Pierce vanished on the fifth."

"That's a long time between victims."

It was spoken by Eric, who remained against the wall.

"Come on," he said. "We're all thinking the same thing my mother thought. All of these boys, my brother included, were taken by the same person."

This was hard on him. Kat saw it in his eyes and in his

ashen face. He was a writer, someone who plied his skills in the world of fiction. His crimes were made up. These were real, and one of the victims was his long-lost brother. It was bound to shake up even the most jaded soul.

"We don't know that for sure," Kat said, not even believing it herself.

Eric approached the board and located the fourth victim. Again, the thumbtack wasn't on a specific town, just a blank area of the map that was shaded green.

"Boy missing from local camp," he said, reading the headline that went with it. "The owner of Camp Crescent, a summer camp for neglected, disadvantaged, and delinquent boys, reported that one of the campers vanished from his cabin during the night. Dwight Halsey, age twelve, lived in upstate New York. Police are searching the woods surrounding the camp under the assumption the boy tried to run away. The article is dated July thirty-first, 1971. Which means he disappeared the night before."

All three of them crowded around the article. The photo that ran with it showed a tall, lanky boy with dark curly hair. He stood in front of what appeared to be a cabin, most likely at the camp he vanished from. Unlike the others, Dwight Halsey didn't look so innocent. His smile was more of a smart-ass smirk, and his eyes contained a mean glint. He looked like the kind of kid Kat warned James to stay away from.

She rounded a corner of the board, stopping at the location where the fifth victim disappeared. It was Centralia, Pennsylvania, and instead of one circle, this town had two, one engulfing the other like a target. In the bull's-eye were two tacks and two strands of string that veered off in different directions. Kat used her finger to trace one of them, coming to a newspaper clipping that showed a stout boy in a shirt and tie sitting in front of a nondescript background. Another school photo.

Above the picture, the requisite bad news: CENTRALIA BOY, 11, REPORTED MISSING. Beneath that was a smaller headline that said, POLICE BELIEVE HE FELL DOWN ABANDONED MINE SHAFT.

Kat scanned the article. The boy's name was Frankie Pulaski. He went outside to play on April 21, 1972, and never came home. Because he lived deep in the heart of Pennsylvania's coal country, the police's first instinct was that a sinkhole had consumed him. It had happened before and according to the article about the sixth and final victim, it happened again on December 11, 1972.

ANOTHER CENTRALIA BOY VANISHES was that headline.

She read from the article beneath it. "A boy from Centralia is missing, police say. William Mason, ten, failed to come home from school yesterday. After an exhaustive search for the boy, who goes by the nickname 'Bucky,' police believe he may have fallen into one of the many mine shafts that dot the area. In April, another Centralia youth, eleven-year-old Frankie Pulaski, also disappeared. The police concluded the boy likely fell into a sinkhole. His body was never recovered."

When she finished reading, Kat stared at the photo of Bucky Mason. He looked like a Bucky—bowl haircut, chubby cheeks, two prominent front teeth that hung slightly over his bottom lip.

She took a step back until she could see the contents of the entire board. The faces of the missing boys looked at her with their myriad expressions. Some happy. Some sad. All hopeful, except for Dwight Halsey and his smirk.

And every single one of them gone.

"You were right, Eric. They're all related."

Kat was certain of it, just as certain as Maggie Olmstead had been when she put together this morbid collage. The scratched-out red circles made it abundantly clear that Maggie had spent a lot of time winnowing down the board's contents to these six cases. There might have been other missing boys on that board at one point, but these were the only ones that mattered to her. The question they now faced was why.

"Nick," she said, "this used to be your thing. What do you make of all this?"

When he worked for the state police, Nick was an expert on the criminal mind. He wasn't a profiler, but he knew enough to understand why people sometimes did unthinkable things. When such a person had targeted the residents of Perry Hollow, Nick had been there to guide her. Kat hoped he could do the same now.

"Clearly, it's a serial killer," Nick said.

Eric cleared his throat. "Killer?"

"There are three types of abductions," Nick replied. "The most common ones are among family members. Custody disputes. Desperate parents. It's usually very obvious early on who the perpetrator is."

"I know," Eric said. "I wrote about one in a Mitch Gracey book."

"The second is acquaintance kidnapping. The victims are mostly teenagers and mostly girls. The perps are normally other teenagers, perverted neighbors, guys who get off on abusing girls."

Nick approached the board, studying it with those green

eyes of his that always seemed to be noticing something Kat had missed. His gaze darted from photo to photo and from town to town, examining the big picture.

"The third type," he said, "are the ones that can't easily be explained away."

Kat knew all about those cases through AMBER Alerts and statewide APBs. These were the kids snatched from the grocery store. The ones who got into the van with the guy offering candy. The ones who, like Charlie Olmstead, rode off on their bikes and were never seen again.

"So," Eric said, a noticeable catch in his throat, "you think whoever did this took and killed all of them?"

Nick nodded solemnly. "If any of these boys were still alive, we'd have heard about it by now."

From across the room, Kat watched as Eric Olmstead took a deep breath and nodded. He lifted the beer to his lips and gulped. Then he excused himself, hurrying out of the dining room, through the kitchen, and onto the back porch. She envied his ability to escape. She wanted to flee the room, as well, and not have to look at the sad gallery in front of her. So many boys. So many victims. Yet she had to look. This was no longer just a matter to be handled by Nick and his foundation. This was now a police matter.

"What do you think the link is?" she asked. "I know there has to be one. You taught me that."

"The first thing I noticed was the ages," Nick said. "Who was the youngest?"

Kat pointed to the photo of Noah Pierce. "He was nine."

"The oldest was twelve," Nick said, gesturing to Dwight Halsey's picture. "That makes sense. Usually killers who prey on children like to stick to the same age range."

"He also stuck to similar locations," Kat added. "All six boys vanished in small towns or rural areas. Charlie disappeared around Sunset Falls. Both Dennis Kepner and Noah Pierce were in parks. Dwight Halsey vanished in the forest. And Frankie Pulaski and Bucky Mason went missing in Centralia."

"So we have who he preyed on," Nick said. "And where."

Kat scanned the red circles on the map, pausing at the two places where more than one crime occurred. The second and third incidents were in or around Fairmount. The fifth and sixth took place in Centralia. Unless the killer liked the locations so much he went back twice, there was a reason they took place where they did.

"He lived there," she said. "In Fairmount and in Centralia."

Despite the grim nature of their conversation, Nick allowed himself a proud smile. He had taught her well.

"Why do you think so?" he asked.

"Fairmount. I've never heard of it and I've spent my entire life in this state. So if I haven't heard of it, then there are a lot of other people who never have, either. Unless they lived there. Same goes for Centralia. A killer doesn't go back to the scene of a crime—"

"Unless he never left," Nick said. "So our perp would have lived in Centralia in 1972. When did the Fairmount incidents occur?"

"Dennis Kepner vanished in 1969." Kat leaned over the board and checked the article for Noah Pierce. Once again, she found herself lifting the fragile newspaper to see the date that was partially printed on the other side. "February fifth, 1971."

She could tell from the date's size and placement that it had been located on the newspaper's front page. And just below it, in much larger type, was the day's top headline:

MAN PAYS THIRD VISIT TO THE MOON.

A small shiver hurried up her arms and seemed to zap directly into her heart, making it beat faster. She thought back to ornery Owen Peale and his recollections about the night Charlie Olmstead vanished. It happened on July 20, 1969.

"The moon," she whispered. "Just like Charlie."

Nick had been watching her with his face scrunched in confusion. "What are you talking about?"

"Charlie Olmstead, the first victim, disappeared the night man first walked on the moon. Noah Pierce, our third missing kid, vanished the same day astronauts landed for the third time."

Through the doorway of the dining room, Kat had a clear view of the kitchen. Sitting on the counter was Eric's laptop. She rushed to it and immediately did a Google search. A few clicks later, she was on NASA's official Web site, looking at the dates of all the Apollo moon landings.

The first was July 20, 1969, which they had already established was when Charlie vanished.

"When did Dennis Kepner go missing?" she called to Nick, who remained in the dining room.

A second passed as Nick checked the board. "November nineteenth, 1969."

Kat looked to the Web site and found the date. November 19 was the same day *Apollo 12* landed on the moon. *Apollo 14*—and Noah Pierce—both occurred February 5, 1971.

"That explains the gap," Kat said.

Nick poked his head into the kitchen. "What?"

"Almost a year and a half passed between the second abduction and the third," she said. "The reason was *Apollo 13*."

The crew of that famous mission never actually made it to the moon. According to Maggie Olmstead's map, no boy from

Pennsylvania suddenly vanished, either. It couldn't have been a coincidence.

Nick returned to the board in the dining room and read the other three dates to Kat—July 30, 1971, April 21, 1972, and December 11, 1972. *Apollo 15*, *Apollo 16*, and *Apollo 17*. Dwight Halsey, Frankie Pulaski, and Bucky Mason.

When Kat returned to the dining room, she looked at the board with fresh eyes. Six successful moon landings. Six missing boys. And one person sticking to a deranged schedule that spanned years.

"We need to tell Eric," she said.

She found him on the back porch, slumped into a lawn chair that looked as bedraggled as he did. His beer bottle, now empty, sat at his feet. He took a drag off his cigarette as he stared out at the backyard. Kat settled into the chair next to him.

"There's something we need to tell you."

Eric's voice was emotionless as he said, "I know. I overheard you and Nick talking inside."

"How much did you hear?"

"That if Neil Armstrong hadn't stepped on the moon that day, my brother might still be alive. Isn't that the gist of it?"

"It is. And I'm sorry."

"When I found out my mother wanted me to do this, I didn't think anything would come of it," Eric said. "I figured I'd hire Nick, give him some money, and let him poke around a few days. I never expected to find out something like this."

Tears began to leak from his eyes. One slipped down his cheek and plopped onto his arm. When Kat absently wiped it away, her hand remained there.

"I know this is hard," she said. "But I promise that Nick and I are going to find out who did this."

Thinking she might have promised too much, Kat said no more. She didn't know if they'd be able to find out who took all those boys. That was ages ago, and evidence and witnesses were probably few and far between. But she at least had to try. Charlie and the other boys deserved that much. So did Maggie Olmstead, whose dogged pursuit of information had led them to that point in the first place. And so did Eric, who was grappling with feelings he never knew existed for a brother he had barely known.

Sitting on the porch, looking out across an expanse of grass that had been rendered brown by the summer sun, Kat leaned over and wrapped an arm around him. She gently guided his head to her shoulder. Then, sitting in stillness and quiet, she let Eric weep.

EIGHT

"Why the hell didn't anyone see this?" Kat said.

Nick didn't have an answer. His best guess was that perhaps because of distance, apathy, or simply poor police records, no one had noticed the pattern. No one had realized that six boys vanished in Pennsylvania, during each of the six moon missions. Most of the incidents looked like accidents, after all, and accidents were less likely to draw suspicion.

"Maggie Olmstead saw it," he said.

"Then why didn't she tell someone?"

Again, Nick didn't know. Maybe she had been embarrassed. Or maybe no one believed her. Having been one of them, he knew how cops worked. Meek housewives who claimed to know something they didn't rubbed them the wrong way. This was especially true forty years ago, when even the best cops had a chauvinistic streak.

All Nick really knew was that his case, the one the Sarah Donnelly Foundation had been recruited to investigate, was about to be taken away from him. If it hadn't been clear after he helped Kat move the wall of victims from the Olmstead dining room to the trunk of her patrol car, it became so with the words Kat spoke next.

"You know this is now an official police matter."

"I know," Nick said. "And just to let *you* know, that doesn't mean I'm going to stop my own investigation."

"I would be disappointed if you did."

They were sitting outside the elementary school in Kat's Crown Vic, waiting for class to be let out. Every other car in line at the curb was a minivan or SUV. Most of them were gray. Nick wondered how James felt about getting picked up from school every day in a police car. The way kids acted nowadays, they'd think it was either badass or embarrassing. He hoped James was on the badass end of the spectrum.

"I've been thinking about your theory that our bad guy lived in Fairmount and Centralia. It's logical. It makes sense."

"It's also wrong," Kat said. "Isn't that what you're getting at?"

That was exactly what Nick was trying to say, and he was pleased Kat had come up with it herself. Upon their first meeting, Nick had to give her a crash course on the thought process of your basic serial killer. Now she knew enough to understand her first theory might not have been the correct one.

"It all comes down to the first victim," Nick said. "In this case, Charlie Olmstead."

Nine times out of ten, victim number one wasn't a random killing. Most serial perpetrators stayed in familiar haunts and acted out only when triggered by something—or someone. That's why the first victim was so vital. Often, the perp had previous contact with them. Catching the bad guy was usually the result of winnowing down where and when that contact had occurred. In the case of Charlie Olmstead, that meant—

"The killer spent time in Perry Hollow," Kat said as she thrummed her fingers along the steering wheel.

Nick nodded approvingly. "That would be my guess. Maybe he didn't live here. Maybe he was just passing through for a spell. But he most definitely saw Charlie before that night. He knew where he lived. He knew where he rode his bike."

"What's the likelihood that whoever did it lived on the Olmsteads' street?" Kat asked.

"I don't know, but it would certainly narrow down our list of suspects."

"I'll talk to the neighbors," Kat said. "The Santangelos. Glenn Stewart. Find out whatever I can about Mort and Ruth Clark. It's the only way we're going to be able to dig something up."

"While you do that," Nick added, "I'll hit the road and see what I can find out from the families of the other victims."

Both of them were quiet as they contemplated the tough task ahead of them. Four decades had passed since these crimes. Even if Nick was able to track down family members of the victims, there was no guarantee they'd remember anything. Police records were most likely sparse and the crime scenes probably paved over by forty years of progress. But the prospect of getting even a hint about what happened excited the hell out of him.

Kat, however, had to play party pooper. "This is bigger than you. Or me. We just might have a ticking time bomb on our hands."

She was talking about China and its three astronauts hurtling toward the moon at that very moment. They were scheduled to land in two days, which was good for China, potentially bad for the people of Pennsylvania.

"You think it could happen again?" Nick asked. "After all these years?"

"Your guess is as good as mine," Kat said. "Whoever did this could be dead. Or out of state."

"Or waiting until Friday."

"Exactly. So you know what needs to be done."

Nick knew. And he didn't want to do it. Just thinking about it gave him a headache.

"If you'd like," Kat offered, "I can do it. I still have her contact information lying around somewhere."

But Nick had the phone number permanently lodged in his brain, a fact Kat was well aware of. It made him the most logical person to do the calling. That and the fact that it was his former boss they were talking about.

"I'll do it," he said.

"Tonight?"

"Yes, for God's sake. Tonight."

He shifted in his seat, his right knee flaring a bit as he moved. Goddamned weather. Looking through the windshield, he saw that dark clouds had replaced the late-summer sun. A second later, the first drops of rain splattered against the glass. The storm had arrived.

By that point, the school's front doors had opened and the first wave of students made their escape. They sprinted through the quickening rain to the curb, where the army of minivans and SUVs swallowed them up. James was part of the second wave. He trotted to the Crown Vic using his backpack as a makeshift umbrella. When he got in the car, Nick tried to give him his usual high-five greeting. James responded with a quickly muttered "Hi, Nick" and a halfhearted slap against his palm.

Nick didn't like kids very much. He found most to be spoiled, rambunctious, and, truth be told, bratty. James was the exception. He was polite, curious, open, and intelligent.

None of those traits, however, were on display that afternoon.

"How was your first day of school?" Nick asked, making another attempt to engage the boy.

James answered with a glum sigh. "Okay."

"Did you learn anything cool?"

"No."

"Where's your lunch box?"

This was from Kat, who was using the rearview mirror to squint at her son. James's answer—an unconcerned "I lost it"—didn't placate her.

"On purpose?" she said. "Or by accident?"

James didn't answer, which Nick took to mean that he hadn't lost the lunch box in question at all. He had outright gotten rid of it. Kat sensed it, too, and shook her head in annoyance as she edged away from the curb and into the street.

The storm had hit full force by that point, a springlike downpour waging battle with an otherwise calm Indian summer. The rain came down in heavy sheets that instantly formed puddles on lawns and overflowed the gutters on the streets.

"So you'll call her when you get home, right?" Kat asked Nick as she jacked the windshield wipers up a notch.

Apparently they were back on that topic again. "The minute I walk through the door."

"You'd better." Kat wagged a finger at him in warning. "Because I'll be calling her just to make sure."

Nick glanced over his shoulder at James, who nodded in unspoken sympathy. In that small gesture, he saw a flash of the old James he had grown to love. It was an acknowledgment on the boy's part that, despite their ages and backgrounds, they were the two most important men in Kat Campbell's life. And both of them knew from experience that they didn't want to be on her bad side.

True to his word, Nick made the phone call as soon as he got back to Philadelphia. Sitting in the Chestnut Street apartment that doubled as headquarters for the Sarah Donnelly Foundation, he picked up the phone and dialed the number he knew by rote.

It was answered on the fourth ring. Slow by her usual standards.

"Hello?" The voice was crisp and formal, just as Nick remembered it.

"Hey, Gloria," he said.

"Nick. To what do I owe this unexpected pleasure?"

Captain Gloria Ambrose had been his boss at the Pennsylvania State Police's Bureau of Criminal Investigation for close to ten years. While never friends or even friendly, they had admired each other's relentless pursuit of justice. Because of this, Nick had assumed Gloria would always have his back in times of trouble.

His assumption had been wrong. Now he was no longer a cop. Nor could he ever become one again, at least not in Pennsylvania and especially not with the state police. It was a raw deal, and hearing Gloria's voice, which contained neither accent nor emotion, brought back all the anger and bitterness that had accompanied his firing.

Nick swallowed hard, trying to keep his emotions at bay. "I was investigating something for the foundation—"

Gloria stopped him. Interrupting was one of her specialties. "How's that going, by the way?"

"Fine."

"I'm so pleased," she replied without a hint of actual pleasure.

"During my investigation, I came across some information you might like to know."

This time Gloria sounded interested. "About what?"

Nick spoke uninterrupted for almost ten minutes. He explained what he and Kat had discovered during the course of the day. He gave all the details he could—names, dates, locations. He even went so far as to tell Gloria that the map and newspaper clippings Maggie Olmstead had compiled were now in Kat's possession, should the state police need them. When he finished, Gloria asked him for something he never thought she'd ever request again—his opinion.

"I think it's a serial," he said. "These incidents are too similar to be coincidence. Then there's the fact that they coincide with lunar landings."

"Who knows about this?"

"Just Chief Campbell, Eric Olmstead, and myself."

One of the names took Gloria off guard. "Eric Olmstead, the writer?"

"Yes. He's my client."

"I'm impressed." Nick wasn't sure, but he thought she might have been telling the truth. Her voice was pitched slightly higher than usual and tinged with what could only be described as respect. But that quality vanished just as suddenly as it had appeared, replaced by Gloria's usual brusque tones.

"Thank you for bringing this to my attention. It was good of you to do so."

"Are you going to look into it?"

Nick knew he shouldn't have asked, but old habits die hard. It was none of his business now, which Gloria wasted no time in pointing out.

"I'm not at liberty to say. Are we finished?"

Nick wanted to tell her that he wasn't finished by a long shot. He wanted to tell her that his foundation was going to solve all the crimes they had given up on long ago. And he wanted to call Gloria all the horrible names he had devised for her in the eleven months since being ass-kicked from the state police. But his dignity—what little was left of it—won out.

"I guess we are."

"Then good-bye, Nick. Do take care."

And that was that. He had called Gloria Ambrose with a minimum amount of fuss and external stress. Kat would be proud. He assumed both women would take his actions to mean he was now done with the case.

He wasn't.

Eric Olmstead had hired him to find out what happened to his brother. First Kat and now Gloria had gotten involved only because he had told them about it. As far as Nick was concerned, this was still his case and he planned to investigate it as such.

Picking up the phone again, he dialed another number he knew from memory. It belonged to a man named Vincent Russo, a cop who worked Philly's South Side. Vinnie's wife had been killed by a hit-and-run driver fifteen years earlier. The man behind the wheel was never caught. Because of their shared pain—and because he liked what Nick was trying to do with the foundation—Vinnie was always willing to do him a favor. That night, Nick needed a big one.

"Nick Donnelly," Vinnie said when he answered his phone. "How the hell are ya?"

"How'd you know it was me?"

"The caller ID never lies," Vinnie replied. "I think I know why you're calling, too."

"Yeah," Nick said. "I need some information."

"Of course you do. Names? Addresses? What?"

"A little of both. You got a pen and paper? There are five of them."

Vinnie let out a low whistle. "I guess you've got a real whopper on the line."

"You have no idea."

"Okay," Vinnie said. "Hit me with them."

Nick took a deep breath. "The first one is in Fairmount," he said. "Last name is Kepner."

NINE

Kat waited until James went to bed before smuggling Maggie Olmstead's map and newspaper clippings into the house. There was no need for him to read the sad headlines that filled the board or see the faces of boys his own age who had gone missing long ago. Dragging it into the basement, the plywood bumping against her knees, she felt a bit like Maggie herself. Their goals were the same: hide the truth from their children for as long as possible.

Once she had the board leaning against the cement block wall, Kat went back upstairs to retrieve her laptop and a glass of wine. She had a feeling she was going to need it. Sitting cross-legged on the chilly floor, she fired up the computer and dove into that swirling vortex known as the Internet.

Her first order of business was to check databases of missing children to see if any of the boys Maggie had singled out were eventually found. None were. Kat then tried to find out if there were any additional abductions Maggie had missed. Just because six boys were taken during moon landings didn't mean the culprit hadn't abducted more over the years. That led to an hour scrolling through gut-wrenching lists of missing kids. Many had been found within hours in the company of estranged family members. Some were never found again. None of them, however, seemed to be related to the six boys tacked onto Maggie Olmstead's board. Different ages, different areas, none of them looking like accidents and none of them taking place around any lunar activity.

Taking a deep breath, Kat next accessed the listing of known pedophiles in Pennsylvania. She narrowed her search, winnowing the list down to those found guilty of sex crimes against young boys between 1969 and 1972. There were a lot of them—too many, in fact—but none of them were murderers.

Her next goal was to look into potential reasons why the boys had been taken. No one decided to abduct boys during lunar landings just for the hell of it. There was something about those momentous NASA missions that compelled the culprit to seek out those kids.

Early in her search, she realized that the abductions could simply have been a by-product of a crazy time in American history. The late sixties and early seventies saw astonishing upheaval. Weeks after Charlie Olmstead vanished, members of the Manson family went on a killing spree in California. A few days after that, Woodstock took place, its message of peace, love, and experimental drugs reverberating around the world.

The sixties came to an end with a concert at Altamont, in which the dark side of the flower power generation was revealed during a set by the Rolling Stones. The shootings at Kent State happened the following May, and by the time Bucky Mason vanished in 1972, the Watergate break-in had occurred, setting Richard Nixon on the road to resignation. Through it all, humming loud in the background like static from a TV set, was the Vietnam war—a seemingly endless parade of bad news and dead soldiers being carried from the steaming jungles of a faraway land.

Kat took a break to refill her wineglass before sinking deeper into the search. Sipping steadily, she read about the effect the moon landings had on the world. Americans cheered when *Apollo 11* landed in the Sea of Tranquility. Enthusiasm was still strong, although slightly more quiet, when *Apollo 12* landed that November. When 1972 rolled around, the nation—having witnessed four more landings in less than two years—had become jaded. When the lunar missions came to an end with *Apollo 17,* no one seemed to care.

Except, Kat suspected, the person who had been snatching boys all across Pennsylvania. To him, the ending of the missions meant no more crimes. Why that happened is what she wanted to find out.

The Internet offered plenty of suggestions. She learned that a startlingly wide swath of the population believed the NASA moon landings were just an elaborate hoax. On the flip side were those who thought that astronauts did walk on the moon but brought something extraterrestrial back with them. Kat assumed both groups were insane, and she wondered if that craziness extended to one of their members targeting little boys.

Then there were the doomsday cultists, who had worried that venturing into space would bring about the end of life on Earth. During her search, Kat stumbled upon an article about a group of religious fanatics in Texas who prepared for the first moon landing by building an underground bunker on their property. When Neil Armstrong took those historic first steps, the men stayed outside, armed with rifles, while the women and children huddled together in the bunker. Some of the children, it turned out, didn't even belong to members of the group. They had been taken from nearby homes. "For their own safety," one of the cult members told police. But those children were returned to their families unharmed within a few hours. The ones unfortunate enough to be a part of Maggie Olmstead's collage were never seen again.

Kat suspected there were hundreds of similar stories and scenarios. She knew from experience that there were horrible people out there doing horrible things. Sometimes, the reason was known only to them, and Kat realized that searching for one was probably fruitless until she got a better idea of what happened to those boys and who could have done it.

She shut off the computer, downed the last drops of wine, and turned the board of victims to face the wall. Upstairs, she made sure all the doors and windows were locked. Then it was on to the second floor, where she would check to see if James was asleep before landing into bed herself.

On the way there, she paused at a framed photograph of her parents, which was hanging in the stairwell. It showed her mother standing in front of a tidy two-story house with an apron around her waist. Kat's father was next to her, wearing his uniform. The house in the picture was the same one Kat lived in now. She had inherited it from her parents.

Staring at the picture, Kat realized she had also inherited something else from her father—the Charlie Olmstead case and all the other missing kids that came with it.

"Thanks a lot, Dad," she muttered. "I would have preferred cash."

Eric spent the rest of the day in a silent daze. After Kat and Nick left, taking that morbid board of pictures and clippings with them, he had wanted to go about his normal business. He tried to write. He made dinner. He called his father again. But everything was filtered through a numbing haze of shock and helplessness. The end result was that his laptop monitor remained a blank slate, his dinner was as flavorless as it was unappetizing, and he decided not to leave another message when his father didn't answer.

Adding to his stupor was the rain that had started soon after he was alone. With it had come an unrelenting grayness that seemed to settle over the town like a damp blanket. The sky was so dark and dreary that Eric never noticed the transition between day and night. Meanwhile, the rain kept coming, steadily pummeling the roof.

Now it was nearing midnight, and Eric decided it was time for him to try to get some sleep. He didn't think it would come. The day had been too surreal for him to fall easily into sleep. Even if he did, he wasn't looking forward to the faces of missing children that were bound to haunt his dreams.

Trudging up the stairs to his old bedroom, he marveled at how his mother had lived for so long with her suspicions, theories, and crazy string-crossed map. He wondered how much time she had spent on her amateur sleuthing and where she got some of those newspaper clippings in the first place. Crawling into bed and closing his eyes, he pictured her slipping into libraries in distant towns while he was at school. He imagined her looking over her shoulder like an unfaithful wife before she stepped into reading rooms or sat before microfilm machines. He wondered how she reacted each time she discovered a new victim to add to her collage and if she ever told anyone about her search.

Hovering in that zone between sleep and wakefulness, he silently apologized to Maggie for not being the son she wanted or needed. For not being good enough to be trusted with her suspicions. For leaving in the dead of night when he was eighteen, leaving only a note on the kitchen counter and two broken hearts in his wake.

I'm sorry, Mommy, he thought. *I didn't know. I'm so sorry.*

A strange noise silenced his thoughts. It was a muted thud, followed by what seemed to be a watery scratch. At first Eric thought he had imagined it. Then he heard it a second time. A third time. A fourth.

He opened his eyes. When the sound occurred a fifth time, Eric realized it was coming from outside, and he padded to the window. The rain, still falling heavily, had dappled the glass until it resembled a mirror that had been shattered to smithereens. But by adjusting his eyes and peering past the drops, he was able to make out Glenn Stewart's house next door and a portion of his backyard.

There were no lights on at Mr. Stewart's house, but Eric knew he wasn't asleep. Instead, he was outside. Eric spotted him through the inky darkness, standing by the line of trees that bordered his yard. At his feet was a small cardboard box. In his hand was a shovel. When he lifted the shovel and sunk it into the ground, it made the exact noise Eric had heard when his eyes were closed.

The shovel continued to rise and fall, going deeper each time. After a few more minutes, Glenn dropped the shovel, picked up the box, and placed it in the hole he had just created. He bowed his head a moment, as if in prayer. Eric counted as he watched, noting the stillness lasted about fifteen seconds. Twenty, tops.

Then, without further hesitation, Glenn Stewart grabbed the shovel and began to bury whatever was in the box.

THURSDAY

TEN

Although the bulk of the rain had stopped during the night, there was enough of a drizzle in the morning to require an umbrella. Kat struggled with hers as she got out of the Crown Vic. An old golf umbrella that had once belonged to her mother, it didn't want to open. When she finally did force it into full bloom, Kat discovered one of the ribs was broken, causing a third of the umbrella to flop down like one of Scooby's ears when he was tired. She decided that, flop or no flop, it would do in a pinch. She didn't expect to be in the cemetery for very long.

Edging around the massive puddles that dotted the gravel parking lot, Kat headed for the wrought-iron arch that was the only way in and out of the cemetery. Passing beneath it, she looked up at the words welded into place more than a century earlier—*Oak Knoll Cemetery*.

The cemetery was the only game in town as far as graveyards went. Most of Perry Hollow's past residents lay within its gates, which had enough room to accommodate most of its present citizens whenever their ends arrived. Kat visited twice a year, once on Mother's Day and once on Father's Day. That morning, three days after Labor Day, was an anomaly. She didn't want to be there, but she had to go. There was something she needed to get off her chest.

Carrying two bouquets of flowers under her arm, she walked to a secluded corner of the cemetery that was studded with ancient maple trees. There were six of them total, their heavy branches grazing each other and creating a leafy canopy. Once under it, Kat discovered that the leaves created enough cover to allow her to lower the umbrella and go about her business.

She laid one set of flowers in front of her mother's grave. Kissing her open hand, she placed it on the section of tombstone where her mother's name was etched. After a brief moment of silence and a whispered "I love you," she moved to the grave beside it.

Kat repeated the ritual of flower placing and hand kissing. But instead of whispering, she spoke aloud at her father's tombstone. She started off by briefly mentioning Lou van Sickle and the state of the police department in general. Then she moved onto the topic of James, who had been named after her father.

That morning she had packed her son's lunch in a brown paper bag, just as he requested. She figured it would make him far happier than the previous day. She was wrong. James was just as moody as he had been during the lunch box controversy.

Things only got worse—and more baffling—when she dropped him off at school. Instead of heading directly into the building, he meandered, as if delaying his entrance as much as possible. Kat, thinking maybe he was embarrassed to be dropped off in a decidedly uncool police car, pulled away from the curb. If James wanted space, she'd give it to him. She wasn't going to be one of those moms who couldn't take a hint when they were humiliating their children. But as she drove away, a quick glance in the rearview mirror revealed James approaching the trash can at the school's front door. Just before stepping inside, he lifted his lunch bag, held it over the garbage, and let it drop inside.

Kat didn't know what prompted his actions. Probably the same thing that caused him to intentionally lose his lunch box the day before. But whatever was going on, it wasn't good. And as she drove from the school to the cemetery, her thoughts settled on one thing.

"I'm worried, Dad," she said. "I think he's having a hard time at school. Kids are probably teasing him, and he's not equipped to handle it. And I don't know what to do. You would know. You were always good at that kind of thing."

In hindsight, her father had been too good at keeping kids off her back. The result was that not many people wanted to be her friend, let alone boyfriend. There was no faster way to spinsterhood than being the daughter of the town's police chief.

When she was done talking about James, she moved on to the real reason for her visit.

"You're not going to believe what landed in my lap," she said. "Charlie Olmstead. Crazy, right? Turns out he might not have gone over the falls after all. Even worse, he wasn't the only kid who vanished."

As Kat spoke, a wave of anger washed over her. Its presence surprised her, as did its strength. She agreed with Nick that times were different back then, and that her father and Deputy Peale couldn't be blamed for not thinking Charlie's disappearance was part of a larger crime spree. But she also couldn't let her dad off the hook entirely. Her conscience wouldn't allow it.

"Why didn't you look closer?" she asked the granite slab that bore her father's name. "Maybe you could have caught someone. It might not have been enough to save Charlie, but it could have saved five other boys."

Kat knew there'd be no real answer as to why her father didn't investigate further. The only thing she could do about it now was investigate herself. Which she intended to do tirelessly.

Moving out from under the dry sanctuary of the maple trees, Kat didn't even bother with the umbrella. The drizzle had softened into a light mist, which was easily dealt with on the long trudge back to the car.

About a hundred yards from the parking lot, another grave caught her attention—a recent addition. Time hadn't yet worn down the gentle mound of dirt, which was still untouched by grass. The headstone, colored a crisp slate gray, looked fresh from the quarry. Kat halted as soon as she saw the name that had only recently been etched into it.

Maggie Olmstead.

Approaching the grave, Kat wished she had brought another bouquet of flowers. Instead, she came equipped with nothing but a promise.

"I'm going to find out what happened. I swear to God, I am."

Unlike with her parents, she felt foolish talking to the grave of a woman she had barely known. She averted her eyes, as if not looking at the grave would lessen her sense of embarrassment. She focused instead on a patch of grass to the right of the tombstone. Like the rest of the cemetery, it was badly in need of mowing. Crabgrass sprouted up as high as her ankles, and at first she didn't see the marble marker that rested among the blades. When Kat did take note of it, she assumed it was a placeholder for someone else—a final resting place already reserved.

Bending down, she tugged up a few handfuls of slick grass

to get a better view. A few rogue blades stuck to the marker itself, and as Kat wiped them away, her fingers ran over a name and date that had been etched in the marble many years earlier.

CHARLES OLMSTEAD, 1959–1969

It was a sight Kat hadn't expected to see. She had no idea what people did for loved ones who vanished without a trace. There was no body to bury. No certainty the person was really dead. Every so often Kat felt the urge to ask Nick what his family had done when his sister was missing. She never followed through on it. Some things were best left unanswered.

As for Maggie Olmstead, she had given her missing son a grave site. Kat didn't know when. She suspected Eric didn't, either. But its presence in Oak Knoll Cemetery raised a question she couldn't shake, even as she returned to her car, tossed the bum umbrella in the trunk, and drove off. It remained with her, unspoken, until she reached the Olmstead residence. Then, as she burst through the front door, she finally let it out.

"What, if anything, did your mother have buried instead of your brother's body?"

Eric was naked.

Actually, he was wearing a towel. But seeing how it was draped over his left shoulder, Kat didn't think that really counted. Especially when he was standing in front of her, caught at the bottom of the stairs.

For a fraction of a second, neither of them reacted. Both were too shocked—Eric for suddenly being so exposed and Kat for seeing him that way. When they did move, it was quick and reflexive. Eric whipped the towel in front of him and started to wrap it around his waist. Kat averted her eyes and lifted a hand over her face for good measure.

"Not sure if you know this or not, but there's been a great invention called knocking," Eric said as he knotted the towel at his hip.

"I didn't expect you to be—" Kat was too mortified to say the word.

"Naked?" Eric said. "Well, in case you're wondering, I'm not a nudist. I just got out of the shower and came downstairs to get clean underwear out of the dryer. And you can look now. I'm decent."

When Kat faced him, she thought *decent* wasn't the best word to describe Eric Olmstead at that moment. *Surprisingly sexy* would have been her choice. The towel still left little to the imagination, and Kat found herself staring at him, her face getting flushed.

"I—I'm sorry," she stammered. "You're right. I should have knocked."

Yet she hadn't. Not that she minded the view, but the whole situation made her more than a little weak in the knees.

"I'm going to wait outside until you get dressed," she said with finality. "And while I'm out there, I'll try not to die of embarrassment."

Outside, Kat collapsed onto the front step. She felt dizzy, hopefully from humiliation and not because of long-dormant urges being zapped back to life. Yet she suspected it was the latter. Seeing Eric naked made her feel like a nun at a Chippendales show.

Fanning her face with her hand, she thought back to high school. Eric hadn't been as good-looking then. She was sure of it. He had been cute, of course. That's what had attracted her in the first place. But the way he looked now was on a whole different level. If he had been that hot while they were dating, she was pretty sure her virginity wouldn't have survived the relationship intact.

Or maybe it would have. Eric's actions hadn't given her much of a say in the matter. They had never gone any further than making out, when he abruptly ended things.

The breakup, if that's what you could call it, happened in early June, the day after Eric graduated. The night before, Kat had been in the bleachers of the high school gymnasium, proudly watching her boyfriend accept his diploma. After the ceremony, they went to a party on the banks of Lake Squall. There was a bonfire. And beer. And Madonna blasting out of someone's boom box. Kat and Eric sat on a large rock by the shore, the lake lapping at their ankles.

"Kat," he said abruptly, "I think I love you."

She had leaned against him, squeezing his hand. "That's good. Because I know I love you."

It was a perfect moment, one of the few Kat had ever experienced in her life. When they kissed by the lake that night, it was like she was living a fairy tale come true. She went to bed that night swooning, convinced that she and Eric were going to be together forever.

The next day he was gone.

His mother had been the one to break the news. Standing in the doorway with a pained look on her face, she told Kat that Eric had left during the night. There was no note. Only empty dresser drawers where his clothes should have been, a picked-apart shelf missing his favorite books, and a fresh space in the hall closet that had once marked the spot of the suitcase he packed everything in.

Maggie Olmstead had been composed while she spoke. Only when she stopped did the sobs break through: rough, guttural ones that terrified Kat. She sprinted off the porch and down the street, sobbing herself, not stopping to consider all that Eric's mother was going through. Kat was too young and heartbroken to comprehend that for the second time in her life, one of Maggie's sons had vanished in the night.

"So what's so important that you had to burst in on me naked?"

Eric plopped down next to Kat on the porch. The towel was gone, replaced by jeans, sneakers, and a T-shirt bearing the name of a bookstore—Murder by the Book. Even in that modest getup, he still looked good.

"I was just in Oak Knoll Cemetery."

"Why?"

She gave Eric the same answer she had given Mayor Burt Hammond the day before when he asked her about the bridge overlooking Sunset Falls. "That doesn't concern you."

"I think it does," Eric said, goading her. "After all, you did just see my—"

"Parents."

"Beg pardon?"

Kat pressed a palm to her cheek. Her skin was hot to the touch. She was blushing again. "My parents. I was visiting their graves."

She told him about stopping at his mother's grave, too, and about the marker next to it that bore Charlie's name. "Do you know if your parents ever had a funeral service for him?"

"If they did, I was too young to remember it," Eric said. "I never knew about any grave marker, and I was probably standing right next to it during my mother's funeral."

"What concerns me is what's beneath it."

Sometimes people who put a grave marker in a cemetery

bury something with it. The usual choice was a photograph of the deceased, along with one or two personal items. Kat assumed something similar had been done with Charlie's grave.

"Are you saying you want to dig it up?" Eric asked.

"Yes. But before I can order an exhumation, I need permission from the deceased's next of kin, usually a parent."

Eric let out an ironic chuckle. "Good luck getting in touch with my father. I still haven't been able to reach him."

"Then it's up to you to decide."

It was obvious the idea made Eric uncomfortable, especially when he changed the subject. "Don't we have to go ask Lee and Becky Santangelo about the night my brother vanished?"

Actually, that was Kat's next stop. But she wanted an answer from Eric first, so she pressed him for one. "Maybe your mother buried something that's important to our case."

"Like what?"

Kat had no idea. But she knew she'd feel a hell of a lot better once she did.

"Tell me you'll at least think about it."

"I am thinking about it," Eric said. "And what I'm thinking is that I should try to call my father again later today. He might be able to tell us what was buried there."

"What if you can't reach him?"

"Then you'll be the first person I tell once I make my decision."

ELEVEN

Nick hoped cows liked the Beatles, because the ones grazing on the side of the road were being blasted with them. Driving with the windows down and the *White Album* blaring, he was on his way to Fairmount. From what he could surmise, the land between there and Philadelphia was one huge cow pasture. Sure, he had steered through a small town or two—most of them carbon copies of Perry Hollow but without the charm. Mostly, though, he saw cows, cows, and more cows. Black ones. Brown ones. White ones. It made Nick long for a purple one, just to mix things up a bit.

Now he was five miles outside of Fairmount. At least that's what the road sign was telling him. Nick kind of doubted it. All he saw on the horizon were more cows.

On his stereo, "Sexy Sadie" ended and the rebellious crunch of "Helter Skelter" began. Nick cranked up the volume while simultaneously flexing his right leg. He had been driving for three hours, and his knee was killing him. He could only imagine what kind of agony he'd be in if he had been using that leg to work the pedals.

After Nick busted his knee beyond repair, there was concern on his part that he'd never be able to drive again. His right leg, after all, was his driving leg. But a solution soon presented itself, one used for years by amputees. He had his car modified, with the gas and brake pedals shifted to the left. It was strange at first, letting the right leg sit idle while the left one did all the work. Even more frustrating was getting his left foot up to speed on the quick reflexes necessary for driving. It took him a month to get the hang of it, although the learning curve included a few fender benders and one unfortunate run-in with a plate-glass window at a 7-Eleven.

But now he was a pro, which was good, because he had a shitload of driving to do in the next two days. Vinnie Russo had been able to locate the Fairmount home of Dennis Kepner's mother, Sophie; the camp where Dwight Halsey disappeared; and the Centralia address of Bucky Mason's father, Bill Sr. As far as Vinnie could tell, there were no known survivors of Noah Pierce and Frankie Pulaski. Not exactly the result Nick had hoped for, but three out of five wasn't bad.

Up ahead, the pastures ended and Fairmount began with almost no transition between the two. One moment, Nick saw a cow dropping a few patties. The next, he was looking at the parking lot of a Dairy Queen. Soon he was gliding down the town's main thoroughfare, seeing the usual parade of drugstores, banks, and beauty parlors.

According to Vinnie's information, Sophie Kepner still lived in the same house from which her son had left and never returned. While spending forty years in the same home sounded crazy to some, Nick had learned enough about small-town Pennsylvania to know it wasn't uncommon. Its residents put down roots. If they settled in a town, chances were they'd stay there.

Nick found the Kepner house with little effort. Just like Perry Hollow, the town's relatively small size made it easy to navigate. Pulling up to the curb, he saw that Sophie Kepner lived among a series of row houses that lined the block. Her dwelling—forty-two was the number on the door—was in the middle, a redbrick abode with lace curtains in the windows and mums on the front stoop.

Across the street was the park where Dennis was last seen. As far as parks went, it wasn't much. Small duck pond. Gazebo in need of a paint job. A bike trail that approached a thick cluster of pine trees where a young woman was now walking a golden retriever. But its splash of green in an otherwise drab part of town no doubt appealed to the children who lived there. Nick easily pictured Dennis hopping off the front stoop and sprinting into the park's embrace.

Sliding out of the car, he leaned on his cane and surveyed the park. The woman walking the dog had temporarily disappeared from view. Quite a big feat for such a small patch of land. Nick's gaze flitted from gazebo to pond to trees, detecting no trace of her. When she eventually emerged into view again, it was from among the pines themselves. She had been following the bike path, which cut directly through the cluster of trees. Nick didn't know if those trees had been there in 1969. But standing in Dennis Kepner's old neighborhood of open streets and uncovered front stoops, he was certain they were the easiest place to grab someone unnoticed. Especially if that someone was a ten-year-old boy.

The woman walking the dog noticed Nick watching her and quickened her pace, trotting to the stretch of row houses that also sat on the opposite side of the park. Turning around, Nick saw an elderly man peeking out of one of the windows in the building behind him. A few stoops away, a young mother balanced a baby on her knee while eyeing him with suspicion. Apparently, it was a watchful street, which only supported his case that the trees were the most logical abduction site.

Nick moved down the street and up the front steps of number forty-two. A cat sat in the picture window next to the door, swishing its tail back and forth. It stared at Nick with feline disinterest as he rang the doorbell.

Footsteps sounded on the other side of the door. Heavy and uneven, they were accompanied by a hollow thudding. Nick recognized it immediately as the noise of a cane coming into contact with a hardwood floor. He heard it himself every day.

The door was opened by a woman who appeared to be in her seventies. Short in stature and heavy in build, she had a thinning white perm and a wary smile. In her left hand was the cane, which was more utilitarian than Nick's. No fancy handle. No expensive wood. Just a sliver of metal to help her get through the day.

"Mrs. Kepner?"

"Yes."

"Sophie Kepner?"

"That's right." Her smile grew pinched. It physically pained her to be standing there. "Can I help you?"

Nick introduced himself. He offered his card. He explained who he was, where he was from, and that, if she didn't mind, he wanted to ask a few questions about her son's disappearance. When he was finished, Mrs. Kepner frowned. She also looked confused, as if she hadn't understood a single word he'd just said.

"Who are you again?"

"Nick Donnelly, ma'am."

"And why are you here?"

Nick wasn't one of those people who thought anyone over

sixty-five was batty in the brain, but Mrs. Kepner's profound confusion made him wonder if something was wrong with her mental capabilities. It happened to the best of them.

"I'm investigating the case of a boy who disappeared in 1969 from a town called Perry Hollow," he said. "I have reason to think it was related to the disappearance of your own son."

Sophie Kepner sighed in agitation. "How many of you are there?"

It was Nick's turn to be confused. "I'm afraid I don't understand."

"People asking about Dennis," she said. "One of you is already here."

Nick looked past the woman into the depths of the house. At the end of the hall was a small dining room with glass doors that overlooked a sad, tidy backyard. To the left of the door was a rickety set of stairs that Sophie probably had a hell of a time trying to climb at night. Across from the steps was what appeared to be a living room. Nick saw floral wallpaper, framed photographs, the end of a couch with a lace doily on the arm. Inside, a chair creaked from an unseen corner of the room. A figure edged into view, someone tall, wide, and possessing the muscular build of a California governor.

He didn't need to see the person's face to know who it was. Nick could recognize that massive body from a mile away. It belonged to Tony Vasquez, one of his former colleagues. Instead of the trooper's uniform Nick last saw him in, Tony wore a black suit that could barely contain his muscles. Approaching the door, he stood beside Mrs. Kepner and smiled at Nick.

"Donnelly. I was wondering if you were going to show up."

When they worked together, Nick liked and respected Tony. He was brave. He was determined. And as an avid bodybuilder and Mr. Pennsylvania finalist, he could probably lift a bus off you if the need arose. Then shit happened, Nick was fired, and when the dust settled, Tony had acquired Nick's old job.

"Lieutenant Vasquez," Nick said, using Tony's new title and his old one, "what are you doing here?"

"Working on a tip from a concerned citizen."

"Do I have to talk to him, too?" Mrs. Kepner asked Tony.

"We have all the information we need." Tony shook her hand and patted her arm. "Thank you so much for your time."

It was obvious Tony had been there awhile. Nick had known Gloria would follow up on the information he gave her. He just didn't think it would be so fast. The speed of the investigation—not to mention Tony's involvement—was a clear sign that, like Nick himself, she thought the disappearances were more than mere coincidence.

Sophie Kepner closed the door, leaving Nick with nothing to do but follow Tony off the stoop. As he trailed the trooper-turned-lieutenant onto the sidewalk, Nick realized he had more than a string of missing boys to investigate.

Now, he had competition.

TWELVE

"Will iced tea be acceptable for the both of you?" Becky Santangelo held up the pitcher of tea for their approval. "It's the only thing I could muster on such short notice."

In reality, the pitcher, glasses, and ice had been brought

outside by a weary-looking housekeeper in white Keds and a faded blue cardigan while Mrs. Santangelo simply watched. Still, the meaning of her words was clear—they should have told her they were coming.

Mustered iced tea and attitude aside, Becky didn't appear harried or put out. In fact, she looked like a woman who was constantly expecting guests. Well preserved for someone edging past seventy, she sat on the veranda in a yellow chiffon dress and a single strand of pearls. Her clothes, pearls, and posture reminded Kat of women only seen in Technicolor movies that featured plantations and horse racing.

Yet there was also an air of faded glamour about her, like a heroine in a Tennessee Williams play. The upswept hair, colored a shade of blond not found in nature, was falling loose in the back. The dress, besides being far too youthful for a woman Becky's age, was slightly threadbare at the shoulders. And when she offered a crisp smile, the rest of her face barely moved. Plastic surgery. From the looks of it, Kat assumed Mrs. Santangelo had gone under the knife multiple times.

Taking a dainty sip of tea, Becky patted Eric's knee. "Look how you've grown up, Mr. Famous Author. So handsome. Whenever I buy one of your books, I tell the clerk that I knew you when you were knee-high to a grasshopper."

Mrs. Santangelo either had a spotty memory or else she was trying to feed them a heaping helping of bullshit. According to Eric, she had barely spoken to him in his entire life. Still, she seemed pleased to see him, probably because it gave her something to brag about to other visitors when they were brought iced tea on the veranda.

"But for the life of me," she continued, "I don't understand why you're asking me about your brother after all these years."

"We have reason to believe his disappearance wasn't an isolated incident," Kat said.

Becky's hand fluttered to her pearls. "Other accidents? I had no idea."

"It wasn't an accident," Kat told her. "At least, we don't think it was."

"That's terrible. Just terrible."

"Our reason for coming here is to see what you or your husband remember about the night Charlie vanished."

Still fingering the pearls, Becky looked surprised by both the request to question them and the assumption that she or her husband knew anything worthwhile. "My husband spoke to the police about it long, long ago. I don't see what I could possibly add to the matter."

Kat had a few suggestions, starting with the identity of the woman Maggie Olmstead claimed to have seen in the window that night. But that one would have to wait. She needed to work her way up to the big questions.

"Chief Campbell is just making sure all her bases are covered," Eric said. "Just in case something was missed the first time around."

Becky softened at the idea after he explained it. Naturally. Kat wondered what else his celebrity could get her to do.

"I'd be happy to answer any questions you have," she said. "But it was such a long time ago."

"What do you remember about that night?" Kat asked.

"Nothing of value. I wasn't home. I only learned about poor Charlie when I returned the next day. He was such a good boy. Always running over here to talk to Lee or taste one of my cookies. He loved my peanut butter cookies."

"Where were you that night?"

Becky didn't hesitate, giving Kat the same information that was in the police report. "My sister's house. She lived in Harrisburg at the time."

"And where was Mr. Santangelo?"

"Lee was here at the house. And I don't see what any of this has to do with Charlie."

Kat backed off when she noticed a flicker of worry in Becky's eyes. If she got spooked too early, she'd clam up and tell them nothing.

"You said Charlie liked to talk to your husband. Was he here often?"

"All the time. He loved hearing Lee's stories."

"What kind of stories?"

Becky, who had been preparing to take a sip of tea, lowered her glass and gave Kat another strangely immobile smile that was anything but friendly. "Before my husband served this great state for twenty years, he served his country first."

"I'm aware of Mr. Santangelo's accomplishments," Kat said.

"Charlie was keenly interested in my husband's work. He would spend hours in the trophy room."

Kat cleared her throat. "Trophy room?"

"Yes," Becky said. "I could show you, if you'd like."

Rising from her chair, she grasped Eric's hand—a gesture that didn't go unnoticed by Kat—and led him off the veranda into the house. Kat followed, pushing quickly through the kitchen, where the housekeeper was scrubbing the countertops, down the hallway, and into what at first appeared to be a sitting room. The drapes were drawn, shrouding the room in darkness. When Becky whipped them open, the morning light tumbled across walls covered with framed photographs, clippings, and other memorabilia.

Becky clutched Eric's hand again and pulled him to an oil painting that dominated one wall. Depicted in a swirl of color was Lee Santangelo wearing a uniform and leaning against the side of an airplane. Next to the portrait was the photograph on which it was based.

"The photograph appeared in *Life* magazine," Becky said. "Of all the airmen who could have been photographed, Alfred Eisenstaedt chose Lee."

Kat moved in to get a closer look. The photograph, she had to admit, was far superior to the painting it had spawned. The portrait was nice, but it failed to capture Lee Santangelo as well as the photo did. Arms crossed, hat rakishly askew, he resembled a matinee idol who had stepped right off the silver screen.

Lee looked just as debonair in all the other photographs, which traced his career from military pilot to potential astronaut to state legislator. Only the details changed. Black-and-white soon blossomed into color. The uniform went from military formal to NASA chic to three-piece suit dull. Lee's hair seemed to grow in each picture, transforming from fifties buzz cut to seventies shag.

"Charlie especially enjoyed hearing about my husband's training for the Apollo program." Becky pointed to a picture of Lee and Buzz Aldrin sharing a laugh outside an airplane hangar. "NASA wanted Lee to go to the moon. They said he was one of the best candidates they'd ever seen. But he thought he could better serve the people as a lawmaker."

Kat had heard a different story. In that version, Lee had

indeed been one of several pilots considered by NASA, but he was eliminated swiftly and early. He went into politics solely because he didn't know how to do anything else. Kat wondered what that kind of rejection did to a man. Was Lee bitter about it? Probably. Bitter enough to take it out on a few kids every time a successful Apollo mission took place? Maybe.

Becky moved to a photograph clipped from a newspaper that showed Lee, still in uniform, standing with a delicate beauty in a white gown and sash.

"This was the night we met," she said. "Miss Pennsylvania Pageant, 1962. I was second runner-up, which is just as much of an honor as winning the crown."

Kat studied the caption beneath the photo. CAPT. LEE SANT-ANGELO IS INTRODUCED TO MISS BUCKS COUNTY REBECCA BATE-MAN. Surrounding the photo were more pictures. Lee being sworn in, with Becky by his side aping Jackie Kennedy in a pillbox hat. Lee at the White House with Richard Nixon. Lee collecting the key to some unnamed city. Lee talking to a group of kids at a school, at a camp, at a church. Each frame bore a small plaque indicating the photo's date and location. PERRY HOLLOW ELE-MENTARY SCHOOL, 1969. ST. PAUL'S METHODIST CHURCH, 1972.

"Thank you so much for sharing this," Kat said, not mean-ing it. "It was very illuminating."

"I'm pleased you enjoyed it," Becky replied, also not meaning it. "Will there be anything else?"

"Well, I'll need to talk to your husband. I'd like to hear what he remembers about the night Charlie Olmstead vanished."

Standing in the middle of the room dedicated to his life, Becky Santangelo laughed. It was an inappropriate burst—practically a snort—that reverberated off the walls and rattled the frames upon them.

"I'm afraid you're a little late for that."

"Has he gone for the day?" Kat asked.

"Of course not."

"Then may I see him?"

"I'd prefer it if you didn't."

She took in Kat's uniform, badge, and handcuffs, which dangled from her duty belt like some piece of Goth jewelry. The contemptuous sniff that followed indicated that Becky thought she wasn't properly ladylike. Kat didn't give a damn. She loved her uniform, her badge, her cuffs.

"Let me put it this way," she said. "I'm not asking to see your husband. I'm demanding it."

Becky sniffed again. "Fine. But you're going to be disappointed."

She was right.

A sinking feeling hit Kat as soon as Becky ushered them into the upstairs bedroom where her husband was located. Lee Santangelo sat in an easy chair so large that he was barely visible. Kat could only see the sleeve of a sweatshirt resting on the chair's arm. Poking out of it was a gnarled hand dotted with age spots.

The only other furnishings in the room were a hospital-regulation bed, complete with side guards, and a flat-screen television that had been muted. On the TV was a nature documentary showing dolphins frolicking among silvery schools of fish.

"I've found he responds to the colors," Becky said. "He couldn't care less about the sound."

Kat stepped tentatively into the room. She could see Lee's face now, pale and alarmingly gaunt. His skin, as thin and translucent as wax paper, clung to his skull, and the veins on his forehead protruded so much that Kat could make out their colors—muted reds and blues that pointed upward to a shock of ivory hair.

"Mr. Santangelo? I'm Chief Campbell with the Perry Hollow police."

Lee didn't respond, forcing her to edge around the easy chair and block his view of the television. Not that Lee seemed to mind. He wasn't really focused on the screen. Instead, he seemed to be looking beyond it, staring out at some other world only he could see.

Alzheimer's, Kat guessed, and Mr. Santangelo had been eaten away by it. When she touched his hand, Lee's eyes snapped to life. Confused pupils took in the sight of her, trying in vain to process who she was and what she was doing there. His jaw dropped open and he emitted a gurgling noise as he tried to form words. The best he could come up with was, "Beck."

His wife swept into the room. "I'm here, dear. This is Chief Campbell. You knew her father, James. He was the police chief, too."

"Beck," Lee said again.

Kat backed away from him, uncertain of her next move. Her plan had been to ask Lee what he was doing the night of July 20, 1969, and, more important, who he was doing it with. That plan was now shot to hell. Even if Lee could remember that night, there was no way he'd be able to tell her about it.

"He was diagnosed five years ago," Becky said. "It's all been downhill from there. He used to have good days. But not anymore."

Kat's reply, a meek "I'm so sorry," did nothing to appease Mrs. Santangelo.

"Now you know our little secret," she said. "Few people do, so I would appreciate your discretion."

Kat nodded quickly. "Of course."

They left the room, meeting up with Eric, who waited just outside the door. Clustered on the landing, Kat said, "Mrs. Santangelo, I need to ask you a few things about what your husband was doing on the night Charlie Olmstead vanished."

"I already told you," Becky said. "He was here."

"Alone?"

"Yes."

"Are you sure?"

They were on the staircase now, descending in single file. Becky, who brought up the rear, stopped at the halfway point. "What are you implying?"

Kat wasn't implying anything. She was coming right out with it. "We're pretty sure there was someone else here with him that night."

Becky lifted her head a little higher as she resumed her descent down the stairs. At the bottom, she marched to the front door and held it open for them.

"I'm sorry, but I don't care to discuss this anymore."

Eric stepped forward, trying to do damage control. "I know this is hard to talk about. But if there was someone else with him, we really need to know about it. Maybe she saw something unusual. Something that would help us find out what happened to my brother."

"Lee was alone that night." Becky remained by the door, still trying to force them out. "I said it then, I say it now, and I'll keep saying it until the day I die."

"I understand you wanting to preserve your husband's legacy," Kat said. "It's not our goal to tarnish it. We just want to talk to the person he was having the affair with."

Affair. She hadn't intended to utter the word that until

now had gone unspoken. But she did, and it practically hung in the air like cigar smoke.

"How dare you!" Becky said, seething. "You barge into my home and violate my privacy. Then you have the gall to accuse my husband, who served his country in so many ways, of something as tawdry as infidelity."

"But my mother said she saw someone upstairs," Eric said. "A woman."

"I know what your mother said. She told anyone who would listen that my husband was screwing around behind my back. But I said nothing, even when she went to the police. Lord knows, I could have said plenty about her. Everyone on this street knew she was crazy."

"Don't talk about my mother like that," Eric warned.

"I'm only telling the truth. Your father tried to act like nothing was going on, but we could hear them, Lee and I. The yelling. The fighting. It was no wonder your brother was here all the time. He couldn't stand to be around your mother."

Her words, however angry, had the ring of truth. Kat remembered Owen Peale talking about how mad and distant Ken and Maggie Olmstead had seemed, sniping over who was to blame for Charlie's disappearance. She thought of that single, mysterious word that seemed to sum up everything that was wrong between them—*bathtub*.

Eric sensed it, too, and moved toward the open door. Becky blocked him.

"I'm not finished," she said. "Do you want to know what made her like that?"

Eric's reply was a firm, "No."

That didn't stop Mrs. Santangelo, who poked an outstretched finger into Eric's chest. "It was you. Everything was fine until you were born. And then something in your mother just snapped."

Eric grabbed her hand, wrapping his fingers over her knuckles. Becky gasped. Kat did, too, and for a moment she thought Eric was going to crush the woman's fingers with his grip. He was strong enough to do it. He looked angry enough, too.

"I don't care what you say about my family. What matters to me is that you're hiding something, Mrs. Santangelo. And I won't rest until I find out what it is."

He released her hand, walked out the door, and crossed the front lawn. Once he reached the street, he kept walking, moving with purpose toward the heart of town. Kat wanted to follow him. She felt as if it was her duty. But from his quickening gait, she knew Eric needed to be left alone.

The visit, she realized, had been fruitless. Now it was too late to ask any more questions. Too much had been said already. That left Kat with no recourse but to leave as well. On her way out, she slipped past Becky Santangelo, who—for the first time that morning—had been stunned into silence.

THIRTEEN

Eric struggled for breath as he entered Oak Knoll Cemetery. His anger had manifested itself in uncontrollable heaves that he felt deep down in his lungs. The anger was so strong it threatened to suffocate him. Yet he continued to walk, gasping loudly as he marched among the rows of graves.

Once he reached his mother's headstone, he bent at the waist and took a series of deep, slow breaths. Each one calmed him down a notch. After about a dozen, his emotions were under control and he was able to stand upright once more.

"That bitch," he muttered.

Unlike Kat, he hadn't expected good things to come from the visit to the Santangelo residence. There had to have been a good reason, after all, for the decades-long feud between them and his mother. He just didn't realize how strong those emotions still were until Becky unleashed her tirade about his mother.

"That lying bitch."

Even as he cursed, Eric knew Becky Santangelo was only partly to blame for his anger. After all, she was only speaking the truth.

That realization had hit him when she jabbed her finger into his chest. Feeling its meager pressure against his skin, Eric knew she wasn't lying. His mother had been crazy—from grief, from loneliness, from the past. That's what fueled his anger. Although Mrs. Santangelo was a worthy target of his wrath, Eric knew he was really just mad at himself. For making excuses to himself about his mother's erratic behavior. For writing it off as eccentricity. And most damning of all, for leaving her alone to fall deeper into behavior she couldn't control.

Shame heated his cheeks as he thought about the night he left Perry Hollow. The plan had been in the works for several months. He had been accepted to NYU, although his mother had insisted Penn State was all she could afford. Eric fooled her into thinking he was fine with that. But secretly, he had already informed NYU of his intention to enroll there. Through furtive calls at pay phones and letters stolen from the mailbox, he wrangled as much financial aid as possible. He found a summer job at the New York Public Library through the friend of a cousin of a friend. He even went so far as to rent a room sight unseen until he was able to move into student housing in the fall.

The goal was to slip out the night after graduation. He would hitch a ride to the bus station in Mercerville and then let Greyhound shuttle him into Manhattan. There he would spend the summer toiling away in anonymity, far away from Perry Hollow. He told himself he wanted a fresh start in a new location, that he wanted to be known as Eric Olmstead and not as just the kid whose brother fell over the falls all those years ago.

That much was true. But the main reason he had to get away was because he couldn't stand to live with his mother anymore. Not under the same roof, with all that silence.

Whenever he looked back on his childhood, which wasn't often, Eric thought of the suffocating silence that seemed to hang over everything. Silent dinners. Silent birthdays. Silent Christmas mornings where the only noise was the slow tearing of paper as Eric unwrapped his few gifts. He wanted a place with nonstop noise. He wanted to be lulled to sleep by the sound of police sirens and taxis honking and drunks shouting in the streets.

The only thing that interrupted his plans was a pretty girl named Kat Campbell. He had seen her around school—a freshman who already seemed bored by the daily cliques and gossip of high school life. While she was attractive in a fresh-scrubbed, girl-next-door kind of way, Eric had been taken by her innate toughness. He noticed how she went out of her way to befriend the outcasts and how she never showed fear in front of anyone. Not teachers. Or the principal. Or the senior with dorky glasses reading Raymond Chandler when everyone else acted too cool to read at all.

When they did connect, it was sudden and explosive. Eric

went from being intrigued by her to liking her to loving her. Very swiftly, his clandestine plans started to change. Two months into his relationship with Kat, he started to rethink the wisdom of spending the summer before his freshman year in a strange city surrounded by people he didn't know. After three months, he wondered if Penn State was a better choice. It was a good school, after all. Plus, it was closer to home, which meant he'd be closer to Kat.

The day before graduation, he had come home from a particularly great date with Kat. They had gone to the movies—*Ferris Bueller's Day Off,* of all things—and then made out for a long time in his car outside the theater.

Too long, as it turned out.

His mother was waiting up for him. She sat on the couch, surrounded by open envelopes. His correspondence with NYU littered the coffee table. His mother had discovered every last bit of it. In tearful shrieks, she accused him of wanting to abandon her, just like his father. Eric assured her that was no longer the plan. He hugged her. He told her he'd never go anywhere, that he'd always be there for her.

He was lying.

While his mother clung to him, her tears soaking his T-shirt, Eric knew he had to get away as fast as he could. If he didn't, it would always be like that, with his mother clinging to him, trying in vain to make him always stay her little boy. And Charlie's ghost would always be there, an unseen, unmentioned entity who flourished in the suffocating silence of the house.

The next day Eric barely paid attention to his graduation ceremony. He was too busy mentally going over all the things he had to do that night. He accepted his diploma with a smile.

He posed for photos with it afterward. He hugged his mother, kissed her cheek, and promised he'd be a responsible young adult at the party that was soon to follow.

The party was when Eric realized that in order to escape his mother, he'd have to leave Kat, too. He also knew it would break her heart. It certainly shattered his. Yet he pretended there was nothing wrong. He danced. He drank. He sat on a rock at the edge of the lake with his girlfriend, knowing that in the morning, she would most likely hate him. That was when he told her he loved her. He didn't know how she'd respond. He didn't know if she felt the same way. But he needed to say it, if only to provide Kat with one last, happy memory before all the bad ones about him came her way.

Later that night he enacted his plan. Soon he was in New York City, going to school there and eventually deciding to live there. He scrawled most of his first novel on yellow legal pads in a coffee shop down the street from his first apartment. He got married. He got divorced. He wrote more books. He hit the bestseller list. He accumulated a lot of money and a fair amount of fame.

Through it all, he slowly repaired his relationship with his mother. It took some time—years, actually—but it was worth it. She forgave him. He forgave her. And when she needed him in the last weeks of her life, he was there.

After her death, he was still there, trying to fulfill her last wish. With Kat's help, to boot. Eric moved past his mother's grave to the patch of grass next to it. Kneeling, he saw the grave marker Kat discovered earlier that morning. He placed an open hand on the ground in front of it. Something was under there. There had to be.

Running his palm over the grass, Eric's thoughts drifted to his other neighbor. He hadn't told Kat about seeing Glenn Stewart burying something during the night. He didn't want to sound like his mother, spouting another conspiracy theory to a doubting cop. Plus, since Kat had literally caught him with his pants down, it was the last thing on his mind that morning. But now that it was back in his thoughts, he realized his neighbor had no earthly reason to be out in the middle of a storm that bad, shovel in hand. It seemed especially strange when Eric considered how much of a recluse Mr. Stewart was.

The only reason he could think of was that circumstances beyond his control had forced Glenn to go outside. After all, he had seen them heading to the falls the previous day. He most likely heard them, too, talking about Charlie, about his disappearance, about what could have happened all those years ago.

Despite having made a fortune writing about them, Eric wasn't a big believer in suspicion or conspiracies. He generally took people at face value, unlike Mitch Gracey, whose motto was "Never believe anything you hear." It had appeared in the first Gracey mystery and ultimately became a line in all of them. Fans would be disappointed if it didn't.

Yet when he thought about his neighbors, Gracey's worldview started to make sense. Clearly, Becky Santangelo hadn't given them the whole truth. She was hiding more than just her gray hair and crow's-feet. Eric now suspected Mr. Stewart was covering something up as well. Evidence of some sort, perhaps. Maybe something he had kept all those years, for reasons unknown. But now that he knew Kat and Nick were digging into his brother's disappearance, he had to get rid of it.

Eric stood and placed a hand on his mother's headstone. Like Glenn Stewart the night before, he bowed his head.

Then he vowed to find out everything his neighbors were hiding.

FOURTEEN

Tony Vasquez moved too damn fast. Nick could barely keep up with him as they walked the perimeter of the park across the street from the Kepner household. Gripping his cane so tightly his knuckles were white, he tried his best. But each step Tony took required two from him just to cover the same amount of ground.

"Can you slow down a little?"

Instead, Tony came to a complete stop. "A year ago, it was me trying to keep up with you."

"A year ago, I also had a real knee."

Lieutenant Vasquez—Nick still felt weird just thinking it—resumed walking, although at a slower pace. For that, Nick was grateful. Adding to his gratitude was the fact that Tony was sharing information with him, which Nick knew was against the rules under the Gloria Ambrose regime.

"Sorry if I'm going too fast," he said. "But we're short on time here."

"Why?"

"You've seen the news. You know what's happening to-morrow. Gloria is worried that whoever took those boys will strike again."

"And you?" Nick asked.

"I think it's better to be safe than sorry. So that's why I'm here."

"What did you find out from Sophie Kepner?"

"Mrs. Kepner—a nice woman, by the way; very helpful— was home the day Dennis disappeared. It was mid-November, chilly but sunny. Dennis came home from school and said he wanted to run out to the park to play with some friends. Sophie Kepner told me she wasn't going to let him. She knew he had homework and thought he should do that before going outside. Dennis told her he didn't have any, which turned out to be a lie."

According to Tony, it was a lie that cost the boy his life. His mother relented and Dennis hurried outside. From the living-room window, Sophie Kepner watched him cross the street and enter the park.

"It was the last time she ever saw him," Tony said.

They were at the gazebo, on their way to the duck pond. Nick looked to the street, taking in a reverse view from the one he had seen when he first arrived. He saw his car parked at the curb and the Kepner household. A few doors down, the woman with the baby still sat on the stoop, watching the morning slowly transform into afternoon.

"Around what time did all of this occur?"

"Three thirty," Tony said. "Maybe a little after."

"Did anyone see Dennis after that?"

"The police report was pretty thorough. They asked everyone up and down the block. Only his mother saw Dennis enter the park. No one saw him leave."

Tony had already looked at the police file on Dennis Kepner. Of course. By this point, the new lieutenant probably had copies of all the reports about all of the boys. Nick really was playing catch-up.

"What else did the report say?"

"That in 1990, one Maggie Olmstead of Perry Hollow contacted the Fairmount police department. She claimed the Dennis Kepner case was related to one involving her son."

At least Nick now had confirmation that Maggie did tell the police about her suspicions. Since he and Tony were still looking into it, clearly nothing had been done.

"I guess they didn't believe her," he said.

"Not really. They did some poking around. Called Perry Hollow PD. Tried to talk to the chief."

"Kat's father?"

Tony shook his head. "He had just died. There was no chief at the time, which is apparently another reason this slipped through the cracks. Perry Hollow PD was in disarray. All the Fairmount guys learned was that the Charlie Olmstead case had been ruled an accident years ago. With the Kepner boy, they suspected from the beginning that abduction was involved."

Which, as far as Nick knew, was different from the cases involving the other boys. He thought of the waterfalls, unfriendly forests, and abandoned mines police assumed had swallowed them. "Why did they think that?

"They searched every inch of this park and found nothing." Tony raised his arms and swept them outward. "And there's not a hell of a lot to search. They also brought in bloodhounds, which lost the boy's scent as soon as they entered the park."

Nick looked to his left, where the duck pond sat. It was small—about the size of a hotel swimming pool—and probably not very deep. Still, he had to ask, "Did they dredge the pond?"

"If you count stepping in there with waders on and kicking around, then yeah, they dredged the pond."

"Did anyone consider that maybe he just ran away from home?" Nick asked.

"I asked Sophie Kepner that same thing. She said Dennis was as happy as a ten-year-old could be. He had friends. He was doing fine at school. There was no household strife he was dealing with."

"So no reason to flee his happy home?"

"None," Tony said. "Plus, we both know runaways are usually older. Midteens and beyond. The kid was just ten. And runaways also take things with them. Clothes. Money. Personal items they can't live without. According to Mrs. Kepner, the only thing missing from Dennis's room were the clothes he was wearing and a model rocket."

"A rocket?"

"The police report described it as wrought iron, painted white, about four inches tall. Dennis had scratched his name on the side with his father's pocketknife. One of the boy's teachers told police he had brought it to school that day, on account of *Apollo 12* landing on the moon. She said Dennis had it with him when they watched the moon walk on TV in the school auditorium. It usually sat on his nightstand, which is why Mrs. Kepner later noticed it was missing."

"What does she think happened to it?"

"That Dennis took it with him into the park. And it disappeared. Just like him."

Hearing this prompted another question from Nick, although one not directly related to Dennis Kepner. "One thing I'm not clear about is why you're telling me all of this."

Tony stopped again. He looked at Nick, eyes slowly drifting to the cane he no doubt had chipped in money to buy.

"Because you got a raw deal, Nick. Everyone knows it.
And you're the best investigator I know. So your help in this
matter would be greatly appreciated."

"Does that mean I'm once again working with the state
police?"

"Unofficially, yes," Tony said. "Officially, no. Because Gloria would kill me, even though you did the right thing by telling
us what was going on. We owe you. Big-time."

Nick should have told him that calling Gloria Ambrose
had been Kat's idea, but he didn't want to spoil Tony's generous mood. "When did the police give up on the Kepner case?"

"They never really did. You know how it goes."

Yes, Nick knew how it went. Cops looked for days, which
turned into weeks, which eventually became months. They vowed
to keep looking. They promised families they wouldn't stop. But
time moves on and man's inhumanity to man marches in lock-
step along with it. More crimes take precedence. More murders
occur. Time continues to tick by. Before long, decades have
passed and an unsolved mystery remains just that.

"So what's next on your agenda?" Nick asked Tony.

"I'm going to Lasher Mill State Park. It's about fifteen
minutes out of town."

"I know," Nick said. "It's my next stop, too."

The park, where Noah Pierce vanished more than four-
teen months after Dennis Kepner, made him curious. It was
February when Noah disappeared and, according to the newspaper article about him, snowy. He knew the boy, a native of
Florida, wanted to play in the snow. But his grandparents lived

in Fairmount, which because of its close proximity also had snow. So why the unnecessary trip?

"What was the park's appeal? I mean, it was most likely too cold for hiking."

"For hiking, yes," Tony said. "But not for sledding."

Nick didn't need to ask how Tony knew this. Looking at the police report on the Pierce boy was the only way.

They had reached the part of the path that dove directly through the pines. From the way the trees' branches intertwined, it looked more like a tunnel than an open-air walkway. Adding to the tunnel effect was the way the path curved slightly to the left. Standing at the entrance, Nick couldn't see the exit on the other side.

He and Tony headed into the thick of it. The lower branches of the pines reached out and brushed their legs. Nick swatted them away with his cane.

"Did the file on Dennis Kepner mention these trees?"

"Yeah," Tony said. "It mentioned how a couple of officers were on their hands and knees sifting through pine needles."

"So these were around in 1969?"

"Unless it was raining pine needles, then I guess they were. Why?"

Nick told him about losing sight of the woman with the dog earlier as she walked the very same path. "From the Kepner side of the street, this section of the park is a visual dead zone."

"I wonder," Tony said, "how it looks from the other side."

He veered off the path, cutting through the thicket on the right. The land there was slanted, rising until it was about three feet higher than the path. Nick followed, even though he knew he was going to get whacked in the face by a branch.

He was wrong. He was whacked in the face by two branches.

The second one came as Tony burst out of the trees. Nick did the same, although since he had sap in his eyes, he really wasn't paying attention to where he was going.

"Nick! Watch out!"

Tony's shout came from behind him. Approaching from the left was the unmistakable blare of a car horn. Nick jerked his head in the direction of the noise, seeing a UPS truck about ten feet away. He felt a tug on his collar as Tony yanked him backward.

Looking down, Nick saw that as soon as the trees ended, the street began. There was no grass berm or sidewalk. Just a length of street lined with row houses on the other side.

"Dude, what the hell are you doing?" It was the UPS driver, who had stopped the van in front of them. "You could have gotten killed."

Nick raised a hand to signal he was okay. "Sorry about that. My fault."

Looking up at the truck, he noticed how it temporarily blocked out the row houses across the street. He assumed the vehicle also did the same thing for anyone watching from those homes. He couldn't see them. They couldn't see him. And if he climbed into that truck right now, he was all but certain that anyone on the other side of it couldn't see him leave.

"Hey, Tony," he said. "I think I know how Dennis Kepner vanished."

FIFTEEN

When Kat knocked on Glenn Stewart's door, she didn't expect an answer. Which was good, considering she didn't get one. Had it been someone else's house, she would have assumed no one was home. But since it was the town's recluse she was dealing with, she knew Glenn was there.

Only he wasn't responding, not even when she pounded on the door a second time and called out, "Mr. Stewart? This is the police. I need to talk to you."

Once again, she got the same haunted sensation as the day before. Dead-end streets always felt a little abandoned, but on this one the feeling was especially acute. She wondered, not for the first time, if it was Glenn Stewart's presence that made it this way or the other way around. Perhaps he only became reclusive because the lonely cul-de-sac demanded it.

She knocked one more time, knowing it was fruitless, and stepped off the porch. Moving backward toward the street, she craned her neck to look up at the rickety house Glenn called home. Its absurd height and proud dilapidation made Kat think of the Addams Family. Only they would have had more fun with the place. A guillotine in the front yard. A cauldron of boiling oil on the roof, ready to drop on unwelcome visitors. Mr. Stewart was content to just let it rot.

Kat waded into the knee-high weeds that made up the house's yard. Her presence stirred up the army of animals living within it. A rabbit sprinted out of hiding and took shelter underneath the porch. Late-summer grasshoppers leaped from the blades and descended a few feet away. A garter snake, fattened by all the available bounty, slithered toward the woods that ran along the edge of the yard.

She moved around the side of the house and into the backyard, where the grass was lower and the wildlife less prominent. But it was louder there, with the roar of Sunset Falls blasting through the woods. Kat caught glimpses of it through the trees, streaks of water descending rapidly.

There wasn't much to see in the backyard—a woodpile, a clothesline, a meager strip of garden that proved Glenn Stewart stepped outside at least sometimes. He also apparently drove. A rusted Volkswagen van sat under a carport that had seen better days. Kat didn't know if the van was in running condition—it certainly didn't look drivable—but it had to have been at some point.

Peering upward again, she saw the widow's walk perched on the center of the roof like an antique hat. It was higher than the trees and probably provided a good view of both the waterfall and the bridge just upstream from it. Had Glenn been up there that night, he could have seen Charlie Olmstead pedaling innocently on his bike toward the falls.

But he had told the police he was asleep at that hour, an alibi that could neither be confirmed nor denied. He could have been lying, of course. He could have been up on that widow's walk, watching the neighbor boy make his way toward the bridge. Then he could have climbed down from his perch, rushed through the woods, and snuck up behind the unsuspecting boy.

"What are you doing here?"

The voice, suddenly breaking the silence of the yard, startled Kat.

"Mr. Stewart? Is that you?"

"I asked you a question."

The voice wasn't angry. It didn't contain enough emotion for that. It was more flat and weary, as if its owner had been expecting her presence for a very long time. Shielding her eyes, Kat tried to pinpoint where it was coming from. Rows of windows ran along all three stories of the house. Most of them were closed. One, on the second floor, was open, but the shade had been drawn.

"I'm Chief Campbell, with the Perry Hollow police."

"I know," the voice said. "And you still haven't answered my question."

"I'm here to talk about Charlie Olmstead."

The shade covering the window—as yellowed and brittle as parchment—rose slowly. Mr. Stewart stood just beyond it, a shadowy figure with no discernible features. The only thing Kat could see clearly was an animal nestled in Glenn's arms. Much longer than a cat, it had slick brown fur dotted with patches of white. Tiny paws swatted the air, and when the animal poked its head into the light, Kat saw a band of black across its eyes.

Glenn Stewart was holding a ferret.

"That's a beautiful animal."

The shadow in the window moved slightly, head tipping forward in a nod. "The compliment is appreciated."

"May I come inside and see it?"

"You may not."

"It would be helpful if we could speak face-to-face."

"We are," Glenn replied. "In a sense."

Kat sighed. "Did you know the Olmsteads well?"

"No. As you can tell, I prefer not to socialize."

"Why is that?" Kat knew there had to be a reason. Agoraphobia was the most likely one. Plain old insanity also could have been the cause.

"Personal preference."

"Do you ever go outside?"

"I do," Glenn said. "But not in the daytime. I don't particularly care for the sun."

"How do you get your groceries?"

"They're delivered to my door every Tuesday. You can ask the manager at the Shop and Save."

"When was the last time you left the house?"

"Chief Campbell, these don't sound like questions about Charles Olmstead."

"Fine," Kat said. "In 1969, you told my father you were asleep when he disappeared. Is that true?"

"If I said it to the police, then it must be."

"And you didn't see anything that night? Hear anything suspicious?"

"If I had," Glenn said, "I would have reported it to your father."

Kat was keenly aware that he was being annoying on purpose, hoping he'd wear out her patience and make her leave. What Glenn Stewart didn't know is that she was the mother of an eleven-year-old boy with special needs. Patience was the chief job requirement, and she could wait out behavior that would bring other mothers to tears.

"Why weren't you watching the moon landing like everyone else?"

"Why would I?"

"Because it was historic," Kat said.

"It was foolish," Glenn countered. "Man wasn't meant to go to the moon. Not back then and certainly not now."

"Why do you say that?"

"Because it's not God's will. Of all the creatures on earth, humans are the only ones who think they're better than nature, that they can overcome it. Of course, they're wrong. Any attempt to prove otherwise is a violation of what God created."

"A violation?"

"Of course," Glenn said. "Some things are best left undisturbed. If God had intended us to walk upon the moon, he would have given us that ability."

"But he did give us that ability," Kat replied. "Through science, knowledge, and critical thinking, man learned that ability."

"I don't think we're discussing the same God. Not that it matters. We've spoken enough. Good day."

The shade began to descend slowly, blocking Mr. Stewart's silhouette and the ferret still in his arms. Before it was fully down, Kat blurted out, "I have one more question."

The shade halted its descent. Glenn Stewart's voice emanated from the six-inch space between the shade's bottom and the windowsill. "Yes?"

"What happened to you in Vietnam?"

"Enlightenment," Glenn said. "Glorious enlightenment."

He lowered the shade the rest of the way, leaving Kat alone in his yard. Resigned to defeat, she trudged to the front of the house. When she reached the street, she found herself facing the former Clark residence. The FOR SALE sign in the yard swayed slightly in the breeze. The photograph of Ginger Schultz, Perry Hollow's only Realtor, moved with it, a blur of chubby cheeks and bad perm.

Kat crossed the street and steadied the sign. She then pulled out her cell phone and dialed the number emblazoned across the bottom of the sign. Ginger herself answered with a perky and unabashedly scripted "Schultz Realty. Let me find you a dream home."

Kat already had a dream home, thank you very much. Yet she pretended otherwise as she greeted her old school friend.

"Ginger? It's Kat Campbell. There's a house for sale in town that I want to take a look at."

Some people are born to be Realtors. Ginger Schultz was one of them. Plump and friendly, she expressed awe and excitement about everything from Kat's uniform to the azalea bush outside the former home of Mort and Ruth Clark.

"It's beautiful in early summer," she said while unlocking the front door. "Absolutely gorgeous."

Ginger held the door open and Kat stepped inside, taking a good look around. The house was devoid of furniture, carpeting, even color. Their footfalls rose from the hardwood floors, bounced off the ceiling, and died against walls painted a blinding white.

"There are so many things you can do with this space," Ginger said as they moved to a living room as clean and bare as a monastery. "It's so versatile. I assume that's what you're looking for. Versatility. You never did tell me why you're interested in this place."

Kat wasn't quite sure herself. She didn't think the Clarks had anything to do with Charlie Olmstead or any of the other missing boys, and she was certain there'd be no clues to be gleaned from the house even if they did. She was more interested in the sight lines their home offered. If the Clarks had intriguing views of the Santangelo residence or Glenn Stewart's house, she wanted to know what they were.

"James and I are getting tired of our place," she lied. "We're thinking about finding something with more space."

"This has oodles of space. I think you two would love it here."

In the kitchen, Kat gave a cursory glance at the cupboards and peeked under the sink just for show. Then it was upstairs, where she bypassed the bathroom for the two bedrooms. The largest one fronted the street, with two windows that faced the homes across from it. The window on the right provided a diagonal view of the Olmstead house. Kat peered out of it, looking for signs that Eric had returned. She saw nothing.

She moved to the window on the left, which offered a head-on view of Glenn Stewart's place. Its large, eyelike windows blankly stared back.

"This house was built in 1940 by the original owners," Ginger said.

"Mort and Ruth Clark?"

"Yes." Ginger giggled. She did that almost as much as she raved about how wonderful everything was. "You've really done your homework about this place."

The second bedroom was smaller than the other one, with a slightly vaulted ceiling and a quaint octagonal window near the door. While Ginger prattled on about how it would be a perfect room for James, Kat approached the window. It overlooked the side of the yard that faced the creek. There wasn't much there—a small strip of grass that quickly stopped at a thick wall of trees. Slips of the creek beyond could be seen through the branches. Kat heard the rush of the water, too, with the roar of Sunset Falls dull in the distance.

Turning her head to the right, she could make out a sliver of the street and the mouth of the path that led through the woods. Craning her neck, she saw a bit of the bridge, which practically blended in with the trees. She assumed it was possible that whatever happened to Charlie Olmstead could have been seen from that window.

Kat was about to move from the window when she caught a glimpse of something else in the yard. It was on the far edge of the property, sitting in the spot where the lawn conceded defeat to the trees. Painted white and boasting a roof of green shingles, it looked like some kind of shed. Only sheds were usually bigger. The one in Kat's backyard was large enough to hold a lawn tractor, a spare tire, and a collection of sporting equipment that she and James never used. This structure looked like it wouldn't even be able to contain one of her son's sleds.

"What's that building over there?"

Ginger giggled yet again and said, "You spotted the springhouse. It's useless now, of course, but it's a real conversation piece. Adds so much character."

Kat didn't hear the rest. She was too busy descending the stairs and looking for the back door. By the time Ginger emerged from the house, Kat had already crossed the yard and was well on her way to the mysterious structure. Once she reached it, Kat could instantly see it was definitely not a springhouse.

The door didn't budge when she tried to open it. Neglect could be an amazing lock sometimes. So could wood rot. The shack had seen plenty of both.

"There's no reason to look inside," Ginger said once she caught up with Kat. "Think of it as decoration."

"Was this part of the original house?"

Hesitation slowed the Realtor's voice. "I believe it was added a few years later."

"I'll be right back."

Kat marched out of the yard and across the street, where her Crown Vic still sat parked in the Olmstead driveway. Popping the trunk, she pulled out a crowbar and carried it all the way back to the Clarks' mystery shack.

Without shooing Ginger out of the way, she shoved the crowbar between the door and its frame and gave a hearty push. The door hesitated and the hinges protested, but soon it was open, letting Kat take a good look inside. What she saw was an empty structure sitting on a concrete foundation. In the center was a smooth door that looked like the hatch of a submarine. Kat gave a tug on the handle, discovering that the door was heavier than she expected. It was made of lead, most likely, and built to withstand a giant impact.

Behind Kat, Ginger stood frozen in the doorway. "I was going to tell you about it. Eventually."

"What is it?"

"A bomb shelter," Ginger said. "According to my records, the Clarks built it in the fifties. It's the main reason this house hasn't sold. It freaks out most potential buyers."

Kat was sure as hell unnerved by it. It brought to mind nuclear Armageddon, terror and chaos—things she didn't care to think about. Its presence also shed an unflattering light on the home's former owners. What kind of people lived in such fear that they built an underground bunker on their property?

"Is anything still down there?"

"I don't know," Ginger said. "I've never looked."

Kat gripped the handle of the door. "Help me open it. We're about to find out."

With Ginger's assistance, Kat managed to heave the door open, revealing a circular hatch with a metal ladder clinging to the side. Peering into it, Kat saw only the ladder's first three rungs. The rest were engulfed by darkness.

Kat removed the flashlight from her duty belt and pointed it inside the hole. The meager circle of light it created illuminated the rest of the ladder, which descended about ten feet. Handing the flashlight to Ginger, she said, "Hold it steady and keep it pointed down."

"You're not really going to go down there, are you?"

"Of course I am."

Kat stepped into the hole and tested her weight against the ladder's first rung. After yesterday's close call on the bridge, she didn't want to leave anything to chance. When the first rung held her up, she tested each subsequent one, slowly making her way deeper into the bomb shelter.

It was much colder at the bottom—so frigid it felt like she had descended into a freezer. It was also dark. Kat couldn't see a thing.

"Drop the flashlight," she called up to Ginger. "I need more light."

Standing by the ladder, she held out her hands. When Ginger dropped the light, Kat caught it easily. Swooping it back and forth, she saw that the shelter itself was a large cylinder. Roughly ten feet long, its walls arched overhead, broken every few feet by support beams that resembled ribs. Along one side, empty shelves had been suspended from the beams. Beneath those was a long bench. On the other side of the shelter, three flats rose along the wall, one above the other. Each was about six feet long, and they shared the same support beams at their corners.

Bunk beds, in case they had to be down there a long time.

The mattresses had long since been removed, but Kat easily pictured them there, stacked on the flats just like in a crowded train compartment. It wasn't comfortable by any means, but it would do in case of an emergency.

Making her way back to the ladder, Kat imagined herself and James having to share such confined quarters. Sometimes they had enough trouble staying in the same house, let alone a room as large as a prison cell. Being cooped up like that would make them both stir-crazy, and there was even room for a third.

Kat stopped, left foot on the bottom rung. Clearly, Mort Clark had built the shelter because he was worried about all the things everyone else was worried about in the fifties. Commies. Bombs. Aliens. If such unthinkable things occurred, he wanted to have a place where he and his wife would be safe.

Yet there were three bunks in the bomb shelter. Not two. That meant Mort was concerned about someone else besides his wife. Why else would he have an extra bunk in his bomb shelter? Who that person was and what it could mean, Kat had no idea.

Climbing out of the hatch and slamming the door shut behind her, she thanked Ginger for showing her the place.

"It's lovely, but I think I'm going to pass."

Ginger frowned. "You don't like the house?"

Kat liked the house just fine, even though she had no intention of buying it. What she didn't like was that she still knew next to nothing about the people who had once lived in it.

For lunch, Kat fetched a pizza from a cut-rate place next to the Shop and Save and took it back to the station. She and Lou shared it, each of them sitting on opposite sides of her desk and grabbing a slice. It was skimpy on the pepperoni and heavy on the grease, but Kat didn't care. She was so hungry that card-board with tomato sauce would have felt like a feast.

"How much do you know about the Clarks?" she asked Lou between bites.

"Not very much. Mort used to work for the mill. And Ruth made a mean lemon meringue pie."

"That's not really the information I was looking for."

"You ever try to make lemon meringue?" Lou asked. "That's not a skill to be trifled with."

"I was hoping for someone who knew more about them."

"They're out there. In fact, they get together every morning at the diner."

Lou was talking about a group of old-timers who crowded a corner booth every weekday at the Perry Hollow Diner. They were called the Coffee Crew, although Kat wasn't sure if they came up with that name themselves or were given it by the diner's frazzled waitresses. Consisting of retirees and former mill workers, it was a constantly evolving bunch. Members died off and were replaced by new faces. Only one man seemed to always be there year after year. As a result, he was the group's de facto moderator, always prompting a discussion of the weather or a complaint about the government.

"Norm Harper?" Kat asked.

"The one and only," Lou said. "I guarantee you can catch him there tomorrow."

She hoped that good old Norm, who rivaled Lou herself in gossip prowess, would be able to shed some light on Mort and Ruth Clark. Kat still didn't think they had anything to do with the missing boys. They were far too old for something like that, especially considering the fact that Bucky Mason, the last boy on their list, vanished in late 1972. But she was uncomfortable with her lack of knowledge about them. They were a giant question mark, as out of reach as Lee Santangelo and just as unknowable as Eric's next-door neighbor.

"Would Norm also be able to tell me something about Glenn Stewart?"

Lou cocked an eyebrow. "You think he's somehow wrapped up in all this?"

"I think he has the potential to be. He's been cooped up in that house for so long that I'm not sure anyone remembers what he was like before Vietnam. Or knows what happened to him when he was there."

"He moved here in 1966," Lou said. "Was shipped off to Vietnam in 1967. Came back crazy a year later. Norm should be able to fill in the blanks."

Kat mentally made plans to intercept Norm Harper at the diner the next morning. Maybe the offer of a free breakfast would refresh his memory. She then reached across her desk and grabbed more pizza.

"Are you sure you want that second slice?" Lou asked.

"Yes. Why wouldn't I?"

"Well, now that Eric Olmstead's back in town, you might want to watch what you eat a little bit. Don't want the melons to get so ripe they spoil, if you catch my drift."

"I think I do," Kat said. "And I'm kind of repulsed."

Lou clucked in that motherly way that made Kat feel simultaneously exasperated and blessed. "Don't be prudish. Everyone knows you and Eric were hot and heavy for a time in high school. And now he's back. You're spending a lot of time together. And, from what I hear, he's looking mighty fine."

Kat couldn't disagree on that point. She knew from her brief, humiliating glimpse that morning that Eric looked more than fine. Still, she had to nip this particular rose of gossip in the bud before it bloomed all over Perry Hollow.

"I'm simply helping him find out what happened to his brother."

"That's very noble," Lou said, snapping the pizza box closed over Kat's hand. "But there's more to it than that. You know it. I know it. And I hope Eric knows it, too."

Kat wriggled her hand from beneath the box's lid, sliding out a slice of pizza. She held it in front of Lou defiantly, ready to take a massive bite. She didn't get the chance. Instead, her phone rang, forcing her to set the pizza down on her desk, where it was promptly snatched up by Lou.

Glaring at her, Kat answered the phone. "Chief Campbell."

"Rumor has it you're investigating Charlie Olmstead's disappearance."

Normally when a caller didn't identify himself, Kat assumed it was Nick. This time, however, it was someone else. But, just like with her friend, she recognized the voice.

"Mayor Hammond," she said. "As a matter of fact, I am. So the rumors are true."

"Would you care to tell me why?" Burt asked. "For a police department in dire need of another officer and new patrol cars, looking into a forty-two-year-old case seems like an odd use of manpower."

Kat could have told the mayor about how it was looking less and less likely that Charlie went over the falls. Or about the other missing boys. Or about the small but very real possibility that another kid could go missing the next day when China's astronauts took their first steps on the moon. Instead, she said, "There's been a new development in the case."

"That doesn't give you the right to bother Becky and Lee

Santangelo about it," Burt said. "Becky just called my office hopping mad."

"So you want me to stop investigating just because the town's most important resident got angry?"

"That would be my preference, yes."

Kat pressed a hand to her cheek. It was warm. No doubt from the anger steadily building up inside her. Other than her ex-husband, only Burt Hammond managed to get her so mad so quickly.

"Well, I won't do it," she said. "Besides, I'm not the only person investigating it. The state police are involved. So you're going to have to talk to them."

"The state police?" The mayor sounded flummoxed by the news, which slightly cooled Kat's anger. "What the hell kind of new development are you talking about?"

"I'm not at liberty to say. But you can tell me what you remember about the Olmstead boy's disappearance."

"Nothing," Burt said. "It was decades ago."

Kat had a feeling the mayor wasn't telling the truth. He seemed to be hedging, which was never a smart thing to do when talking to a cop. Police sensed it the same way a dog smelled bacon.

"Yes, but you were alive at the time. How old were you in 1969? Seventeen? Eighteen?"

"I was nineteen," the mayor said. "And I don't recall anything other than the fact that the boy fell over the falls and was never seen again."

"Other people remember more," Kat told him. "Which is why I'm not going to halt the investigation, no matter how much you want me to."

"You're the chief of police." Burt's voice was tinged with

sarcasm. "You do what you want. But I'm warning you. Don't bother the Santangelos again."

He hung up without another word. Holding the suddenly silenced phone, Kat noticed that Eric had entered the station and was now standing at the threshold to her office.

"That looks familiar," he said. "I spent the past hour the same way."

"I guess you couldn't get in touch with your dad."

Eric shook his head and stepped into the room. He was calmer than when Kat had last seen him and was moving with a renewed sense of purpose.

"But I promised I'd tell you when I made a decision about Charlie's grave marker."

"And?"

Eric gave her a half smile that was more sad than amused. It was obvious he didn't like or want to be in this position. Yet he was, and he responded with appropriate authority.

"Whatever is down there, let's dig it up."

SIXTEEN

The last place Nick wanted to be was in another park, especially one a hundred times the size of Fairmount's little green. All that open land. All those trails, trees, and pathways. It meant only one thing—more walking.

"You ready?" Tony asked as Nick emerged from the car.

"No."

The trip to Lasher Mill State Park had taken them barely

fifteen minutes. Even with Tony driving, it wasn't enough time for Nick to rest his leg. His knee, which had seen more action in the past two days than the previous two weeks, was still throbbing. But he had to push on.

Tony agreed with his theory about Dennis Kepner's abduction. They both thought the boy had been grabbed in the thicket of trees, dragged to the street that ran behind it, and tossed into a vehicle parked at the curb. Nick had been hoping for a similar setup at the state park to explain how Noah Pierce could have vanished just as easily.

No such luck.

The area surrounding the rectangular parking lot was a wide swath of grass. Three sides of it were studded with picnic tables, fire pits, and open grills. That afternoon, all of them were empty. The fourth side was open lawn that sloped for several hundred yards to the shore of a massive lake. Nick spotted a boat launch at the bottom, also empty, and to the far right, a crumbling building that had once been painted red but was now a weathered rust color. Sitting on a stone foundation, it jutted over the water.

"That used to be a gristmill," Tony said with the authority of a tour guide. "This whole area was once a working mill. When it closed during the Great Depression, it was turned into a state park. Hence the name."

Leaving the parking lot, they set off down the long slope to the lake. Nick's knee practically screamed at the beginning of the descent. To drown it out, he tried to picture the entire area covered in snow. It was probably pretty, if you were into that kind of thing. Snow-drenched treetops. The icy white expanse of the lake spreading out below. And this never-ending

slope that his knee hated but that every kid would love, especially if they had a sled handy.

"The day Noah vanished was a Friday," Tony said. "It had
snowed the night before. School was canceled. And this spot
was notorious for its sledding."

Nick's mental image of the scene grew more crowded. He
pictured kids and parents alike streaking down the hill and continuing out over the frozen lake—every kid's wintertime dream.
Only it had turned into a nightmare for one of them. Because
among the crowd, unrecognizable in a parka, ski cap, and
gloves, was someone who had more than fun on his agenda.
And thanks to the failure of *Apollo 13,* his wait had been very,
very long.

They had reached the lake and were standing on its rocky
bank as water licked at their shoes. The opposite shore looked to
be a mile away. Definitely not far enough for a sled to reach, no
matter how fast it was going and how much ice it glided over.
Whoever took Noah Pierce did it in the immediate area.

"What are the details?" Nick asked Tony. "Since you seem
to already know them."

He sat down on a nearby rock, stretched out his leg, and
listened as Tony told him everything from start to finish. Noah
Pierce, age nine and an only child, had been sent to stay with
his grandparents in Fairmount while his parents finalized a
particularly nasty divorce. On that fateful Friday, they drove
out to Lasher Mill State Park with a thermos of hot chocolate
and a Flexible Flyer sled strapped to the roof of their station
wagon. It was cold, so Noah's grandparents parked facing the
lake and sat inside the car, listening to the radio as they watched
the boy go up and down the hill.

"They lost sight of him," Tony said, even though Nick had already assumed that. Losing sight of a child was always the first chapter in an abduction story. "They said he was wearing a black snowsuit. Just like every other kid sledding that day."

According to Tony, Noah's grandparents got out of the car and looked for him. Others soon joined the hunt, including a park ranger. No one knew where he had gone because no one had been watching him. All they found was his sled, abandoned near the old gristmill.

"That evening," Tony said, "several hours into the search, the park ranger took a snowmobile out onto the frozen lake. He discovered a hole in the ice about a quarter mile from shore. The immediate assumption was that Noah had fallen in and drowned."

"End of story?" Nick asked.

"Not quite. The police started to question that theory when spring arrived, the lake thawed out, and no body appeared."

Nick shook his head. Replace the lake with a waterfall and Tony could have been reciting the story of Charlie Olmstead's disappearance.

"You mentioned his parents were going through a messy divorce," he said. "Did the report say how messy?"

"No custody disputes, if that's what you're thinking."

It was exactly what Nick had been thinking. A staggering number of abductions in the United States were committed by parents locked in battles over custody. Some fled the country and made national headlines. Most were settled by the local police. In the case of Noah Pierce, it was a moot point.

"Both of his parents were in Florida at the time," Tony said. "Friends, coworkers, and divorce attorneys all confirmed it."

"And his grandparents?"

"They were clean. Other parents in the park testified to seeing both of them get out of the car with Noah, give him his sled and hot chocolate, then get back inside the vehicle. Neither of them left it until an hour later, when they realized they no longer knew where he was."

"And they didn't know anyone else in the park?" Nick asked.

"Nope."

"Then the culprit was most likely a stranger. What did the police think?"

"The dipshits still concluded that he drowned."

As much as he wanted to, Nick couldn't entirely blame everything on the police. This was, after all, the work of a sicko with a thing for little boys and a keen interest in NASA's landing schedule. Besides, America was a different place back then. In 1971, people still left their doors unlocked at night and trusted their neighbors. They didn't warn first graders about stranger danger. Milk cartons didn't yet carry the faces of the missing.

"So we've got a hillside full of kids and one stranger among them," Nick said. "By the end of the day, there was one less kid and the stranger was gone."

"How do you think he did it?"

Nick shoved the tip of his cane into the ground and pushed off the handle until he was standing again. He faced the hillside, Tony's car parked at the top in the distance. "How far away do you think that is?"

Tony squinted and eyeballed the hill. "Two hundred yards. Maybe two fifty."

"How old were Grandma and Grandpa?"

"According to the report, he was sixty-three. She was sixty."

"Experts say vision starts to worsen around age sixty," Nick said. "If it hasn't already. So maybe one of them couldn't see all that great to begin with. Add in all that blinding snow, all those kids running around in dark snowsuits."

Tony caught on quickly. "They could have been watching the wrong kid for a while. And they probably didn't see Noah leave with someone else."

Nick knew that whoever took Noah Pierce didn't just drag the boy kicking and screaming to his car. Even a blind grandparent would have noticed that. If they hadn't, there sure as hell would have been several other parents who did.

"He had to be discreet," Nick said. "He had to quietly and carefully lure the boy somewhere first. Maybe he told him he was a family friend."

Early on, kidnappers had learned that kids didn't trust strangers. But they *did* trust people their parents knew. If a stranger claims to be friends with a child's parents, there's a 50 percent chance that kid will go along with whatever he says.

"Sounds solid," Tony said. "But where would he do this?"

Nick looked past the lieutenant to the dilapidated gristmill that sat at the lake's edge. "The only place that was available."

Up close, the mill looked like a stiff breeze could knock it over. A notice nailed to the wall said it had been condemned sometime during the Clinton administration. Giving them a third warning that they shouldn't enter, the door had been padlocked.

Nick looked for other ports of entry but found nothing. There were no other doors and the only windows within reach were too small to squeeze through. Sitting over the lake, the mill's stone foundation had wrought-iron grates on two sides that allowed water to pass under it. They couldn't even swim beneath it and look for a way in from below.

"What do you think we should do?" Tony looked at Nick expectantly. "We're breaking the law if we go in there."

"We're also investigating the disappearances of six kids," Nick said. "I think that trumps trespassing."

"What about vandalism?"

Tony nudged Nick out of the way, grabbed his sidearm, and shot the padlock twice. The first bullet heavily damaged it. The second obliterated what was left. Surprisingly, the mill remained standing. Perhaps that was a sign they should enter after all.

Newly freed, the door creaked open, allowing Nick to use the tip of his cane to clear most of the cobwebs that crisscrossed the frame like a safety net. Beyond the door was a dim room that reeked of mildew and bird shit. The floor was covered with withered leaves and long-lost feathers of former occupants. A set of stairs rose along the wall to a second level. In the far corner, a trapdoor had been built into the floor that opened to the water—the nineteenth-century equivalent of a trash chute.

"Looks dangerous," Tony said. "Maybe I should go in first."

"You shouldn't go in at all," Nick replied. Of the two of them, Tony was the one who needed to avoid stepping into rickety wooden structures. It would be like an elephant trying to cross a bridge made of toothpicks. "Besides, I've been in old mills before."

When he took a step inside, the floorboards did more than creak under his weight—they screamed. Still, Nick moved forward, gingerly making his way into the center of the mill. Beneath his feet, wide gaps between the floorboards provided glimpses of the lake water just inches below. Above his head were large holes in the ceiling where the wood had rotted through. Beyond them, he could see the mill's rafters and more holes in the roof.

Standing amid the squalor, Nick understood how the mill could appeal to a child. It was like the biggest, baddest play fort ever created, with the sky above and water below. Not to mention places to climb, nooks to explore, trouble to get into. It probably had taken zero effort to lure Noah Pierce inside.

"Is there anything interesting in there?" Tony called from the doorway.

"Interesting? Yes," Nick said. "Helpful? No."

He had reached the corner and was standing on the trapdoor in the floor, which had also been padlocked. It seemed slightly more sturdy than the mill's floorboards, especially when Tony entered. His first step inside rattled the entire structure.

"Do you think this is where the boy was taken?"

"Maybe," Nick said. "I doubt we'll ever know."

Tony took another step. Just as it had with Nick, the floor beneath him screamed its displeasure. "You're probably right," he said.

"Then let's get out of here. Maybe we'll—"

Nick was going to say that maybe they'd have better luck at their next stop, but the splash he created cut him off. Actually, a yelp came just before the splash—a startled cry Nick managed to croak out just before his fall. A fraction of a second before his cry had been the groan of unstable wood under pressure and a sharp crack as the trapdoor he was standing on split in two.

The water overtook him immediately. There was no in-between stage, no slow progression into the drink. One second he was dry. The next he was engulfed.

The water was colder than he expected. Deeper, too. As he touched bottom, Nick put his hands over his head, hoping they would break the surface and he could gauge the depth. No such luck. That meant the water was at least seven feet deep. Most likely more.

On two sides of him were the grates built into the mill's foundation, preventing easy escape. The upside was that they let in much-needed light. Nick saw slick tentacles of weed reaching upward. A rock sat next to his foot, round and covered with algae. A few feet above him was the surface and, beyond that, the floor of the mill.

Pushing off with his good leg, he rose quickly to the top but to the left of where he wanted to be. When he tried to break the surface, he was stopped by the floor above him. He hit it with full force, his skull slamming against the wood and knocking what little air he had left out of him.

A tightness had formed in his chest by the time he sank to the bottom again. It only got worse as he pushed off a second time and rose upward. This time he shoved his hands in front of him, bracing for impact. When his palms felt rough wood, he eased his face closer to the underside of the floor.

There was about six inches between the floor and the water—just enough room for his face to breach the surface and allow him to take a desperately needed breath. Gasping for air, he peered through a crack in the floorboards. Tony was on the other side, lying on his stomach and peering right back at him.

"Donnelly? You okay?"

"I think so."

Think was the key word. Nick had no idea if he was okay or not. The suddenness of his plunge and the chill of the water had left his whole body numb. He couldn't even feel the pain in his right knee. But the numbness didn't make his bum leg work any better, and soon he felt himself being dragged back under by his waterlogged clothes.

Nick fought against the pull, paddling as best he could in such tight quarters. It was useless. He managed one more gasping breath before slipping under again. Above him, he heard Tony crawling across the floor, the water distorting the sound. It only added to the disorientation he felt beneath the surface. The floor was above him instead of below. He didn't know which way was right or left. Then there was the tightness in his chest, which his few gulps of air had only seemed to make worse.

He soon found himself at the bottom again, ass planted firmly in the muck of the lake's bottom. When he tried to push toward the surface, the weeds wrapped around his wrists and grabbed at his ankles. Nick thrashed his arms. He kicked his legs.

All that work did was to twist him around until somehow he was on his side, shoulder being sucked into the mud. The undulating weeds pushed into his face, brushing against his cheeks and covering his nose. He pushed it out of the way, seeing the rock he had first landed next to. His hand knocked against it, the rock rising slightly and spinning with impossible ease. It settled into the mud again, a different side of it facing Nick.

That side had two rounded holes in the center. Slightly

beneath them was another hole. Below that, studding its bottom, was a row of teeth.

Nick was staring at a skull.

Fighting the weed, Nick glimpsed the bottom half of the skull. It had detached and sat half buried in the mud. Nearby, he saw three ribs arch out of the muck. Next to it was a skeletal hand, weed growing between its fingers.

Nick felt another hand press against his chest. But this one was alive, attached to a muscular arm that wrapped around him and yanked him upward.

Tony Vasquez had jumped in and was pulling Nick to safety. As they neared the surface, Tony got behind him and shoved. Up ahead, Nick saw the square hole in the floor he had fallen through. Propelled by Tony, he reached it quickly, grabbing the trapdoor's frame and pulling himself out. Tony soon followed, breaking through the water and doing the same.

Inside the mill, both men lay side by side on their backs, legs still dangling beneath the surface. They breathed heavily, their chests rising and falling in unison. As soon as he was able to, Nick spoke.

"There's a skeleton down there."

Tony sat up, surprised. "Seriously?"

"Seriously. And I'm pretty sure it once belonged to Noah Pierce."

SEVENTEEN

Kat parked outside the elementary school, early for once. Checking her watch, she saw she had fifteen minutes until the bell rang. Plenty of time to sit back and think without interruption about the Olmstead case. She turned on the radio, mostly for a little background noise, and was greeted by a news report.

"So far so good for China's three astronauts," a female newscaster said in a rushed voice that was apparently mandatory for radio personalities. "Officials from NASA who are advising the Chinese space mission say the second day of spaceflight is going smoothly. While there's no firm time yet for a lunar landing, reports from China's state-run television said it could be as early as Friday afternoon."

Kat changed the station, replacing the news with some eighties music that Nick would have found repulsive. She didn't want to hear about the astronauts' steady progress to the moon. All it did was remind her that her own progress was at a virtual standstill. It also made her regret scheduling the exhumation of Charlie's grave until that night.

At the time, she had thought she was making a wise decision. Carl Bauersox would be on the clock by then and would be able to help with the task. Also, darkness would most likely keep away curious onlookers wondering just what the chief and her deputy were digging up in Oak Knoll Cemetery.

Kat, of course, didn't know what she would unearth in a

few hours. She hoped it would be something useful. She needed all the help she could get. There was always the possibility that Nick had found something, although Kat assumed his road trip wasn't going well, either. She tried to call him twice that afternoon, but he never answered his phone. The last she heard from him was that morning, when she received a typically profane text message: TONY IS HERE! FUCK!

She whipped out her cell phone and was in the process of calling Nick a third time when someone tapped on her window. It was Jocelyn Miller, the principal of Perry Hollow Elementary. A wisp of a woman in a gray pantsuit, she motioned for Kat to roll down her window.

"Sorry to bother you, Chief. But I need a word."

As chief, Kat was often asked to speak to students about safety, obeying the law, and the importance of community police. In rare instances, she was even brought in to scare the crap out of a misbehaving kid who hadn't been fazed by detention. Then there was the annual assembly about avoiding predators and never trusting strangers. For the next talk, Kat considered bringing in Maggie Olmstead's collection of newspaper clippings to use as a visual aid. If that didn't get through to the kids, nothing would.

"No bother at all," Kat said. "Is it assembly time again?"

"Actually, it's about James. I know he went through a lot last October."

"He did," Kat replied. "But his therapist says he's doing well."

"That's fantastic news."

The principal didn't sound like she meant it. Her half-sincere tone made Kat sit up and flick off the radio. "Is something wrong?"

"Maybe," Jocelyn admitted. "Has he been acting differently at home?"

The question required no thought. James was definitely acting strangely. He was quiet. More subdued. And then there was the missing lunch box from yesterday and the lunch he had so casually trashed that morning.

"He has," Kat said. "I noticed it ever since school started. Is he acting differently here?"

"I haven't witnessed anything. Neither have his teachers. But we think he might be having problems."

"What kind of problems?"

"With a classmate," Jocelyn said. "More specifically, bullying."

Kat kept a straight face. She needed to. But, inside, it felt like her heart was sinking into the depths of her stomach. Ever since James entered first grade, she knew the possibility existed that it could happen. She feared, expected, and doubted it all at the same time. But now the principal was confirming what she suspected: her son was being bullied.

"Who's the classmate?"

Jocelyn shook her head. "I'm not at liberty to say."

"If I know who it is, I can talk to him and his family. Maybe bring a stop to it. I am the police chief, after all."

"Which is exactly why I can't tell you."

Jocelyn's message was clear from her body language—hands clasped primly in front of her. She didn't want Kat driving to this kid's house and cuffing him until he promised not to pick on her son. It was exactly what Kat wanted to do.

"Can you at least tell me what happened?"

"Neither boy is talking," Jocelyn said, "so we don't know the full situation. Something to do with stolen lunches."

That cleared up why James had thrown his lunch away before entering the school that morning. It was a preventative measure—destroying the lunch before it could be stolen. Kat now knew with certainty that James was lying when he said he had lost his lunch box the day before. In reality, it had been taken from him, most likely because fifth-graders didn't use lunch boxes. Yet Kat had insisted he take it to school with him. Knowing she had played a role, however small, in the whole thing made her tremble with guilt.

"What should I do?"

"Talk to him," Jocelyn said. "See if he'll open up to you. Many kids going through things like this want to talk about it. It helps to get it off their chests. But they're also too embarrassed and afraid to broach the subject. That means you need to bring it up."

Kat waited until dinner to follow Jocelyn Miller's advice. Even then, most of the meal had passed in silence before she just blurted out, "Are you having problems at school?"

James, who had just taken a bite of mashed potatoes, shook his head.

"Are you sure?" Kat pressed.

This time James spoke, the mashed potatoes gray and gooey on his tongue. "I'm sure. Honest."

So much for the principal's theory about kids wanting to discuss their problems.

"You know you can talk to me, Little Bear. If something is going on at school, it might help to tell me about it."

"Nothing's wrong."

Part of Kat's job was trying to figure out who was lying and who was telling the truth. Usually, it was easy. Liars avoided eye contact. They stayed frozen in place as they spoke. They tried too hard to summon honesty in their voices. James was displaying all three characteristics, so she asked him one last time.

"Positive?"

"Positive."

"Then how is the fifth grade going? You didn't say much about it yesterday."

"I didn't get the chance."

Kat felt another twinge of guilt. The night before, she and Nick had spent the dinner hour discussing Charlie Olmstead and the other missing boys, much to her son's boredom.

"You have the chance now. I'm all ears."

"It's different," James said.

"Different how? Harder? More intimidating?"

She knew it was too many questions, but she was so happy that James actually seemed to be opening up that she couldn't stop herself.

"I guess," James said. "Math is harder."

Kat's cell phone, which had been silenced for dinnertime, started to vibrate. It sat an arm's length away on the table, its buzz causing the nearby silverware to rattle. She ignored it, even though it was most likely Nick finally returning her call.

"Do you think it'll be too hard?" she asked James.

"I'll get the hang of it."

The phone continued to go off. Each vibration shimmied it closer in Kat's direction. She had to will herself to not reach out and grab it. Instead, she leaned toward it, trying to glimpse the caller ID. But whoever was calling had given up, and no name or number was visible. The phone once again sat in silence and stillness.

"What about science?" she asked. "Will you be studying anything neat?"

"I hope so. We might get to dissect a frog."

Her phone jumped to life again, vibrating its way even closer to her elbow. Whoever was calling, desperately wanted to talk to her. She needed to answer.

"I'm sorry, honey," she told James. "I really need to get this."

James folded his arms across his chest and stared at his plate. "Fine."

Grabbing the phone, Kat got up from the table and moved into the kitchen before answering. "Hello?"

"We found him." It was Nick, of course. "At least, we probably did."

"Found who?"

"Noah Pierce. Tony and I discovered a skeleton at the state park where he disappeared."

He talked quickly, explaining the events of the day and concluding with the grim discovery beneath an abandoned gristmill. As he spoke, Kat heard a constant hum in the background.

"Where are you?"

"In the car with Vasquez," Nick said. "We're heading to the county morgue. The state police brought in a forensic anthropologist to look over the bones. We're meeting her there. What's new on your end of the investigation?"

Nothing was new, and Kat admitted as much. She was going to talk about Becky Santangelo, weird Glenn Stewart, and the Clarks' bomb shelter but decided against it. None of it was very exciting. Especially when compared with possibly finding the remains of one of the six missing boys on their list.

"I need to go," she said. "Carl and I have some business to

attend to. Call me if you find out anything else tonight. If not, I'll talk to you tomorrow."

She ended the call and returned to the dining room. James was exactly where she had left him, in the very same position.

"Nick says hi."

James's voice was barely above a murmur. "No he didn't."

Kat sighed. James was mad at her because she interrupted him to answer the phone. Her punishment for the transgression was going to be a night of pouting.

"I'm sorry about that. But sometimes work doesn't stop when I come home."

"You're always working." Again, it was a mumble that Kat had to strain to hear.

It was hard being the child of a police chief. Kat knew that firsthand. Her childhood had been a series of missed soccer games and late-night kisses on the forehead long after she had gone to sleep. When she was growing up, her father was absent from the dinner table more often than not and rarely tucked her in at night. The only difference between her and James was that her mother had been around to do those things in his absence. James had no such luxury.

"I'm sorry, Little Bear. I truly am."

She was even more sorry about what she needed to do next, which was to leave for a large portion of the night. Because she couldn't get a babysitter on such short notice, James would have to leave with her. Normally she would have taken him to Lou van Sickle's house, where he could play with one of her grandchildren. But Lou had plans that night, leaving her with only one option.

"Why can't I stay here?" James asked after she told him they were leaving for an hour or two.

"Because I can't find a babysitter and you're not old enough to stay home alone."

"I am so."

Kat wasn't going to have this argument, especially when her days were spent looking for boys who went missing when they were James's age. If it was possible, she'd choose to never let him out of her sight.

"Hurry up and grab your homework," she said. "We need to go."

"Where are we going?"

"To meet a friend of mine. A very old friend."

Kat Campbell had a son.

For some reason, this blew Eric's mind. Years ago he'd heard from his mother that she had married a fellow cop. A startlingly short time after that, word got out about her divorce. But he never heard about a son, especially one with Down syndrome.

But there he was, sitting on his couch as Eric stared at him. The boy stared back, daring him to be a stupid adult and say stupid things. He saw that look in a lot of kids—that I'm-hard-to-impress glare—and it never ceased to unnerve him.

"You mom said you might have some homework to do."

"It's done."

"Then is there anything you'd like to watch on TV?"

"Not really."

When she dropped James off, Kat assured him she'd only be gone two hours tops. Eric, who had been stunned to learn she had a son to begin with, told her that was no problem. She was, after all, trying to find information about his brother. Since Eric preferred thoroughness over speed, he said she should take her time. But five minutes after she left, he was regretting his words.

"How do you know my mom?" James asked.

"We used to be friends. A long time ago."

"You're not friends now?"

"We are," Eric said. "Just not as good as we used to be."

"Were you her boyfriend?"

Checking his watch again, he saw that only another minute had passed. It was going to be a long, awkward night. And although he had turned away from James and was now facing the window, he could still feel the heat of the boy's curious gaze.

"I was," Eric said. "When we were in school."

"Did you two kiss?"

"I think we're done with the questions now." Eric stared out the window at Glenn Stewart's house. His neighbor was home, of course, as evidenced by a single lit window on the second floor. Soon James joined him in gazing at the rectangular glow of the window in the house next door.

"Where did my mom have to go?" he asked.

This was a question Eric knew how to answer. "She's digging for something."

"Digging?" James crinkled his nose. "For what?"

"A clue."

"About what?"

Eric let out a rueful chuckle. The boy was definitely Kat's child. They shared the same stubbornness, the same unquenchable thirst for answers.

"About my brother," he said. "He disappeared many years ago. Your mother is trying to help me find out what happened to him."

James didn't ask a follow-up, and for a moment Eric thought the questions were over. Then the light went out in Glenn Stewart's window, prompting James to say, "I think whoever lives there just went to bed."

Mr. Stewart was such a mystery that he could have been a vampire for all Eric knew. Yet he had a feeling the boy was right. No other lights flicked on in other rooms to take the place of the one that had just been extinguished.

"Why are you watching that house?" James asked.

"Because the man who lives there might also know something about my brother."

"Like what?"

"I don't know." Eric thought about what he had witnessed in his neighbor's yard the previous night. Glenn Stewart in the rain with a shovel. Putting the shoe box into the ground. Saying his silent prayer in the dead of night. "But I think I saw him bury it."

"Is that what my mom is digging up?"

"No. She's somewhere else."

"Then why don't you do it?"

It was a valid question—and an even better suggestion. While Glenn slept, Eric could sneak into his yard and quickly dig up whatever had been buried there. Of course an eleven-year-old boy would be the one to come up with it. Even more appropriate was the fact that the boy was none other than Kat Campbell's son.

"Maybe I'll do that," Eric said.

"Can I help?"

"Sure. You can help."

As they headed to the garage to find a shovel, Eric couldn't help but smile. Sometimes the apple really didn't fall far from the tree. As Kat and her deputy searched the ground in the cemetery for hints about what happened to Charlie, he was about to do the same with her son. And he hoped both search parties unearthed something worthwhile.

EIGHTEEN

Dusk had firmly taken hold of Oak Knoll Cemetery by the time Kat passed through its front gate. There was enough light to see by but not enough to make out many details. The dimness seemed to erase the names on the gravestones, creating rows of blank slates that stretched from one corner of the cemetery to the other. Creeping between them, Kat pointed her flashlight at each headstone until she found Maggie Olmstead's.

"We're here," she said.

Behind her were Carl Bauersox and Earl Morgan, the cemetery's groundskeeper. Both men carried shovels, which they set down in front of the grave.

Earl, who was a far cry from the cemetery's previous groundskeeper, waited expectantly in dirt-smeared jeans and a green John Deere cap. "What are you looking for again?"

Truth be told, Kat had no idea. Digging up the grave site was just her attempt to leave no stone unturned. She didn't expect to find any earth-shattering clues or definitive proof about what fate had befallen Charlie Olmstead. But there was also a chance they'd discover something small that could help them in their quest.

"Hope," she said. "We're looking for hope."

Dropping to her knees, she smoothed a hand through the grass until she found Charlie's grave marker. She then rested her flashlight on top of it, the beam illuminating the grass. Earl pulled four wooden pegs from a satchel slung over his shoulder, placing them at the corners of the grave site. Next out of the satchel was white twine, which he strung from peg to peg, marking out the area where they'd be digging.

"This should do it, don't you think?"

Carl eyed the patch of grass. "It depends on what's down there."

"I hope something small and close to the surface," Kat said. "If this is going to be a waste of time, I don't want to be here all night doing it."

Shoving a hand into the satchel, Earl removed a spade and started the unenviable task of removing the grass from over the site. He did it quickly and thoroughly, using the spade to carve the grass into evenly spaced sections. He then pried up the squares of green and set them aside in a tidy pile.

Kat removed a plastic trash bag that poked out of the satchel and spread it on the ground to the right of the grave site. Their plan was to pile the loose dirt on top of it, which would make it easier to fill in the hole when they were finished.

With the prep work finalized, Earl picked up one shovel and handed the other to Carl. They stood on opposite sides of the rectangle of exposed earth. Then, on the count of three, both of them dug in.

Eric lifted the shovel out of the ground and dumped the contents off to the side. He didn't worry about being tidy with his digging. Since the ground was freshly turned, there was no need to be. His goal was speed.

And not getting caught, of course.

"You still keeping a lookout?" he asked James, who stood a few feet away, facing Glenn Stewart's house.

"Yeah," the boy said. "Coast is still clear."

"Good. Keep looking. If you see a light come on, just run back to my house. I'll take care of everything else."

Eric felt uneasy about bringing James along. Kat would be livid if she ever found out, which is why he had made James promise not to tell her. But the extra set of eyes helped, and James seemed to be relishing his role as official lookout.

"I feel like a pirate," the boy whispered. "This is fun."

"Glad you're enjoying it," Eric whispered back. "Now, no more talking. He might hear us and wake up."

James nodded and ran his pinched thumb and index finger across his mouth—the universal symbol for zipping his lips. He then turned back to the house, hand over his eyes like Captain Jack Sparrow surveying the sea.

Just to be sure, Eric also eyed the house, moving his gaze from the first floor all the way up to the widow's walk on the roof. Every window was dark. The only noises were the drone of the nearby falls and Eric's shovel as it invaded the ground once again.

That was followed by another noise—a slight crunch of steel on cardboard.

James heard it, too, and whirled around to face him. "What was that?"

"That," Eric said, "is what we're looking for."

Carl was the one who found it. After digging for about ten minutes, he plunged his shovel into the dirt and struck some-

thing hard and impenetrable. The unexpected force of the collision made the shovel vibrate.

"You hit something," Earl Morgan said, stating the obvious.

Carl dropped the shovel and shook the numbness out of
his arms. "It seems that way."

Something big and heavy, by the sound of it. As Earl used
his shovel to clear away larger patches of dirt, Kat got down
on her knees and used her hands to sweep away the rest. Running her grime-smeared palms over their find, she realized it
was a child's coffin.

Earl saw it, too, and said, "You told me there was no one
buried down there."

"There isn't. At least, there shouldn't be."

The top half of the coffin was mostly intact, its lid firmly
in place. The bottom half had succumbed to time and nature,
swamping the interior with dirt. Leaning over the coffin's upper lid, Kat had a flashback to the previous year. Opening all
those coffins built by the Grim Reaper. Seeing all those grue-
some surprises. She had thought those days were over.

Lifting the lid slightly, she tried to peek inside but couldn't.
There wasn't enough light to see by. In order to get a good
look, she had to open the entire coffin. Taking a deep breath,
she yanked on the lid. It creaked just as loudly as the door leading to the Clarks' bomb shelter earlier that day. But, just like
that stubborn door, the lid eventually yielded.

The first thing Kat saw was dirt, which had flowed in
from the breached bottom half. It filled the upper portion of
the coffin, making the satin pillow that sat there look like a
white island in a sea of brown. Resting on top of the pillow
was an unmarked tin box.

It was in remarkably good shape for something that had spent the past four decades in the ground. Only a few blotches of rust marred the lid. When Kat picked it up, something inside rattled.

"Aren't you going to open it?" Carl asked.

It was certainly tempting. But what the box contained was personal. It had enough meaning to Maggie Olmstead that she chose to bury it in lieu of her son. If it was going to be opened, it needed to be done by family.

"No," Kat said. "That's a job for Eric."

Sitting cross-legged on the damp grass, Eric rested the shoe box between his knees. The impact of the shovel had dented the lid slightly, but it was otherwise intact. That was a good thing. He would have been angry with himself had he damaged whatever was inside.

James stood behind him, looking excitedly over his shoulder. "Go on. Open it up."

Removing the lid, Eric peered inside. James did, too, craning his neck for a better view. What they saw was both surprising and more than a little sad.

"What is it?" James asked.

"It's a ferret," Eric replied.

He gazed down at the animal that lay on the bottom of the box. Its fur was light brown, punctuated with bits of white. A band of black surrounded its closed eyes. The way it was positioned, curled into a tight ball in one of the box's corners, made the animal look like it was sleeping. But Eric knew better.

James, still curious, asked, "What happened to it?"

"It died."

"How?"

"I don't know."

The only thing Eric did know was that invading Glenn Stewart's yard had been a bad idea. Clearly, the ferret had been his pet and he had braved the storm the night before because the animal, having just died, needed to be buried. Hence the late-night digging and the quick prayer when it was over. What Eric had spied from the window was nothing more than a lonely man saying good-bye to a beloved companion. Knowing that his suspicions had gotten the best of him made him sweat with shame.

James crowded him from behind. "Can I touch it?"

"No."

Eric yanked the box away, causing the dead ferret inside to slide to another corner. Something else slid with it. He had missed it earlier because it had been hidden beneath the animal. Now it was exposed, sitting askew against one of the ferret's front paws.

A flat disk, it was roughly the size of a plate from a child's tea set. Eric picked it up and turned it over in his hands. It was made of clay and surprisingly heavy for its size. One side was unadorned. The other had been coated with a thin layer of white paint. Dark traces of clay could be spotted through the paint job, giving the whole thing a blotchy, stubbled look. It wasn't until Eric examined it at arm's length that he realized what the disk resembled.

It was a full moon.

"What's that?" James asked in a manner that came close to resembling awe. For him, this really had become a treasure hunt.

"Just a piece of clay."

"Can I have it?"

"No can do," Eric said. "We need to leave it where it is and bury the animal again. Quickly."

Eric returned the disk to the box and put the lid over it. Climbing to his feet, he grabbed the shovel and used it to widen the hole he had pulled the box from. When it was big enough, he laid the box inside and, with much guilt, began to rebury it.

He was almost finished when James tugged on his arm and whispered, "He's awake."

Eric looked to the house, where a light had brightened a second-floor window. He caught sight of a silhouette behind the glass, apparently looking out over the yard.

"Go," Eric hissed to James. "Run."

The boy sprinted away, streaking from Glenn Stewart's yard. Eric soon did the same, running with the shovel as fast as he could until he was back in his own yard. He caught up with James on the back porch. There was a giddy smile plastered on the boy's face as he breathlessly said, "That was so cool! Do you think he saw us?"

Eric shook his head. "I don't think so."

It was a lie. Eric knew without a doubt that Glenn Stewart had seen both of them. He also had a dreadful sense that his neighbor knew exactly what they had been up to.

NINETEEN

The bones lay on the stainless-steel table like parts of a jigsaw puzzle ready to be pieced together. The skull Nick had found in the water sat at the head of the table. Just below it was the lower jaw with its row of browned teeth. The rest of the bones that state police divers had found were arrayed below that in a fair approximation of what a full skeleton would look like. Ribs in the middle. Two arms—one of them broken in half at the elbow—resting alongside them. Legs pointing to the bottom of the table.

Years underwater had stripped the skeleton clean. There were no traces of skin, organs, even tendons. Time had wiped away most of it. Fish had done the rest. All that remained were the bones.

Nick took a slow walk around the table, studying them. The hand of the right arm, the one that was in two pieces, lay flat against the table's surface, fingers slightly spread. The left hand was balled into a fist, the bones of its fingers tight against each other. He had just reached out and touched it when a woman sailed into the autopsy suite, leaving its double doors swinging wildly behind her. She looked first at the skeleton and then at Nick.

"Are you in charge?"

Lieutenant Vasquez, who had been sitting quietly in the corner, stood. Like Nick, he was still damp from their unexpected dip beneath the mill. Unlike Nick, he had removed his shirt and approached the woman with a bare-chested swagger. The show-off.

"I am," he said, extending a hand and introducing himself.

"Lucy Meade. We spoke on the phone." To Tony's disappointment, the woman had gone back to looking at Nick. "Who's he?"

"Nick Donnelly. He's helping out with the case."

"If you want to help," Lucy said, speaking directly to Nick, "then don't touch my fucking bones."

The way she verbally took possession of the skeleton informed Nick that she was the forensic anthropologist brought in to examine the remains. She was younger than he was expecting—early thirties, tops—and too pretty for someone who spent most of her time with the long dead. Her eyes were blue. Her auburn hair was tied back into a ponytail. She wore jeans, Nikes, and a CIA T-shirt.

"You were once with the CIA?" Nick asked.

Lucy Meade covered the shirt with a white lab coat she pulled from a hook next to the door. "Yes, but not the one you're thinking of."

"What other CIA is there besides the Central Intelligence Agency?"

"Culinary Institute of America," Lucy replied. "I was going to be a chef."

"What happened?"

"Bones are more interesting."

She shooed Nick away from the table with a flick of her hand and swooped in to replace him. Then she took a long look at the bones arranged in front of her.

"It's a boy," she said. "Taking a wild guess, I'd say he was no older than eleven."

Nick was impressed. "How can you tell?"

"Pubic bones." Lucy pointed to a series of bones held to-gether in a butterfly shape. "There's hardly any wear and tear of the pubic symphysis, indicating the skeleton belongs to someone who died very young. The pelvis is narrow and deep, telling me it's a male."

"That sounds like our boy." It was Tony, who had put on his shirt and joined them at the table.

"And just who is 'your boy'?" Lucy Meade used air quotes as she said it, a gesture that normally annoyed the hell out of Nick. In her case, however, he found it charming. Mostly be-cause she was smart. And pretty. And didn't hesitate to throw her weight around.

"Noah Pierce," he said. "Nine years old. Went missing in 1971."

"Where did you find him?"

"In the lake next to the state park where he disappeared."

"We'll need a dental anthropologist to try to match the teeth with dental records," Lucy said, "but I have a feeling this really is your boy."

"Would you be able to determine how he died?" Nick asked.

Like the others, he also was going on the assumption that the bones pulled from the water had once belonged to Noah Pierce. What he really wanted to know was who killed him and why. But since there was no way Lucy would be able to tell them that, Nick would gladly settle for a cause of death.

"Maybe." Lucy's eyes never left the bones on the table. She looked at them the way an art critic studied a Picasso—curious, probing, searching. "It depends on how he was killed. Since you found him in the water, wouldn't logic dictate that he drowned?"

Nick and Tony had discussed that possibility while toweling off in the back of a CSU van at Lasher Mill State Park. Both already knew that serial criminals rarely drowned their victims—the horrible truth being that it was less fun for them that way. When a victim of a serial killer was found in the water, there was a good chance it was merely a dumping ground and that the victim was killed by other means.

Snapping rubber gloves over her hands, Lucy moved to the head of the table and picked up the skull. She held it at eye level, tilting and turning it.

"I don't see any sign of skull fractures or contusions," she said. "I'll spend the night doing a more thorough examination, but off the bat it doesn't look like any blunt force trauma was involved."

Lucy set the skull down as gently as she had picked it up. She then moved to the side of the table, swiping a stray lock of hair behind her ear as she bent over the bones. She looked at each one closely and methodically, gaze skipping from rib to rib.

"What are you looking for?" Nick asked.

"Damage to the bones that could have been made with a weapon. Stabbing victims sometimes have slices on their bones made by the knife blade. Shooting victims have notches from where the bullet passed through. The good thing about the remains belonging to someone so young is that there's not a lifetime of skeletal damage to make things confusing."

Nick morbidly thought of his own leg and how it would have looked after four decades underwater. He suspected the titanium pins would still be there, unless the fish had been especially ravenous. It would certainly be enough to throw off even someone with Lucy Meade's expertise.

"With children," she continued, "there are fewer fractures to contend with. Fewer broken bones. The bad part—"

Nick volunteered an answer. "Is that the remains belong to a kid."

Lucy looked up from the table and smiled sadly. "Yes. That's exactly it."

She resumed her examination of the skeleton, pressing her fingertips against the bones of the right leg and running them down to the toes. Then she moved to the other side of the table, doing the same to the left leg, fingers now working upward.

"So tell me, Mr. Donnelly," she said, "is this one of your foundation's cold cases?"

Nick, whose gaze had been following Lucy's hands, now looked at her face. It remained mostly blank, her eyes squinting with concentration. Had she been studying his face, she would have seen surprise that she knew who he was.

"Partly," he said. "We sort of stumbled upon this one."

"Which is why you're back to helping the state police."

"Exactly."

At last, Lucy looked at him again. "I've read a few articles about you and your mission. I admire what you're trying to do. Call me if you ever need help with a case. I'd be glad to offer my expertise."

"I appreciate that."

"Or," Lucy added, "call me if you just want to grab a beer sometime. I'd be happy to do that, too."

Tony, who was standing behind her, gave Nick an excited thumbs-up. Because he was facing Lucy, Nick couldn't react to the gesture. But, inside, his stomach was doing happy somersaults. He fully intended to make that phone call once he was done with the current case.

"I'll definitely keep that in mind," he said.

Lucy didn't respond. She was too busy leaning over the left arm splayed on the stainless-steel table. Something about the clenched hand had caught her attention, and she drew in close until her nose was almost touching the knuckle of the index finger.

"I think he's holding something," she said.

She flipped the arm over; pressing the wrist against the table with her left hand, she began to peel back the fingers with her right.

The pinkie finger was first. The joints cracked loudly when Lucy separated it from the others—a sickening popping sound that made Nick wince. Once it was flat against the table, Lucy instructed him to put on a pair of rubber gloves.

"Hold the finger down," Lucy told him once the gloves were on.

Nick pressed down on the bone as she moved to the ring finger. As soon as she pulled on it, the finger snapped off and clattered to the table.

"Fuck."

"That's one way of doing it," Nick said.

Lucy frowned. "The wrong way."

Although clearly flustered, she didn't hesitate to move on to the middle finger. It made the same cracking sounds as the pinkie, although louder. When its knuckles had been bent to the table, Nick also held it down. He did the same once the index finger was unfurled. Soon he found himself staring into the now-open palm.

The object sitting in the hand was unidentifiable at first glance. Decades of mud and algae clung to its surface, making it look more like a turd than anything else. When Lucy slid it out from beneath the thumb, it left a smear of dark slime behind.

"It's heavy for something so small," she said.

Lucy made her way to the sink along the wall and began to wash it off. Picking up a nearby scrub brush, she scoured it for a good five minutes. Every so often, the grime that coated the object made an audible *splat* as it fell into the sink's basin. When it was clean, Lucy turned around and showed it to them.

"What is it?" Nick asked.

"Honestly, I have no idea."

She passed it to Nick, who examined it. The object was about a few inches long and indeed heavier than it looked. If he had been asked to guess what it was made out of, he would have said wrought iron. Fortunately, he didn't need to guess.

"It's a model rocket," he said.

The paint job had been wiped away, leaving just a basic rod with a top that tapered into a rounded tip. What looked to be two small fins jutted out at the bottom. But the main thing that allowed Nick to identify it wasn't the shape or size. It was the letters that had been carefully scratched onto the side.

He held the rocket to the light and angled it until the letters could be seen by Tony and Lucy. What they spelled was a first and last name.

That name was Dennis Kepner.

TWENTY

After his experience in Glenn Stewart's yard an hour earlier, Eric wasn't sure if he wanted to open the box Kat brought back from the cemetery. He still felt guilty about digging up his neighbor's dead pet and remorse about invading his privacy. Staring at the tin box sitting on the dining-room table didn't help matters. If anything, it only reinforced the lesson he had learned next door—that some things were meant to stay buried.

"Are we really doing the right thing here?" he asked.

Kat sat next to him, nodding gently. "Isn't this what your mother wanted?"

Eric's mother wanted him to find Charlie. He wasn't sure she ever imagined that digging up things she had once buried would be a part of that. But apparently it was. Now he had to decide whether to go through with it or not.

To her credit, Kat remained patient as he thought through his dilemma. She had sent James home with Carl Bauersox, asking the deputy to keep an eye on him until she returned. Eric was certain she wanted to do that sooner rather than later. He was also pretty sure that, having been the one to unearth the box, she wanted to see what it contained.

After another minute of silence ticked by, Eric said, "I guess it has to be done."

Without giving it any more thought, he removed the lid and looked inside the box. A photograph of his brother stared back at him. Again, it was Charlie's final school portrait—an image Eric had seen far too many times in the past few days. He picked it up and stared at it a moment, taking in his brother's sad eyes, jug-handle ears, and wary smile.

"There's something else in the box," Kat said.

Eric set Charlie's picture aside and peered into the box once again. Sitting on the bottom, where it had been hidden by the photo, was a key. Once bronze but now tarnished to a dull dark brown, it was smaller than modern keys. The teeth were more pronounced, the ridges less deep. Nothing was attached to it—no ring or chain—and nothing indicated what the key could be used for.

Eric, however, had a good guess.

Grabbing the key, he jumped up from the table and headed out of the dining room. Behind him, Kat could barely keep pace as he rushed upstairs, stopping at the door to Charlie's room. With shaking hands, he slid the key into the hole. It fit perfectly. When he turned it, a slight click emanated from inside the door.

Charlie's room was now open.

Standing in front of the unlocked door, Eric let out a joyous whoop. That was followed by some celebratory hopping up and down. He grabbed Kat, who had at last caught up to him, and pulled her into the dance.

"It's the key!" he shouted. "We're in!"

He drew Kat close, enveloping her in a bear hug. He pulled her face close to his. Then, without thought or warning, he kissed her.

Kat wasn't expecting the kiss. But when it came, she realized that she had wanted it. From the moment she had laid eyes on Eric again, she wanted it. After barging in on him naked earlier that day, when she had peeked more than she cared to admit, she knew she *really* wanted it.

So when that first sudden peck on the lips was over, she silently indicated she wanted another by placing a hand on the back of his head and pulling him close again. Halfway through that second go-round, she started kissing him back.

They had kissed before, of course. Long, long ago. When they were dating, one of their favorite pastimes was finding new places to park and make out, places her father and his deputy didn't know about. But they had been kids then. Now they were adults, and Kat was pleased to see that Eric's style had changed and matured. His kiss was somehow simultaneously forceful and gentle. There was a hunger to it that Kat liked.

Eric snaked an arm around her lower back and lifted, pulling her against him. The resulting collision of their bodies made her weak with desire, and she found herself grabbing onto the door handle for support. When Eric moved his lips to her neck, the pleasure she felt caused her to twist the handle.

Like the initial kiss, the opening of the door was a surprise. Both of them had been leaning against it, shoulders adding pressure to the wood. When the door went, they went with it, tumbling into the room in a heap of intertwined limbs.

Kat landed on her back, head knocking painfully against the floor. Eric fell on top of her, although his arm remained beneath her body. She felt the bump of it running along her lower back. When he slid his arm out from under her, it was colored a dark gray from the dust.

Every movement they made only kicked up more dust. By the time they had helped each other to their feet, they were engulfed by a cloud of it.

"Jesus," Eric said, swatting in vain at the dust particles floating in front of his face. "I can barely breathe."

Neither could Kat. The dust was overwhelming. Dipping a hand into the front of her uniform, she yanked the collar of her T-shirt until it was over her nose and mouth. Eric did the same with his own shirt as both of them peered through the dust cloud into the depths of the bedroom.

Kat's first impression was that it looked like everything in the room had been drained of color. The bedspread. The curtains. The toys littering the floor. All of it had been rendered gray by the dust. Moving deeper into the room, she passed a dresser cloaked in it. She swiped a finger across its top, revealing a streak of its original color—a shade of blue that stood out even more against the unrelenting dust.

There were cobwebs, too. Strung from the bed to the nightstand. Clinging to the radiator. Large strands of them swooped from the ceiling like crepe paper that had been hung for a party and never taken down.

"How long do you think it's been since someone was in here?" Kat asked.

"Probably 1969." Eric tried the light switch by the door. It did nothing. The bulbs had all died long ago. "Right before they buried the key."

Looking around, Kat thought it was more like the moment Charlie disappeared. The room had the aura of something suddenly abandoned, as if Charlie ran out of the room one night and no one had entered since. No organizing possessions. No clearing out. And certainly no tidying up. She could easily see the disarray of daily life present in the room, even though the boy who had inhabited it was no longer alive.

Kat walked to a desk pushed against the wall. Scattered over its surface were uncapped pens and worn-down pencils that had been used to mark nearby pieces of paper. She picked one up using her thumb and forefinger, trying to shake away the dust and cobwebs. Through the layer of gray that remained, she saw hand-drawn pictures of stars, a rocket, and, of course, the moon.

A fair amount of space-related paraphernalia could be found scattered around the room. A papier-mâché planet dangled from fishing line over the desk. On the dresser was a series of model rockets, arranged by height, and sitting next to the window was a small telescope perched on a tripod.

Eric was nearby, examining the nightstand. There was another model rocket there, along with a lamp and a framed photograph. He began to wipe away the decades of dust that obscured the photo.

Kat moved to the window and did the same, swiping it in a circular motion until there was a clear oval of glass. The view it offered was a nice one. She saw a patch of the front yard, followed by the street itself. On the other side sat the Santangelo household, lights ablaze in almost every window. Kat knew not much had changed on the cul-de-sac since 1969. What she was looking at now was pretty much exactly what Charlie Olmstead would have seen back then. She imagined the space-crazed kid spending hours peering through his telescope, watching the sky, the street, the neighbors.

She examined the telescope. The lens cap was on it, blocking the blanket of dust that covered everything else in the room, including the telescope's eyepiece. Kat blew on it a few times, each breath sending up tiny puffs of dust. When the eyepiece was relatively clean, she bent down and squinted through it.

The first thing she saw was Lee Santangelo. The telescope was aimed directly at his bedroom window, giving Kat an up-close view of his blank face. The glow from the nearby television colored his skin a pale blue. The only things that moved were his eyes, which darted back and forth, following the action onscreen.

Kat adjusted the telescope until more of the room came into focus. She saw Lee's easy chair, the television, and a corner of the railed bed nearby. Peering inside the Santangelo house, she wondered if the stars in the sky were the only things Charlie had gazed at through his telescope. From the looks of it, he also did some spying on his neighbors.

On the other side of the room, Eric gasped. "Kat, look at this."

Still holding the freshly cleaned photograph, he turned the frame until Kat could see the picture inside. It was of a cluster of schoolkids sitting on the floor and looking up in admiration at a man speaking in front of them. The man was Lee Santangelo in all his former glory—young, virile, handsome. He seemed to be smiling down at a boy in the front row. That boy was Charlie Olmstead.

"The photo is signed." Eric pointed to the inscription before reading it. "Always look to the sky. Your friend, Lee."

Kat looked through the telescope again, inching it slightly lower until she could see into the room beneath Lee's bedroom. It was the odd museum devoted to his life and career, lit brightly like the rest of the house. Kat focused the telescope, zeroing in on the photographs covering the wall. She stopped at one in particular, one that she had completely bypassed earlier that day without giving it a second thought.

"I can't believe I didn't piece it together."

"What are you talking about?"

"The pictures," Kat said. "In Lee's house. They told us everything we needed to know."

She was out of the bedroom within seconds. A minute later, she was out of the house itself and crossing the street. Eric caught up with her as she stepped into the Santangelos' yard, marching up the grass to the front door.

"I don't understand what's going on," he said.

Kat grabbed the large brass knocker and used it to pound on the door. "You will in a minute."

Becky Santangelo answered the door in a satin nightgown and matching robe. Like the yellow chiffon number she had entertained them in that morning, it was both young and inappropriate for a woman her age. Making the outfit more ridiculous were the slippers she wore. Colored a light shade of purple, they had kitten heels and small tufts of white at the toes.

"You again." Becky didn't even try to sound happy to be seeing them. "Have you come here to interrogate me one more time?"

"I want to see the pictures," Kat said. "Of your husband."

"After your behavior this morning, I think your intrusion—"

Kat cut her off. "I don't give a damn what you think."

She pushed on the door, forcing Becky to step aside. Once inside the house, she made a beeline for the trophy room she had just seen through the telescope. All the pictures on the wall stopped her fierce momentum. There were so many of them, depicting so many different eras. She circled the room a moment, getting her bearings, before finding the patch of wall she was looking for.

The first photograph she zeroed in on was a copy of the one Eric found in his brother's room. The plaque affixed to the bottom of the frame indicated it was taken at Perry Hollow Elementary School in 1969.

The photo next to it showed a similar scene. In it, Lee stood outside a stone church, shaking hands with an elderly woman as a group of kids looked on. The plaque on the photo said ST. PAUL'S METHODIST CHURCH, 1972. The church's name also appeared in the photo, on a sign to the right of Lee Santangelo. Beneath the name, in small white letters, was its location— Centralia, Pennsylvania.

"Centralia?" Eric said. "Isn't that where two of the boys vanished?"

Kat nodded grimly. "It sure is."

"What boys?" It was Becky Santangelo, standing in the doorway with a look of pure fear on her face. "I don't understand what's going on."

"Six boys went missing in the late sixties and early seventies," Kat said. "And we think your husband could have had something to do with it."

Behind her, Eric said, "We've got another hit."

He was staring at a photo a few feet away—another image of Lee in front of a room of kids. Only these boys weren't as admiring. Some of them looked pretty rough as they sat in what seemed to be a large lodge. In the background of the photo was a window, revealing trees and the rooftops of log cabins. Etched onto the accompanying plaque were the words CAMP CRESCENT, 1971.

Kat edged closer to the photo, peering at the faces of the boys in the audience. In the second row was a boy of about twelve with hard eyes and a sharp smirk.

Dwight Halsey.

"Holy crap," Kat said, tapping the picture. "He's in the photo! He and Lee most likely met."

"I don't understand why that would be considered suspicious," Becky said. "My husband traveled all over Pennsylvania. It was part of his job."

"Do you know if he was ever in a town called Fairmount?"

"Probably. He's most likely set foot in every town in the state."

"Mrs. Santangelo," Kat said, "we know someone else was with your husband the night Charlie vanished."

Becky's chin rose in defiance. "That's just a vicious lie."

"I don't think you understand how serious this is," Kat said. "We're talking about six boys who disappeared during Apollo moon missions. You're husband, a rejected astronaut, had contact with at least two of them."

"That doesn't mean Lee killed them."

"No," Kat replied, "but it makes him our prime suspect. So unless there was someone else here with him, someone who could provide a decent alibi, I'm going to have to arrest your husband for the abduction of Charlie Olmstead."

Becky glanced at the large oil painting of Lee in uniform. From the intense way she looked at it, she appeared to be seeking the image's guidance. Holding the collar of her robe tight against her throat, she stared at it, fighting off tears.

"I can't tell you," she blurted out. "I'm sorry. I just can't."

Kat marched past her and into the hallway. "Then I'm sorry for what I'm about to do."

Becky made a desperate grasp for her sleeve. Kat shook it off and headed toward the stairs, climbing them with purpose.

She stayed that way—head high, back straight—as she moved down the hall. Then it was into Lee Santangelo's bedroom.

He was still in his giant chair, his face a blank canvas being painted by the colors of the television. Lee didn't look at Kat when she stood in front of him, nor did she expect him to, not even when she pulled out the handcuffs.

"Beck," he chirped. "Beck."

When his wife reached the room, breathless and bug-eyed with worry, Kat slapped one of the cuffs around Lee's wrist.

"Lee Santangelo, you have the right to remain silent."

Becky gasped. "What are you doing?"

"I told you," Kat said, cuffing Lee's other wrist. "I'm arresting him."

"This is madness." Becky ran to her husband, examining his shackled wrists. "He's a sick man. You can't take him to jail. He could die in there."

Kat understood that. Which is why she didn't actually plan to throw Lee Santangelo in jail. Her intention was to scare the truth out of his wife. It worked.

"I can prove he didn't hurt those boys," she said.

"How?"

"With evidence. I have evidence he didn't touch them."

"Then show me."

"I have to find it first," Becky replied. "But I will. I promise. Just please take those god-awful handcuffs off him."

Kat relented. If Lee had been in better health, she would have had second thoughts about unlocking the cuffs and letting them fall away from his wrists. But she knew he and Becky weren't flight risks. Even if he did have something to do with those missing boys, justice could wait one more day. Late evidence was better than no evidence.

"You have twenty-four hours," she told Becky. "If I don't see proof by this time tomorrow, I won't hesitate to drag your husband to jail."

TWENTY-ONE

For the second night in a row, Eric slept uneasily. He seemed to spend hours precariously balanced on the precipice between sleep and wakefulness. When he did manage to drift off, the nightmares crept in. He had one about Lee Santangelo, looking like he did forty years ago, standing over the bed, ready to grab him. Another one starred Charlie—or at least the ghost of him, Eric couldn't tell—roaming around his bedroom, kicking up plumes of dust.

The only good dream of the night featured Kat. It was a re-creation of their kiss by Charlie's unlocked door; only this time both of them were naked. When the bedroom door inevitably swung open, they fell not onto the floor but into a warm, white light so sensual it woke him up.

His eyes snapping open, Eric tried to ignore his obvious arousal. He and Kat hadn't discussed the real, live lip-lock after leaving the Santangelo residence. There had been more pressing matters to deal with. But alone in the dark quiet of the bedroom, he couldn't stop thinking about what it all meant. More important to a man who hadn't had sex since before leaving Brooklyn, he wondered when—or even if—it would happen again.

It wasn't unusual for his mind to race like this. It happened quite often when he was working on one of his Mitch Gracey books. In the thick of the writing process, he'd often lie in bed as his thoughts pulled him further away from sleep instead of the other way around. That night, the only difference was that Eric had no book to work on. Mitch Gracey's voice had been silent for months.

Instead, he thought of Charlie. And Mr. Stewart. And the terrified look on Becky Santangelo's face as Kat slapped cuffs around her husband's wrists. After about a half hour of this, his mind grew hazy, ready to surrender to sleep—and possibly more bad dreams—once again.

Then he heard the noise.

The sound made him sit up, ears straining to identify it. It wasn't like the one he heard the night before, when Glenn Stewart's shovel striking the ground had cut through the hum of the rain. This noise was sharper, louder.

When he heard it again, Eric still couldn't tell what it was. But he could definitely identify where it was coming from—downstairs.

Someone else was in the house.

Eric slid out of bed slowly, careful not to make too much noise. He didn't want to alert the intruder to his presence. Crossing the room on tiptoes, he paused at the bedroom door. It was already closed, but Eric locked it for good measure. Better to be safe than sorry.

He pressed his ear to the door and listened. The noise downstairs had started again. This time Eric recognized it.

Footsteps.

Coming closer.

Approaching the staircase.

Eric remained motionless at the door, hoping whoever was downstairs would think the house was empty and go away. He didn't want to move. He didn't want to breathe. He gulped for air and held his breath.

The footsteps below changed their tone, growing lighter, less forceful.

And closer.

The intruder was ascending the stairs in a slow and unsteady progression. There were lengthy pauses between each step, signaling uncertainty about the climb. When Eric heard the telltale creak of the fifth step, he knew the intruder was halfway to the top.

He surveyed the bedroom, looking for something he could use to defend himself. His options were slim—a duffel bag, a pair of sneakers, a coffee mug he had forgotten to take to the kitchen that morning. The heaviest item in the room, he realized, was his laptop.

Eric crept to the desk and picked it up. He held it sideways, the way someone would use a book to squash a spider. He felt stupid sneaking back to the door with the laptop held in front of him. If Mitch Gracey were real, alive and standing in the room with him, he would have rolled his eyes with contempt.

But Eric didn't care. Nor did he care that he was about to use a very expensive computer as a weapon. The fact that he had written nothing of value on it in the past month eclipsed all second thoughts.

Reaching the door again, Eric unlocked it. The intruder had reached the top of the stairs and was making his way down the hall. Every tentative footstep echoed off the walls, slicing through the silence of the house.

Hand poised at the doorknob, Eric waited. On the other side of the door, he heard breathing. Heavy. Labored. Definitely a man.

Eric didn't know who the man was or what he wanted. But he knew what had to be done.

He needed to fight.

Yanking the door open, he raised the laptop over his head and rushed into the hallway, prepared to strike. When he saw the intruder, all thoughts of fighting back ceased.

The man in the hallway wasn't a threat. Hell, he could barely stand. Using the wall to prop himself up, he gazed at Eric through heavy lids. The stench of alcohol swirled around him. Cutting through it were even more unsavory smells—sweat, piss, the alarming whiff of decay.

"Dad?" Eric said. "What are you doing here?"

His father was too drunk to answer. Staggeringly drunk, in fact. If the smell didn't tip Eric off, the way his father could barely stand did. When he started to slide down the wall like a string of spaghetti not fully cooked, Eric grabbed him by the arms and guided him to his mother's old room.

Once there, Eric helped his father collapse onto the bed. Watching his father's unwashed head loll back and forth on the white pillowcase caused a twinge of guilt. His mother wouldn't have wanted this. She wouldn't have let Ken back into the house, let alone the bedroom they had once shared. If anything, she would have made him sleep on the back porch.

But it was too late for that. His father was in the bed, no doubt stinking up the sheets, and Eric was exhausted. On his way out of the room, he heard Ken stir in bed. Turning around, he saw that his father was sitting up and—shocking for his condition—almost lucid.

"Eric," he said. "I'm sorry."

"Sorry for what?"

His father had done so many shitty things in his life that he hoped this wasn't an umbrella apology. If he was finally saying sorry, Eric wanted specifics.

"For Charlie," his dad said.

"Why would you be sorry about that?"

His father didn't answer the question. He fell back onto the bed, eyes closed and arms splayed. But he wasn't asleep. Not quite. Just before drifting off, he murmured five words.

"Don't try to find him."

FRIDAY

TWENTY-TWO

Nick spent the night in a Super 8 motel ten minutes outside of Fairmount. Tony did, too, although in a room bought and paid for by the state police. Nick's had been put on his already-overwhelmed Visa card. Good thing for him the room was cheap. Something more expensive—a Days Inn, perhaps—would have put him over his credit limit. At least he got free coffee out of the deal. Tony brought it from the lobby to his room at 6:00 A.M.

"Here," he said, shoving the cup at Nick. "I figured you'd need this for your drive."

"Where am I going?"

"Camp Crescent."

Nick was confused. He thought it might have been from caffeine deprivation. But two mighty gulps of coffee later it still didn't make sense.

"Aren't you going, too?"

"I can't," Tony said. "We got the dental records of both Noah Pierce and Dennis Kepner. A dental anthropologist from Harrisburg is driving up later this morning. Hopefully by the afternoon, we'll know which of the boys was found beneath the mill."

Until they found the model rocket, Nick had been certain

the remains he discovered belonged to Noah Pierce. Now, he wasn't so sure.

Neither was Tony.

"I called Gloria," he said. "She's ordered a full search of the state park, just in case it was Dennis that we found. For all we know, the remains of the other boys could be there, too."

Nick didn't need to ask Tony if he had told Gloria Ambrose about his involvement in the investigation. If he had, there was a good chance he wouldn't be talking to him now.

"So while you guys search Lasher Mill State Park, you want me to poke around the camp where Dwight Halsey disappeared?"

"Exactly," Tony said. "Just be discreet about it."

Nick thought he could handle that. He liked the idea of Tony beating the shrubbery at a public park while he got to do the investigating. It was a refreshing change of pace.

He showered, shaved, and yanked his clothes from the rod where they had been hung out to dry the night before. They were as stiff as cardboard and had a funky smell that was part lake, part mildew, and part cheap hotel. Once in the car, he rolled the windows down in an attempt to air them out.

According to the directions, Camp Crescent was located in the heart of a large swath of forest two hours southeast. Instead of music, Nick spent the drive listening to news reports about the Chinese astronauts' progress. The lunar landing was slated for about four that afternoon, with a moon walk to take place roughly an hour after that. If someone was planning on abducting another little boy when it happened, the time to prevent it was running out.

The entrance to the camp itself was a good five miles off

the main highway, at the end of a pothole-riddled road enclosed by trees. When Nick pulled up to it, he found no sign marking it as the location of Camp Crescent. All he saw were a metal gate blocking the road and at least four separate signs warning trespassers to stay away. Since Nick wasn't really a trespasser, he got out of the car and, with the help of his cane, crawled under the gate.

There was more road on the other side, which sliced deeper through the trees. Eventually, the road split and a weathered sign sat in the middle of the fork, finally welcoming him to Camp Crescent. Next to it was a smaller sign with arrows pointing to various locations within the camp—cabins, mess hall, latrine. Nick followed the one directing him to camp headquarters.

The headquarters turned out to be a two-story cabin built in the Adirondack-style. The foundation was fieldstone. The exterior support beams were peeled logs. A rocking chair sat on the porch that wrapped around the side of the building. Although the structure had clearly seen better days, the chair signaled that someone still used it from time to time. So did the uncovered furniture Nick spied through the smudged windows. But when he knocked on the door, no one answered.

Walking along the porch, he moved to the back of the cabin. An overgrown meadow stretched from the porch to a thin line of pines about a hundred yards away. Through the trees, he glimpsed a bit of lake and a boat dock that was now mostly submerged.

In the middle of the meadow was a circle of rocks. A few benches surrounded it, only one of which was still fully intact. A fire pit, Nick guessed. From when Camp Crescent used to be a real camp. It certainly wasn't anymore. Nick didn't know when or why, but the camp had closed up shop long ago.

He stepped off the porch and into the meadow, heading toward the remains of the fire pit. He got about three steps before he heard a familiar noise behind him. He remembered the sound well from his days in the state police. Once someone heard the hammer click of a 12-gauge shotgun, they didn't forget it.

A man's voice accompanied the click. "Who the hell are you and what are you doing here?"

Frozen in place, Nick said, "I'm with the state police."

He knew it was the best way to get the man to lower the gun, even though it wasn't entirely the truth. Semantics went out the window when someone had a 12-gauge aimed at your head.

"Turn around."

Nick rotated slowly, coming face-to-face with the man holding the gun. He appeared to be in his early seventies, with a bald head and a wild, sand-colored beard. His solid frame hinted that he had been strong once, although most of the muscle was now gone. As he held the shotgun, the skin on the man's upper arms drooped in wobbly flaps.

"What's your name?"

"Nick Donnelly. What's yours?"

"Before I tell you anything, how 'bout you tell me why the state police is coming around here snooping."

"Does the name Dwight Halsey sound familiar?" Nick asked.

"What about him?"

"Did you know him or not?"

The man lowered the gun and hung his head with it. "Yeah, I knew him. That goddamn boy ruined my life."

* * *

His name was Craig Brewster, and he owned the land Camp Crescent sat upon. He ran the camp, too, back when it really was a working camp and not a pile of rotting timber. Now he lived in its former headquarters during the warm months and rented an apartment in Philadelphia in the winter. He was seventy-two, unmarried, and needed a pacemaker to keep his heart from stopping.

He told Nick his sad tale from the back porch of the cabin he now called home. Nick imagined he sat there quite a bit, surveying everything he owned—and all he had eventually lost. According to Mr. Brewster, the blame rested with one kid who vanished in 1971.

"Were you here the night Dwight Halsey vanished?" Nick asked.

Craig nodded. "Of course."

"And do you remember any suspicious activity going on? Anyone acting strange?"

"No, sir. Not until the next morning when we realized he had run away."

"Do you mind if I take a look around the camp?"

"Not at all," Craig said, pushing himself out of his chair. "I'll give you the grand tour."

They walked the perimeter of the meadow, veering left onto a dirt path that led to a wooded area. Among the trees, the other structures that made up the camp sprouted from the forest floor like giant mushrooms.

"My father was a big fan of the outdoors," Craig said. "He taught me a lot. I learned at an early age that two things make you strong—discipline and nature. I've always followed that advice."

He told Nick that he joined the army at age nineteen. After he was honorably discharged, he found work as a guard at a juvenile detention facility. His father died in 1969, leaving him a lot of money, which he used to purchase one hundred acres of forest.

"I saw a lot of bad boys in juvie who were good boys deep down. They just didn't have the upbringing I did. I thought they could benefit from a place like this, where they could fish and hike and just be kids. Nothing turns a boy into a man better than the outdoors. That's how Camp Crescent was born."

"Interesting name," Nick said.

"It's symbolic. A crescent moon is just a sliver, barely formed. But over time it grows, becoming a full moon that brightens the night. The boys who came to this camp were the same way—small, unformed, but with the potential to be bright lights."

They paused at a wide, low-slung building constructed of logs. A sign over the door indicated it was the mess hall—incredibly apt, considering its condition. Half the roof was missing, having caved in ages ago. Growing through the remains of the rafters was a large maple tree.

"I opened the camp in 1970," Craig said, "taking in boys who had been in trouble with the law or were on their way there. It did them some good to be outdoors. Waking up at dawn, going to bed at dusk. Learning how to get along with others. It made a difference, and I was proud of that. Then the Halsey boy showed up."

"When was this?" Nick asked.

"June 1971. He didn't take to the camp like the others. Hell, he didn't take to it at all."

"Not a fan of the great outdoors?"

"Not to speak ill of the dead," Craig said, "but he was a city punk through and through. Full of lip. Lots of attitude. Had a police record a mile long, and he was only twelve. Shop-lifting. Vandalism. Got kicked out of school for showing up with a knife."

He didn't need to go on. It was clear Dwight Halsey was no angel.

"How'd he get along with the other kids?" Nick asked.

"Not too well. Right off the bat, he started causing trouble."

Nick recalled the photograph of Dwight from Maggie Olmstead's collection. The boy looked mean in it, like he was in the process of challenging the photographer.

"What kind of trouble?"

"The usual. You know how boys can be at that age. Taunt-ing. Name-calling. A few fistfights. He got into one the day he ran off. Had a pretty big shiner, if I recall."

He guided Nick deeper into the camp, which was in just as much disarray as the mess hall. Passing the meager latrine, Nick saw that the walls and roof had crumbled, leaving a row of toilets sitting out under the open sky.

"How do you know Dwight Halsey ran off?"

"Because he hated it here," Craig said. "He said as much every day. So when the other boys in his cabin reported him missing the next morning, I automatically assumed he made a run for it."

"And got lost in the woods?"

"That's what we figured. Me and the police that came to investigate thought the same thing. The woods surrounding this place are deep, Mr. Donnelly. It's not too hard to get lost in there. And once you get turned around like that, chances are pretty slim you'll get out alive."

"But if he was trying to run away, why didn't he just follow the road?"

"Sometimes we don't know why boys do what they do."

They had reached an area circled with cabins, most of which had collapsed in on themselves. Those that were still standing had a broken-windowed look of deep neglect. Craig led Nick to one of the survivors, although the pine shingles on the roof were overrun with moss and the door was missing.

"This is the cabin he was staying in."

Nick stepped into the doorway but made no move to actually enter. He had learned his lesson at the mill the day before. In addition to cobwebs, bird nests, and a dead mouse on the floor, he saw two sets of bunk beds built into the wall. Previous occupants had scratched their names into the cabin wall. Among them were a Bobby, a Kevin, and a Joe. Nick looked for a Dwight but couldn't find one.

"Each cabin held four boys," Craig said. "Close quarters, but it taught them how to get along. Dwight was in bed at curfew. I know because I checked the cabin myself."

"What time was curfew?" Nick asked.

"Ten. Reveille was at six the next morning. By that time his bunk was empty and he was gone."

"Did he take anything with him?"

"Not that I'm aware of. All of his stuff was still stowed under his bunk."

"If you were going to run away from someplace and never come back," Nick said, "wouldn't you take your belongings with you?"

Craig Brewster stroked his beard as he mulled over the question and then dismissed it. "Not if it meant waking up the other boys in the cabin. He needed to go quietly."

"So the other boys in the cabin didn't see or hear anything?"

"No, sir." Craig sighed. "The police already asked me these questions a long time ago. They talked to the boys. They talked to the camp counselors. No one saw a thing and everyone thought the same thing—that Dwight fled into the woods and died there."

"How do you know he's really dead?"

"Because he never resurfaced," Craig said. "And if he had, my life would have turned out a whole lot differently."

He started to lead Nick back to camp headquarters, explaining how Dwight Halsey's disappearance was instant bad publicity for the camp. The next summer the camp hosted only half the number of kids it had the summer before. In 1973, it was even less. After ten more summers of barely scraping by, the camp closed for good.

"It was the only thing I could do," Craig said. "I tried to rent or sell the place to another camp, but no one wanted it. This land was forever stained by that Halsey boy and I lost everything."

Nick wanted to feel sorry for the camp owner yet couldn't bring himself to do it. Something about the man struck him as insincere, as if he only really regretted how Dwight Halsey's fate affected the camp and not what happened to the boy himself. The feeling grew more pronounced when Craig said, "You never told me why, after all these years, the police are suddenly interested in Dwight Halsey again."

"Between 1969 and 1972, six boys of similar ages vanished in similar locations," Nick told him. "All but one of them looked accidental. All of them happened at the same time man was walking on the moon. Dwight Halsey was one of them."

Craig's face grew so pale that Nick expected even his beard to change color. "You're telling me that Halsey boy didn't run away?"

"That's correct," Nick said. "Someone most likely abducted him. Just like the other boys."

"Then what did he do with them?"

Nick blinked. In that brief moment of darkness, he pictured the bones from the lake arranged across the stainless-steel table. That was all that was left of either Dennis Kepner or Noah Pierce. And, he suspected, all that was left of Dwight Halsey. Somewhere.

"He killed them," he said.

"But that just doesn't make sense. Why would someone pick the Halsey boy to kidnap and kill?"

"That's one of many things we don't know," Nick said. "But why wouldn't they?"

"He was a strong boy. Could handle himself in a fight."

"But you said he had a black eye the day he vanished."

"He did," Craig said. "But you should have seen the other kid. If you wanted to come into a camp and take a kid, there were other, weaker targets."

Nick had a feeling that Dwight, like all the other boys they were hunting, was simply a victim of being in the wrong place at the wrong time. He imagined him waking up in the middle of the night to take a leak and being jumped on his way back from the latrine. Or sneaking out to the boat dock for a late-night smoke, only to be surprised by someone already there. Many wrongful deaths could be chalked up to bad timing.

"We're not even sure someone came in and took him," he said. "Whoever did this might already have been here."

"You think it could have been a worker?" Craig asked, once again growing pale.

"Perhaps. Do you still have the employment records from 1971?"

"No," Craig said, a little too quickly for Nick's liking. "They're long gone."

"Do you remember having problems with any of your employees? Maybe a counselor who paid a little too much attention to the kids? Something along those lines."

A dark, angry expression crossed the camp owner's face, like a storm cloud rolling over a meadow. "Are you saying that what happened to Dwight and those other boys is somehow my fault?"

"Of course not. But it could be the fault of someone you hired."

"The workers here were good people, Mr. Donnelly. I made sure of that. Some of them I knew from my days as a guard. Others were college kids. None of them were killers."

Nick raised his hands in a gesture of innocence. "I'm sure you did. None of this was your fault."

Craig Brewster's face brightened again. The storm cloud was gone as quickly as it had appeared.

"I trust you," he said, although Nick wasn't sure he really meant it. "I'm just a little sensitive about it, even after all these years. I went through a lot after Dwight vanished like that. I'm sorry it happened, and I'm sure as hell sorry it happened here."

They had reached the meadow and the fire pit again. Making their way back to the main cabin, Nick asked how easy it would have been to trespass onto the property in 1971. Craig shrugged his response.

"Not too difficult, I imagine. It's a ways off from the main road, but easy to get to if you put your mind to it. And, of course, if you know where you're going."

Nick knew what he was getting at. Getting into the camp wasn't hard. He had been able to do it with a bum knee and only one cup of coffee under his belt. Someone in better shape would have had an even easier go of it. But in order to reach Camp Crescent, you needed to be aware of its existence. That meant whoever took Dwight Halsey back in 1971 didn't stumble upon the place by accident. He knew what it was, where it was, and, most important, what kind of potential victims were waiting there.

TWENTY-THREE

Norm Harper blew his nose, took a quick peek at his handkerchief to see what surprises it yielded, then stuffed it back into his shirt pocket. Old men could get away with such things. Norm was so old that he could do this mere inches above his early bird special and no one watching would bat an eye.

"Mort and Ruth Clark. I remember them. Good people."

"So I've been told," Kat said.

She was sitting across from Norm at the Perry Hollow Diner, two booths down from his usual spot in the corner. The other members of the Coffee Crew—five ancient men wearing plaid, khaki, and Aqua Velva—were still there, shooting Kat dirty looks because she had the nerve to pull away their perpetually disgruntled leader.

For his part, Norm didn't seem to mind being culled from

the herd. Judging from his blow and show earlier, he felt just as comfortable with her as he did with his friends. Kat wasn't sure if this was a good thing.

"How well did you know them?" she asked.

"About as well as I know everyone in this town. You see them around. You make small talk. You hear gossip."

"And what was the gossip about the Clarks?"

Norm picked up a fork and dug into his breakfast of eggs, bacon, and toast. "That Mort was a little bit paranoid."

Kat had figured that one out for herself. Anyone who went to the trouble of building a bomb shelter beneath their yard worried too much.

"And Ruth?"

"Fine woman," Norm said. "Made the best lemon meringue pie in the county, no question."

Taking a sip of her coffee, she was beginning to regret initiating her chat with Norm Harper. So far, he had nothing new to offer, and her time could have been better spent elsewhere.

On James, for instance.

That morning had been the usual routine of rushing and bumbling. When Kat slapped together James's lunch, she hoped it wouldn't be for naught and that he'd be the one eating it that day. She even used a Magic Marker to scrawl his name on the brown paper bag, in the hopes it would deter any would-be thieves.

It ended up not mattering. After she dropped him off at school that morning, James repeated what he had done on Thursday. Kat didn't witness it herself. James was too smart for that. So she pulled away quickly and let Lou van Sickle, who had also secretly parked at the curb, do the witnessing for her.

They met up in the diner parking lot, where Lou confirmed

what Kat had feared—that James once again dropped his lunch in the trash before entering the building. He seemed resigned to the fact that the bullying would continue and that there was little Kat could do about it.

"I wouldn't worry too much," Lou told her before heading to the station for the day. "Boys will be boys."

"But why do they have to be mean boys?" Kat said.

"Because," Lou replied, "human nature dictates it."

Yet Kat still felt that she had to intervene somehow. She knew James needed to learn how to fight his own battles. There'd come a day when she wouldn't be around to fight them for him. But it pained her to know that while her son was being tormented at school, she was stuck at the diner watching Norm Harper slurp down a fried egg.

"So that's all you remember?" she asked. "That Mort and Ruth were good people?"

"That's about it. Shame about what happened to their daughter, though."

A daughter. The word set off a reaction in Kat's brain similar to the effect of a grenade tossed into water. At first, there was a light splash, in which she understood that's who the third bunk in the bomb shelter had been reserved for. Then the detonation came, and a hundred different questions bubbled to the surface.

"Why didn't you tell me the Clarks had a daughter?"

Norm dug into another egg. "You weren't asking about her."

"I am now. What was her name?"

Norm lifted the egg to his mouth and gulped it down, leaving a smear of Day-Glo yolk stuck to the corner of his mouth.

Kat didn't tell him about it for fear he'd use his already-soiled handkerchief to clean it away.

After he swallowed, Norm said, "Jennifer, I think."

"Are you sure?"

"Pretty sure."

"I need you to be certain," Kat said.

Norm leaned out of the booth and called to his cronies in the corner. "Fellas, what was the name of the Clark girl?"

"Janice," one of the old men replied. Another one said, "Janine."

"It was Jennifer," Norm said. "Certain of it."

"And what happened to her?"

"She died, of course," Norm replied, as if everyone knew this fact.

"How?"

"Poor thing drowned to death."

"When?"

"Late fifty-nine, I think. This was down in Florida. The Keys. Word is she went out one morning for a dip in the ocean and never came back. They found her a few days later, washed on shore like a boat wreck. Poor thing. Barely nineteen."

"Why was she in Florida?"

"She was living there for a spell," Norm said. "With the Olmsteads."

"Ken and Maggie Olmstead?"

"The very same. They all went down to Florida together in early fifty-nine. The Olmsteads returned that July after Jennifer died and Maggie had Charlie. They were real broken up about it."

"I didn't know they were close."

"Maggie and Jennifer? They were like this," Norm said, crossing his fingers. "As close as sisters."

"And that's all you know about her?"

Norm nodded. "It's hard finding out much about those who die young. Their secrets tend to die with them."

Kat had to agree. Whatever there was to know about Jennifer Clark had died either with her or with those she was close to. But there was another person living on that cul-de-sac who was still alive and kicking, but just as unknowable.

"What about Glenn Stewart?" she said. "What do you know about him?"

"Quite a bit," Norm said. "We were friends for a spell. Attended the same church. Back before the war, of course. After the war, I don't think anyone really got to know him."

"Why do you think that is?"

"Most likely because he got shot in the head."

"When was this?"

"In 1968, I think." Norm grabbed a triangle of toast and slid a corner of it through a puddle of egg yolk on his plate. "The story differs with whoever's doing the telling. I heard the Vietcong shot him during an ambush and I heard he shot himself after going crazy in the jungle. I can see how that place would drive you crazy, so I'm leaning toward the second version of events."

"How did he survive?"

"He got lucky," Norm said. "Or unlucky, depending on how you look at it. Either way, it left him looking pretty strange, which is why I think he doesn't like to go outside anymore."

"So you've seen him?" Kat asked.

Norm told her he had seen Glenn Stewart once since he

returned home from Vietnam, which was one time more than most anyone else in Perry Hollow.

"It was right after he got back," he said. "I stopped by one day. He let me inside, but only briefly."

"How did he act?"

"Strange. But calm."

Glenn Stewart was the same way when Kat had talked to him. Apparently, not a lot had changed in four decades.

"What did you two talk about?"

Norm shrugged as he took a sip of his coffee. "Small talk, at first. Who was still in town, who wasn't. Then it got weird."

"Weird how?"

"Well, he kept talking about the moon."

A second grenade went off in Kat's head, sending up another wave of questions. It was surprising that she didn't have a headache. She was certain that one more information bomb would make her entire brain explode.

"The moon? What about it?"

"How great it was. How it, and not the sun, was the source of life on Earth. Crazy talk, really. But he said it with such seriousness that I knew he really believed it."

"Believed what?"

"I'm not sure, exactly. Like I said, it was weird. I asked him if he'd be going back to church. He said no and started telling me about how he had changed beliefs while over in Vietnam."

"Religious beliefs?" Kat asked.

"Yes. He said he met a few Vietnamese while recuperating and they converted him. He seemed in awe, too. Kept talking about—"

Kat knew what he was about to say. "A glorious enlight-enment?"

Norm snapped his fingers. "That's exactly right."

Quickly, Kat grabbed her wallet and slapped a twenty on the table in front of Norm. It would pay for his breakfast and her coffee, with a big tip for their harried waitress. "I need to go," she said. "Thanks for the information."

"Find out everything you needed?" Norm asked.

Kat had, and then some. She now knew that Mort and Ruth Clark had a daughter, that the Olmsteads were there when she died, and that their neighbor, the elusive Glenn Stewart, most likely worshipped the moon.

The kitchen looked like it had been raided by a starving grizzly. When Eric entered it, he found the refrigerator door ajar, an overturned carton of juice dripping orange stickiness onto the linoleum. Two cupboards were open. So was the silverware drawer. Yet as far as Eric could tell, no food had been taken. His father's target was the alcohol, and he had consumed—or spilled—every last drop.

Cleaning up the mess, Eric discovered an empty wine bottle rolling beneath the kitchen counter. A six-pack of beer he had purchased two days before had become a no-pack. All the liquor bottles his mother had left behind—most of them at least ten years old and containing only a few ounces of spirits—had been drained and lined up near the sink.

As for Ken, he was still asleep upstairs. Eric heard him stir only once, and that was to make a crazed dash to the bathroom, where some of what he had consumed during the night had come back to haunt him. Eric tried to ignore the noise as he went about cleaning the kitchen with a sad resignation only the children of alcoholics possessed.

Eric didn't know what came first—Ken's drinking or his divorce from Eric's mother. By the time Eric was four, both had been well established. Growing up, Eric spent one miserable week each summer with his father. Every June, Ken would pick him up in his rig and whisk him to whatever trailer home or backwoods hovel he was staying in at the time. Always, there was a woman involved—trashy yet kindhearted gals who bleached their hair and liked a good time. Their names and their faces changed, but they were mostly the same.

Once the kitchen was in reasonably good shape, Eric stepped onto the front porch and lit a Parliament. As expected, his father's rig was there.

Ken was too old to still be driving a truck for a living, yet that didn't stop him. He said he couldn't afford to retire, which was undoubtedly true. But pushing seventy-three, he couldn't keep living a life on the highway much longer, either. Especially in an ancient rig like the one he owned.

Black with orange flames spreading across its sides, it was an unruly beast of a vehicle. Eric remembered going for a ride in it when he was younger. The noise, rumble, and sheer power of the rig had terrified him. Or maybe the fear came from the fact that he was pretty sure his dad had been half-lit while driving it. He suspected his dad drove that way a lot. Whenever Eric's phone rang late at night, he immediately assumed it would be someone notifying him that Ken had finally killed himself that way.

That morning, however, the rig was parked neatly at the curb. Eric took it as a sign that his father had waited until coming inside to start his bender. There was some consolation to be had in that, no matter how small.

Eric took one last drag on his cigarette and prepared to head back inside. As he turned around, he accidentally kicked something that had been placed to the right of the door. It was a shoe box, similar to the one he had dug out of Glenn Stewart's yard the night before. But this one was clean, covered not with dirt but with that morning's mail.

Picking it up, Eric felt leery about opening yet another box. It was starting to feel like the whole investigation into his brother's fate had been reduced to peering into box after box after box. Yet curiosity got the best of him—as it always did—and he lifted the lid.

Inside, he found a reel of film sliding around the bottom. Stuck to it was a Post-it note written in a feminine hand.

Turning around, Eric looked past the truck to the Santangelo residence across the street. He focused on the first-floor window that faced his own house. He now knew it was the room devoted to Lee Santangelo's accomplishments, a bit of self-importance his mother would have found insufferable. And just behind the glass was the pale face of Becky Santangelo, staring back at him.

Under her watchful gaze, Eric picked up the box and carried it inside. Once he closed the door, he took another look at the note Mrs. Santangelo had attached to the film reel.

Your proof, it read. *When you're finished, burn it.*

TWENTY-FOUR

The professor's name, Luther Edmond Reid III, intimidated Kat. So did the fact that he taught at Princeton University. And that he was considered America's leading expert on the religions of Southeast Asia. All of it—name, place, profession—conjured up images of a bearded man in a smoking jacket who read thousand-page books written in Sanskrit just for fun. When he answered his phone with a deep-voiced "*Namaste*," Kat knew she was talking to someone far removed from Perry Hollow.

She had discovered Professor Reid through a process possible only in the age of Google. Curious about the religion that had so moved Glenn Stewart during his time in Vietnam, she turned to the Internet. Her first step was to do a search of the words Vietnam and religion. That yielded several thousand results, most of them regarding things like Tết or Wandering Souls Day. After clicking on a few and seeing nothing about moon worship, she narrowed her search.

Thus, *moon* was added to the previous two words, fetching only a few hundred results. None of them looked very promising. She next tried *glorious moon*, which led her to a book called *Religions of Southeast Asia*. Its author was Professor Reid, who had his own Web site. That led to her calling directory assistance at Princeton, where she was hopscotched from department to department, finally reaching the esteemed professor himself.

"I'll admit, I'm surprised by your call," he said. "Many people don't even know mooncentric religions exist."

"I didn't until today."

"Most people are more familiar with sun worship, Earth worship, plus the big ones like Christianity and Judaism. But there are a handful that pay the same respect to the moon."

Kat, who wasn't much for religion in the first place, could at least understand someone putting their faith in something as powerful and vital as the sun. The moon, not so much.

"Why the moon?"

"There are different reasons," the professor said. "Lunar cycles play a big part of it. Unlike the sun, the moon is constantly changing, suggesting the work of a higher power. Then there's the basic symbolism of it being a literal light in the darkness."

"Does such a religion exist in Vietnam?"

"Yes, but barely." Professor Reid paused a moment, filling the silence with frantic typing on a keyboard. "It doesn't have an official name, although it's generally referred to as *mặt trăng vinh quang*. That loosely translates to 'glorious moon.' "

Which was very similar to the glorious enlightenment Glenn Stewart mentioned to both Kat and Norm Harper. She had a feeling Professor Reid was leading her in the right direction.

"Do a lot of people follow it?"

"Hardly any. Maybe a hundred people or so. Probably less. It's an ancient, agrarian religion that's practiced mainly in small, isolated villages."

"And what exactly is this practice?"

Professor Reid stopped typing and Kat heard one last click from his end of the line. A few seconds later, a similar click sounded on her computer.

"You've got mail," the professor said.

Kat opened the e-mail. It contained no text, just three photographs. She scrolled through them as Professor Reid spoke. The first showed a full moon rising over a steaming tangle of jungle plants.

"*Mặt trăng vinh quang* is based on the idea of the full moon, which is perceived to be the moon in its purest form. A child born during a full moon is considered blessed, so much so that some followers have been known to try to slow down or speed up labor in order to make this happen."

The next photograph showed an open hand holding a clay disk that had been painted white.

"What's that in the second picture?" Kat asked.

"It's basically a good luck charm," the professor said. "It's left with the dead to ensure a blessed afterlife. Those buried with a clay moon are thought to be guaranteed a place in heaven. Those buried without it are doomed to roam the earth in ghostly form."

"We're not talking about the same heaven Christians believe in, right?" Kat asked.

"Correct," the professor said. "Believers of *mặt trăng vinh quang* go somewhere else."

"Where?"

"Do you still have the e-mail up?"

"Yes," Kat said.

"Look again at the first photo."

Kat scrolled up a bit, landing on the photograph of the full moon hovering over the jungle. There were no stars in the picture, only a pregnant orb dominating the darkness. Kat stared at it, letting the professor's words settle over her thoughts like dusk.

"Wait a minute," she said. "When they die, they think that they go to the moon?"

"Yes. Their spirits are supposedly carried to the moon, where they spend eternity bathed in warm, white light."

Glenn Stewart had called the moon landings a violation. Although Kat was baffled at the time, it now made sense. If he was a follower of *mặt trăng vinh quang,* then he had good reason to think poorly of NASA's lunar missions. They were basically landing rockets on his version of heaven. Adding insult to injury, another landing was scheduled to take place that very afternoon.

"Since you're the expert," Kat said, "do you really consider this to be a legitimate religion?"

"As a scholar, it's not really my place to classify or pass judgment on the beliefs of others. But in this case, I can safely say *mặt trăng vinh quang* basically amounts to a moon cult."

Those two words—one innocent, one not—gave Kat a chill when she heard them pushed together. Knowing Eric's neighbor could very well be a member created a second chill. What the professor said next created an outright shiver that Kat felt from the tips of her toes to the top of her head.

"The fact that you're inquiring about it concerns me. While most followers are nothing but peaceful, a few have been known to be very dangerous."

"Dangerous how?"

"Please look at the last picture."

Kat scrolled through the e-mail until she came to the third and final photo Professor Reid had attached. A black-and-white shot, it showed a young boy sleeping on a bed constructed of stone, leaves, and tree branches.

"That was taken in May 1940 in a tiny village near My

Lai," the professor said. "There were two full moons that month."

"A blue moon?"

"That's right," Professor Reid replied. "The second full moon is called a blue moon in most parts of the world. Followers of *mặt trăng vinh quang* think differently. They refer to it as *xấu mặt trăng*—the bad moon. They consider that second full moon to be an imposter not containing the spirits of their loved ones."

"What does it contain?"

"Evil entities that can only be chased away with one thing."

Kat examined the photograph again, spotting details she had missed the first time. There were white flowers affixed to the platform. The boy, ten if he was a day, lay flat on his back with his hands folded over his chest. Tucked under his fingers was what looked to be a flat circle of clay—a moon charm made for the dead.

"Please tell me I'm not looking at a human sacrifice."

"I wish I could," the professor said. "But I can't. It was believed that only the death of someone young and without sin could appease the bad moon."

Kat closed the e-mail with a sharp tap of the mouse. She couldn't look at the picture anymore. Just thinking about it both frightened and saddened her in equal measure.

The fear rose to the forefront, however, when Professor Reid said, "If you know a follower, and I suspect you do, I urge you to use caution. As I told you, most of them are nonviolent. But on a day like today, a hard-core believer might not be so peaceful. In fact, he could be more dangerous than you or I can fathom."

* * *

A minute after she got off the phone with Professor Reid, Kat received another phone call, this time from Eric Olmstead. She didn't want to talk to him. Honestly, she didn't have the time. She needed to talk to Glenn Stewart, face-to-face, and find out exactly what he had come to believe while recuperating in Vietnam. But when she answered the phone, the seriousness of Eric's voice stopped her cold.

"You need to come over," he said. "Now."

When Kat reached Eric's house, she found a rig in the street and a film projector in the living room. Both of them looked out of place. The truck, Eric told her, belonged to his father, who was sleeping off a bender upstairs. The projector apparently had been his mother's because he found it in the basement.

"The film," he said, "belongs to Lee and Becky Santangelo."

Kat eyed the projector. It was square and bulky, like most things built in the middle part of the twentieth century. Eric had wiped away most of the dust, but some remained—streaks of gray on the projector's brown surface. The reel of film had been spooled through it and was ready for viewing.

"Have you watched it yet?"

Eric shook his head. "I waited for you."

He had turned the projector to face a bare patch of wall near the television. While he started it up, Kat closed the curtains and drew the blinds until the living room was dark enough to see the square of light projected on the wall. Eric flicked a switch and the movie began.

The first image to appear was of a hallway, the walls and floor tilting sharply to the right. After a slight bump, they righted themselves briefly before slipping to the left. Soon they became blurs of saturated color as the camera was carried through the hall and down a staircase.

The movement resembled the point of view of someone who was either very drunk or very seasick. It made Kat feel the same way, especially when the camera apparently slipped, the lens lurching downward toward the floor in one quick, stomach-churning move.

Whoever was holding the camera righted it at the bottom of the stairs. The view was of the entrance hall to Lee and Becky Santangelo's house. Kat recognized the location but not the décor, which was done up in late-sixties chic—shag carpeting, wild colors, geometric patterns on the wallpaper. The only sign of good taste was a vase of white lilies sitting on a side table near the door. It was also where the camera was headed. There was one last blur, this time in the form of a lily slapping the lens, before the camera came to a rest on the table.

The perch provided a waist-high view of the front door and about a third of the entrance hall. It also finally allowed Eric and Kat to see who had been manning the camera. That would be Lee Santangelo, who entered the frame from the left and moved quickly to the door. Dressed in only boxer shorts and an unbuttoned white shirt, he looked to be partially hiding behind the door even as he opened it.

At first, Kat couldn't see the person standing on the other side. It was dark there, for one thing, and Lee had really only opened the door a crack. But when the visitor took a step forward, Kat recognized her wide, searching eyes and face drawn tight with worry.

Maggie Olmstead.

Eric gasped his surprise. Standing next to the projector, he wordlessly reached out his hand. Kat took it and gripped it tight as they watched his dead mother converse with Lee San-tangelo. There was no sound with the film, just flickering images from long ago. Yet Kat knew what Maggie and Lee were talking about.

Mrs. Olmstead was looking for Charlie.

Onscreen, Maggie tilted her head, trying to get a better view inside the house. Lee stepped in front of her, blocking her view of the camera and, incidentally, the camera's view of Maggie. Eventually, Lee tried to shut the door but was stopped, most likely by Maggie. After a few seconds more, the door closed for real and Eric's mother was gone once again.

Just as in life, the film carried on without her. Lee picked up the camera on his way back from the door. What followed were more streaks of off-kilter hallways, more sudden lurches from one focal point to another. During one particularly dizzying moment, Kat saw nothing but the blurs of Lee's bare feet as he ascended the stairs. Then it was into a bedroom—the same room Lee Santangelo still occupied, although in a far different state.

When the camera settled down again, it was to give the viewer a glimpse of a television. Unlike the widescreen, high-definition set currently filling that room, this television was a tidy square of black-and-white images. Pointed at the TV, the camera remained steady, as if in awe of what was happening onscreen.

On the television, two astronauts were bouncing impossibly high on what could only be the surface of the moon. The footage was grainy, made even worse by the age of the film itself, but it was still an amazing sight. No wonder Lee had stopped whatever he was doing to capture the moment. Kat would have done the same thing.

After a few seconds, the camera jerked to the right, away from the television and toward the window. Someone stood naked before it, peering outside—no doubt the woman Eric's mother had seen from the yard. Only it wasn't a woman. Even with their back to the camera, Kat could tell it was a young man. The shoulders were broader than a woman's. The hips not as rounded. The person at the window was all bone and sinewy muscle. The only thing remotely feminine about him was his hair, which brushed his shoulders.

"My God," Eric said. "All this time the mystery woman was a mystery man."

"Yep," Kat replied. "No wonder Becky Santangelo didn't want to talk about it."

The man turned around when he noticed the camera. He approached Lee quickly, head bobbing out of frame, hand thrust forward to block the lens. There was another blur as the camera changed hands, with Lee now the focus of its gaze. He yanked off his shirt and fell back on the bed, giving the camera a lustful grin as he caressed his crotch. He reached for the camera with his free hand, causing yet another dizzying spin as the young man once again came into view.

He stood still a moment, letting the camera get a good look at him. His unruly hair draped over his eyes. His skin, especially his face, was deeply tanned, signaling that he had spent most of that summer out in the sun. But the tan wasn't dark enough to cover one notable feature—a dime-sized mole on his chin.

The scene abruptly ended, the square of light replacing it on the living-room wall. A whirring sound emanated from the projector, which had run out of film. Eric switched it off while Kat continued to stare at the wall, stunned.

The glimpse of the boy's face had been brief. A few seconds, tops. But it was enough. She now knew what the Santangelos had been hiding all those years. She also knew who had been with Lee that night, and his name was Burt Hammond.

TWENTY-FIVE

Nick was in the car when he got a phone call from Tony Vasquez. Since holding the phone with one hand and steering with the other was a recipe for disaster, he waited to answer until he was safely stopped on the side of the road. He switched off the CD player—"Lucy in the Sky with Diamonds," in honor of his new forensic anthropologist friend—and picked up the phone.

"What's up?"

"Dental records gave us a positive ID of the body under the mill," Tony said. "It's Noah Pierce."

"How does Lucy think he died?"

"She can't be sure," Tony said. "After a more thorough examination of the remains, her best guess is that he was strangled to death. Anything more violent most likely would have left some trace on the bones, not to mention blood in the mill itself, which would have been seen by police at the time. And you and I both ruled out accidental drowning."

So a stranger hadn't lured Noah into the mill and then into a car, whisking him away from his grandparents. Instead, the sick fuck had strangled the boy right there in the mill, most likely before anyone realized he was gone. An open trapdoor and a dumped body later, and one nine-year-old kid was gone forever.

"Why was Noah holding Dennis Kepner's toy rocket?"

"Beats the hell out of me," Tony said. "What do you think?"

"That Dennis had it with him when he was snatched from the park," Nick said. "The perp then used it to lure Noah into the mill."

Tony took a stab at humor to lighten the mood. "Do you always have to show me up?"

"You can tell Gloria it was your idea," Nick said.

"What about the camp Dwight Halsey vanished from? Dig up anything useful there?"

Nick briefly recounted his talk with Craig Brewster and the strange, sad story of Camp Crescent, including how the police and the owner automatically assumed Dwight had met his fate in the surrounding forest. When he was finished, Tony asked, "And what's your opinion?"

"That he might have died in the woods, but at the hands of someone else."

It was becoming all too clear that was how most, if not all, of the crimes occurred. Nick no longer suspected someone abducting the boys and holding them captive for days. He assumed they were all killed quickly, perhaps right where the culprit found them. The only incident that didn't back up that theory was Dennis Kepner's disappearance. Nick chalked that one up to the killer knowing that neighbors could be watching.

"Listen," Tony said, "it's still pretty crazy where I'm at. The press got wind of the body and want some explanation. Gloria is hounding me about it, too. Oh, and get this, I just got word from the police in Fairmount. There was a whole other file on Dennis Kepner that they failed to tell me about."

"What's in it? Anything new?"

Tony let out a frustrated sigh. "You're assuming I got a chance to look at it already. How did you do this job and not go crazy?"

"Screw Gloria," Nick advised. "Throw something small to the newshounds. They'll gnaw on it for a day or so. But check the new Kepner file. I'll track down Bucky Mason's father and see what he remembers."

He was hoping to sneak that in without the overwhelmed lieutenant noticing. No such luck.

"Nick, maybe I should send a trooper there instead. Gloria—"

"What did I just tell you about that?"

"That's easier said than done," Tony said. "She's still my boss. And she'll be mad as hell if she finds out you're interviewing family members as part of this investigation."

"Fine," Nick replied. "Send a trooper. But whoever it is will have to drive pretty fast."

"Goddamn it, Donnelly. Are you already there?"

Nick wasn't. But he sure was close. He estimated he was only a few miles outside Centralia.

"Just let me talk to him. We're both on the same side here. We both want to find out what happened to the boys and who did it. I want to do my part."

"Fine," Tony said. "But be professional."

"Hey, I'm always professional."

Lieutenant Vasquez couldn't help but chuckle. "Nick, you weren't professional even when you were a professional."

When the call was over, Nick edged back onto the road and contemplated the GPS system built into the dashboard of his car. It disagreed with his assessment that Centralia was close by. According to its map, there was nothing up ahead. No roads. No buildings. Nothing. But Vinnie Russo, Nick's source, didn't lie. If he said Bill Mason Sr. was alive, well, and living in Centralia, then it was a certified fact.

He hoped.

The second signal that something was amiss came a mile down the road, when Nick saw a sign warning motorists of hazardous smoke and toxic fumes in the vicinity. The odor was next—a foul mixture of smoke and sulfur that smelled simultaneously of cigarette butts and rotting eggs. Gagging, Nick closed the windows and shut off the air conditioning. It was of no use. The stench had already invaded the interior of the car.

A half mile later, the smoke welcomed him to Centralia. It was an insidious cloud that sprouted on the side of the road and snaked through a forest of dead trees for as far as Nick could see. Occasional tentacles wafted across the road like fog banks, and Nick had to slow down as he drove through them.

Emerging on the other side of the smoke, he saw that the road swerved sharply to the right. Directly ahead was another road, although a concrete barrier prevented him from driving on it. Even if the roadblock hadn't been there, a large fissure in the road would have stopped him. Roughly three feet wide, it stretched down the entire length of asphalt, turning most of the road into rubble. Occasional wisps of smoke rose from the crevasse.

Nick had no choice but to turn right, which led to more smoke and dead trees. He eventually passed a gated cemetery, smoke twisting among the graves. It made Nick think of hell on Earth, and he whispered a prayer for the poor souls who had been buried there.

The smoke eventually cleared. The sulfurous stench did not. Nick could still smell it, thick in the air all around him. He studied his surroundings, trying to get his bearings. What he saw was a town that looked as if it had been wiped off the map. Rolling down streets that contained no houses, Nick saw hints that someone had once lived there. Stop signs stood sentinel at the corners. A bit of driveway, slowly succumbing to weeds, led to an open field. At another bare lot, a mailbox, flag up and door down, waited for a delivery that would never come.

When Nick glanced left, he saw the steeple of a church just above the trees. He veered the car in its direction, hoping it would lead him to someplace occupied. But when he reached the church, he realized that God—and his followers—had abandoned it long ago. Weeds blocked the front door, which had been padlocked, and a gaping hole marred the roof. The cross had fallen off the steeple and was now sunk upside down in the ground next to the church itself. Hell on Earth indeed.

Moving past the church, Nick finally caught sight of a house. Well, half a house. What had once been a duplex was now only a single unit—a tall and ridiculously narrow structure colored dark gray by the smoke. One side appeared normal, with windows, shutters, and a single chimney sprouting from the roof. The other side had no windows, just an expanse of vinyl siding and what appeared to be five exposed chimneys rising to the eaves. They were brick support beams, Nick realized, built to keep the house standing when its other half had been torn down.

He idled in front of the house a moment, taking it all in. There was no mailbox out front, nor was there a number next to the door. But someone still lived there. An American flag hung from the porch railing. Below it, leaning against the foundation, was a message that had been spray-painted on plywood. DON'T BOTHER US!

Nick didn't really have a choice. Either it was the home of Bill Mason Sr. or that of someone who might be able to point him in the right direction. He just hoped whoever lived there didn't own a shotgun. He'd seen enough of those for one day.

Hopping onto the porch, he was about to knock when a voice rose from the other side of the door. It was a woman's voice, old but firm and full of spitfire.

"Whoever you are should read the sign and go the hell back to wherever you came from."

"I'm not here to bother you," Nick said. "I'd just like to ask you a few questions."

"Are you with the government?"

"No. I'm working with the state police. I'm looking for information about a boy who vanished from here in 1972."

The door swung open immediately, revealing a short woman wearing jeans and a sweatshirt. Her hair was gray, her face weathered and hard.

"Which boy?" She looked up at Nick with eyes the same color as steel. "Frankie or Bucky?"

TWENTY-SIX

Perry Hollow's town hall was a building with delusions of grandeur. Sitting squat and heavy at the end of Main Street, it looked far more important than it really was. Kat was all for imposing architecture, if it was warranted. But running up the hall's marble steps, she knew that a building devoted to waste management and dog licenses didn't warrant Corinthian columns.

The mayor's office was on the second floor, forcing Kat to climb more steps with a half-spooled film reel under her arm. But since it was a lazy Friday morning, no one was around to notice the strip of celluloid curling from her armpit. Chalk one up for bureaucracy.

When she hit the second floor, Kat turned left and entered the mayor's office. The tiny waiting area bearing the American and Pennsylvania flags was empty. So was the receptionist's desk, which allowed Kat to march into Burt's inner sanctum and toss the reel of film onto his desk.

Burt looked up, startled. "What the hell is this?"

"You don't recognize it?"

"No.

Most of the film had come unspooled and curled across his desk blotter. Kat grabbed a section and stretched it taught in front of Burt's face. "Let me refresh your memory."

The mayor squinted, eyeing the frames one by one. It only

took three to make his face go white. By the time he saw a fourth, Burt Hammond looked like he was about to puke.

"Where did you get this?"

"You know where," Kat said. "And I think you know when it was filmed."

"That was a long time ago."

"It was July 1969. The night Charlie Olmstead disappeared. You were there, Burt. On his street. Now, you're going to tell me what you saw that night or this film will be on YouTube by the end of the day."

Burt remained silent. The only sound he made was a slight gurgle as he swallowed hard. He closed his eyes and took a deep breath. When he opened them, Kat saw only the whites. His pupils had rolled back into his head as he slumped forward.

Kat rushed to his side and tried to keep him upright. Instead, Burt listed to the right and fell out of his chair, taking her with him. When they thudded to the floor, it became clear to Kat what happened.

The mayor of Perry Hollow had passed out.

Eric knew he wouldn't be welcomed by Becky Santangelo. Other than Kat, he was probably the last person she wanted to see. Yet there he was, standing at her front door, rapping on it with the brass knocker.

When Becky answered, Eric nodded politely. "May I come in?"

"I'd prefer it if you didn't."

She wore a black designer sweatsuit, made for someone far younger, that hugged her buttocks and pushed up her breasts.

Although she had made sure to do her hair and makeup, she still looked exhausted. Her eyes were sunken and ringed by dark circles—the look of someone who was bone-tired.

"I just wanted to thank you for trusting me with that home movie," Eric said.

Becky's shoulders lifted into a weary shrug. "It's not like I had a choice."

"You didn't. Still, it must have been hard for you. And I just wanted to let you know that your secret is safe with me."

To Eric's surprise, Becky emerged from the house and lowered herself onto the porch steps. She patted the empty space next to her, urging him to sit.

"I saw you smoking on your porch this morning," she said. "Care to let a neighbor bum one?"

Eric produced two cigarettes. He lit Becky's first and then his own. After a minute of silent smoking, she said, "I should have just told the truth a long time ago."

"I understand why you didn't. It would have destroyed your husband's career."

Becky let out a quick laugh that was startling in its bitterness. "He should have thought about that before filming himself screwing around with those boys."

"So there were more of them?"

"A few," Becky said. "Movies, that is. Only the Lord and Lee know how many boys there were. I found the film reels decades ago. Lee had locked them in a trunk in the attic. I think he forgot they were even there."

"Did you confront him about it?"

Becky shook her head. "There wasn't any point. We were

your typical married couple. Lee was the solid, upstanding citizen with secrets. I was the dutiful wife who pretended I didn't know about them."

Instead, Eric knew, she continued dressing up. And decorating. And adding more framed photographs to the cluttered wall of Lee's trophy room.

"But you knew even before you found the home movies, didn't you?" he asked. "You knew the moment my mother said she saw a woman in your bedroom window."

He watched Becky closely while what began as a slow shake of her head transformed into a nod.

"I guess I did," she said.

"Did you ever think about leaving him?"

"Of course," Becky said as she exhaled a long stream of smoke. "But as the years passed, I came to understand that marrying Lee Santangelo was my only real accomplishment. Other than being a beauty queen, I had no skills and no money of my own. If I divorced him, I'd have nothing. So I stayed. Even more, I made it my goal to preserve his name. It's all I've got left."

Eric realized he preferred this version of Becky Santangelo to the strident woman he had always known. It made him wish he had grown up seeing this Mrs. Santangelo, instead of the cold stranger who lived across the street.

"I need to ask you something," he said. "Do you really think my mother was crazy?"

"I think she was hurting. Both before your brother disappeared and especially after. And I'm truly sorry I didn't try to help her in any way."

Eric appreciated the sentiment, even if it was too late to do anything about it. Besides, it wasn't Becky Santangelo's place to

254 | TODD RITTER

intervene. The one person who could have helped his mother the most was now asleep in her old bed.

He didn't know why Ken had abandoned his mother. Eric assumed it was the same reason that he, too, had left—he just couldn't live like that anymore. But he had never known about the problems before Charlie disappeared. His father, on the other hand, did. And the fact that he left so quickly and never came back seemed like the greater betrayal.

"You told me you often heard my parents fighting. Did you ever hear what it was about?"

"I wish I could tell you," Becky said. "I only knew that they were fighting. That's when your brother would stop by. Or else he'd go to the Clark place. Whenever he crossed the street, we knew something was going on with your parents."

Eric thought back to the previous day, during a far different conversation he had with his neighbor. "You said before that it didn't start until I was born."

Becky Santangelo looked away, ashamed. "I shouldn't have told you that."

"But is it true?"

"From my limited viewpoint, it was. They seemed happy until you were born. But I'm not saying that had anything to do with it."

She didn't need to. Eric could draw his own conclusions. What he didn't understand was why his birth had caused such a rift between his parents. Since he had gone a lifetime not being offered an answer, Eric knew the only way he'd get one was if he asked for it.

He looked to his house across the street. Ken was still asleep inside. If not, then he was certainly experiencing one hell of a hangover. While he had vowed to wait until his father woke to start in with his questions, Eric realized he had waited long enough. Forty-two years, in fact.

Saying good-bye to Becky, he crossed the street quickly. Once inside, he headed up the stairs and into his mother's old bedroom. Ken was still asleep, curled up on his side. A thin stream of drool hung between his mouth and the pillow.

"Dad." Eric nudged his father's shoulder. "Wake up."

Ken rolled over, the line of drool now stretching across his cheek, and opened his eyes. He seemed surprised to be there. From the way his gaze darted around the room, Eric assumed he had no recollection of the night before.

"Where am I?"

"Home," Eric said. "And you're going to tell me what really happened between you and Mom."

Burt Hammond gained consciousness with a can of Mountain Dew and a few slaps to the cheek. The soda came from a vending machine down the hall. Kat provided the slaps. It was the least she could do.

Soon the mayor was back in his chair. He still looked pretty rough, but the color was coming back to his face and the soda was greasing up his vocal cords.

"What do you want?" he asked Kat. "Is this about the police budget? If so, I can do something to get you those patrol cars."

Kat instantly wanted to slap him again. "Is that what you think this is about? Blackmail?"

"You've got the upper hand."

"I want to know what you saw that night. I don't give a damn about anything else."

"And you're not going to tell anyone else about this?" Burt asked.

256 | TODD RITTER

Kat shook her head. "Not if you're honest with me."

"Fine." The mayor took a lengthy swig of soda. "I used to mow Lee Santangelo's lawn. That's how it started. I became friendly with him. He'd invite me in for a glass of lemonade or let me use their swimming pool to cool down. One day, while I was going for a dip, Lee joined me."

"How long did it take to get from the pool to the bedroom?" Kat asked.

"Not long," Burt said.

The ashen shade had returned to his face, and Kat worried that he was going to pass out again. Instead, Burt began to weep, which wasn't much better. At least she got to slap him when he fainted. With the tears, all she could do was offer him a tissue.

Burt accepted it and wiped his red-ringed eyes. "This is so humiliating."

"You can skip ahead to the night of the movie," Kat said. "I don't need all the details."

Nor did she want them. She just needed to know what, if anything, Burt Hammond saw on his way to and from the Santangelo residence.

"We set a date," he said. "The night of the moon landing. I knew about Lee's past. I figured he'd want to watch it. He said he didn't care and neither did I."

"What time did you get there?"

"About ten thirty, I think. I walked there and I wasn't wearing a watch."

"Did you see anyone else?"

"Not at first," Burt replied. "I waited in the yard a little bit, trying to muster the courage to go inside. After about five minutes, I saw a man."

Kat felt another one of those explosive shocks she had experienced earlier when talking to Norm Harper. Only this time, it was less like a grenade and more like an atomic bomb. The effect was an immediate rush of surprise that left her entire body numb. Someone else was on the cul-de-sac that night. Someone that no one but Burt Hammond knew about.

"Did you recognize him?" she asked.

"No. I knew it wasn't Ken Olmstead and I knew it wasn't Mort Clark. He was a stranger."

"Can you describe him?"

"I didn't get a good look. It was dark and we were both in the shadows."

"Was he alone?"

"Yes."

"Did he see you?"

"No. He just milled around in the yard, like he was thinking about going inside but didn't have the courage." Burt coughed out an ironic laugh. "I could relate."

"And that's everything you saw?"

"Mostly. At one point, he went up to the door and almost knocked but changed his mind. Then he went back to the yard and stood there a while."

"What I want to know," Kat said, "is why you didn't tell the police about it. You saw a strange man on Charlie Olmstead's street the night he disappeared, yet you said nothing."

Burt sniffed and looked to the ceiling. He was crying again. "I didn't think they were related."

"I don't believe you."

"I swear. People were saying what happened to Charlie was an accident. I didn't think there was anything suspicious going on."

Kat's fingers instinctively curled into fists as the raw burn of anger built up inside her. She wanted to punch Burt. Hard. More than anything, she wanted to pummel him with her fists and tell him that while he was crying from humiliation, there were six sets of mothers who cried because their boys had vanished. He could possibly have prevented those tears. He might have been able to spare those women—concerned moms like herself—a lifetime of pain and questions. But Burt Hammond had stayed quiet, and Kat wanted to make him hurt because of it.

"Maybe you didn't know at first," she said. "But by the next day you had to have heard that people were looking for Charlie Olmstead."

Burt shook his head. "I didn't think they were related. Honest to God."

In a flash, Kat was in front of the mayor, gripping his tie, and pulling his face close to hers. "Admit it, you son of a bitch. You realized it, yet you said nothing, even though you saw a complete stranger waiting outside the Olmstead house."

The mayor's face was turning crimson. His mouth opened and closed rapidly, like a fish that had just been tossed onto land.

"You don't understand," he gasped. "He wasn't at the Olmsteads."

Kat let go of the tie, its silk slithering across her palm as Mayor Hammond fell back into his chair. "What do you mean?"

"I knew about Charlie," Burt said, smoothing a hand over his neck. "I knew he went missing that night. But I didn't think the man I saw had anything to do with it."

"Why not?"

"Because this guy wasn't anywhere near the Olmstead house."

Kat's entire body stiffened. "You said he was waiting around the yard."

"Yes," Burt said, still massaging his neck. "But not the Olmsteads' yard. He was waiting outside Mort and Ruth Clark's house."

TWENTY-SEVEN

"This used to be a nice town," the woman said. "Until the mine fire."

The man sitting next to her piped up. "Even after that, it was livable. Then the ground started opening up and everything went to hell."

They were polar opposites, that man and woman. She was short and rail-thin—a series of sharp angles attached to one another. He was large, both in height and girth. When he walked across the room, the entire house trembled. They had been neighbors for years, friendly but not friends. Then their sons disappeared, their spouses soon followed—hers to divorce, his to lung cancer—and Marcy Pulaski and Bill Mason Sr. found themselves with only each other.

It wasn't the most romantic story Nick had ever heard, and the couple didn't try to embellish it. They were both clear-eyed about what their relationship was—two people united by loss, grief, and the thinnest of hopes that they'd see their boys again. Now they lived together in half a house, their two lives squeezed together.

The walls were covered with photographs of both Frankie Pulaski and Bucky Mason, as if they had been part of one big, happy family. The furniture was arranged in a similarly haphazard fashion, with chairs that belonged to one clan clashing with the couch from another. Covering it all was a thin layer of gray Nick had at first assumed was dust. It wasn't until he swiped a finger over the coffee table that he realized it was something worse—soot.

"When did the fire start?"

"Early sixties," Bill said through his cough. "No one knows the exact date."

"How did it start?"

According to Marcy, Centralia had been built above a closed anthracite mine. This being Pennsylvania's coal country, that wasn't much of a surprise. What did surprise Nick was hearing how the townsfolk decided to use the vacant mine shafts as a landfill and stuff them with trash for decades.

"One day," Marcy said, "it ignited."

She told Nick how the fire hit a vein of anthracite, flaring to epic proportions. "Once that happened, the town was a goner. We just didn't know it yet."

"They tried to put it out so many times we lost count," Bill added. "Nothing worked. The fire was too big to be tamed."

Nick learned that over the next decade, the residents of Centralia played the hand they had been dealt. Life went on as normal, with school, church, work, and play. They noticed the ground becoming increasingly warmer. In winter, snow never stuck to the roads or sidewalks. Still, they soldiered on the best they knew how.

"The first hole opened up in 1971," Bill Mason said. "It just appeared overnight. A big pit in someone's backyard spitting out smoke."

Marcy closed her eyes and shook her head slowly, as if reliving the bad memory. "Another one happened soon after. And then another."

As the mine fire grew, it started to erode the ground above it. The oxygen from one crevasse only fueled the flames, which led to another crevasse, which spurred the fire on more. And so it went, a vicious cycle that threatened to consume an entire town.

"People started to clear out real quick after that," Marcy said. "My husband and I talked about leaving, too. We didn't know where we were going to go. This town was all we knew. But we were worried about Frankie and his safety."

She stopped to choke back a sob. When Bill Sr. took her hand and gave it a tiny squeeze, Nick thought it might have been the kindest gesture he had ever seen. The two of them may have come together in grief and desperation, but there was true love there. He could tell.

Marcy collected herself enough to talk again. "He went out to play one day. I told him to stay in the yard, but I knew where he was going. Straight to the sinkholes."

"Weren't they covered or cordoned off?"

"Some of them were too big to cover," Marcy said. "They put up some warning signs and wrapped some fence around it, but that didn't keep the kids out."

Bill nodded in agreement. "Each new hole in the ground was like catnip to the boys in town. Bucky went to them, too."

Nick knew he would have done the same thing at that age. To a young boy, a smoking hole in the ground was something exotic and dangerous that broke up the bleakness of life in a coal town. He imagined a whole cluster of kids surrounding it, tossing rocks into its depths and daring each other to scoot closer to the edge. Maybe Frankie and Bucky had gotten too close and tumbled in, but Nick didn't think that was the case.

"At what point did you think Frankie fell in?"

"Immediately," Marcy said. "When he didn't come home for dinner, my first thought was that something bad had happened. A boy in town had fallen through the ground a couple of weeks before. He managed to grab the roots of a nearby tree and yell for help. He got lucky."

"And the police?" Nick asked. "They thought the same thing?"

Marcy waved a hand in disgust at the mention of the police. "They didn't know what to think. The first thing they asked me was if I thought Frankie could have run away from home."

"And could he?"

"He was a happy boy," she said. "He might not have been the smartest or the most popular kid, but he was happy. And I loved him."

When she sobbed again, Nick could tell it was sorrow that couldn't be controlled with a pause and a deep breath. It was a bubble of sadness that rose from deep within. Marcy put a hand over her mouth to stifle it, but it did no good. The sob gurgled out of her until she fled the room, crying.

"It's still hard to talk about," Bill said once she was gone. "I know it was a long time ago, but it still hurts."

Nick knew the feeling well. Most days were fine. Others weren't. And then there were those dark times when something trivial—hearing his sister's favorite song on the radio, seeing her favorite color—would bring on a sudden explosion of grief.

"Was it the same way with Bucky?" he asked. "Did the police think he ran away?"

"By that time, no. It was the same situation. He came home from school, went out to play, never came back. But since it happened with Frankie earlier that year, the cops assumed the same thing had happened to Bucky."

"What do you think?"

Unlike his companion, Bill Mason seemed immune to the sadness of the situation. Still, it was there. Nick saw it in his deep-set eyes, in the way he lifted his shoulders in a listless shrug.

"I thought what the police thought," he said. "They made a huge fuss when both boys disappeared. Search parties and spotlights and bloodhounds running around everywhere. We gave them one of Bucky's shirts to sniff. Marcy and her husband used a pair of sneakers. Both times, the dogs took off and followed the scent to the same place."

Nick knew what that place was. "A sinkhole."

"That's right." Bill said. "So I think they fell in. Marcy, she's not so sure."

"What does she think happened to them?"

"That they were taken. It's why we're still here."

He told Nick that almost everyone in Centralia had moved out by the mid-eighties. Those few who stayed behind watched their neighbors' empty homes get demolished. When Marcy's house was condemned, she moved into the other half of Bill's duplex. When that half was condemned and torn down, she moved in with him, which explained why Vinnie Russo hadn't been able to locate her. Nothing remained in her name.

"Why isn't this half condemned?" Nick asked.

"The state tried to kick us out. The first time, we told

them we weren't going. The second time, I made it clear we weren't going." Bill pointed to a Winchester rifle hanging above the fireplace mantel. "After that, they left us alone."

Nick admired their tenacity, even if he couldn't understand it. "Why do you want to stay so bad?"

"What if Marcy is right and the boys were taken? And what if one of them ever tried to come home? If we left Centralia, they wouldn't know where to find us. So we stay. Marcy wouldn't have it any other way."

"Do you know why she thinks the boys were taken?"

"Only that she says Frankie was too smart to fall into a sinkhole," Bill said. "Bucky was, too. But I'd bet on an accident over a kidnapping any day. Accidents happen all the time. Kidnappings don't."

But they do happen, in places far nicer than Centralia. Perry Hollow, for example. And Fairmount and state parks and camps for disadvantaged youth.

"This was a good town," Bill went on, "filled with good people. Neighbors looked out for one another. There's no way someone could come in here and start taking kids."

"Well," Nick said, "there's a chance it could have been someone who was already here."

"One of the neighbors? Never."

"How do you know?" Nick countered. "Who lived in the other half of this duplex?"

"A bunch of people. I rented it out. Most just leased it for a year or so. Newlyweds. Single dads. Young couples. People like that."

In other words, the same type of people who could have been living in a row house on a side street in Fairmount. Nick opened up his mental file and retrieved Kat's initial reaction about the hometowns of the missing boy. She had thought the perp lived both in Fairmount and Centralia, the areas in which there were two consecutive victims. He was inclined to agree. Next, he dug deeper into the mental file, pulling out the years of each case. The Fairmount boys—Dennis Kepner and Noah Pierce—went missing in 1969 and 1971. Frankie and Bucky both vanished in 1972. It was completely within the realm of possibility that whoever did this moved from Fairmount to Centralia during the time in between.

"Where did Marcy and her husband live?"

"Two houses down," Bill answered. "On the same side of the street."

"Was that also a duplex?"

"No, sir. This was the only one on the block."

Nick normally didn't jump to conclusions, but listening to Bill Mason practically made him leap at one.

"Do you remember who was living on the other side of you when Bucky vanished?"

"Vaguely," Bill said. "I remember he was real supportive. Took part in the search party. Helped make up flyers. Was real nice to both me and my wife."

"And was he the same tenant months earlier, when Frankie disappeared?"

Bill Mason, God love him, didn't even take a moment to think about it. "Yes. Yes, he was."

"Do you remember his name?"

"I think it was Brewster," Bill said. "Craig Brewster."

TWENTY-EIGHT

Holding his coffee mug with both hands, Eric's father took a sip and swished the liquid around before swallowing. Next, he stuffed a doughnut into his mouth, the crumbs sticking to the gray stubble that he called a beard. Once the doughnut was gulped down, it was back to the coffee and the swishing and the swallowing.

"Dad." Eric grabbed the plate of doughnuts before his dad could reach for another one. "Quit stalling."

"I'm not stalling. I'm hungry."

In truth, Ken Olmstead looked frighteningly thin with his jeans and Henley shirt hanging off his frame like the clothes of a scarecrow. When he tried in vain to snatch another doughnut, the wrist that poked out of his sleeve was broomstick-thin.

His dad's appearance worried Eric. So did his silence when Eric asked how things were going with Lorraine, his girlfriend. Then there was his smell—a nostril-stinging odor that didn't go away even after he had showered. If Eric had to guess, he'd say his father was homeless and living out of his rig.

Such a guilt-inducing prospect made Eric push the doughnuts back across the dining-room table. His father grabbed two of them, and Eric waited for him to inhale both before asking, "Last night you told me not to try to find Charlie. Why?"

"Because it's a waste of your time."

"Mom didn't think so."

Ken's face took on a pinched look, as if a bolt of pain had

just flashed through his body. It might have been the usual hangover headache, but Eric suspected it was something else. Like an unwanted memory.

"Your mother wasn't well," he said. "She was a strong woman who endured a lot, but deep down she was sick."

That was the same word Becky Santangelo had used, too. After crazy, of course. Eric assumed *sick* and *crazy* actually meant the same thing and that his neighbor had merely softened her tone the second go-round.

"What was wrong with her?"

"Maggie was a good woman. Smart. Feisty. Pretty as a spring morning. But she wasn't well. Not after you were born. The doctor called it the baby blues, whatever that meant."

The noontime sun, spilling through the dining-room window, spread across the table between them. Listening to his father, Eric focused on the way the blinds sliced through the sunlight, creating a pattern reminiscent of a prison cell. His father's recollections only bolstered that thought. From the way Ken talked, it sounded as if his entire family had been taken prisoner by his mother's illness.

"She was sad all the time," his father said. "Sometimes she showed no interest in you kids. She had trouble feeding you and bathing you. Sometimes she'd just give up and I'd come home to find you screaming in your crib. Your mother would be asleep on the couch or upstairs in bed. Charlie would be at the neighbors, mostly, or playing outside. He could get out of the house. You couldn't. And it worried me. Especially after that day in May."

"What happened then?"

"Your mother almost killed you."

Eric would have appreciated a warning. Of all the things

his father could have said, that was the one he didn't see coming. He had been taking a sip of coffee at the time and the shock made him gulp, the piping hot coffee scalding the back of his throat.

"She didn't mean to do it," his father said. "I know it wasn't her fault. It was the sickness that did it."

He pushed away from the table and wandered to the front door. Eric followed, not understanding what was happening until his father turned and faced the stairs. Then it became clear—his father was reenacting that long-ago May day.

"As soon as I walked through the door, I heard water running." He pointed to the ceiling. "It was the bathtub upstairs."

Ken edged toward the steps, climbing them slowly. Eric did the same while trying to imagine what his father heard that day. A quiet house. The steady rush of water into the tub. The squeak of the stairs as he ascended to the second floor.

Once they were in the upstairs hallway, his father stopped at Charlie's old room. The door was open, revealing a space so dust-choked even the midday sunlight couldn't brighten it. Ken stood in the doorway, gaze sliding over the entire room. From the sad flicker in his eyes, Eric guessed his father had never expected to see it again.

"Charlie was outside playing. I passed him in the driveway when I came home." Ken continued down the hall, glancing first at Eric's childhood—and current—bedroom. "You were supposed to be in the nursery. But your crib was empty."

The next stop, in both his father's recollection and in present day, was the bedroom Ken and Maggie had once shared.

"The door was open, just like it is now. And I saw your mother, fast asleep in bed."

"Where was I?" Eric asked.

His father backtracked, pausing at the door to the bathroom. "In there. The door was closed, but I knew you were inside."

He crept into the bathroom on unsteady legs, like a man approaching the gallows. Looking to the bathtub, his voice bounced off the tiled wall behind it as he said, "The tub was half full. You were in it. Underwater. I don't know for how long, but you were already starting to turn blue."

Eric felt like he was still underwater. The details of the story—Ken yanking him from the tub and flipping him over as water drained from his mouth, the bumbling attempts at CPR, the sirenlike wail Eric emitted once he could breathe again—created a numb, floating sensation. By the time his father finished, Eric found himself leaning against the bathroom sink for support and gasping for air.

"Your mom cried for two days straight," Ken said. "She felt awful about it all. She swore to me that she would never, ever willingly hurt you. I knew it was the truth. But I also knew that, somewhere deep in her brain, was a feeling she couldn't control. Like a small part of her wanted to get rid of you."

Eric needed to get out of that bathroom. He couldn't stand looking at the bathtub where he had almost died or seeing the light blue wallpaper that only enhanced his feelings of being underwater. Shaking the numbness from his limbs, he started back downstairs.

"I'm sorry if this is upsetting you," his father said once they returned to the dining room. "That's why we never told you about it."

Eric lied and told him he was fine. In reality, he was anything but. If this didn't send him sprinting into therapy, nothing would.

"Your mother loved you more than anything in the world," Ken said. "I want you to know that. She wasn't well when that happened. But she got better. She changed the night Charlie vanished. As soon as she found out he was gone, she grabbed you and refused to let you go. Those baby blues suddenly went away. Losing Charlie made her afraid of losing you, too."

"I understand postpartum depression," Eric said. "But why did it happen only after I was born? Didn't Mom feel the same way after she had Charlie?"

His father shook his head, although Eric wasn't sure if he was answering the question or refusing to. "I don't want to talk about it anymore. It's upsetting you."

"If there's something you're not telling me, I want to know about it. Why wasn't Mom depressed after giving birth to Charlie?"

"Because she's not the one who gave birth to him."

Eric froze when he heard the news. Yet another numbing surprise in a day that had been filled with them. "What the hell are you saying?"

"I'm saying," his father replied, "that Charlie wasn't our son."

Kat sat in the basement of the Perry Hollow Public Library, surrounded by a hundred years' worth of old newspapers. The back issues of the *Perry Hollow Gazette* had been unfolded and pressed into bound volumes so heavy it strained her arms when she lifted them. Luckily, each behemoth contained three months of papers, and Kat only had to pull four of them off the shelf—January through December, 1959.

Since Norm Harper told her the Olmsteads had returned to town in July, Kat pushed winter aside and headed straight for spring. When she opened the volume, her nose was tickled by the musty smell of age and neglect. Motes of dust sprang from the pages as she flipped through the issue for April 1, 1959.

She found the obituaries halfway through the section. It was a single column of print, bearing only two names. Neither of them was Jennifer Clark.

The search continued, with Kat flipping rapidly through April and then into May. The names and faces of the dead flashed before her—men in crewcuts and women with cat's-eye glasses, most of them now long-forgotten beneath weathered headstones in Oak Knoll Cemetery. She slowed down once she reached Memorial Day. Turning the pages carefully lest she miss an obituary, she worked up to the middle of June without success. Then, on the front page of the June 20 edition, she found something.

Instead of an obituary, it was an article about Jennifer's drowning. The story mentioned how the Perry Hollow native had been living with friends in the Florida Keys. It talked about a hurricane that had blown through two days before, causing rough waves and widespread damage. And it talked about how young Jennifer Clark had stepped out into the ocean and wasn't seen again until her body washed ashore.

A picture accompanied the article—a yearbook shot that showed a pretty young woman with straight hair, a pale, open face, and a slightly sad smile.

A woman who looked very much like Charlie Olmstead.

Kat inhaled sharply, stunned at the resemblance. They had the same eyes. The same ears. The same mouth. Finally, the realization hit her. Maggie Olmstead wasn't Charlie's biological mother.

Jennifer Clark was.

Breathlessly, Kat rifled through the next few pages of the newspaper. She stopped once she reached the obituary page. Jennifer Clark's was at the top. It was short and sweet, as far as obits went, simply listing her date of birth, the date of death, and the names of her parents. There was no mention of a memorial service, just a sentence saying that she had already been cremated.

The only surprising bit of news was contained in the obituary's final sentence. Fortunately for Kat, it was exactly the information she was looking for.

"In addition to her parents," the sentence read, "Ms. Clark is survived by her fiancé, PFC. Craig Brewster."

TWENTY-NINE

The stench of smoke and sulfur didn't fully leave Nick's nostrils until he was thirty miles outside of Centralia. Even then, he still caught occasional whiffs of it, thanks to the way it clung to his skin and clothes like drugstore aftershave. It made him want to stop the car, get out, and twirl around in the fresh air.

But Nick couldn't stop.

He needed to drive as fast as he could, ignoring the speed limit and barreling toward a quiet, abandoned spot in the middle of the woods. He needed to get to Camp Crescent.

Nick's cell phone rang when he was about ten minutes away from the camp. He answered it with one hand, fumbling to pick it up while keeping his eyes on the road and his other hand on the wheel.

"Nick?"

It was Kat. Hearing her voice made him realize he hadn't talked to her since the night before. It had been a busy twenty-four hours, and as a result, she had no idea about the identification of Noah Pierce's remains or the discovery of Dennis Kepner's toy rocket. And she certainly didn't know about the owner of Camp Crescent, who was now their prime suspect.

"I've got big news," he told her.

"So do I," Kat said. "I think I know who took Charlie Olmstead. His name is Craig Brewster."

Nick stood corrected. Kat did know about Craig Brewster. "How did you know that?" he asked.

Maintaining his breakneck speed, Nick listened to her talk about bomb shelters and sex films and the daughter of Mort and Ruth Clark. Most of it confused him—especially the sex film part—but as Kat spoke, it became clear both their investigations had pointed them to the same man. It now made Craig Brewster look doubly guilty.

When she finished, Kat asked, "How did *you* find about him?"

Actually, Nick had learned of him twice—three times if you counted Kat. The first time came courtesy of Bill Mason. When Nick called Tony Vasquez with the news, the lieutenant shared something from the recently discovered police report about the Dennis Kepner case. It turns out Mr. Brewster had also lived in Fairmount at the time, four doors down from the Kepners.

"Are you heading to the camp?" Kat asked after listening to Nick's tale.

"I'm practically there."

Nick had made plans to meet Tony at the entrance to Camp Crescent, hopefully with some state troopers to back them up. Nick would sit back—not by choice—while Tony and his men in blue raided the camp and brought Craig Brewster in for questioning. If he was feeling chatty, they might have a confession to all six crimes by sunset.

"What can I do?" The question was vintage Kat—always wanting to be a part of the action.

"Right now, all you can do is wait," Nick said. "I'll call you as soon as Tony slaps the cuffs on Mr. Brewster."

He ended the call and surveyed the highway. Up ahead was the turnoff that led to Camp Crescent. A state police patrol car blocked the exit. Inside was a trooper with a clenched jaw and aviator shades. He waved Nick through after he gave his name.

Nick passed through two more state police checkpoints on the stretch of dirt road between the highway and the camp. Their mission was twofold—to keep any unauthorized vehicles from coming in and, more important, to keep Craig Brewster from getting out.

Six more patrol cars sat outside the entrance to Camp Crescent, along with Tony Vasquez's unmarked vehicle and a SWAT team van. The place was crawling with troopers loading their firearms and strapping on body armor. A handful had gathered near the metal gate that blocked the road, watching a SWAT team member dismantle it with a circular saw.

Nick parked at a safe distance and got out of the car. Tony was by his side in an instant.

"We're going to head up there soon," he said, tightening a Kevlar vest across his chest. "You stay here and I'll report back once we bag the bastard."

Nick followed him. "I should go with you. I'm the only one here who's seen the camp. I know the layout. This Brewster guy gave me the grand tour earlier today."

Tony shook his head. "Sorry, Nick. Gloria would have a shit fit if she found out."

"I understand," Nick said. "It makes sense. I merely saw all of the places Brewster could potentially be hiding. But with all that Kevlar on, you should be fine if the guy decides to use the shotgun he was carrying."

Tony didn't reply. He merely walked over to the SWAT van and whispered something to the team leader. When he returned, it was with a second Kevlar vest, which he tossed in Nick's direction.

"You can be a real pain in the ass, Donnelly."

Nick leaned his cane against the car and slipped into the vest. "I know."

"I'm not sure what you think you can get out of this," Tony said, watching him straighten the vest and tighten the straps at the sides. "You know you can never be a cop again."

"I'm not doing it for me," he told Tony. "I'm doing it for Charlie Olmstead."

Kat wasn't good at waiting. Not in airports. Not in doctor's offices. And certainly not for phone calls regarding the arrest of a man who might have killed six little boys. The nervous energy struck as soon as she got off the phone with Nick. To pass the time, she hopped on to the Internet, only to be greeted by an unwanted headline on CNN's Web site: CHINESE ASTRONAUTS TO LAND ON MOON WITHIN THE HOUR.

She logged off without even reading the article. The headline told her everything she needed to know.

Thrumming her fingers along the surface of her desk, she reviewed everything she knew about Mr. Brewster. At one point, he had been engaged to Jennifer Clark and, if her resemblance to Charlie was any indication, had gotten her pregnant. The resulting baby ended up with Ken and Maggie Olmstead, through reasons unknown.

Then there were the crimes themselves. On July 20, 1969, Craig came to Perry Hollow and took Charlie. That made a little bit of sense. Kat could easily see a father shut out of his son's life going to extreme measures to retrieve the boy. But what did he do with him after that? And what about the five others who were missing? Why did Craig Brewster target them?

When the phone rang, Kat lunged for it. She answered with a breathless "Please tell me you got him."

The caller wasn't Nick. It wasn't even a man. Instead, Kat heard a hesitant female voice say, "Chief Campbell?"

"Speaking."

"This is Jocelyn Miller."

"Sorry about that," Kat said. "I was expecting an important call."

"Well, consider this an important call."

The principal's tone was stone-cold serious, and it made Kat feel like her heart was simultaneously sinking into her stomach and leaping into her throat. Physically impossible, yes, but psychologically common.

"Did something happen with James?"

"Yes," Jocelyn said. "There's been an incident. You need to come to the school immediately."

Nick rode in Tony's car, following the SWAT van as it rolled slowly through the forest. They kept the speed to a minimum in the hope it wouldn't alert Craig Brewster to their presence until they got closer. Surprise was their friend. Otherwise, Camp Crescent's former owner could be greeting them with a few hellos from his 12 gauge.

The plan was for the SWAT guys to enter the camp's former headquarters first. Since the building now served as Craig's main residence, it was where they'd most likely find him. Tony and a few troopers would move in after them and do the cleanup work—the cuffing, the Mirandizing, the hauling to the police car.

Nick was to remain in the vehicle unless it was an emergency. Tony was adamant about that point. But as the trees cleared, revealing the camp spread out before them, he pressed a Glock into Nick's hands.

"Just in case," he said.

Nick accepted the gun without a word and tucked it into the waistband of his pants.

The convoy picked up speed once they reached the sign welcoming them to Camp Crescent. Soon they were barreling toward the headquarters, the SWAT van kicking up bits of gravel that bounced off Tony's windshield. Members of the SWAT team started leaping out of the vehicle before it screeched to a halt next to the cabin's front porch. One of them burst through the door as if it was made of construction paper. Two others immediately followed. Another group stomped across the porch to the other side of the cabin, their boots sounding like hoofbeats against the floorboards.

"It's go time," Tony said as he threw open the car door. Before hopping out, he turned to Nick. "Remember. Emergencies only."

Nick gave a sarcastic salute. "Go get him, tiger."

He watched Tony and his group of troopers disappear

into the cabin. Through the windows, he could see SWAT guys bursting into rooms and searching behind doors, in closets, under furniture. A few had reached the second floor and were doing the same thing. Nick heard the barking of orders and the slamming of doors—the music of the hunt.

While the SWAT guys continued to make noise, Nick noticed movement on the lower left-hand side of the cabin. It was a basement window, flapping open about two feet off the ground. Poking through it were twin cylinders of steel—the barrel of a shotgun being pushed outside. Right behind it was a head, then shoulders, then a torso. It was Craig Brewster, squeezing through the window to make his escape.

Shotgun lodged under his arm, he crawled away from the cabin on his stomach. After about ten yards he climbed to his feet and started to sprint deeper into the camp. Nick got out of the car, yanked the Glock from his waistband. He assumed this was the kind of emergency Tony was referring to.

"Hey!"

He hoped the yell would either make Craig stop or get the attention of the troopers inside the cabin. It did neither. Instead, the suspect gained speed while the SWAT team made more noise. Nick shouted again before resorting to the last thing he wanted to do.

He started to run.

The first step hurt. The second and third hurt like hell. All the steps that followed hurt like fucking hell. Nick's knee felt like it was on fire—an all-encompassing pain that brought tears to his eyes.

Yet he couldn't stop, not with Craig heading into an area thick with trees. If the camp owner made it to the woods, they'd never be able to find him. So he continued on, trying to minimize the pain. He still used his cane, stabbing it into the grass as he moved. But it only slowed him down and didn't blunt the pain that was now shooting up and down his entire right leg. He let go of it, the pit bull handle dropping to the ground as he continued on without it.

Shedding the cane made his leg hurt even more. But it also made him faster. By gritting his teeth and letting out a ferocious grunt with each step, he was able to gain on Craig, who had run into the pine-dotted area where the camp's cabins were located.

By the time he reached the area, Nick's face was drenched with sweat. So were his clothes, which had started to cling to his skin. His chest rose and fell as he panted for breath. And his knee, well, Nick didn't want to think about the damage down there.

Turning in an awkward hop-step, he took stock of his surroundings. He was in the middle of a small clearing, surrounded by five cabins. There was no sign of Craig, which meant he had either sprinted impossibly fast into the woods or was now hiding in one of the cabins. Nick assumed it was the latter, and examined each of them.

Of the five, two were merely the remains of cabins—collapsed walls, crumbled roofs, weed-choked entrances. The other three were better hiding places. Although ravaged by time, they were still standing. Which was more than Nick could say about himself. He was leaning on his left leg so much that he was afraid he'd tip over.

He picked the cabin to his immediate right and shouted at it.

"Craig! You should just come out now! The other guys are going to be here any second and they're meaner than I am."

He risked a glance over his shoulder toward camp head-quarters in the distance. The SWAT search had moved from the cabin to the surrounding area. To get their attention, he thrust the Glock into the air and fired.

Craig Brewster fired back.

Nick didn't see which cabin it came from. He only heard it—a thunderous blast that echoed through the trees—and felt it. The rush of air seemed to come from all directions, raining buckshot. Nick leaped to the ground, covering his head.

Behind him, he heard distant shouting and rapid foot-falls coming from the rest of the camp. Tony and the SWAT team. They had heard the gunfire and were now coming to the rescue. No matter how fast they got there, it wouldn't be fast enough.

Lying on his stomach, Nick squirmed through the dirt. The cabins were quiet again. Craig could have been in any of them. Or none of them. Nick didn't know for sure.

Craig fired again. The blast, which hit the ground to Nick's right, sent clumps of earth spinning through the air. Bits of it landed on his face as he rolled in the opposite direction. Another shotgun blast followed, this time to Nick's left, forcing him to roll back to his original spot.

Gripped by panic, he flipped onto his back, legs apart and bent at the knee. It hurt like hell again, but Nick held the position, raising his head and shoulders off the ground. He thrust the Glock straight ahead, pointing it between his knees.

He aimed at the cabin in front of him. Its door was open, a gaping mouth waiting to spit out another scalding blast of buck-shot.

Nick fired first. Two shots. Right into the cabin.

Sounds rose from inside the cabin to his left. A bump. A click. A half-caught breath.

He twisted his body and popped off two shots into that one, not caring that the sounds might have been coming from somewhere else or part of his imagination. He did the same thing with the cabin to his right.

One shot.

Two shots.

Then a brief moment of silence before the SWAT team flooded the area. Flat on his back, Nick watched their boots stomp across the forest floor as they swarmed each cabin. When he looked up, he saw Tony Vasquez standing over him.

"Were you hit?"

Nick shook his head.

"Good."

Tony helped him to his feet and handed him his cane. Nick clutched it the same way a crack addict held his latest stash. He wasn't ever letting go of this puppy again.

All around them, the SWAT guys emerged from the cabins, reporting that all was clear. Only one cabin failed inspection— the second one Nick had shot into. A member of the SWAT team poked his head through the open door and bellowed, "He's in here!"

Tony rushed to the cabin. Nick hobbled. Stepping inside, he saw four bunk beds, a dead mouse, and the names Bobby, Kevin, and Joe carved into the wall. It was the cabin Dwight Halsey had vanished from, and slumped in a corner was Craig Brewster.

The shotgun lay on the floor at his feet. Tony swooped in and grabbed it while Nick got a better look at Mr. Brewster. He was still alive, but barely. Each breath was a ragged stream that hissed through his beard. A hand was on his chest, clutching at his heart.

Nick looked for signs of bleeding. There weren't any. The bullets had missed him, meaning something else took Craig down.

"We need to get him to a hospital," Nick said. "He's having a heart attack."

THIRTY

Jocelyn Miller's office was a glass-walled cube that sat just inside the front entrance to Perry Hollow Elementary School. Like specimens in a petri dish, anyone sitting in the office could be seen by those entering and exiting the building. So when Kat rushed into the school, the first thing she saw was the back of James's head as he sat inside this administrative fishbowl.

Kat got a look at the front of him once she entered the office. His head was tilted back, nostrils stuffed with tissues in an attempt to stem a bloody nose. Drops of crimson spattered his shirt.

"Little Bear? What happened?"

Deep down, she already knew. The bullying James had been experiencing at school had been taken to another, more dangerous level.

"Chief Campbell?" It was Jocelyn Miller, standing outside the windowless room where her desk was located. "May I have a word?"

Kat joined the principal in the office, slamming the door behind her. "Who did this to him?"

Jocelyn offered her a seat. Kat remained standing. She was too angry and racked with guilt to sit.

"I'd like to talk about James," the principal said.

"And I want to talk about the punk who beat him up." Kat started to pace, crossing the office in restless strides. "My son is out there bleeding and you're going to tell me who did it."

"I've been an educator for twenty years," Jocelyn said with infuriating calmness. "In that time, I've observed a lot of children. I think I know them pretty well. They're emotional creatures. Quick to anger. Quick to get upset. But also, thankfully, quick to be happy again."

"Could you please just tell me what's going on?"

Jocelyn raised a hand, asking for patience. "Sometimes, kids do things that they know are wrong. Lying. Cheating on tests. Sometimes they steal. And sometimes they bully other kids. Why do you think that happens?"

"I have no idea," Kat said.

"The first reason is that kids don't understand the consequences of their actions. They just know the benefits."

"And the other reasons?"

"They're more complex. And they're related. Care to guess what they are?"

Kat didn't, especially not where the kid hitting her son was concerned. Whoever it was, and most likely his parents, were no-good trash, pure and simple.

"Anger and poor parenting," she suggested.

"Close," Jocelyn said. "It's more like power and attention. Children know they have no control over this world. They're always being told what to do, what to eat, when to go to bed. It's for their own good, of course, but they don't know that yet. So they sometimes pick on others because it's something they can control. And sometimes they do it because they feel like they're not getting enough attention at home. The bad behavior and the bullying are often a subconscious plea for attention from their parents."

If the principal's goal was to wear Kat down, it worked. She plopped into a chair, saying, "I just want to know what happened. Tell me the name of the punk who's been picking on James and I'll take it from here."

Jocelyn crossed her arms, leaned back in her chair and contemplated Kat. "I can see why there's a problem."

"Excuse me?"

"A problem," Jocelyn repeated. "With James."

"James is just fine. It's this other kid who's been taking his lunches and hitting him that's the problem. Yet for some reason I'm the one sitting in the principal's office being given the emotional profile of a bully."

"Chief Campbell." The principal's voice rose just a notch, enough to make Kat sit at attention. "Your son just sent another student to the hospital. So, in my experience, James is the bully."

Eric remained seated for the rest of the afternoon. He was too stunned to move. Or eat. Or drink. He barely had enough energy to stare at the patch of sunlight brightening the dining-room table, which moved and stretched as the day progressed. Sometimes there'd be silence, long pauses in which the sunlight edged forward an inch or two. But for the most part, the dining room was filled with the sound of his father's voice, revealing just how he and Maggie had come to take possession of a little boy they named Charlie.

His mother, he learned, had lived in their house her entire life, growing up across the street from her best friend, Jennifer Clark. The two were inseparable. They shared clothes, makeup, secrets. When they were older, the girls would sometimes sneak away to Sunset Falls, where they sipped beer until they got dizzy.

One night, a boy from nearby Mercerville came with them. His name was Ken Olmstead.

"Your mother was the prettiest girl I ever saw," Eric's father said. "I was in love with her the first time I laid eyes on her."

They were an item all through Maggie's senior year and engaged by the time she graduated high school in 1958. They were married that August and made plans to move to Florida. Ken had distant family there, who offered to rent them a small house in the Keys starting in January 1959. There, they would build a life together, just the two of them.

It didn't work out that way. Jennifer Clark came with them.

She had started dating a young man in the army named Craig Brewster. They saw each other infrequently, with Craig burning through weekend passes just to visit her. But it was enough time to get engaged and definitely enough time for her to get pregnant, which she confessed to Maggie on Christmas Eve.

Jennifer was scared. Of what her parents would do. Of how the world would treat a shamed woman. According to Ken, Eric's mother came up with the solution—Jennifer could have the baby in Florida and put it up for adoption. That way no one in Perry Hollow would ever know.

She agreed, and the three of them moved to the Keys. Craig joined them that March, when he was honorably discharged from the military. It was cramped in that small house on the beach. Work was scarce and money was tight. But when Ken talked about it, there was a sad nostalgia in his voice that Eric had never heard before. It was the tone of a man recalling the happiest time of his life.

The happiness didn't last.

As the weeks passed and Jennifer's stomach extended, she began to have doubts about giving up her baby. She also had doubts about Craig, who didn't seem eager to make an honest woman out of her. There were fights, which echoed in the tiny house all through the night and into the dawn.

"We heard every word," Ken said. "Your mother and I would lay in bed and swear to each other we would never fight like that. Little did we know that, eventually, we would. Only worse."

June rolled around, bringing hurricane season with it. As one lashed the island, Jennifer Clark's unborn child decided it was time to greet the world. There was no hospital on the island; nor was there access to one. The hurricane had closed all routes to the mainland. Jennifer Clark had to give birth at home, with Maggie serving as terrified midwife.

Listening to his father, Eric closed his eyes and let his writer's imagination take over. He pictured lightning casting incandescent flashes across the room where Jennifer lay in a sweat-soaked bed. His mother had boiled water, because that's what they did in the movies, although she didn't know why. Both girls—even though married or pregnant, they weren't yet women—wept with fear as Jennifer grunted through another contraction and Maggie wiped her brow. The wind didn't shake the house so much as push it.

Eric then imagined his father and Craig Brewster in another room. Pacing. Not talking. Craig maybe stepping outside to feel the rain sting his face while he wondered what the hell he had gotten himself into. Then it was back to more pacing and not talking until, through the paper-thin walls that were peeling paint because of the humidity, an infant's wail broke through the sounds of the storm.

Once the baby was born, Eric's parents left Jennifer and Craig alone. The goal was to let them make a decision—keep the baby and raise it together or put it up for adoption and go their separate ways. By the time the sun rose over a storm-battered island, Jennifer had told Craig that she wanted to be a wife and mother. He told her that he had reenlisted in the army and was heading back to base in a few hours.

"Craig left without even holding the baby," Ken said. "And Jenny, well, she was devastated. The morning after Craig left, she was out of bed. Your mother told her she needed her rest, but Jenny insisted on going outside. She wanted to dip her toes in the ocean, she said. That was all. Just go to the beach and think."

Jennifer gave Maggie a long hug and a peck on the cheek before she left. It was the last time Eric's mother ever saw her.

No one knows what really happened in the roiling ocean. There were no witnesses, no random passersby who saw Jennifer walk into the water and slip beneath the waves. It could have been an accident. It could have been suicide. All Ken knew was that her body washed ashore a day later, which is all that really mattered.

Between her disappearance and discovery, Maggie cared for the still-unnamed baby as if he had emerged from her womb. She bathed him, fed him, and made makeshift diapers out of bedsheets, using sewing skills she had picked up in home economics classes. When the police came around to talk about Jennifer, they asked Maggie who the child belonged to.

"Your mother told them he was ours," Ken said.

Maggie didn't discuss the decision with him. She didn't even warn him it was coming. Instead, she calmly told the police the partial truth—that the infant had been born during the full thrust of the hurricane and that Jennifer's disappearance prevented them from going to the nearest hospital when the storm had passed. She didn't feel the need to mention Craig Brewster, currently on his way to Fort Rucker in Alabama, or the true identity of the infant's mother.

The police easily accepted that explanation and even drove them to the hospital, where the baby got a checkup. On the birth certificate, Ken and Maggie Olmstead were listed as his parents. When it came time to pick a name, they chose Charles, in honor of Ken's grandfather.

"The only time we talked about it," he said, "was when we got back from the hospital. Your mother swore it was the right thing to do. She said Jennifer would have wanted us, and not some strangers, to raise the boy. I wasn't sure it was a good idea. I was afraid someone would realize what we had done."

They passed the first test when Mort and Ruth Clark flew down to Florida to cremate their daughter and scatter her ashes into the sea. Maggie told them the same story she gave the police. When they saw the newborn in her arms, they said he looked just like her.

The second test came a few weeks later, when they decided

to return to Perry Hollow. They moved in with Maggie's parents, who were stunned to learn about their new grandchild.

"We told them we kept it a secret because there were complications and we weren't sure if the baby would survive," Ken said. "Who knows if they believed us. But they never asked about it again."

Soon Maggie's parents moved out, leaving them the house. Charlie grew up across the street from his true grandparents and Maggie eventually got pregnant for real, giving birth to Eric.

"The rest," Ken said, "you know about."

Finished at last, he stood and stretched, the cracking of his joints filling the silent dining room. Then he headed to the front door, where he had kicked off his boots the night before. The sound of him slipping them on prompted Eric to speak.

"But I *don't* know the rest," he said, confronting Ken by the door. "There are a lot of gaps to your story."

"I told you my memory isn't what it used to be."

When Ken headed upstairs, Eric doggedly tailed him to his mother's bedroom. "What about Craig Brewster? Did you ever hear from him again?"

"Only once," Ken said. "The day after Jennifer was found, I called his base to give him the news. When he asked about the baby, I told him the truth. He said we were doing the right thing."

He picked up his denim jacket, which had been tossed onto the floor the previous night. He stuffed a hand into the pockets, digging for his keys. Now that he had spilled all the family's secrets, he was preparing to leave again, even though he had no place to go and Eric still had another day's worth of unanswered questions.

"Why didn't you tell the police you weren't Charlie's real

father? Surely, Craig would have been the prime suspect if you had."

"Craig wanted nothing to do with him, that's why. When I told him we had Charlie, he vowed never to bother us."

His father edged into the hallway, Eric right behind him. "That doesn't mean he didn't come and take Charlie. I can't believe you just assumed he was innocent."

"Charlie died," Ken said. "He walked to the creek, fell in, and went over the falls. End of story."

"*Walked* to the creek? I thought he rode his bike."

Ken tried to cover his mistake. "That's what I meant to say."

Eric's mind began to race—a dizzying spin that brought back everything he knew about Charlie's disappearance and his father's role in it. The fact that he never told the police about not being Charlie's birth father. The way he asked Kat's dad to stop investigating the incident. The way he just admitted he knew Charlie had walked to the falls, even though his bike was found at the base of it. All this led to a conclusion that made Eric sick deep down in the pit of his stomach.

He noted their location in the hall, right in front of Charlie's dust-filled bedroom. The door was still open. The key remained in the lock.

He took a step, forcing his father to take one backward. After another step, Ken was standing in the doorway of Charlie's room. One more, and he was inside.

"What are you doing?" Ken asked.

Eric lunged for the doorknob. Soon the door was closed and he was fumbling with the key. The knob twisted in his hand—his father turning it on the other side. Eric held it steady and turned the key.

Ken was now locked inside.

"For Christ's sake, Eric, let me out!"

The door shimmied as his father jerked the handle. Eric leaned against it, listening to his father's angry huffs on the other side.

"I'm not going to let you out," he said. "Not until you tell me what you did with Charlie."

Nick sat in the waiting area outside the emergency room, watching TV. On the screen, he saw a pockmarked expanse of gray surrounded by a sky as dark as death. Accompanying the visual was the voice of a news anchor who sounded as awestruck as Nick felt.

"You are looking at a live picture from the surface of the moon," he said. "Just minutes ago, the three Chinese astronauts who blasted off early Wednesday touched down in the Sea of Tranquility. They plan to exit their lunar module in an hour or so for the first moon walk in almost thirty-nine years."

Somewhere in the depths of the hospital, a medical team was trying to keep Craig Brewster alive. Outside the hospital, some of the cops who had been at Camp Crescent milled about the parking lot, smoking, laughing, and generally shooting the shit. The rest of them were still at the camp, looking for clues about what Craig might have done with the other boys.

The only person near Nick was a fresh-faced nurse sitting behind the check-in desk and reading a tattered paperback. Nick couldn't help but notice the name of the author—Eric Olmstead. He chuckled when he saw it, prompting a sweet smile from the nurse. Nick could tell she thought he was cute. He chalked it up to the cane. Women seemed to love men with a weakness.

Nick pulled out his phone and dialed Kat's number. He

immediately got her voice mail. He had tried calling her once on the way to the hospital and again after he arrived. Both times he had left messages. Kat's failure to call him back was worrisome.

The nurse piped up. "You can't use cell phones in here."

Nick tucked the phone back into his jacket. "Sorry. My bad."

He was about to turn back to the TV and those unreal images of the moon, when Tony Vasquez emerged from the hospital's inner sanctum. As a member of the state police, he was allowed to go back there. Nick was not.

"Craig's still critical," Tony told him. "Completely unresponsive. We're not going to be able to question him for at least a day or so."

"When you do," Nick said, "ask him why he decided to use me for target practice."

"I'd rather find out what he did with the bodies of those kids."

Nick nodded in agreement. "You're right. That's a better question."

The automatic doors leading outside slid open as a man entered the emergency room. He wore the gray, oil-stained uniform of an auto mechanic. In his early fifties, he looked wan and worried as he made a beeline to the check-in desk.

"I'm here to see about my father," he said. "I was told he had a heart attack."

Nick and Tony both stood. At the desk, the nurse asked, "Patient's name?"

"Craig Brewster."

They approached the man quickly from behind. He was

stating his name—"Kevin Brewster"—when Nick tapped him on the shoulder.

The man turned around, confused. He had a pale face, small nose, ears that jutted from the sides of his head. His eyes were sad. His smile was slightly lopsided. It was a face Nick had seen before, only in black-and-white and printed on newspaper.

And although its owner had just said he was Kevin Brewster, Nick knew without a doubt that he was standing face-to-face with Charlie Olmstead.

THIRTY-ONE

Tony asked the questions. The man who called himself Kevin Brewster answered them. Nick's job was to listen.

"What is your name?"

"Kevin Brewster."

"Was that the name you were born with?"

"I want to know what happened to my father."

The three of them were in an examination room just off the waiting area. Kevin sat on the examination table, hands in his lap, legs swinging beneath him. Tony paced the room as he tossed out his queries. Nick was in the corner, scribbling everything down on a prescription pad he had flirted from the hands of the nurse at the check-in desk.

"He had a massive heart attack," Tony said. "He's in ICU as we speak."

"Will he survive?"

"We don't know."

"Can I see him?"

"Not right now."

"But soon?"

"If you answer some questions," Tony said. "Now, is Kevin Brewster the name you were born with?"

"No." A slight hesitation. "I once was known as Charlie."

"Charlie Olmstead?"

"That's right."

"When did Charlie become Kevin?"

"The night I met my real father."

Nick halted his pen, leaving a skid mark of ink across the page. "Maggie and Ken Olmstead weren't your parents?"

Kevin shook his head. "Craig Brewster is my father. He said the Olmsteads stole me when I was a baby."

"Who was your mother?" It was Tony, whose stern gaze in Nick's direction indicated that he'd be the only one asking questions.

"I don't know."

"Mr. Brewster never told you?"

"He said she died. That was all."

"When was this? Right after he abducted you?"

"He didn't abduct me. I went willingly."

"Willingly?"

"Yes."

What Kevin told them—and what Nick furiously wrote down—was that on July 20, 1969, he went to Sunset Falls. On his way back to the house, a man in the street stopped him.

"He told me his name. He then said he was my real father."

"And you believed him?"

"Not at first. But he showed me a photograph. It was of him on a beach. He was with a woman and the Olmsteads. He told me the woman was my mother and that she died soon after giving birth to me. Then he said Mr. and Mrs. Olmstead stole me. That's when I started to think he was telling me the truth."

"Why?"

"Because I looked nothing like them. But I looked like the woman in the photo. The woman I was told was my real mother."

"So you left with him? Just like that?"

"No."

"Then he took you by force?"

"I didn't say that," Kevin snapped. "He asked me if I believed him. I said maybe. He asked if I wanted to spend some time with him to see if it was true. Again, I said maybe."

While Tony seemed content to let the man formerly known as Charlie Olmstead draw out the story, Nick was getting impatient. "Tell us why you left with him."

"He said the Olmsteads didn't want me anymore."

"And you bought this?" Nick asked.

Kevin glanced in his direction. "I know it's hard to understand. But imagine you were in my shoes—a ten-year-old boy in a family that was falling apart. Ken and Maggie Olmstead were fighting all the time. There was a baby. I've forgotten his name, I'm afraid to say."

"Eric," Nick said.

"That's right," Kevin said with a fond smile. "Eric. I knew that Ken and Maggie seemed on the verge of divorce and that the baby was caught in the middle. I remember being worried about him."

"What about you?" Tony asked.

"I seemed not to matter. I spent a lot of time outside, playing alone or bothering the neighbors. They didn't seem to miss me. So when my father—my real father—said the Olmsteads didn't want me, it had the ring of truth."

"So you left with him that night?" It was Tony, back to being the sole interrogator.

"I did, but only after he said the Olmsteads knew that I'd be with him."

"Did you realize he was lying?"

"No. Was he? I never found out."

"Where did he take you that night?"

"To some land he owned in the woods. Next to a lake. It was beautiful there. He had built a cabin and we slept in sleeping bags on the floor. He asked me about my likes and dislikes. What I dreamed of becoming. How I was doing in school. We talked the entire night. In the morning, he asked me if I wanted to stay another night."

"Did you ask about the Olmsteads?"

"I did. He told me I had their permission to stay the entire week if I wanted to. I told him I did."

"What did you do there?"

"We fished a lot. We roasted marshmallows and he told me ghost stories. And we worked. He told me he was in the process of building a camp on that land and that he'd appreciate my help. We cleared brush. We built more cabins. It was hard work, but I didn't mind. I enjoyed being with my real dad. So when the week was over, he said the Olmsteads allowed me to stay another week. And then another. Then he said they wanted me to stay the rest of the summer."

"Didn't you miss them?" It was Nick again. He knew he

was pissing Tony off, but he just couldn't help it. "They did raise you, after all."

"At first I did. In the back of my mind, I always thought they'd eventually come to the camp and get me. When they didn't, I actually got angry. It was proof that my father was right and that they didn't want me anymore. So I stayed."

"But what about school?" Tony asked. "Didn't you think about going back in the fall?"

"No," Kevin said. "Because by that point, my father told me that the Olmsteads had moved."

"Did he say where?"

"No. Just that they were gone. So I went to live with him. He gave me a new name. To signal a new start, he said. It was weird at first, but I eventually got used to it. Especially after going to a new school. Everyone there called me Kevin. No one knew I had once been Charlie. After a few months, it was like Charlie had never been my name."

"So you spent the rest of your life as Kevin, Craig Brewster's son?"

"I did."

"And he was good to you?"

"He was."

"No abuse? No sexual assault? Nothing like that?"

"No. Never. He's a good, kind man."

"Did you ever see him with any other boys?"

"What do you mean?"

"At any time, were there other boys living with you? Maybe identified as distant cousins or the children of friends?"

"No. It was just the two of us."

Nick had another question. Instead of blurting it out, he

wrote it down on the prescription pad, tore off the page, and handed it to Tony to read. He did, with mild annoyance.

"Did you ever try to find the Olmsteads?"

"No."

"Why not?"

"I had no reason to. At some point after I went to live with my father—I can't remember if it was a few weeks, a few months, or a few years—he told me that they were dead."

"All of them?"

"Yes. Ken and Maggie. Even the baby. I didn't ask for details and he didn't give me any. He said that there was a tragedy, they all died, and I was now officially his son."

"How did this make you feel?"

"Sad, of course." Kevin looked to Nick again. "Like you said, they raised me. And they were good to me. I cried when I heard the news. I wanted to go to their funerals, but my dad said they were already buried. Instead, he took me to the lake. I painted their names on three rocks and dropped them into the water. I had my own burial."

Nick tried to stop himself. He really did. But as he listened to Kevin talk about his former family, the urge to speak expanded in his chest until it had to burst out.

"They're not dead," he said. "Maggie Olmstead is, but just recently. The others, Ken and Eric, are still alive."

The news stunned Kevin Brewster. What little color there had been in his cheeks drained away and his mouth dropped open.

"I don't believe you."

"I've met Eric," Nick replied. "He's looking for you right now. Your mother spent her whole life trying to find out what happened to you."

"Maggie Olmstead is not my mother."

"She was," Nick said. "Once upon a time. And your father, this Craig Brewster, he lied to you."

"Prove it." Kevin hopped off the table. Tony intercepted him and edged him back in place. "My father wouldn't lie to me like that."

Nick left the room. Back in the waiting area, he headed straight for the nurse. She was on the phone, the paperback at her elbow. Nick picked it up and mouthed four words, "May I borrow this?" When the nurse smiled and nodded, he took the book into the examination room and handed it to Kevin Brewster.

"Who wrote this?"

Kevin read the cover. "Eric Olmstead."

"That's the same Eric Olmstead who was your brother. In his mind, he's still your brother. He always has been and he always will be."

Nick flipped the book over, revealing an author's photograph on the back cover. It was a black-and-white image of Eric, who seemed to stare out at his former brother. "He's alive, Charlie."

"It's Kevin," the former Charlie said.

"Yes. Kevin. But you were once Charlie Olmstead. You were once part of a family that loved you. When you left, they missed you. They still miss you. And they'd love to see you again and know that you've been safe all this time."

Kevin Brewster started to cry. Nick didn't know what actually prompted it. Maybe his words. Maybe the picture of his long-lost brother. The cause didn't matter. The important part was that he realized he had been lied to all those years ago, and that clarity made him weep until his body was wracked with sobs.

"Where is Eric now?" he asked, trying to stop the tears.

"Perry Hollow," Nick answered. "Probably a half hour away."

Kevin Brewster, who seemed to be changing back into Charlie Olmstead with each passing second, wiped his eyes.

"Take me to him," he said. "I want to see him."

THIRTY-TWO

One hour.

Kat couldn't dislodge the number from her head. Sixty minutes of discussion about James's problems, although the conversation had been pretty one-sided. Jocelyn Miller barely let Kat get a word in edgewise, which made her feel both angry and foolish. And duped, of course. She couldn't forget about feeling utterly duped by her son.

According to the principal, the deception began on Wednesday, when James entered fifth grade carrying his lunch box. A student in his homeroom—a smart-alecky runt named Randy Speevey—immediately teased him about it. James, who had at least six inches on Randy, grabbed his lunch, opened it up, and saw it was so much better than the one Kat had packed. So he tossed his lunch box, ate Randy's lunch, and then lied about it.

He did it again the next two days. When Kat and Lou saw him throw his lunch into the trash outside the school, they had assumed it was to prevent it from being stolen by others. In reality, James had simply been tossing it in favor of Randy's. The principal said James probably would have kept on doing it if

Randy Speevey hadn't tried to stop him. Denied his better lunch, James beat him up, causing a black eye, a cracked rib, and a sky-high doctor's bill that Kat was now obligated to pay.

"You're grounded for a week," she told James. "Starting the moment we get home."

They were in her Crown Vic, stopping and starting in the late-afternoon traffic on Main Street. School had let out while Kat was stuck in the principal's office. Now it was rush hour, when it seemed like every car in Perry Hollow was heading somewhere.

"No computer," Kat continued. "No TV. No video games. No iPod."

"What about school?"

There would be no school, either. At least not for a week, which was the length of the suspension Jocelyn Miller handed down.

"I can't believe you hurt that boy," Kat said. "I taught you better than that."

James crossed his arms in defiance. "I told you someone would make fun of me."

"That doesn't mean you needed to take his lunch and beat him up. You could have just asked for better lunches and I would have done my best."

That's all she wanted him to understand—that she was trying to raise him the best she could under stressful circumstances. It was hard being the only parent of a child with special needs while simultaneously watching over an entire town. In a way, Perry Hollow was like a second kid, sometimes more needy and unruly than James.

"You just need to talk to me more, Little Bear. And I'll listen."

James frowned. "No you won't."

"What do you mean by that?"

Kat's cell phone, clipped to her duty belt, began to vibrate. She had silenced it during her meeting with Jocelyn Miller, letting it buzz throughout the hour-long ordeal. Grabbing the phone, she saw that Nick had called eight times. This was attempt number nine. He had news about Craig Brewster. Huge news, Kat assumed. But she couldn't answer it, not with James staring at her with a dejected look on his face.

This is what he was talking about. The phone calls. The long hours. Being shuffled off to Lou's house or Carl's place or anywhere there was a responsible adult willing to look after him for a few hours. Kat had vowed to change all that ten months earlier, after she and James had come face-to-face with the serial killer known as the Grim Reaper. But her old ways had crept back without her realizing it.

"It's about this, isn't it?" Kat said as she held up the phone. "Not lunch boxes or problems at school. It's about how you think I'm choosing my job over you."

She remembered what Jocelyn Miller had said about bullies subconsciously seeking attention from their parents. James had become one of those kids, doing whatever he could to make Kat notice him.

"Is that what you want?" Kat asked. "My attention?"

James nodded.

Kat lowered her window and tossed the phone out of the car, where it clattered into the street. A UPS truck in the oncoming lane ran over it, the phone crunching under its wheels. Kat was too angry to care.

"There," she said. "You have my undivided attention."

The tense silence that followed lasted all of a minute.

Then the police radio crackled and Lou's voice boomed out of it. "Chief? You there?"

Kat could easily get rid of her phone, but the police radio was another matter. There was no way she could avoid answering it, no matter how much James pouted.

"I'm here, Lou. What do you need?"

"Two things, actually," Lou said. "The first is that the Chinese astronauts are walking on the moon. It's all over the Internet. On the TV, too. I figured you'd want to know, just in case."

Kat snuck a glance at her side mirror, where she could still see the shattered pieces of her cell phone in the street. Man was once again on the moon and she had no idea if Nick and Tony had found Craig Brewster.

"What's the second thing?" she asked.

"I just got a call from Glenn Stewart."

"Seriously? What did he want?"

"He called to complain about a domestic situation taking place next door."

Kat gasped. "That's Eric's house."

"It is," Lou said. "And you should get over there. Mr. Stewart said he heard a lot of yelling."

Kat swerved off Main Street and headed toward Eric's house. Once on the cul-de-sac, she saw that Ken Olmstead's rig was still parked at the curb. She brought the Crown Vic to a halt behind it.

"I'll be right back," she told James before jumping out of the car. "Lock the doors behind me. And if you move an inch, you're grounded for another week."

Inside, the house was quiet. If yelling had occurred, it was now over. Kat didn't even hear talking. The only noticeable noise came from Eric's cell phone, which blared from somewhere in the living room. Kat poked her head inside and saw the room was empty. She did the same with the kitchen and the dining room before climbing the stairs.

At the top, she found Eric in the hallway, sitting with his back against the door to Charlie's bedroom.

"Eric? What are you doing up here? And where's your father?"

He jerked a thumb at the door behind him. "In there."

"You locked him inside?"

"I had to," Eric said. "He was going to leave."

"Then you should have just let him go."

"But he was hiding something. About Charlie."

"It's okay," Kat said. "They found out who did it. Nick and the state police. Hopefully they've arrested him by now. All that's left is to find out what he did with the other boys."

"So it's over?" Eric spoke haltingly, as if in disbelief. "Really over?"

"I need to call Nick to confirm it," Kat said, "but it's pretty much a done deal. Now, let's unlock the door and let your father out."

Eric opened his hand, allowing her to pluck the key from his palm.

"This person they've arrested, who is he?"

Kat slid the key into the lock. "He ran the camp where Dwight Halsey disappeared. He was once engaged to Jennifer Clark, Mort and Ruth's daughter."

"Craig Brewster?"

"Yes." Kat turned the key, the lock clicking free of the door. "How did you—"

The door was yanked open. Kat, who had been gripping

the doorknob, went with it. She tumbled into the room, sliding along the dust-covered floor. Ken Olmstead jumped out from behind the door, leaping over her. As he left the room he lowered his head, ramming it against Eric's stomach in the hallway.

They hit the wall hard, Eric taking the brunt of the blow. His arms flailed at his sides. His head bounced off the wall. Dazed from the impact, Eric went limp. Ken grabbed him by his shirt collar and thrust him into the bedroom.

Kat was once again on her feet and racing toward the door. She caught Eric as he fell inside, trying hard to keep him upright. In front of her, the door slammed shut. She lunged for it, catching the handle.

It was too late. On the outside, Ken Olmstead was turning the key. She and Eric were now the ones locked inside.

"I'm sorry," Ken said through the door. "I didn't want to do this. But you'll never be able to understand the things I've done."

Kat pounded on the door, slapping it with both hands. "Mr. Olmstead, we can sit down and discuss this. It might not be as bad as you think."

"I'm sorry," he said again. "Tell Eric I did it for him."

Pressing an ear against the door, Kat heard his footfalls echo rapidly through the hallway. They became more muted when he reached the stairs. A few seconds later, the front door opened and closed.

Eric was at the window, trying to get it to open. "He's getting away."

Kat joined him, fingers trying to burrow beneath the window frame. It was stuck. No surprise, seeing how it had been closed for more than forty years.

Outside, she heard the low rumble of an engine. Ken

Olmstead's rig, revving to life. Still struggling with the window, she watched the rig tear away from the curb and head toward the end of the cul-de-sac. Ken made a U-turn before speeding off in the other direction. When it passed her patrol car, she saw James sitting in the front seat. Just like her, he was watching the truck's departure with surprise and confusion.

"James!" Kat smacked at the window, trying to get her son's attention. "Up here!"

But James wasn't looking in their direction. His head was turned, following the truck's progress as it belched out diesel smoke. Kat and Eric did, too, watching hopelessly as the truck made a wide right turn at the other end of the cul-de-sac and vanished from view.

Ken Olmstead—as well as any secrets he still possessed—was now gone.

"What did he tell you?" Kat moved from the window to the door, twisting the handle in vain.

"He said Charlie wasn't my real brother."

Kat already knew that. It was surprising, yes, but not worth assaulting your son and fleeing an officer of the law.

"What else?"

"I'm pretty sure he knew Craig Brewster took Charlie that night."

Now that, Kat thought, was something worth running about. Which meant she had to stop that truck, by any means possible. But the first order of business was to get the hell out of that bedroom.

Backing up, she counted to three. Then she took off into a sprint, slamming into the door with her right shoulder. She had used that move once before, eight months ago. It hurt then and it hurt now. But on this occasion, just like the last, the pain was worth it. The force of the blow cracked the door frame. One swift kick later and the door was open.

Eric let out an impressed whistle. "Damn."

"Just wait," Kat said, "until you see what I do to your father."

The rig came out of nowhere, rounding the corner and swerving into Nick's lane. He slammed on the brakes, skidding to a halt as the truck righted itself. When it passed, Nick noted its exterior in case he ever saw it tearing through Perry Hollow again. Black paint. Orange flames airbrushed along the side. There was also a distinct groan to the engine, a telltale rumbling that grew more pronounced as the driver shifted gears.

"He must be in a hurry."

It was spoken by either Charlie Olmstead or Kevin Brewster, depending on how you looked at it. Nick could only think of him as Charlie, and addressed him as such. The man sitting next to him didn't seem to mind. Not that he talked all that much. The comment about the truck was the first thing he had said in more than fifteen minutes.

Nick made a left turn onto the same street the truck had suddenly burst from. "This is where you used to live. Does any of it look familiar?"

Charlie gazed out the window. "I'm not sure. Driving through town was like déjà vu. I recognized some things, but it's like I couldn't remember from where."

If he was nervous, he didn't show it. But from the wide-eyed way Charlie took everything in, Nick could tell the whole experience was probably one giant mindfuck.

Charlie caught sight of the Olmstead residence. "My God. It hasn't changed at all."

Turning into the driveway, Nick saw Kat's patrol car parked in the street. Even though she had ignored his calls all afternoon, he was glad she'd be there to witness the reunion. Unless Tony had managed to reach them from the hospital, Kat and Eric still didn't know that Charlie was alive. Seeing him was going to blow their minds.

"You ready to go in?" he asked Charlie.

"I think so."

They got out of the car. Charlie headed for the house, but Nick paused at Kat's Crown Vic. James was inside, sitting with his arms crossed. Nick rapped on the window with the tip of his cane.

"Hey, kiddo. What are you doing here?"

"Waiting for Mom." James had his iPod in hand, shuffling through the digital jukebox like he'd never get to play with it again.

"She might be a while. Do you want to come inside?"

James didn't look up. "She told me to stay in the car."

"Suit yourself, I guess."

Nick turned back to Charlie, who rotated in the middle of the lawn, trying to see everything at once. "This whole street is exactly the same. The Santangelos lived there. The Clarks next door to them. And crazy Glenn Stewart's house."

Looking up at the house next door, Nick saw the curtains in a second-floor window flutter, as if rustled by a light breeze. But there was no breeze, light or otherwise. Nick had a feeling that the movement came from Glenn himself, who was once again spying on them. He wondered if the neighbor recognized Charlie after all these years and, if so, how he was reacting.

But the reaction he was most looking forward to was Eric Olmstead's. As they stepped onto the front porch, he felt a pang of envy. Eric was about to meet the sibling he thought had died decades ago. It was something Nick often fantasized about. How would he react if he found out his sister was still alive? How would Sarah look? Eric, the lucky bastard, was about to experience something straight out of Nick's dreams.

They entered the house just as Kat was storming down the stairs. Eric was behind her, trying to keep up. Nick stepped out of the way, revealing Charlie standing in the doorway.

"Surprise," he said.

Kat watched the reunion from a discreet distance. Nick was by her side. Both knew enough to stay out of the way and let Eric and Charlie get reacquainted. It didn't matter that they weren't related by blood. Nor did it matter that their separation most likely came at the hands of Ken Olmstead. The important thing was that, after forty-two years, they were together once again.

At first, Eric didn't know how to act. He took an awkward step forward, jaw dropped in disbelief. When he held out his hand, Charlie shook it. Then he tugged Eric close, wrapping him in a strong embrace.

"I thought you were dead," Eric said. "We all did."

Charlie released him reluctantly. "I'm here now."

Then, as they moved into the living room, both men began to cry. Kat felt tears of her own pooling in the corners of her eyes and threatening to overflow. When one slipped down her cheek, she swiped it away. There was no time for tears.

"We have to catch Eric's dad," she whispered to Nick. "He just left."

"Was he in a black truck?"

"Yes," Kat said. "Also known as his getaway car."

"Is he mixed up in all of this somehow?"

Maybe, Kat told him. Maybe not. She didn't know. But the fact that Charlie was alive and well when five other boys weren't made her think Craig Brewster wasn't responsible for the other abductions.

"What if the other boys were taken not by Craig but by someone looking for Charlie?"

"Like Ken Olmstead?" Nick said.

"Exactly. We need to track him down and find out just what kind of role he played in all of this."

As they rushed to the door, Kat peeked into the living room. Eric and Charlie sat on the couch, silly grins slapped on their faces. They had a lot of catching up to do. A lifetime's worth. They wouldn't miss her and Nick.

"We should take two cars," she told Nick once they were outside. "It'll double our chances of catching Ken."

Nick was already halfway to his, cane thudding on the grass. "He turned right. Probably heading toward Old Mill Road on his way out of town."

He climbed into his car and pulled out of the driveway. Then, tires squealing, he took off down the street.

Kat reached the Crown Vic, intending to do the same. She slid behind the wheel, keys at the ready. She was about to start the car when she noticed the passenger seat. It was empty. An iPod sat in the middle of the seat, a pair of white earbuds tangled next to it. On the floor was a backpack. But the boy who owned them was nowhere to be seen.

James was gone.

THIRTY-THREE

Kat got out of the car, slowly at first, more annoyed than concerned. She had told James to stay in the Crown Vic. Demanded it, in fact. And as she edged into the center of the street, she felt a too-familiar sense of anger wash over her. Now he was in even more trouble.

Scanning the street for places where he could be, Kat knew he couldn't have gone far. It was only a cul-de-sac—four houses clustered together in a forgotten corner of town. And anywhere near Eric's place could already be ruled out. If James had been there, in the yard, say, or on the back porch, she would have noticed.

"James?"

She thought about checking the path that led to Sunset Falls and immediately dismissed the idea. It was too covered with brush and foliage to catch his attention. The same could be said for the yard of Mort and Ruth Clark's old house. The bomb shelter hidden beneath it would be irresistible to a kid his age—if he knew it was there. And James most definitely did not.

That left the Santangelo residence and Glenn Stewart's house as the only two places he could be. Kat headed toward the Santangelos' place, simply because it was the least forbidding of the two.

Crossing the street, she called his name again. "James?"

She said it calmly, without panic. There was no need for panic. Yet.

But the lack of a response concerned her. James was the type of boy who would call back if he heard his name. No matter how mad he was. No matter how surly he was feeling.

"Little Bear?"

Kat said it louder this time, with a tinge of worry she hoped James would pick up on when he heard her. If he heard her.

She thought of Maggie Olmstead and the mothers of the other missing boys. How long did it take them to get worried? When did they realize something was amiss? If her feelings were any indication, then the answer was soon. James hadn't even been gone five minutes and already she was buzzing with anxiety.

By that time, she was at the edge of Lee and Becky Santangelo's vast yard, crossing it as the grass whispered between her feet. Once on the porch, she realized her hand was trembling as she rapped on the door. She shoved both hands in her pockets and turned back to the lawn.

Waiting for Becky to come to the door, she pictured a much younger Burt Hammond mowing the lawn. Then she imagined Lee Santangelo inside, watching, thinking of ways to get him inside. Once he did, he grabbed the camera.

The resulting tawdry home movie wasn't illegal—Burt was old enough, Kat knew, but still awfully young—yet it made her think about other young men he might have invited into his bed.

As Becky opened the door, it occurred to Kat that the Santangelos' film only served as an alibi for the night Charlie Olmstead disappeared. Lee's whereabouts when the other boys vanished were still unknown. Kat knew he had been to Camp Crescent and Centralia. Most likely Fairmount, too. There was a chance—slim, yes, but a chance nonetheless—that he had something to do with the others' disappearance.

"Can I help you, Chief?" Becky asked.

"Have you seen a little boy? He's ten. Big for his age."

Kat looked past her into the house, scanning the dim hallway for signs of her son. She knew Lee was no longer capable of grabbing a boy off the street. But his wife was. Becky with her brittle manners and refusal to show her age. Maybe she had seen James on the street and lured him inside, perhaps with the cookies that Charlie Olmstead had loved so much. And once James was inside—

She was being paranoid. Becky Santangelo had nothing to do with James, just as she had nothing to do with those other missing boys. If she or Lee had been guilty, they wouldn't have displayed framed photos of the locations of their crimes. And Becky wouldn't have answered the door now.

"Today?" she said. "I haven't seen a boy on this street since Eric Olmstead left town."

"Are you sure?"

"Positive. Have you checked Glenn Stewart's place? Your son probably isn't there, but stranger things have happened."

Her words set off alarm bells in Kat's brain. Clanging off the insides of her skull, they reawakened all the things she had forgotten during the craziness of the day. Things like Norm Harper talking about Glenn Stewart's religious conversion in Vietnam and Professor Luther Reid explaining *mặt trăng vinh quang*. All those words with sinister meanings. Glorious enlightenment. Human sacrifice.

Bad moon.

"I need to go," Kat said. "If you see my son, please tell him I'm looking for him. And that I'm worried."

The sound of her voice appalled her. Accented with a

noticeable quaver, it was the voice of a woman far more stressed than she thought she was. This wasn't mere worry, Kat realized. It was panic. And it was fully taking over.

Nick knew Perry Hollow. Not as well as Kat, but better than any other outsider. He knew cutting through Pine Street was faster that taking car-clogged Main. He knew that when Kat and Carl Bauersox were busy, a driver could go twice the speed limit and blow through every Stop sign. And he knew the quickest way in and out of town was Old Mill Road, which passed the lake before bisecting soybean fields on the way into Mercerville.

Since Ken Olmstead also knew Perry Hollow, Nick assumed that was the route he took. But time, not to mention distance, was running out. Five miles ahead, Old Mill Road ended, turning into Route 58. A mile beyond that was the interstate. If Ken Olmstead hit the open highway, Nick would never be able to catch up with him.

Following the rig's presumed path, he tried to calculate what kind of a head start it had and how fast he'd need to go to catch up. Nick sucked at math. But he was good at driving. You didn't need to think when driving. You just needed to pound the gas pedal and go.

That's exactly what he did. By the time he reached Old Mill Road, he was going seventy. A mile later, he was topping seventy-five. He glanced in the rearview mirror, hoping to see Kat's car. It wasn't there. He was on his own.

On his left, Lake Squall passed in a watery blur. Then it was through the fields, where the road was a flat straightaway. He didn't encounter many vehicles, just a rust bucket of a truck that he easily passed.

The speedometer hit eighty as he crossed the border between Perry Hollow and Mercerville. Signaling his arrival was a large sign next to the road that welcomed him to town. Nick grimaced at the sight, only because it meant he was getting closer to the interstate.

And that Ken Olmstead was closer still.

Just beyond the sign, the road rose sharply, making its way over a small hill. Halfway up the incline was a Cadillac, as wide as a barge and just as slow. Nick was behind it instantly, tailgating the vehicle in the hope it would go a little faster. When it didn't, Nick knew he needed to pass it as fast as possible.

He veered left into the opposing lane, the crest of the hill looming ahead of him. About a hundred yards from the top, he was side by side with the Caddy. Fifty yards from the top, he had pulled ahead, his rear tires parallel with the Cadillac's front ones. Soon he was cresting the hill. The road, previously in front of him, suddenly dropped away, revealing an expanse of sky and the valley below.

There was also a tanker truck. Rolling over the hill in the opposite direction, it was coming right at Nick.

He jerked the steering wheel to the right, cutting off the Cadillac. In the rearview mirror, he saw its driver slam on the brakes. The Caddy fishtailed onto the side of the road, kicking up a cloud of gravel. The tanker roared past at the same time, blasting its horn.

When the horn died out, it was replaced by another sound rising from the bottom of the hill. The noise—the guttural grinding of an engine trying to get up to speed after switching gears—was the same one Nick had heard in the car with Charlie. In the distance, where the road flattened out again, was a black rig with orange flames airbrushed across its side.

Nick had located Ken Olmstead.

* * *

Kat jumped off the Santangelos' porch and ran across the yard, the bad thoughts continuing to crowd her brain. She thought of the faces on Maggie Olmstead's plywood board. All those smiling boys who vanished without a trace. She recalled the photo Professor Reid e-mailed her. It showed a boy—one James's age, she couldn't forget—killed to appease the moon god. It was crazy that anyone anywhere could do such a thing. Crazier still was the possibility that someone from her town could be capable of such deeds.

But insane people existed, she knew. Including people in Perry Hollow. And a poll of the townsfolk would likely conclude that there was no one more strange than Glenn Stewart.

Once on the street, Kat shouted James's name again. It was a last-ditch attempt to get him to appear. There was still a chance he had wandered off on his own. Still the possibility that this was all a ruse to punish her for grounding him.

But she doubted it, especially when James again failed to appear. He had been taken. Just like the other boys had been taken. But instead of Craig Brewster, Charlie Olmstead's captor, Kat was certain this was the work of Mr. Stewart.

Approaching his house, she peeked into the backyard. The rickety car port was there, doing a bad job of shielding the elements from the Volkswagen van parked beneath it. The van should have been the first sign that Glenn wasn't entirely homebound. He might not drive it anymore, but once upon a time he did—steering it all the way to Fairmount and Centralia and the deep woods where Camp Crescent was located.

Kat pictured him behind the wheel, opening the door to invite unsuspecting boys inside. Dennis Kepner and Dwight Halsey. Frankie Pulaski and Bucky Mason. According to Nick, Noah

Pierce had been killed on the spot, his body dropped into a watery grave beneath an abandoned gristmill. They had all been taken for one reason—the glorious moon that Glenn seemed to revere.

When Kat reached his house, she ran onto the front porch, unholstering her Glock as she moved.

Then she heard the shrieks.

There were two of them, high-pitched and loud, coming from the other side of the door. Kat's heart raced at the sound. She recognized them. More chilling, she knew who was making them.

It was James.

Quaking with fear, Kat tried the front door. It was unlocked, thank God. Without wasting a second, she twisted the handle, calling for James.

Then, Glock at the ready, she burst inside.

Nick's left foot squeezed the gas pedal against the floor. His right trembled with anticipation. He was getting closer.

In the distance, the rig also picked up speed. Even from a half mile away, he heard the groan of the engine. Like Nick, Ken Olmstead was trying to drive as fast as possible.

The truck blew past a sign on the side of the road. Thirty seconds later, Nick did the same thing. It was a blue and red highway sign, telling him the interstate was up ahead. Nick guessed it was now two miles away. Maybe even less.

Looking toward the road again, he saw he was gaining on the truck, slowly but surely. Once a half mile apart, he was now a quarter mile behind the rig and gaining. But Nick knew it might not be enough. Once the truck got to the interstate, there'd be more traffic to deal with and the chances of actually getting

Ken to stop would drop dramatically. If he was going to halt the rig, it had to be in the next minute or so.

He flicked on the headlights, flashing them in the hope Ken would see them and stop. When that didn't work, he honked the horn, slamming the heel of his hand until there was a steady blare.

Up ahead, the rig grew closer. Nick was right on its tail. He muttered at it through gritted teeth. "Stop, you motherfucker. Why don't you stop?"

He knew the answer. The interstate was right ahead. Nick could see the overpass up ahead as the highway crossed the road. Just before that, the entrance ramp veered right, sweeping upward to meet it.

An orange light flared in the back of Ken Olmstead's truck. It was the turn signal, blinking steadily as the truck edged toward the entrance ramp.

Gripping the wheel to steady himself and the car, Nick lifted himself up from the seat until he was standing on the gas pedal. The car jerked forward, engine revving in protest. He ignored the sound, swerving to the right. He hit a rumble strip on the road's shoulder, tires buzzing, car vibrating. Then he was off the road, bouncing through weeds with the rig right next to him.

Nick blasted the horn again. The orange flames on the side of the rig were about six inches from his window. Then they receded a bit, falling behind until they were parallel with his back windows.

He was passing the rig.

With a grunt and one last stomp on the gas, Nick pulled ahead of the truck. He veered back onto the entrance ramp, the rig's grille perilously close to his rear bumper. Up ahead, the ramp flattened out, connecting with the highway. It was his last chance to stop the truck.

Nick slammed on the brakes. His tires squealed along the road as momentum propelled the car forward. When his front wheels gripped the road, the back ones kept going, screeching along the asphalt. Nick felt his seat belt tighten across his chest, pinning him back down to the seat as the car rotated.

It came to a stop in the middle of the ramp, perpendicular to the road. To his left, the approaching rig also slammed on its brakes. The engine, going so fast for so long, shuddered at the sudden deceleration. The truck followed suit, swerving back and forth unsteadily.

Nick slid across the front seat, banging his right knee on the steering column. The pain that shot through his entire body made him want to stop. But he couldn't stop. The truck, brakes screaming, was just outside the window, getting closer, closer, closer. He scrambled into the passenger seat, lunging for the door handle.

He tugged on it and the door flew open. Nick slithered out of the car, hoping he could roll away from the inevitable impact.

It never happened.

Lying on the ground, he looked to his car. It was still in one piece. Sitting up, he saw the truck on the other side of it. It had come to a stop inches away. Somehow, a collision had been avoided.

That didn't make Ken Olmstead any less pissed off. Hopping out of the rig, he marched around Nick's car, shouting, "What the hell are you doing? I could have goddamn killed you and myself in the process."

Nick climbed to his feet. It was hard without the cane, which was still inside his car, but he managed. Standing with his weight on one leg, he faced Ken Olmstead.

"I'm Nick Donnelly."

Ken gave him a blank stare. "So?"

"I was hired to find Charlie," he said. "And I did."

THIRTY-FOUR

Kat found herself in a small entrance foyer that led to other points inside Glenn Stewart's house. Directly in front of her was a staircase that rose to the second floor. To the right sat a darkened dining room. To the left, a soft red light glowed from a parlor. Kat followed it, just as another shriek sliced the air.

Glock still raised, she pushed into the parlor. It was remarkably clean, considering the house's exterior appearance, and decorated in an Asian theme. A bamboo screen covered one corner. On the walls were watercolor images of mountains and pagodas. Red Japanese lanterns hung from the ceiling, providing the glow.

The only piece of furniture not fitting in with the décor was a small bookshelf pushed against the wall. Kat saw volumes of Shakespeare, modern classics, even a copy of *The Art of War*. One shelf was devoted to the works of a single author— Eric Olmstead. Glenn owned a copy of every book he had written, all in pristine condition.

James was on the floor in front of the bookshelf. Sitting on his shoulder was a slithery mass of brown and black fur. A ferret, which scurried across the back of his neck to his other shoulder. When the animal's bushy tail brushed his face, he shrieked once more with delight.

"James?"

He froze when he saw her. "He told me to come in."

"It's true," Glenn Stewart said. "I saw him and urged him to come inside."

His voice rose from a dim corner behind Kat. He was a shadowy figure, sitting in an overstuffed chair with ethereal stillness.

Kat stepped in front of her son. "James, let the animal go."

"But, Mom—"

"Let it go!"

James released the animal, which skittered past her legs. The ferret jumped into Glenn's lap, where it received a tender pat on the head.

"They're gentle creatures," he said. "A little rambunctious, but nothing too bad. This one lost his companion just the other day. He's still grieving."

Kat glanced back at James. "Little Bear, I need you to get up and go to the door."

James didn't protest. Frightened and confused, he climbed to his feet and hovered by the doorway, waiting for further instructions.

"Now, go to the hallway," Kat told him. "Wait by the door. If something happens to me, run outside to Eric's house and tell him to call Carl. Understand?"

James's reply was a scared and silent yes.

"Good. Now go."

Kat waited until James was gone before pointing the gun in Glenn Stewart's direction. "What the hell were you doing with him?"

"I know you mistrust me," Glenn said. "But he was perfectly safe. In fact, he's safer here than he is out there."

"What's out there?"

"Danger, of course. A world of danger."

"Is that why you don't go outside?"

"Partly," Glenn said. "But looking like I do, I suspect most people would prefer me to stay inside."

It was too dark to see him clearly. All Kat could make out was a silhouette, shoulder rising and falling as he continued to pet the ferret.

"You don't look too unusual to me," Kat said.

She detected a note of amusement in Glenn's response. "You're very kind. But you've yet to see the full picture."

He stood. Kat took a cautious step backward and aimed the Glock at Glenn's chest, prepared to shoot if necessary. But there didn't seem to be a need. All he did was move forward into the light, giving her a clear view of his face.

From the nose down, Mr. Stewart looked normal. Handsome even, with full lips and sharp cheekbones that narrowed to a strong jaw. Above the nose, it was a different story. The left side of his face boasted a thin brow and an eye colored a startling shade of blue. The eye on the right was missing. So was the brow. In their place was a patch of skin as smooth as wet clay. Rising above it was a thick, pale scar that sliced through his forehead and into his hair.

Kat kept her gaze steady. "What happened to you in Vietnam?"

"My Lai happened. I assume you've heard of it."

Kat certainly had. In March 1968, hundreds of civilians were killed by a unit of the United States Army. The victims were unarmed. Many of them were women and children.

"Some people think you shot yourself," she said. "That true?"

"I don't suppose it really matters now. The important thing is what happened to me afterward."

"*Mặt trăng vinh quang*," Kat replied. "You learned about that in the hospital?"

Glenn nodded. "It opened my eyes to so many things, even though it's a very misunderstood religion."

"I can see how people wouldn't get that whole human sacrifice part. Is it true?"

Glenn's voice was pained as he said, "It is, I'm afraid. There are some who used to practice such things. But I'm not one of them. Most good followers aren't."

"Then what do you believe in?"

"That life is sacred. Including my own. That one needs to find peace with himself before he can find peace with the world. I'm still working on that, even after all these years. And that no matter what we do, bad things exist in the outside world. I should know. I've seen them."

"In Vietnam?" Kat offered.

"Yes. There, of course. But also here, in Perry Hollow. On this very street, in fact."

"Did you see anything the night Charlie Olmstead was taken?"

"I did," Glenn said. "I lied to your father about it. Not because I wanted to, mind you. I needed to. For the sake of everyone on this street."

"What did you see?"

"Sit down," Glenn said. "And I'll tell you."

It felt weird having a brother again. Good but weird—like a recurring daydream you can't believe is actually coming true. Eric couldn't stop grinning. And crying. He felt overjoyed, despondent, thrilled, and subdued all at once.

"I don't know what to talk about," Eric said. "I don't know where to start."

"Family," Charlie suggested. "Are you married? Do you have kids?"

"Divorced. No kids. You?"

"Divorced. A daughter, although it's been a while since I've seen her."

They went back and forth like that, swapping forty-two years' worth of information about jobs, homes, likes and dislikes. Eric learned that Charlie was a mechanic in Chester County who liked country music, Harleys, and a good bourbon. He told Charlie about the highs and lows of a writer's life, about living in Brooklyn, about the famous people he's met. They learned their differences—Charlie was an ace centerfielder in high school, Eric not an ace at any sport—and their similarities, such as the fact that both of their ex-wives were named Laura.

Then the topic turned to Eric's family, whom Charlie insisted on calling Ken and Maggie Olmstead.

"I heard Maggie passed away," he said. "How did she die?"

The mention of his mother made Eric sad again. She would have loved to have witnessed this conversation. The fact that it was her final wish made it all the more poignant.

"Cancer. Ovarian."

"I'm sorry to hear that. From what I remember, she was a great lady."

"What else do you remember about living here?" Eric asked.

Charlie mulled the question over, hand absently stroking his chin. Watching him, Eric saw traces of the boy he had known only through decades-old photographs. Same awkward ears. Same sad eyes. Same crooked smile when he said, "I remember Mrs. Santangelo's cookies. Are the Santangelos still around?"

"They are," Eric said. "So is Glenn Stewart."

"The Clarks are long gone, right?"

"Of course. But you—"

Eric halted when he realized Charlie still didn't know that Mort and Ruth Clark had been his maternal grandparents. He didn't have the heart to tell him just yet. They'd have plenty of time to discuss things that happened before he was born and after he left.

"Did you know," Charlie said, "that the Clarks had a bomb shelter built under their yard?"

"Really?"

"That's another thing I remember. I used to play in it when I was a kid. And the falls. Jesus, when I was ten, I loved walking out on that bridge and seeing Sunset Falls."

"It's still there," Eric said. "The bridge, too."

Charlie's face lit up. "We should go there."

"Now?"

"Yeah. Come on."

He was off the couch in a flash, heading toward the back door. Eric followed, at first with reluctance. But his attitude began to change once they were in the backyard, rushing through the grass. By the time they crossed onto Glenn Stewart's property, he was having a blast.

Charlie was faster than he was, practically sprinting across Mr. Stewart's yard. He seemed to know so much more than Eric did about the area, from the Clarks' bomb shelter to the place where Glenn buried his pets. ("I'd spy on him when he did it," Charlie said as they passed the spot Eric had dug up the night before.)

Running behind him, struggling to keep up, Eric felt annoyance and admiration in equal measure. He was jealous of what Charlie knew and glad he was sharing it with him. He was in awe of him and just a little bit intimidated. In short, for the first time in his life, he knew how it felt to have a big brother.

They hurried around the far side of Glenn Stewart's house, the roar of Sunset Falls growing louder. Eric glimpsed it through the trees, a heady tumble of whiteness stretching three stories.

"I'd go this way to sneak out to the falls," Charlie told him as they emerged at the end of the cul-de-sac and headed through the trees. "That way no one could see me."

Since Eric had traversed the grown-over path earlier in the week, he went first. Charlie followed close behind, peeking over his shoulder for glimpses of the waterfall itself.

"There's the bridge," he said excitedly. "I figured they'd have torn it down by now."

"They're going to soon," Eric said.

His brother slapped him on the shoulder. "So that's all the more reason to take one last trip across it."

They had come to the sawhorse blocking the bridge. Charlie leaped over it. Eric ducked beneath it. Yet another difference between the two.

"Be careful," Eric warned as Charlie hurried onto the bridge itself. "It's not stable."

Charlie heeded the warning, stepping carefully onto the bridge's first few boards. "Can it hold two people?"

"Two, yes," Eric said. "Three, probably not."

By that time, he was on the bridge, too, trying to follow Charlie's footsteps. He stepped over the gaping hole that Kat fell through a few days earlier. Some of the other planks creaked beneath his weight, and the entire bridge shimmied slightly, but overall, it seemed stable. At least stable enough to hold them up as they stood shoulder to shoulder against the railing, watching the inexorable flow of the creek.

"You having fun?" Charlie asked.

"Yeah," Eric said. He was having the time of his life. "You?"

Charlie put his arm across Eric's shoulders. "Definitely, brother."

Noise suddenly rose from the woods to the right—the sound of twigs snapping and branches being whipped out of the way. It was followed by footsteps, loud and fast on the dirt path leading to the bridge. Someone was running toward them.

Eric turned toward the sound, seeing Kat Campbell burst through the trees. She had her gun out, raising it once she reached the cusp of the bridge.

"Charlie, put your hands in the air and back away from him."

But it was Eric who lifted his hands, holding them waist-high in front of him. "Kat? What are you doing?"

"Get off the bridge, Eric."

"I don't understand. What's happening?"

Eric saw a blur of motion on the edge of his vision, as

quick as a lightning strike. He felt one of his brother's arms wrap around his neck, pulling him backward, choking the air out of him. Then he was slammed against the side of the bridge, the railing pushing into his ribcage. Charlie was behind him now, holding him in place.

"I'll kill him if you come any closer!" he yelled to Kat. "You hear me? I'll toss him off this bridge just like I did when he was a baby."

THIRTY-FIVE

Nick rode in Ken Olmstead's rig, although not by choice. When Ken got word that Charlie was back in Perry Hollow, he immediately started to leave, giving Nick only enough time to grab his cane and limp into the truck with him. He left his car on the entrance ramp, where it would no doubt be hit, scratched, or otherwise impounded.

Whatever damage occurred, Nick knew it would be worth it. Because as he drove, Ken told him everything that happened on July 20, 1969.

"It was supposed to be a quiet night," he said. "After dinner, Maggie put the baby to bed and then went to sleep herself. Her naps had become a nightly ritual."

"Where was Charlie?" Nick asked.

"He was also napping. At least he was supposed to be. Maggie and I had already agreed to let him stay up to watch the moon landing. We knew history was going to be made that night. Instead, everything fell apart."

According to Ken, the beginning of the end was signaled by a tentative knock on the door a little after 10:00 P.M. Ken answered it quickly, fearful the sound would wake up everyone else. He assumed it was Mort and Ruth Clark, whose TV always seemed to be on the fritz, asking to watch the moon walk with him. But when Ken opened the door, he saw not his neighbors but a man standing on the front porch.

A man he knew.

A man he hadn't seen in more than ten years.

"It was Craig Brewster," Ken said. "He told me he wanted to see his son. Back when Jennifer died, he told Maggie and me that he'd never bother us. But there he was, standing at my door begging to see Charlie."

"But why then?" Nick asked. "After all that time?"

"His father had died a few days before, and ever since then he couldn't stop thinking that he had made a huge mistake leaving Jennifer and letting us take Charlie. He said he came to town with the intention of telling Mort and Ruth Clark everything, but he couldn't get the nerve to actually ring their doorbell."

Ken said he listened, patiently at first. He let Craig tell him about his job guarding juvenile offenders. About his rapport with them. About how he wanted to open a camp for them using land he had just inherited.

"He said he was a changed man. But that he was lonely. Said that there was a hole in his life that he never noticed until his dad passed away."

"And he thought being Charlie's dad could fill that void?" Nick asked.

"He said he didn't want to take Charlie away from us," Ken continued. "He just wanted to meet him and see how he had grown. The problem was that Charlie didn't know who he was."

The truck, which had been traveling at top speed, slowed as it started the climb up the hill they had just come down only minutes before.

"You never told Charlie about him or his real mother?" Nick said.

"We couldn't tell anyone. Not with Charlie's real grandparents still living across the street. Everyone, Charlie included, needed to think he was our boy. Otherwise, it would have been a disaster. The Clarks could have sued for custody. The police could have arrested us for kidnapping. We had no real right to raise him. It didn't matter we were the only ones who had cared for him in the days after his birth. The law was the law, and what we had done was illegal."

"How did Craig take the news?"

"Not good," Ken said. "He kept telling me Charlie had a right to meet his real father. That he needed to know he wasn't our son. His voice got louder. So loud I expected him to wake the whole house."

Instead, Ken said, he only woke Charlie.

"His bedroom was located directly above us. He might not have heard every word, but he heard enough. I yanked Craig outside, telling him to keep his voice down. While we were out there, Charlie must have crept downstairs and slipped out the back door."

"He was running away?" Nick said.

"Not quite," Ken answered. "He had the baby with him."

Ten minutes later, as Ken still argued on the front porch with Craig, they heard the sound of running cut through the rainy night. It was Glenn Stewart, bursting out of the darkness with Eric in his arms.

"I grabbed the baby. He was soaking wet. When I asked Glenn what happened, he told me Eric had almost drowned."

"Drowned?" Nick replied. "In the creek?"

"I looked at Glenn and saw he was drenched, too," Ken said. "And that's when I knew what had happened. I knew Charlie had done it before Glenn even told me."

"How?"

"Because he had tried it before. In May. That time it was in the bathtub. Only I thought Maggie was responsible. I blamed her for everything."

They had reached the top of the hill and were now starting their descent. The truck groaned from the sudden acceleration, the noise almost drowning out Ken Olmstead. It didn't help matters that Ken spoke softly, with a hollow tone to his voice. He sounded to Nick like a man who was dead inside.

"I went inside and looked in Charlie's room, hoping that Glenn was lying and I'd find him there fast asleep. But he was gone, just as I knew he would be. So I went downstairs, grabbed a flashlight, and headed to where I thought he'd be hiding."

"Where was that?" Nick asked.

"The bomb shelter Norm Clark had built under his backyard. Charlie loved going down there and playing. Soldier. Astronaut. Alien invader. It was like his own private hideout."

"And was he there?"

"He was," Ken said. "Craig went with me, and I had him hold Eric while I went down there. I found him sitting on one of the cots Mort had put down there, his legs swinging beneath him. When I shined the flashlight in his face, Charlie didn't even flinch. I asked him if he dropped Eric into the creek. He told me yes. I told him that Eric could have drowned. Or worse, gone over the falls."

"What did Charlie say?"

"He said, 'I know. That's why I did it.'"

Nick closed his eyes and clutched his stomach. The thought of a little boy—a ten-year-old, for Christ's sake—purposely trying to kill his infant brother repulsed him. When his sister was murdered, it felt like a part of him had died with her. He couldn't imagine someone intentionally causing such pain.

"I asked him why he did it," Ken said. "Charlie told me it was because Maggie and I wanted to get rid of him."

"And did you?" Nick asked.

"Of course not. I loved Charlie with all my heart. But pointing that flashlight at his blank face, I didn't feel any of it. Instead, I felt anger and guilt and fear. Especially fear. I looked into Charlie's eyes and I saw nothing. No remorse. No emotion at all. It felt like I was looking at a monster. He had tried to drown Eric twice. I have no idea why. I didn't back then and I don't now. But I knew he would try again. I was certain of it."

According to Ken, he climbed out of the bomb shelter, leaving Charlie below. Taking the baby from Craig's arms, he told him what Charlie had said and how he had looked. Ken admitted that he was afraid of him. It sounded absurd. A grown man terrified of his son. But Ken was deeply terrified. And he didn't know what to do.

"I couldn't call the police. Not after Charlie had learned that me and Maggie weren't his real parents. They'd charge us with kidnapping and possibly take Eric away from us, too. But I couldn't take Charlie back home and hope it never happened again. That's when Craig said he would take him."

"Where?"

"To live with him," Ken replied. "He said he'd be able to whip Charlie into shape. Just like he did with the boys at the detention center. Just like he planned to do at the camp he was going to build."

Out his window, Nick saw a sign telling them they were leaving Mercerville. It went by in a blur. They were now back within Perry Hollow's borders.

"I didn't like the idea," Ken continued. "I knew Maggie would like it even less. She was fiercely devoted to Charlie, even though she often didn't show it. I remembered how tender she had been with him in the hours after his birth, how she treated him like he was her own. She had never stopped. In her mind, Charlie *was* her son. But he wasn't. Eric was our real son. Charlie was just a baby we had taken in out of pity. A favor for friends. Now one of those friends was offering to take him back."

"So you accepted?" Nick said.

"It hurt to do it. It hurt so bad. But I needed to think of Eric. I needed to keep him safe. And giving Charlie to Craig seemed like the best option."

"But you knew Maggie would try to find him if you did."

Eyes still fixed on the road, Ken gave a little nod. "The only way she'd let Charlie go, is if she thought he was dead."

"So you went back to the house and got Charlie's bike?"

"I did," Ken said. "I carried it to the bridge and tossed it into the creek. I was hoping the police would see it and assume Charlie had fallen in and gone over the falls."

For the most part, his plan had worked. But the lack of tire tracks didn't go unnoticed by Deputy Owen Peale, who later told Maggie Olmstead. That, in turn, set off decades of searching for a son who was never really missing in the first place.

"Once the bike was in the water," Ken continued, "Craig climbed into the bomb shelter and introduced himself to Charlie. I took Eric back to the house. I never saw Charlie again."

"When they were gone, that's when you called the police?" Nick asked.

"I told them Charlie was missing. Then I woke Mort and Ruth Clark to help with the search. No one suspected a thing. At that moment, Charlie was officially gone."

Ken sobbed. It rose from the depths of his chest and left his body in a burst of anguish. "And I killed him. I killed one of my sons to save the other."

"You did the right thing by getting Charlie away from Eric," Nick said. "But you should have told the police the truth."

Because Charlie was indeed a monster. Although he was whisked away from his baby brother, he had tried to kill again. And he succeeded. With Dennis Kepner, who lived four doors down from him. With Noah Pierce, whom he most likely lured into an abandoned mill using Dennis's toy rocket. With Dwight Halsey, his cabin mate at Camp Crescent. With Frankie Pulaski and Bucky Mason, when he lived next to the Mason family in Centralia.

Charlie Olmstead, later known as Kevin Brewster, had killed them all.

Nick looked out his window and saw the glistening expanse of Lake Squall up ahead. They'd be in town soon, speeding through the streets on the way to the cul-de-sac. He hoped it wasn't too late.

THIRTY-SIX

Kat stepped onto the bridge, not knowing if it could hold all three of them. She moved cautiously, trying to see if she could get a good shot at Charlie without putting Eric at risk. It was impossible. Charlie still had him in a choke hold as he leaned against the railing. Eric struggled, using both hands in a vain attempt to pry the arm from around his neck. It did no good. Charlie was bigger and stronger. And, Kat knew, he was serious about throwing Eric into the water.

He had done it before.

Glenn Stewart saw it happen from the widow's walk on the roof of his house. Charlie sneaking through his backyard with a wailing infant Eric in his arms. Charlie cutting through the trees on his way to the creek. Charlie standing on the bridge. Holding his baby brother over the water. Letting go and watching the splash. Glenn saw it all.

Eric would have died if his neighbor hadn't been there. But Glenn told Kat he acted quickly. Running down the bank, he had just enough time to see Charlie scurry away. Then he was at the water's edge, taking a deep breath and diving in.

Glenn said he then hurried to the Olmstead house after pulling Eric from the creek. Pressing the drenched infant into his father's arms, he recounted all that he had seen. Then he went home and remained silent, even when Maggie Olmstead knocked on his door to tell him Charlie was missing. The next day, when Kat's father and Deputy Peale came by, he lied and said he was asleep. During the news stories and search parties, he didn't say a word. And decades after that, when the story of Charlie Olmstead passed into Perry Hollow legend, he kept quiet.

"But did you know what really happened to Charlie?" Kat had asked him.

"No," Glenn replied. "I didn't care. All I knew was that he was gone, and that all of us were better off because of it."

Kat took a second step onto the bridge. It responded with an ominous groan rising from beneath her.

"Let him go, Charlie. He's not the one you want to hurt. Not now and certainly not back then."

"I didn't want to do it," Charlie said as he tightened his grip around Eric's neck. "But I had to. They were going to get rid of me."

"Did your father tell you that?"

"No. But I could sense it. They didn't need me anymore. Not with Eric around."

Kat took another step, heard another groan of the bridge.

"So you thought that if you got rid of Eric, the Olmsteads would keep you?"

Charlie peered at her from over Eric's shoulder. His eyes were like currants, dark and emotionless. "Yes."

Kat's fourth step set off another round of bridge noises. It wasn't going to hold them much longer. A few feet ahead of her was the gap she fell through on Wednesday. She remembered the feel of the surrounding boards as she slipped between them, the coldness on her foot as it hit the water.

"What about the other boys?" she asked Charlie. "Why did you kill them?"

"I didn't plan to kill Dennis. It just happened."

"How?"

"He had a model rocket," Charlie said, as if that explained everything. "He showed it off at school the day *Apollo 12* landed. I wanted it. We met in the park after school and I took it."

A quick shiver rushed up Kat's spine as she thought of James, safe and sound in Glenn Stewart's house. Her son had done the same thing, only over something as silly as a school lunch. She recalled Jocelyn Miller's words: *Kids don't understand the consequences of their actions.*

"He followed me home," Charlie continued. "He kept demanding the rocket back. We fought in the backyard. I hit him with it. Hard. I didn't want to kill him. I just wanted him to let me keep the rocket."

"And the others?" Kat asked. "Were they accidents?"

"They were in the wrong place at the wrong time. Except for Dwight. He had it coming."

Kat didn't ask why he only killed during moon landings. The answer was clear. He chose them because the first moon landing was the moment when Charlie Olmstead died and Kevin Brewster was born. Each Apollo mission after that was a chance for him to re-create that night, to kill off another child just as he had been killed.

"Did you know Eric was still alive?"

"I assumed he was," Charlie said. "I just didn't know where to find him."

"But when you found out he was in Perry Hollow, you needed to come back and finish what you started in 1969?"

Charlie offered a cruel smile. "Something like that, yeah."

"I'm not going to let that happen."

Kat took another step. Charlie reacted by tightening his arm around Eric's neck and slamming him against the railing.

The wood there broke free, snapping like a twig. Chunks of it fell into the creek and began their quick slide toward the top of Sunset Falls.

All that movement made the bridge tilt noticeably, its support beams creaking under the strain. Eric and Charlie remained standing, although barely. Clutching each other, they teetered on the edge of the bridge, bodies swaying to keep their balance.

Kat ran toward them, gun still raised. When she reached the gap in the bridge, she leaped over it, landing hard on the plank next to it.

It broke immediately upon impact.

She yelped, a blast of surprise that echoed off the trees on the other end of the bridge. Her arms flew outward as she dropped through the newly expanded gap. The Glock escaped her grip, landing on the bridge, and sliding in Charlie's direction.

Kat caught herself midfall, legs dangling beneath the bridge, feet once again swishing through the water. From her new vantage point, she could see the gun sitting a few feet away. Then she saw a pair of hands pick it up and point it at her head.

The hands belonged to Charlie. He now had her Glock. And he was going to kill her.

Eric saw everything and understood none of it. The action appeared to him in quick flashes that left no time for comprehension. First there was the railing, splintering apart at his hips. Then water, viewed from above, rushing under the bridge. When Charlie's arm left his neck and traveled to his shoulder, it left Eric not knowing if he was trying to toss him into the drink or keep him out of it. He saw Kat running. Then she was falling, letting go of the gun. Soon Charlie was scooping it up, aiming it at her, trigger finger twitching.

Now Eric needed to stop him. It was the only thing he understood.

"Don't hurt her!" he yelled. "I'm the one you want."

Charlie whipped the gun away from Kat and aimed it at his chest. Eric raised his hands.

"You want to kill me? Fine. But let her go. Please."

He didn't think about what he was saying. There was no noticeable transmission from brain to tongue. Eric just wanted to keep Kat safe, and the only way he knew how was to use the very things he made his living with—words.

"She's done nothing to you," he said. "She was only helping me try to find you. That's all."

Charlie looked at him with a mix of panic and despair. Eric imagined he had the same look on his face when he realized Dennis Kepner was dead. Maybe after he killed all of the boys.

"I just want things to be the way they were," he said. "When I lived here. Before you were born. I was so happy then."

"You still can be," Eric told him. "You can live here with Dad. I'll go away. It will be like I was never born. You just need to let Kat go."

He prayed that Charlie would believe him. That he wouldn't realize there would be no happy ending once they stepped off that bridge.

If that ever happened. Eric wasn't sure it would. Charlie seemed torn, moving the gun between him and Kat, who still clung to the bridge in an attempt to keep herself from slipping into the water.

340 | TODD RITTER

"Let me help her up," Eric said. "I'll help her up, put her on land, and then it'll be just you and me. Then you can finish what you started all those years ago. I'll be gone and you'll be happy."

Charlie thought it over, still aiming the gun at Kat. Then Eric. Then back again. Finally, he settled on Eric, pointing the Glock at his heart. Eric knew he was too close to miss. The bullet would tear through his chest like a rocket. If he was lucky, he'd die instantly. If he wasn't, then he'd go slowly, bleeding out on this godforsaken bridge.

Eric pleaded with him. "Let her go first. If you're going to do it, let Kat go."

As he spoke, a deep rumble rose to his left. It came from the cul-de-sac, the sound of an engine cutting through the wall of trees along the creek. Eric knew the sound. It was his dad's rig, roaring toward them. Charlie heard it, too, and faced the noise.

Eric took advantage of the distraction and ran forward, tackling Charlie. Caught by surprise, Charlie flew backward, gun spiraling from his fingers and skittering across the bridge. Then they tumbled together, falling to the bridge's surface.

Their landing jarred the entire span, which seemed to spring to life, shaking in all directions. Lying on top of Charlie, Eric felt the bridge tilt wildly to the left. Then it listed right, making them slide with it.

Beneath them, a support beam buckled under the pressure. Eric heard it snap—a panic-inducing *crack* that briefly blocked out all other sounds. The truck. The falls. Kat's labored breathing as she managed to climb back onto the bridge.

Then, just as Eric feared it would, the bridge began to collapse all around them.

THIRTY-SEVEN

Nick held on tight as the truck made a left turn onto the cul-de-sac. They were going so fast and Ken had jerked the wheel so sharply that Nick thought the truck would tip over. He felt his side of the vehicle lift off the road, rising with the turn. But they made it through unscathed, the truck settling back down on all tires. Once out of the turn, Ken jacked up the speed again, shooting like a bullet down the cul-de-sac.

Looking out the windows, Nick saw they were zipping past Ken's old house. In front of Glenn Stewart's place, he spotted James standing next to a man with a smooth patch of skin where an eye should have been.

Seeing the rig, the man pointed to the path at the end of the cul-de-sac. Ken nodded and stepped on the gas pedal.

"Brace yourself," he said.

Nick shrank in his seat, covering his face with his arms. Even then, he could see they were approaching the wall of trees at a furious pace. The only clear spot was the meager path that led to the bridge and the stream. That's what Ken was aiming for, and Nick had no clue if they were going to make it.

The bounce over the curb threw him up from his seat. He hovered a fraction of a second before being yanked back by the seat belt. In front of him, branches slapped the windshield as the truck rushed through the trees. One—as thick and strong as a Louisville Slugger—shattered the glass, splintering it until it resembled a spiderweb made of ice. To Nick's right, a tree took out the side mirror before scraping along the door.

Ken slammed on the brakes as the trees cleared. The truck skidded forward, knocking against one tree and then another, before coming to a stop at the edge of the bridge.

Only the bridge, Nick saw, was gone.

What remained of it was now breaking apart in the creek. He saw Kat on her hands and knees, holding on as the bridge floor rocked on the water's surface. Just beyond her, Eric and Charlie Olmstead lay next to each other, trying to do the same.

Charlie managed to stand, somehow keeping his balance. Eric couldn't. He tried to get up, reaching out to his brother for balance. Charlie shrugged him off before pushing him away. Eric rolled across the bridge and fell off the side that faced the falls. Then he vanished, disappearing under the water.

"Eric! No!"

Ken unsnapped his seat belt, threw open the door, and jumped out. Nick did the same, climbing out as fast as he could. When he was on land, he saw Ken run to the edge of the creek, about to dive in.

Someone else beat him to it.

Glenn Stewart had skipped the path and headed straight through the trees. As he moved, he shouted instructions to Ken.

"Find something for us to grab on to. Form a chain and stretch it out over the water. I'll get Eric."

Then, once he reached the water's edge, he dove in.

Tumbling underwater, Eric knew he was about to die. He tried to fight the current and break the surface, but the water was too strong. The pull of the falls kept him under, tugging him along the bottom of the creek. Somersaulting in the depths, he felt rocks scrape his back, his face, his hands.

He saw the remnants of the bridge drifting away from him. Pilings crisscrossed in the water. Beams jutted out of it. Then they were gone, torn from his vision as he was flipped over once again.

He shut his eyes before feeling another impact with the creek bed. The force of the blow knocked the air out of him and snapped his mouth open. Water filled his throat, choking him. The pressure in his lungs was immediate, like a pair of hands inside his chest pushing outward.

I'm dying, he thought.

He knew it without a doubt. If drowning didn't kill him, the drop over the falls would. He couldn't decide which was worse.

Just when he had settled on the plummet from the falls—it was quicker, he reasoned, with less agony—something entered the water to his right.

Or his left.

He was so confused he couldn't tell.

Eric also didn't know what the thing sinking next to him was. When he opened his eyes, he saw only pebbles studding the bottom of the creek. Then the bridge, now even farther away. Then a face.

Glenn Stewart's face. Coming toward him.

His neighbor stretched out his arms, grasping at Eric's shirt. He caught the collar and tugged Eric toward him. Soon their heads were above the surface. Eric opened his mouth and vomited out the swill that had collected there. Then he inhaled—a blessed, full-bodied breath that calmed his inflamed lungs.

Glenn still had a firm grip on his arm and was pulling him to shore. Looking to his left, Eric saw the mouth of the falls about ten yards away, still trying to yank him toward it. The current was strong, but Glenn was stronger. He climbed to his feet, trudging to land and dragging Eric with him.

His father was on the bank, lying on his stomach. In his hand was Nick Donnelly's cane, which he thrust over the water. Holding on to his legs was Nick himself. When Glenn grabbed the cane, the other two pulled, forming a human chain whose only goal was to get Eric out of the water and away from the falls.

Reaching shore, Eric collapsed in the mud and coughed up more water. Ken lay next to him, and he wrapped his arms around him. It was the first time he had hugged his father in years, maybe decades. It felt good.

Flat on his back, Eric looked at those around him. There was his dad, of course. And Glenn Stewart, having saved his life a second time. Nick, however, was gone.

Eric sat up in time to see him scurrying along the bank to the remains of the bridge. His gaze swept across the creek to the pile of wood slowly breaking apart in the middle of it. Kat was still there, trying to gain her balance on a patch of the bridge that had broken free.

With her was Charlie, crouched on the other side.

"Kat," Eric said. "We need to help Kat."

The bridge had become a raft. And not a sturdy one, either. Roughly ten square feet, it rocked unsteadily, water sloshing across its surface. Kat rose to a half crouch, bending her legs and keeping her balance with her hands. Across from her, Charlie

Olmstead was getting into the same position. The Glock sat between them.

When Charlie lunged for the gun, Kat did the same.

They connected in the center of the raft, Charlie pushing her backward. Kat fell, the planks of the bridge hard against her back. Her head hung over the water, hair swirling in the current. When Charlie charged again, she twisted on to her side and curled into a ball as he kicked her in the stomach.

The pain was excruciating. Centered at her abdomen, it spread outward like wildfire, consuming her whole body. When Charlie kicked her again, it hurt so bad that it blacked out her thoughts. Everything going through her head vanished, replaced by pain.

She was vaguely aware of Nick and Eric nearby, the pair of them trying to reach her. It was impossible. She and Charlie were in the middle of the creek, too far to reach without diving in. And that was risky.

Too risky.

Yet they still tried. Eric scrambled out to one of the shattered beams. He wrapped his legs around it while grasping at another one a few feet away. He couldn't reach it.

But Charlie saw the attempt, and it stopped him from landing a third blow to Kat's stomach. He paused, with his leg reared back. It wasn't long—a mere blip of a second—but it was enough time to let Kat grab his leg and pull it out from under him.

Charlie yelped before he toppled backward, just as Kat had done. The impact set the raft in motion. Kat felt it catch the current and start to drift. Soon it was spinning across the water's surface like a rudderless boat.

She knew she needed to swim for it. But she couldn't leave Charlie alone with the gun. He'd pick her off in the water as soon as he got the chance. So she scrambled on top of him, even though her body was screaming in pain. Straddling his chest, she squeezed her legs in an attempt to keep Charlie's arms pinned to his sides. He grunted under her weight as she reared back and punched him in the jaw.

"That's for Dennis Kepner's mom."

She clocked him again. She couldn't stop herself. Thinking about all the pain he had caused kept her swinging.

"And Noah Pierce's."

Another punch. This time in the nose. Kat saw blood spurt out from beneath her fist.

"And Dwight Halsey's."

Two more.

"And Frankie Pulaski. And Bucky Mason."

Kat was crying now. She didn't know how long it had been going on. Maybe as late as the last punch. Probably as early as the first. She let the tears flow. If not for her, then for all those mothers who lost sons at Charlie's hands.

She stood. It wasn't hard. She used Charlie's body as leverage to balance herself. Then she kicked him in the stomach, just as hard as he had kicked her.

"And that's for Maggie. Who never stopped loving you and never stopped looking for you. All that hope. All that love. You didn't deserve it."

The raft had gained speed, heading inexorably toward the falls. Kat looked to the horizon, trying to gauge how much distance there was between them and the waterfall. She guessed fifteen yards. Maybe less. Not much distance at all, especially when each second meant they were one foot closer to the falls.

Kat heard Nick and Eric behind her, begging her to leave the raft. "Swim for it!" they yelled. "Just jump!"

She knew it was her only option. She took a step back, preparing to leap.

A familiar click, sharp and metallic, stopped her. It was the sound of her Glock. Charlie had managed to grab it while she was kicking him. Now it was locked, loaded, and aimed right at her.

Charlie sat up, holding the gun with trembling arms. She was trapped, with the waterfall now only about eleven yards away.

"You can go ahead and shoot, Charlie," she said. "But it won't matter. You'll still be just as dead as I am."

It took one glance at the falls for Charlie to know what she meant. Even if he shot her, he couldn't get away from the current's grip. For the first time, Kat saw emotion in his cold, dark eyes. It was fear. The deep, bone-chilling fear of someone who knew he was out of options.

Ten yards.

"What do we do?" Charlie asked as he climbed to his knees. "How do we keep from going over?"

Kat eyed the Glock. "You put that thing down and we work together."

"How?"

"Drop the gun first."

Charlie let go of the Glock. It hit the raft and bounced off, cartwheeling into the water. "Now tell me how."

Nine.

Kat pointed to the oak branch that reached over the creek about five feet from the water's surface. She had noticed it on Wednesday when she was on the bridge with Eric, identifying it as a person's last chance to escape the falls. She had no idea then that it would be her only hope now.

Eight.

"When we get to that branch, we need to reach up and grab it. Then we slide over onto land."

Kat didn't know if her plan would actually work. There was no way to know if the branch would support both of them until they were hanging from it. But they had to try.

Seven.

She held out her hand. Charlie took it and let her pull him to his feet. They both faced the falls and, standing shoulder to shoulder, prepared to grab the swiftly approaching branch.

Kat raised her hands, holding them over her head. Charlie did the same.

Six.

"Why are you helping me?" he asked.

"Because your mother would have wanted me to."

"Even after everything I've done?"

"Yes," Kat said. "Even after all of that."

Five.

Beneath them, the raft started to bounce. They were running against the rocks on the creek bed as the water got shallower ahead of the falls. The raft was close enough for Kat to see the pool of water thirty feet below. Once again, the rocks there made her think of teeth—sharp, deadly ones ready to gnaw them to pieces.

Four.

"Did Maggie really look for me?" Charlie asked.

Kat nodded. "Her entire life."

Three.

"And did she love me?"

"Yes," Kat said. "More than anything."

Two.

They hit the patch of white water just before the plunge. It jostled the raft, breaking it into pieces. Several planks ripped free and spun over the edge.

One.

The oak branch was now right above Kat. She jumped, catching it with her right hand. Her lower body continued moving forward, tugging her arm until she heard a sickening pop. Her shoulder dislocating. She screamed through the pain, stretching her left hand until it also had a firm grip on the branch.

Below her, Charlie was still on the raft. He had lowered his arms, not even attempting to grab the branch with her.

"What are you doing?" Kat yelled. "Jump! It's not too late!"

But it was. The raft had sailed under the branch, leaving anyone on it without a means of escape. Kat knew it. And Charlie did, too.

"You were right," he called back. "I didn't deserve it."

Kat pulled herself onto the branch. It hurt like hell, and her right arm was pretty much useless, but she managed. Once there, she wrapped her arms and legs around it.

She watched the raft reach the lip of the falls, where it splintered apart. Charlie sank into the water, not even fighting the current as it overtook him. He flopped against the rocks like a rag doll, head lolling, arms and legs splayed.

Then, more than forty-two years after he first vanished, Sunset Falls finally claimed Charlie Olmstead.

THIRTY-EIGHT

In addition to a dislocated shoulder and some bumps and bruises, Kat also suffered three cracked ribs, most likely when she was kicked in the stomach. She didn't mind. It could have been a lot worse. She could have ended up like Charlie. Still, her injuries were enough to put her in the hospital overnight, which is where she learned that Dennis Kepner's body had been found.

The bearer of the news was Tony Vasquez, one of the half-dozen people crammed into her room. James was there, of course, along with Lou, Carl, and Nick. Even Glenn Stewart had made an appearance, although he stood silently against the wall, away from the crush of people surrounding Kat's bed. Still, it was good to see him there. Kat hoped she'd be seeing more of him.

"They dug up the yard where Craig Brewster used to live in Fairmount," Tony said. "They found Dennis's remains a few feet beneath the garden. He had been there all that time."

That left three of the missing boys unaccounted for— Dwight Halsey, Frankie Pulaski, and Bucky Mason. No one had high hopes of finding them. Dwight's body could be any-where in the woods surrounding Camp Crescent. As for Frankie and Bucky, there wasn't any way to search the fiery mine shafts that ran beneath Centralia.

"But their families know what happened to them," Nick added. "Now they have closure. They can finally move on."

It wasn't the happiest of news, but it would suffice. They

knew when they started the investigation that there wouldn't be any happy endings for those boys. They were right. But finding out the truth about what happened was a resolution they could be proud of.

From what they pieced together, Charlie had indeed killed Dennis Kepner over a toy rocket. He then used it to lure Noah Pierce into the gristmill at Lasher Mill State Park, where he strangled the boy before dumping him in the water below. If Dennis was an accident, Noah was a thrill kill—Charlie's first. But there were others, including Frankie Pulaski and Bucky Mason, both apparently shoved into the same sinkhole a few months apart.

That left Dwight Halsey, who shared a cabin with Charlie at Camp Crescent.

"Craig Brewster told me that Dwight had been in a fight before he vanished," Nick said. "Most likely, the person he fought with was Charlie, who got his revenge later that night."

"What about Craig?" Kat asked. "Were you able to talk to him?"

Tony shook his head. "He died. As soon as Nick and Charlie left the hospital, he started crashing. He didn't last an hour."

Kat's heart sank at the news. She didn't know Craig Brewster, so she couldn't mourn his passing. But she *was* sad that they would never find out if Craig suspected Charlie of killing those boys. She wanted to think he didn't, but she knew better. Craig certainly would have realized what was going on, especially as more kids around him vanished. It was too much to ignore.

"So that's that," she said. "Anything else to discuss?"

Carl stepped forward. "Two things, Chief. We found Charlie Olmstead at the bottom of Sunset Falls."

"Dead, I assume?"

"Yes. Dead and washed up onshore."

She closed her eyes and exhaled deeply. She didn't quite know how to feel about that. Even knowing all the horrible things he had done, a small part of her still thought of Charlie Olmstead as an innocent victim. The result was a mixture of remorse and relief.

"What's the second thing?" she asked.

"Burt Hammond stopped by the station."

"What did he want?"

"It was just some budget stuff." Carl's face broke into a wide, happy grin. "Like what kind of features we want with our new patrol cars."

"Dodge Chargers," Lou said, sounding as excited as a kid at Christmas. "The exact ones you wanted."

Kat pretended to be happy. She even forced a pretty good fake smile. She didn't have the heart to tell them that the cars were really a bribe on Burt Hammond's behalf. He was trying to buy her silence about the home movie Lee Santangelo had made. It wasn't going to work. Once she was released from the hospital, she'd tell Burt to spend the money elsewhere. Then she'd break the news to Carl that his beat-up Crown Vic would have to last another year.

After a few more minutes of happy chitchat, Carl and Lou left the hospital to get back to work. Tony soon followed, saying he needed to deal with Gloria Ambrose, who had found out about Nick's role in the investigation.

"I'm about to get my ass chewed out," he said. "I hope you two are happy."

Nick saluted him. Kat blew him a kiss.

Next to leave was Glenn Stewart, who presented her with

two books. One was *To Kill a Mockingbird*. The other was *Goodnight Moon*. Kat accepted both of them graciously, pleased to see that Glenn at least had a sense of humor about things.

"May you have pleasant dreams and a swift recovery," he said before sweeping out of the room.

That left only James and Nick. James was in an overstuffed chair in the corner, where he had curled up during the crush of visitors. Nick stood at the foot of her bed.

"I guess this wasn't a rousing success for the Sarah Donnelly Foundation," Kat said.

Nick shrugged. "Not really. But we helped people, which is all that matters. And you're still alive, which is the most important thing."

"Yeah, and you didn't have to come to my rescue. I told you I was capable of saving myself."

"Maybe next time," Nick said.

Kat wanted to tell him there wouldn't be a next time and that she was done helping his cause. But she knew it would be a lie. She knew she'd be there whenever Nick needed her and that he would be there for her. It's just the way things worked.

"So what are your plans this weekend?" she asked. "Going to try to dig up another cold case?"

"Actually," Nick said, "I'm taking the weekend off. In fact, I need to go pretty soon. I'm meeting someone for a beer."

Kat gasped in mock surprise. "Are you telling me that you're putting crime fighting aside long enough to go out on a date?"

"It's not a date," Nick protested. "It's just a—"

"No matter what you say, it's a date. And I hope it goes well. But shower first. You smell like a wet ashtray."

"Thanks. I'll consider that."

Nick moved to the door, glancing into the hallway for a

354 | TODD RITTER

moment. When he looked back into the room, Kat saw he had a wry smile on his face.

"You know," he said, "you might want to consider diving into the dating pool yourself."

He slipped out of the room before Kat got the chance to ask him what he meant. But it became clear enough when Eric Olmstead entered a few seconds later, carrying a bouquet of flowers.

"Sorry I couldn't come sooner," he said, setting the flowers next to her bed. "Unlike you, I had to wait in the ER for someone to check my injuries. It took forever, but I got a clean bill of health. As an added bonus, I found some nice pamphlets about rehab places for Dad. We talked about his drinking. He knows he has a problem and now he's getting help."

"How's he doing with the whole Charlie thing?"

"To be honest, he's still pretty shell-shocked."

"What about you?"

Eric sighed. "Other than meeting my long-lost brother, finding out he tried to kill me, and then having him try to kill me a second time, I'm doing great."

"It's a lot to take in," Kat said. "For both of you."

"We'll manage. But it means I'll be staying in town a while longer. At least until Dad gets better and settles into the house."

This surprised Kat. All along, she assumed Eric was going to leave Perry Hollow as soon as the investigation was over. "You're not selling it?"

"No," Eric said. "Dad needs a place to live. I have a house. It makes sense. Besides, it's the least I can do."

He fussed with the flowers a moment, rearranging the stems. "Now that this whole thing is over, I was wondering if you wanted to have dinner sometime. Nothing big. Just a—"

Kat knew where he was going with this. Regretfully, she had to stop him.

"I can't," she said. "Not right now."

It pained her to say it. She liked Eric. She liked being with him. She easily imagined them falling into something similar to what they had in high school. And that was the problem. They weren't in high school anymore. They were older and perhaps wiser, with commitments and lives of their own. Besides, Kat couldn't make time for another man in her life. Not when she was already neglecting James, who would always be her main priority.

She looked to the chair in the corner. James was asleep, eyes closed, chest rising and falling in gentle rhythm. He looked so peaceful like that, so innocent. Watching him sleep, Kat had a hard time believing he was capable of hurting anyone, let alone a classmate.

But he had. Over something as silly as lunch. Now, Kat needed to deal with it. She had to spend time with him, to listen to him, to help him become the responsible adult she needed him to be. If she didn't do that, then James's behavior would get worse. It happened. Charlie Olmstead was proof of that.

"James needs me," she said. "And your father needs you."

Eric did a bad job of trying to hide his disappointment. His smile never wavered, but his eyes dimmed ever-so-slightly.

"So nothing can ever happen between us?" he said.

"Not right now. But maybe someday. Someday soon."

Although they had been speaking in whispers, their voices were loud enough to wake James. He stirred in the chair, eyelids fluttering.

"I'm going to leave you two alone," Eric said, backing away from the bed. "Take care, Kat."

Although Kat hated to see him go, she knew she had made the right decision. There would always be a place in her heart occupied by Eric. But her heart was owned by the boy waking up a few feet away.

"You sleepy, Little Bear?"

When James nodded, she slid to the side of the bed to make room for him. He crawled in with her, burrowing under the covers.

"Am I still grounded?" he asked.

"Yes."

Again, it hurt Kat to say it. But she had to be strong. James did something wrong, and he needed to be taught to never do it again. She knew he'd hate it. She knew he'd be mad at her. But it was for his own good.

"I'm sorry for what I did," he said.

"I know. And you'll do bad things again later. We all do. But you're my son and I love you. I will always love you. And no matter what you do, I'll never let go of you."

Kat closed her eyes and pulled James close. Soon they were both asleep, sleeping soundly. James tossed and turned a bit, uncomfortable in her grip. But true to her word, Kat didn't let go.

ACKNOWLEDGMENTS

Most of the towns and places mentioned in this book are ficti-
tious, including Perry Hollow. The major exception is Centralia, a modern-day ghost town that has passed into Pennsylvania
legend. While it is true that Centralia did succumb to a long-
burning mine fire, I toyed with the town's timeline and its geog-
raphy to better suit my story.

With the Apollo moon missions, however, I stuck to the
script. All mission dates and details are according to official
NASA records. If there is an error, it is mine alone and completely unintentional.

Now, on to the thank-yous. I am indebted to my editor,
Kelley Ragland, her assistant, Matt Martz, and everyone at
St. Martin's Press and Minotaur Books. A special thanks goes to
Sabrina Soares Roberts for her eagle eye and for dealing with
my poor attempts at Vietnamese. I also must thank my wonderful agent, Michelle Brower, and Dana Kaye, publicist extraordi-
naire.

On a more personal note, I'd like to send love and thanks
to both the Ritter and Livio families. Your support is inspiring
and greatly appreciated. Same goes for Sarah Dutton, who kindly
read the book and told me what worked and what didn't, and

Felecia Wellington, for reading it and telling me she liked it better than my first book. I'd also be remiss if I didn't mention the friends and family members who saw a lot less of me as I once again fell down the all-consuming rabbit hole of writing a novel.

Finally, the bulk of the thanks goes to Mike Livio for being a fantastic partner, driver, therapist, traveling companion, and sounding board. Once again, all the thanks in the world just isn't enough.